BEST NEW AMERICAN VOICES 2007

GUEST EDITORS OF
Best New American Voices

Tobias Wolff

Charles Baxter

Joyce Carol Oates

John Casey

Francine Prose

Jane Smiley

Sue Miller

BEST NEW AMERICAN VOICES 2007

GUEST EDITOR
Sue Miller

SERIES EDITORS
John Kulka and Natalie Danford

A Harvest Original • Harcourt, Inc.

Orlando   Austin   New York   San Diego   Toronto   London

CONTENTS

PREFACE

When the Best New American Voices series made its debut in 2000, it was praised as a new and important venue for fiction writers. It was then, and remains today, the only annual anthology devoted exclusively to work by emerging writers. Now in its seventh year, the series has become something of a benchmark for writers embarking on their professional careers. Witness the many contributors to past volumes who have gone on to publish successful novels and short-story collections. Among them are: Eric Puchner (*Music Through the Floor*); David Benioff (*The 25th Hour*); William Gay (*Provinces of the Night* and *I Hate to See That Evening Sun Go Down*); Ana Menendez (*In Cuba I Was a German Shepherd*); Timothy Westmoreland (*Good As Any*); Adam Johnson (*Emporium*); John Murray (*A Few Short Notes on Tropical Butterflies*); Kaui Hart Hemmings (*House of Thieves*); Julie Orringer (*How to Breathe Underwater*); the late Amanda Davis (*Circling the Drain* and *Wonder When You'll Miss Me*); Maile Meloy (*Half in Love* and *Liars and Saints*); Jennifer Vanderbes (*Easter Island*); and Rattawut Lapcharoensap (*Sightseeing*). This is far from a complete list.

If the names in the current volume are not as familiar as these, that is certain to change with a little time. Represented here are the best stories written last year by writers enrolled in workshops in the United States and Canada. Nominations come to us from arts organizations such as the Banff Centre for the Arts and the PEN Prison Writing Committee, from summer conferences including Bread Loaf and Sewanee, from MA and MFA writing programs like Iowa and Columbia, and from fellowship programs like Stanford and the Wisconsin Institute for Creative Writing. Workshop directors and teachers send their nominations directly to us. We do not accept submissions. A directory at the back of the book lists all of this year's participating institutions.

Why organize a short-story anthology around the workshop? For the simple reason that the workshop has come to exert enormous influence on literary life and culture in North America. This influence has increased as the general-interest magazine has faltered and as the power of New York publishing has waned. In his book *Writing in General and the Short Story in Particular,* Rust Hills, fiction editor at *Esquire,* observes this remarkable transformation: "If one but stands back a bit and looks, one sees that it is no longer the book publishers and magazines, but rather the colleges and universities, that support the entire structure of the American literary establishment—and, moreover, essentially determine the nature and shape of that structure." Sixty-eight years ago, in 1939, the first writing program in the United States was founded in Iowa City. Today *The AWP Guide to Writing Programs* recognizes about 140 schools offering the master of arts degree in writing; and another fifty or so offering the master of fine arts degree. The Best New American Voices series is, then, a nod in the direction of the workshop. A nod of recognition and appreciation.

Many of these programs are highly selective and justly famous training grounds for our best new talents. Consider, for example, that the following writers all came out of the Iowa program: Flannery

O'Connor, Wallace Stegner, John Gardner, Gail Godwin, Andre Dubus, and T. C. Boyle, to name just a handful. And the Stanford program has produced its own credible national literature with such famous alumni as Robert Stone, Raymond Carver, Evan S. Connell, Tillie Olsen, Larry McMurtry, Ernest J. Gaines, Ron Hansen, Ken Kesey, Scott Turow, Thomas McGuane, Alice Hoffman, Allan Gurganus, Wendell Berry, Harriet Doerr, Al Young, Michael Cunningham, Blanche Boyd, N. Scott Momaday, Vikram Seth, Dennis McFarland, and Stephanie Vaughn. Every writing program has its distinguished alumni. The greater challenge would be listing those contemporary American authors who are *not* graduates of workshops.

For *Best New American Voices 2007* we received hundreds of nominations. We read all of these nominations at least once, as we do every year, and winnowed them down to a much smaller group of finalists that we then passed on to our guest editor, Sue Miller. Sue has selected fifteen stories for inclusion in *Best New American Voices 2007*. Her selections are varied, fresh, and surprising, making for a diverse, multicultural anthology whose contributors have little in common. The stories speak for themselves.

We would like to thank Sue Miller for her thoughtful editorial suggestions, for her alacrity, and for her support for the series. We would like to thank our past guest editors for their ongoing efforts and support: Tobias Wolff, Charles Baxter, Joyce Carol Oates, John Casey, Francine Prose, and Jane Smiley. To the many writers, directors, teachers, and panel judges who help to make this series a continuing success we extend warm thanks and congratulations. To name some others: We thank our editor Andrea Schulz for her patience and guidance; Andrea's former assistant, Jenna Johnson, for her support; André Bernard at Harcourt, Inc., for his continuing support; Lisa

Lucas in the Harcourt contracts department for her attention to detail; Sara Branch, assistant managing editor at Harcourt, once again for her unflagging efforts; Kathi George, for copyediting the Best New American Voices series; and our friends and families for their love and support.

—*John Kulka and Natalie Danford*

INTRODUCTION

Sue Miller

Why do people go to writing programs anyway?

I went because Jayne Anne Phillips told me to.

We were sitting around one afternoon when it came up. Not that I knew her. We'd just been introduced. This was twenty-five years ago. She was a beautiful young woman just out of Iowa, with a book of short stories about to come out, and I was a frazzled thirty-fiveish divorced day-care worker with a son, always trying to find a solitary half hour to write. We'd been brought together by a mutual friend, another writer, whom I knew through a writing class at the Harvard Extension School, and whom Jayne Anne had met at a writing conference. Fran. Fran Schumer.

Fran thought we should know each other and each other's work, so she'd invited us both over on a summer afternoon, and we'd spent some time reading our stories out loud. Then we had some wine or iced tea and Jayne Anne asked me what I was going to do—about my writing, she meant.

I said I didn't know. Just keep at it when I could, I supposed.

I should apply to a writing program, she said.

I said I had no money for a writing program.

No, no, she said. That was the *point*—that they would pay *me* money, money that would buy me time to write.

This was a revelation, but a revelation that more or less got lost in the onrushing and overwhelming flow of disparate responsibilities that was my life at the time—child, house, job, friends. Then, some months later, I saw an advertisement for a writing fellowship at Boston University. There it was, the amount spelled out, almost as much annually as I was making working in day care. I thought of that summer afternoon, I thought of Jayne Anne, with a book ready to go, and it seemed worth a try.

Well, I got the fellowship, and I spent the academic year of 1979 to 1980 in a world new to me, a world where everyone around me cared most of all about fiction, a world where my most pressing concern was producing stories—actually writing—every day.

Never did I stop to think about the pros and cons of going to a program. Never, until later, when I read the cautionary note struck by critics and other writers, warning of the damage being done to the short story by these programs—not only that, but the damage being done to *writers*—did I question the wisdom of what I'd done.

And then I read Flannery O'Connor's *Mystery and Manners* (and it was someone in my class at Boston University who brought this necessary book to my attention. I still find it one of the most helpful—and funniest—books about writing I know). I was startled, I recall, by her critique of the standard workshop in writing, where manuscripts are discussed by the group. She called it "the blind leading the blind." She said the criticism generated in a workshop was "equal parts of ignorance, flattery, and spite." She also said that you had the sense that now that creative writing was so widely taught in university, "you almost feel that any idiot with a nickel's worth of talent can emerge from a writing class able to write a competent story. In fact, so many people can now write competent stories that the short story as a medium is in danger of dying of competence."

My own first editor, Ted Solotaroff, in a wonderful essay called "Writing in the Cold: The First Ten Years," cautions against the *smallness* of the world writers have occupied since the number of writing programs in the United States has burgeoned so rapidly; he warns that the possibility of comfortable living within the academy (what comfortable living? I hear my writer friends cry) means that writers have poked around less out there in the Real World, that they run the risk of a rarefied or arid vision of life. And I imagine we've all been aware of the general bemoaning of the state of the American short story, the regrettable prevalence of a recognizable "workshop story" with all the elements neatly and predictably lined up in place, including the requisite elegantly small epiphany at the end.

I'd argue that these concerns are largely misplaced; though I *do* think that there was a particular and highly recognizable style of writing, a style which the *New Yorker* and the *Atlantic* and *Esquire* all promulgated to greater or lesser degrees at a certain period, and which writing students of that period emulated—the very period when the bemoaning was loudest. And yes, this style was recognizable and elegant and "workshoppy." But it was "workshoppy" because that was what the American short story itself had become for a while—the American short story as it appeared in those glossy magazines—and sometimes in little literary magazines, too. Because they weren't stupid, workshop students, at least those who hoped to make a living by writing, emulated those kinds of stories. But the "workshop" story existed before the workshop did.

We can all stop gnashing our teeth about the dangers of writing programs, I think. For one thing, students go to writing programs with their ideas about short stories largely formed. They don't go, in other words, to learn how to do it. They go because, as in my case, they want to change their lives, to find a way to put writing at the center. They go because they get a fellowship. They go, sometimes, because they hope to make connections that will launch them. They go to learn to sharpen their own work, to edit it. They go to give themselves deadlines, to make themselves work in more disciplined ways than they've managed out there on their own.

For another thing, there is not any longer that sense in the world of writing and publishing, of *a way to do it.* A kind of balkanization of the short story has occurred—as better-paying short-story venues have dried up, as the *New Yorker* has moved into new territory editorially, as quite disparate "little" magazines have taken over the publishing of most of the work in this form. The result of all these changes is that the American short story has changed, has become multifarious, stranger, richer. And as writing programs have sprung up all over the country and the nature of their population has changed—many more students of diverse ethnic backgrounds, for instance, and more older students, who have indeed been out there in the Real World for a while—the writing produced by these programs has been less responsive to any particular aesthetic. I was struck by this when I edited *Best American Short Stories 2002,* and I've been struck by it again in rereading the group of stories I chose for this collection. What should a short story be about? How should it go about making its meaning? This is clearly up for grabs in workshops in America today, as it is in the magazines and journals that publish stories.

Look at this collection. There's a long account of the loss of a particular landscape and its rich history under the pressure of development ("Shadow on a Weary Land"). There's the story of a young Vietnamese refugee in San Francisco, confronting his loss and isolation even as he comes to terms with his homosexuality ("A Correct Life"). There's a group of Russian immigrants, neighbors in Pittsburgh, and the account of the way their interlocking lives are pulling apart as life and the American experience change them ("About

Kamyshinskiy"). There's the tale of a fussy rosarian who takes over his neighbor's garden when she's incapacitated with cancer ("By Any Other Name"). There's a story set in Philadelphia in 1876, a series of letters from a man whose son has been kidnapped to people who have responded to his advertisements ("The Temperate Family").

Nothing is predictable. One story is set on Virgin Gorda ("Wake"), one in a village in China ("Persimmons"). The language varies wildly, from elegiac to wired, from elliptical to elaborate; the narrative stance from denial to confessional. The main characters in "Persimmons" are a group of Chinese men (this is a story told in the first person *plural*), while "Shadow on a Weary Land" features a seventyish former drug addict and inventor, and "Syra" a deported illegal alien from Pakistan. "Ashes" peeks into the mind of a widow more relieved than grieving. The mysteries of family are the concerns of "The Freddies" and "The Inappropriate Behavior of Our Alleged Loved Ones." "Karaoke Night" and "Pompeii Recreated" put parents and children under the microscope. And in "Whatever Happened to Sébastien Grosjean?" and "Winter Never Quits," men who cannot seem to locate themselves, let alone their relatives, struggle to adjust. These tales are startling, inventive, moving, fresh. Not a workshop story in the bunch.

BEST NEW AMERICAN VOICES 2007

ALICE J. MARSHALL

University of Washington

By Any Other Name

In November, when he arrived home from a weeklong tax seminar, something seemed wrong as Smith turned into the driveway. He pushed the automatic button for the garage door, and then pulled the car forward until the tennis ball dangling from a string rested on the windshield. Tools hung from their pegs above his tidy workbench, and the gardening books lined the shelf above, arranged by height.

He stepped out of the car and walked down the driveway into the twilight. The hoses were coiled on their retracting holders. His wife had apparently remembered to sweep up after midweek weeding, so that couldn't be it. The roses flanking the long driveway were all at rest under their winter blankets of mulch.

He lifted his head and looked across the street. That was it. His headlights must have caught the Martins' yard, where, clearly, their roses had neither been pruned nor bedded down properly. He crossed the street in a few quick steps and looked closer. Indeed, they wore their late-summer growth like leggy adolescents whose bony wrists poke through sleeves, too cold for the weather. Here it was, the fourth Tuesday in November, just a few days before Thanksgiving, and winterizing was a good ten days overdue. There was something raw and painful about the roses, and it wasn't right. Nor was it like Mrs. Martin to let them go.

Still, Smith had not gotten where he was in life by fussing over things he couldn't do anything about. He had to assume that the Martins would take care of it as soon as they could. Surely they had simply been away. For Zone 5, or even granting Mrs. Martin's micro-climate argument, Zone 6, it was critical to get the winter protection in place before it got any colder. The canes still hadn't been dead-headed. Those roses needed attention soon, or there would be hell to pay in the spring.

That night at dinner, Smith felt it necessary to mention his concern.

"Of course," his wife answered offhandedly, "she hasn't had the time or energy now that she's started treatments."

Treatments? Smith knew better than to make this inquiry aloud. He had long ago learned in his marriage, as he had in board meetings, that it was always better to feign both knowledge and interest in the subject at hand until either the speaker or his memory filled in the gaps. It was his habit to murmur, "Oh," "I see," or "Of course," in such situations while focusing on a pen that wouldn't write, or looking intently at a report before him. Now he concentrated on extracting a morsel of meat from the chicken thigh on his plate, while in his head he walked down vast corridors of oak filing cabinets, finally stopping at one labeled, "Martin, Mrs., 2004 and prior."

Thus he was able to retrieve a mention of blood counts and a diagnosis having to do with female parts and cancer. See, people thought that he didn't pay attention and didn't remember. Nothing was ever lost, no moment forgotten entirely. He simply filed them away until needed. After all, it did not make sense to keep at one's fingertips information that wasn't immediately useful. Smith dismissed a fact, generally, as soon as he'd safely filed it.

His wife went on about the progression of the illness, mentioning the words *uterus* and *cervix*. He winced. It just didn't seem right that people had permission to look into one's private life this way, so that words and phrases, body parts and functions that were most personal became the subject of dinner conversation.

Now Mrs. Martin's illness exposed her to the neighborhood as if the X-rays and lab results were posted daily on her mailbox. How many ovaries might she be left with? Would she be able to return to "full function"? Innumerable humiliations must be endured, and he felt that this public evisceration must be the worst part of an illness.

As he chewed the morsel of chicken he saw he had taken too long between responsive murmurs, and his wife was looking at him in that way of hers which threatened to know what exactly was going on in his brain. He didn't like that look; it resembled pity. Somehow he didn't think she would be reassured to know that everything he knew about her was filed and cross-referenced, ready to be summoned with the invocation of keywords and phrases such as *anniversary* and *bridge club*.

Desirous of changing the subject, and having completely lost the thread of what his wife continued to say, he blurted, "I could trim up those roses for her. Get them ready for the winter." It popped out of his mouth, and even as he spoke he realized that it was a phenomenally bad idea. He would never have wanted anyone to take care of his roses, and he certainly didn't think that Mrs. Martin would like his methods and his tools in her precious beds. On the other hand, as he looked at his wife, he was pleased to see that she was more or less in shock. She paused with a fork halfway to her mouth and blinked a few times.

"That would be so very considerate, Harold. I wouldn't have thought to ask you, but, you know, the whole neighborhood has been trying to think of ways they can help. We're providing dinners for the family every Friday night for the time being."

She went on, but Smith had turned his mind to the garden. He thought he'd put his passion to bed for the winter with his own roses, but the prospect of another weekend with his fingers in the soil pleased him enormously. Truth was, now that he gave it some thought, he would love to give Mrs. Martin's garden a little going over. He'd always argued with her over fertilizer nitrogen ratios. Here was his chance to see if his preferred mixture would indeed improve the production of blossoms. Mrs. Martin had the only collection of English roses on the street that could compare to his. He had always wondered at the mind behind that rose garden, as her selections were eclectic, to say the least. She put climbers where they couldn't climb and bushy roses where they were impeded by walls. Really there seemed little or no logic to it. He began happily making mental lists: bedding material, fertilizer, check for disease.

The day after Thanksgiving, Smith was up early to begin preparations for their traditional antileftover cocktail party. Once, to his gentle teasing about her endless stream of turkey tetrazzini, turkey soup, turkey sandwiches, and turkey potpie, Marian had said, "Why don't you come up with something better?" Always willing to rise to a challenge, he'd gotten a stack of cookbooks from the library and determined that the traditional tastes of Thanksgiving could meld with pan-Asian flavors. Over the years he'd developed a complex menu, and now he started assembling several types of dumplings: turkey shu mei, yam-sweetened har gow, and gyoza with a spicy sauce of cranberry and star anise. He worked through his tasks happily, listening to the pleasant murmur of crisp British accents on the BBC broadcast as he chopped vegetables. Once done with the preparations, he made a plate of cheese and fruit, ham and rolls, and set it on a tray. He added a small thermos of coffee and a pitcher of orange juice. After retrieving the paper from the driveway, he brought the tray and a pot of coffee upstairs, where his wife waited, having brushed her hair and teeth and donned her cream-colored satin robe. She gave him a broad smile. He set the tray down and slipped into bed next to her. Later, they spent a happy hour reading the newspaper and nibbling their way through breakfast.

Before they'd finished the crossword puzzle, the phone rang, and Marian answered, bringing the caller abreast with the latest on Mrs. Martin's illness. Smith felt very uncomfortable with the conversation, as if he had the caller and Mrs. Martin in bed with him as well as his wife. He escaped into the bathroom to shave and shower. As he let the water stream over his back, he thought, as he often did, that it simply didn't pay to dwell on the female parts of the wives of one's friends and coworkers. Models, yes, actresses, certainly, but friends of his wife? Never. He had trained himself so long and so hard in this discipline that he'd ceased to think of Mrs. Martin as female. Yes, a woman, yes, a human being, yes, Martin's wife. But he would always stop before wondering about the body beneath her silk blouses and wool skirts. James's mother, the best bridge player on the block, a fellow rose lover, all these things she might be, but never a female with breasts, curling fallopian tubes, and a secret uterus.

The guests started arriving at five. He manned the bar, making sure that every drink stayed fresh and everyone tried the shu mei. He'd done all the cooking, but his wife, as always, was the true hostess of the party. She greeted guests and took their coats to the den. He watched with admiration as she moved between knots of conversation, saying just the right thing to everyone, inquiring after their children, their jobs, and their recent concerns. Nearly everyone asked her about the Martins and she replied, frankly but briefly, "It's going to be a long haul. They're doing well considering."

Later in the evening, the Martins appeared at the door. Smith shook Carl's hand, and then helped Mrs. Martin out of her coat. His wife briefly hugged each of them, then kissed Mrs. Martin on each cheek. "Sue, I'm so glad you were able to come. You look lovely. That dress is very flattering!"

Mrs. Martin laughed. "It's amazing what a little weight loss will do!"

Smith smiled politely with the others, although he found the jest ghoulish, to say the least.

Mrs. Martin turned to Smith. "Marian tells me you're going to help out with the garden."

"Well, yes," Smith replied. "I thought perhaps we could discuss your preferences—what your plans are and such. Should I keep a journal for you? Or do you have one going?"

"Oh, I'll just have to trust you," she said lightly. "I'm sure you'll do a fine job. I don't imagine I'll have the energy to think about the roses for a while." Other guests had crowded around, and the Martins were swept away from Smith and into the party. Once, while pouring drinks, he glanced up into the mirror over the mantel, and his eyes locked with Mrs. Martin's as a result of that odd way that mirrors have of throwing glances together. He turned his attention back to the guest holding an empty glass in front of him and didn't see when the Martins left.

On Saturday Smith went to the nursery for bedding materials and a special overwintering supplement he liked to feed his roses. Once home, he loaded up his wheelbarrow and headed across the street to the Martins' front yard. The bushes were in a sorry state. As usual, Mrs. Martin had clipped flowers all fall, not leaving enough spent blossoms to dry and turn to rose hips. This was an essential step to ensure a deep hibernation. It seemed a small price to pay—to give up fresh flowers in your living room just for a week or two and thus provide a peaceful winter slumber and a more productive spring. He got to work with his clippers.

Late in the afternoon, Martin emerged. "I can't say how much we appreciate this, Harold," he said. "These roses mean so much to Sue."

Smith nodded, craning his head up at an awkward angle. He had the sun in his eyes, and Carl was merely an outline, looming before him. Smith couldn't read the expression on his face.

"Here, thought you might be thirsty."

The sun had been beating steadily down and, despite the chilly air, Smith felt overheated, and appreciated the look of the dewy bottle Martin held out. He rose stiffly, whacked the dirt off his knees, and then removed his garden gloves, placing them carefully in the wheelbarrow before turning and taking the offered beer.

"Nice party last night," Martin ventured.

"Glad to see you there."

"Family doing well?"

"Sure." Smith paused. "You know, working out here I've been thinking. It looks as if I might be taking care of the garden for some time, and there are a lot of decisions to be made. I'll keep careful records of what I do."

"Don't worry about it," Martin said. "I'm sure you'll do the right thing."

Smith pressed on. "I'd hoped to talk to Sue last night about her plans for the spring." As soon as he said it, Smith thought that perhaps they weren't thinking that far ahead. Fortunately, Martin didn't answer him. They finished their beers in silence, and Martin returned to the house with the bottles. Smith finished up his work and went home.

The winter wore on and the roses slept. He knew that they were still growing and living, no matter how dead they appeared from the outside. The house across the street remained dark, with Mrs. Martin cocooned in the master bedroom, sleeping, they said, up to twenty hours a day. He had seen her return from one of her treatments, swallowed up in a fur coat, too luxurious and full for her birdlike wrists, her neck rising frail and spindly from the collar. The flesh on her face was stretched tightly over sharp cheekbones, bright spots of rouge oddly orange and not at all the right color for her ashen skin.

From time to time as he worked in the garden, he would notice her sitting in a rocking chair at her bedroom window looking down upon him. She would stretch her face into a thin smile and give a slight wave.

On dark winter evenings, Smith sat up in bed poring over rose catalogs, dreaming of spring. He studied his gardening journals, comparing them with the almanac, to see what sort of winter he could expect, and how wet and warm the spring would be. The Abraham Darby, which had been plagued by mites last season, should still be considered fragile. He played with sketches of his garden, contemplating several moves to accommodate the new roses that he had ordered. If they were to be successful, he would have to plan their placement and prepare the beds well ahead of the bare root arrivals.

By mid-February, Smith's anxiety about Mrs. Martin's bare roots became intolerable. The nursery had already called to say that his were ready for pickup. He didn't know if Mrs. Martin had ordered any, and he certainly couldn't guess where she wanted them planted. He'd thought about calling over there, but Marian made noises that she was not doing well, and shouldn't be disturbed. One night after he and his wife had eaten and cleared the dishes, when he was certain that Martin would be home, he crossed the street and rang the doorbell.

Martin's eyes were dull, as if he were in a fog, but he opened the door wider and asked Smith to come in. He hadn't been in their living room for—what had it been? A year? The house felt hot and close, both dark and too bright. Martin disappeared into the kitchen and Smith could hear ice cubes rattling. He came back with two glasses of ice and a bottle of scotch.

"Well, Harold, how have you been? Your wife?"

"Fine. Fine." Before he realized it, the words were out of his mouth, "And yours?"

"Getting by." Martin poured a generous amount of scotch into the glasses. They each sipped.

Smith brought the subject around to the matter at hand. "It's about the roses."

"Oh, I meant to tell you. I really appreciate your looking in on them. But there's really nothing to do during the winter, is there?"

"Actually, there's a great deal that needs doing," Smith said. "Decisions to be made, you know. I wondered if your wife..."

Martin waved his hand dismissively, a little irritated. "Honestly, Harold, I'm sure you can figure out what to do."

They both looked up as a wavering voice called down the stairs, "Carl?"

Martin stood. "Excuse me, please."

Smith nodded.

Martin went up the stairs. A door opened and closed. Smith sat very still while a low voice was muffled behind the door. He looked around the room at the photos on the end table and the botanical artwork carefully framed. The walls were papered in that over-patterned Victorian style: all lace and flowers. So much to look at that the eyes didn't seem to get a rest. Martin came down the stairs saying, "I'll be just a minute," and disappeared into the kitchen.

Smith could hear the refrigerator opening, something being poured, and the gathering of dishes. He looked around the room again and noticed a bookshelf full of leather bindings. He couldn't resist crossing the room and reading the titles. Most were antiques: Dickens, Kipling, and Shakespeare, small leather-bound poetry volumes, slim copies of Carlyle and Plato. Tucked between two Dickens novels, he found a gardener's diary. It was the expensive sort, with waterproof paper, a supple leather binding, and a cord that wrapped from the back to the front, winding around a little mother-of-pearl button. When he unfastened the cord and opened the book, several dried rose petals fell to the floor. He hastily picked them up, but they shattered in his fingers. He sprinkled the shards between two pages. The journal was crammed with Mrs. Martin's leftward slanting handwriting, loops open and inviting, letters dipping so far below the line that she had been compelled to write on every other one. He flipped quickly through the journal and found magazine clippings of rose varieties pasted on the pages, with notes marching around the edges. Between notations of feedings and mildew treatments were detailed maps of the garden and the rosebushes. Scanning forward to find the last entries, he saw that she'd ordered some classic English roses, and the new David Austin, "Jude the Obscure." He smiled. There were better options. The Jude just wouldn't thrive in this zone. It would have been far more sensible to attempt the Golden Celebration, very similar to the Jude, but much hardier. He heard steps approaching and slipped the book back onto the shelf.

Martin carried a tray through the room, barely glancing at Smith. "Just a moment," he said, and he took the tray up the stairs. Smith went back to the chair with his drink.

Martin's return brought a cloud of hospital smell into the room. He looked gray.

Smith leaned forward. "Should I go?"

"No. No." Martin picked up the bottle and poured another two inches into his glass. "Please stay." He sat down and looked around the room as if he'd been gone a year instead of a few minutes. He blinked several times. "It's nice she wanted something to eat. She hasn't had any appetite. We're coming to the end of treatments now, and she should begin to get stronger."

Smith nodded and made a noise in his throat that he hoped sounded useful or supportive. He asked about work, then the topic moved on to cars. After a while though, there was a muffled crash from upstairs. With a stricken look, Martin dashed up the stairs. That same door opened and closed again.

Time passed. Smith watched the ice in his glass melt. He looked around at the room again, this time noticing the flowered porcelain teacups, each with its saucer tilted up behind it. He drained his scotch and thought about pouring another. He strained to hear something upstairs, but no sound came through the door. After several minutes had passed, it occurred to Smith that Martin wouldn't be coming down. He crossed the room, pulled the leather journal down from the bookshelf, shrugged his coat on, and went out into the cold evening.

Once across the street at his own driveway, he glanced back at the Martin house. He could see into the master bedroom, where Martin helped his wife across the room. They hadn't drawn the heavy drapes, and the sheers offered no privacy at night with a fully lit room. He could see that Mrs. Martin wore a teal bathrobe, very much like the terry cloth one he'd bought for his wife the previous year—on sale at Nordstrom, wasn't it? The kind she liked, big and comfortable, but nothing he would enjoy seeing on her. He could always tell when his wife intended to curl up with a book and not with him—on went the lust-robbing flannel nightgown, heavy wool socks, and that robe. He saw Mrs. Martin pause in her progress across the room and face the window. Before he could be seen, he quickly turned toward home.

A week later, Smith retrieved the bare root plants at the nursery. He nervously approached the clerk to ask about Mrs. Martin's order as well, not certain they would give it to him.

"Oh, how is Sue?" The clerk took the order sheets and handed them to a teenager who went to find the plants in the back. "Is there any news?"

Smith grunted noncommittally. He really didn't know.

"Well, Jenny was in here the other day and said she's started on a new kind of chemotherapy. I guess the other one wasn't working so well. Too many side effects."

He realized he did know something. "Her appetite is improving," he ventured.

"That's wonderful." The clerk beamed at Smith as if he were responsible for Mrs. Martin's progress. She finished the transaction and said, "Don't worry about Sue's roses, we'll send her bill to the house." Smith escaped, put the roses in the car, and drove home.

Later he sat at his garage workbench with a mug of coffee. He carefully marked out the dimensions of his garden on a large sheet of graph paper, making two copies. On one, he marked in the roses and their current locations. On the other, he began tweaking the plan he'd created, consulting his gardening journals, and several rose care volumes. His Sweet Juliet had been beset by fungus this year. Moving her to the eastern edge of the bed might help. The Ambridge Rose, never a tall plant, was being overshadowed by the Heritage, and he thought he would find a place near the front edge of the garden where it could show off its salmon-colored blossoms and sweet myrrh fragrance.

Once satisfied, he sketched another pair of diagrams for Mrs. Martin's rose bed. Then he opened a drawer in his workbench and pulled out the leather journal. It released a spicy scent as he opened it. He began carefully turning the pages, looking for any notes about the varieties Mrs. Martin had ordered.

It was a little like an archaeological dig. For the first several pages, there were careful lists and records of planting, fertilizing, and pest treatments. These logs weren't kept consistently, though, and one page of entries might cover as little as a month, or as much as two years. They gave way to pages of hastily scribbled notes and doodles, jotted, it would seem, during telephone consultations, as phone numbers, nursery names, and catalog ordering numbers were scattered between the sketched flowers.

Then came something unexpected. The first such page held a collage of magazine photos of roses, wound with tiny script, lines from Wordsworth, Keats, Browning, all about roses. The next held what he thought must be an original poem, surrounded by sketches of blooms and buds on a twisting vine that left the border to wind around a portrait of Gertrude Jekyll, the Victorian garden designer. Sprinkled throughout these pages were little diagrams of Mrs. Martin's garden, in which she often drew herself, a tiny stick figure with a floppy garden hat and oversized gloves.

He flipped through the pages slowly, admiring but only skimming similar pages until he found a map dated the previous September. There Mrs. Martin had laid out her plan for the following year with a few practical, useful notes. *Cut Abraham Darby back severely. Constance Spry needs more sun, move against fence in back.* A photo of a new rose, Jude the Obscure, dominated the facing page, from which an arrow traced a line to a central spot on the map of the garden. There were only three words below the picture. *It will thrive.*

Smith sat back and sighed. Why couldn't she have picked something easier? The Golden Celebration was, in all respects, an equal rose, but more resilient, and much better suited to the climate. Why did she insist on the Jude? He looked forward, hoping to find some clue to justify her unreasonable interest in this unsuitable rose, but found only blank pages. Shrugging, he put the journal back in his workbench drawer, pulled out his calendar, and set to work making a schedule for the planting and transplanting that he had to do.

April showers had let up a little and Smith knew that he had to take advantage of this sun break and get out to the Martins' garden. There was a lot of work to do. That morning as he'd finished up his own weeding, he'd seen the Martins pull out of the garage. Mrs. Martin, looking pale but happy, in fact almost plump, waved through the car window as they drove away. Smith knew they had gone into the city for one of her follow-up appointments. She'd been gaining strength now that the treatments were ended, and the neighborhood was aware that today's visit should confirm what they all hoped, and the doctors believed—that she had turned the corner.

The roses were thriving, each branch swelling with life—buds and leaves bursting forth, proof that the prayers and preparation of the winter had paid off. Every plant was blooming, except for the Jude, of course. Despite several more careful readings of the journal, he had found no helpful insight into Mrs. Martin's intended care of the difficult rose. No matter though. The two glorious Othellos covered in bold red blossoms flanked the Gertrude Jekyll like guardians, or, as he'd realized from Mrs. Martin's notes, more like rivals for her affection. The Gertrude started as perfect little scrolled buds, but would soon open into beautiful, large, rosette-shaped flowers of rich glowing pink. Right now they were not yet fully realized, still all potential, ambition, reaching toward the sun. He leaned over and the intoxicating classic old rose scent rushed into his nostrils.

Smith glanced across the street and saw his wife backing out of the driveway. She rolled down the window. "I'm going down the hill to get some ingredients for the Martins' dinner. Do you need anything?"

He shook his head. "All set here." He worked his way down the row of roses and considered his wife. She always thought of people in terms of what she could or should or would do for them. He'd realized this in college, when they'd met. Indeed, it was one of the things that most attracted him to her. If he had in his employ, at his disposal, so to speak, someone who noticed the little, important things about people, who knew how to interact and how to be in relationship, then he would be able to move more easily through the world. He did have the sense to recognize that such an admission would not be taken as flattery or romance. Even now, his wife could never know how deeply he loved her for her ability to bridge the gap between him and the rest of humanity.

It struck Smith that the Martins might enjoy fresh flowers at their table tonight. Mrs. Martin should see that she wasn't the only creature blossoming. He moved through the bushes, carefully selecting some of the strongest and most lovely blossoms: the William Shakespeare, red and full, a classic rose shape with that old rose perfume. He snipped several Abraham Darby, their creamy pink blossoms exuding a fruity smell. He added the Graham Thomas for a yellow splash, and the Winchester Cathedral, for its white blossoms and sensuous scent of honey and almonds. The Jude stood stubbornly bare. Leaves had emerged, but not a single bud swelled. Sighing, Smith turned and looked back across the street at his Golden Celebration, a profusion of blooms, an excellent producer for a first-year plant.

His eyes roamed over the neat rows of roses he'd planted at just the proper interval to allow cultivating and access. They were arranged by height in ranks one after another, the spreading, bushy ones toward the edges, the tallest in the back. He could almost see the lines of the graph paper on which he'd drawn his plans, the careful plans by which he worked the pieces of his life. There was nothing messy, haphazard, or risky about his garden. Everything was careful, precise, and appropriate. Everything worked because he made sure, before he even started, that it would.

At the edge, one cane of the Abraham Darby had worked free until it dangled like a loose thread on a sleeve. *I'll have to peg that,* he thought. Later.

Now, he carried the flowers across the street to his workbench and then started tossing things about in the garage, looking for a jar he could use. He was digging around in the glass recycling when his wife drove in.

"For heaven's sake, dear, what are you doing?"

"Looking for something I can use for a vase."

"Why don't you use a vase then, you goose?" She opened a cabinet along the back wall, and there on the top shelf stood a collection of vases. He recognized many of them from the arrangements he brought home for her in the months when the garden wasn't in bloom. His wife reached for a pink fluted vase and handed it to him.

"I'll get you some ribbon to put around the vase. It will look lovely."

When she returned, he arranged the bouquet, adding one Golden Celebration from his own garden. It should have been the Jude in the center, but he had little hope that it would produce at all this year. He filled the vase with water and dropped in a few pennies to inhibit bacterial growth.

Then he opened his workbench drawer and took out Mrs. Martin's journal.

At that moment his wife appeared with a casserole and several dishes in her arms. "Do you want me to take the roses over with dinner?"

Startled, Smith dropped the journal before his wife could see it. He turned his back to the drawer and shut it behind him. "Isn't it too much for you to carry?" he asked. "How are you going to open the door?"

"I think I can manage." She didn't look as if she could though, with dishes stacked nearly to her chin.

"Let me help," Smith insisted, and he took the salad bowl from her, and picked up the vase in his other arm.

They crossed the street and Marian punched in the code on the Martins' automatic garage door. "They're going to have to get the code changed now," she said. "Nearly everyone in the neighborhood has used it sometime in the last few months."

In the kitchen Marian busied herself making room in the refrigerator for the salad, setting the oven to a low temperature sufficient for keeping the casserole warm. Smith put the flowers in the center of the kitchen table and then slipped into the living room. He could feel the empty house around him. He ran his fingers over the soft leather spines on the bookshelf and pulled out a novel. He opened it to a random passage.

"Harold?"

Smith looked toward the kitchen. "Be right there." He closed the novel and held it to his face, inhaling the musty scent of old stories. Then he put it back exactly where he'd found it. He joined his wife in the kitchen, where she'd set the table with good china and candles. "Isn't that nice?" she asked.

He pulled her to him and rested his chin on the top of her head. "It's beautiful," he said. Then, holding hands, they crossed the street to their own house.

For the next few weeks, he waited impatiently for the Jude to blossom. He'd been in the garden every day patrolling for mites, vigilant

against fungus. He had scoured that damn journal cover to cover trying to find some clue, some plan that Mrs. Martin might have had to
make the Jude work. There was nothing. His imagination failed him.
He just couldn't see how to make it work, and finally he made up his
mind to replace it with a Golden Celebration. The nursery didn't
have any left, but he made a few calls and on Saturday picked one up
in the city.

He put the plant in his wheelbarrow, loaded up a shovel, some fertilizer, and his gloves. Then, thinking this was as good a time to return it as any, he tucked Mrs. Martin's journal atop the load and
brought everything across the street. He put the journal on the bench
by the garden path and set to work. He started cutting a circle
around the Jude with the sharp blade, stepping lightly on the shovel.
He had almost completed the circle when he heard a tapping and,
glancing up, saw that Mrs. Martin stood at the master bedroom window, gesturing frantically. He shrugged to indicate he didn't understand her. Finally she signed for him to wait and he did, resting his
arms on the shovel as he imagined her moving through the house.
She emerged from the front door with surprising speed, her wet hair
plastered to her head, and her legs bare beneath the teal terry bathrobe. He also noticed that her legs were shaved—recalling that as
people get well, they start taking care of themselves more.

"What are you doing with my Jude?"

He began to explain.

As she listened, her dark eyes seemed to harden into little stones.
The color on her cheeks looked more natural now, as if it matched
her skin again. She had run out of the house without anything under
her bathrobe, and the fallen lapel revealed the top curve of one of her
breasts.

Abruptly, she stood up straighter. "I think," she said with an edge
to her voice, "as much as I appreciate what you've done, it's time I got

back to caring for my own garden." Smith looked at her for a long moment, and then the information seemed to find its place in his files.

"We have certainly been happy to do everything we could to help," he said quietly. "Marian and I are very grateful that you are getting well."

Mrs. Martin nodded, clutched her bathrobe to her, and turned, then saw the journal for the first time. She bent to pick it up from the bench, and as she stood, gripping the little leather book with her thin fingers, she gave him an acid look, long and hard. Then she walked into the house, closing the door behind her. After she left, Smith tamped down the earth around Jude the Obscure. He honestly didn't think it would survive the season, but after all, it wasn't his garden.

From that time on, Mrs. Martin spent more and more afternoons in her garden, her bright sun hat bobbing among the roses like an over-sized blossom. She returned to the monthly neighborhood women's gatherings. Smith would see her when she came to meet Marian for their daily evening walk. They went farther out and back every day.

Smith loved summer in the garden, but also took time to tour the countryside for the rose shows. His wife was pleased to join him, and they planned a trip that would drop them at the Sylvia Beach Inn down the coast on their anniversary. There they settled themselves on comfortable couches, with her feet in his lap, and worked their way through a few novels each. Smith read forgettable mysteries, but his wife was captivated by Trollope, Brontë, and Dickens.

One morning in August, when Smith went to retrieve the paper from the end of the driveway, he glanced toward Mrs. Martin's house to find that Jude the Obscure, tall, healthy, spreading his arms wide to the world, outshone everything in the garden. Blooms stood on every branch, as if they'd exploded in riotous life simultaneously. He crossed the street to look more closely, and noticed that Mrs. Martin had created paths between her roses out of bright stones, marbles, and pieces of glass pressed into the soil. They accounted for the subtle sparkle he had noticed that seemed to light her roses from below. He knelt to get a closer look and imagined her bending to the work, selecting each pebble and scrap of glass according to her heart's design. The morning sun had warmed the roses above him, around him, and Smith could smell Jude's exotic perfume. Intoxicating, like sweet wine and deep amber honey, the smell almost made him feel faint. He ran his hand over the mosaic surrounding the Jude. She had been moving among these roses, her hands had held the canes; her knees had been dimpled by these stones.

He stood and stepped back, glancing as he did at the sun reflected off the bedroom window. There was no way for him to see past that light, or to tell if Mrs. Martin was watching him.

ELLEN LITMAN

Wisconsin Institute for Creative Writing

ABOUT KAMYSHINSKIY

At eight A.M. Alyosha Kamyshinskiy is going for a run. Before going, he stands in the middle of the kitchen and drinks a cup of coffee in one long gulp. The kitchen smells of garbage. Alyosha picks up a dry-erase marker. On the white refrigerator door he writes, "Clean the goddamn refrigerator."

Alyosha's daughters are asleep. They don't work and don't go to college. They sleep until noon, and the family dog suffers. The dog steals shoes—hides them under the couch, won't give them up. They live in a sprawling apartment with rotting floors and bad insulation. The windows don't lock. It is expensive, but the landlord allows dogs.

Alyosha Kamyshinskiy is a mild man. In his spare time he likes to look at art, read gentle poetry—a sleigh, a moonlit trail, the melancholy trot of a troika. Since he lost his job two months ago, there's been a lot of spare time. Every morning at eight, he goes for a run.

He runs long and hard, and his sneakers hit the pavement in a rhythmic, dependable pattern. Lines spin in his head. *White snow, gray ice...A blanket made of rags... City in the noose of a road...* It is a song, though not the kind of song Alyosha would ever admit to liking. It's what his daughters listen to, glib Russian rock bands—angular faces, angular lyrics. *Those who live by their own rules...And who will die young...* The girls like songs about death. Their mother died a year ago from cancer, but that didn't affect them the way you'd expect. They sleep and gossip and don't work, while Alyosha buys groceries and takes care of the apartment.

Alyosha Kamyshinskiy runs down Bartlett Street, across Murray, all the way to Schenley Park, and the song follows Alyosha. Today, he thinks, today he will start living by his own rules.

At nine A.M. Kostya Kogan is leaving his wife, Marina. They are finishing their last breakfast together—cereal with milk and fruit, thin shavings of strawberries and bananas. They each drink a glass of grapefruit juice. The children have gone to school, and Kostya's suitcase is packed, waiting by the front door.

"You can't come back," says Marina. She collects the cereal bowls and takes them into the kitchen. The silverware rattles sharply against the china. "This time, you cannot come back."

"You're kicking me out?" says Kostya. He follows Marina into their birch and stainless-steel kitchen, leans against the smooth veneer of the kitchen island.

"You're leaving us," explains Marina. "You're leaving us for the woman who used to dance with a snake at the Moscow Nights. Do you want a sandwich before you go?"

"Do I want a sandwich?"

"Of course you want a sandwich. You think the Sinitsa woman will make you a sandwich?"

She reaches for the metallic refrigerator door, and the children's photographs, affixed with bright plastic magnets, wink at Kostya. Mishka is in third grade and having trouble with math. Verka is turning thirteen in two weeks; she likes ice-skating and rap. In the Kodak photographs their faces are the succulent color of an apricot.

"Turkey or ham?" says Marina.

"At least don't sell the house," says Kostya. "At least till the children finish school."

"I can't afford the house," says Marina.

"I'll pay the mortgage," Kostya tells her. "Just promise you won't sell."

Marina wraps the sandwich in wax paper and adds a small carton of orange juice. She puts it all in a brown paper bag.

"I couldn't live without you," says Kostya. "You know that's why I come back."

"This time you don't." Marina strokes his cheek. "I'm late for work. Let yourself out." She kisses him quickly on the lips. "You're having a baby with the Sinitsa woman," she reminds him. "And don't forget, you have two shirts at the dry cleaner's."

At ten A.M. Seryozha Rodkin tries to sleep. This week he works the night shift, which would be perfect if only he could fall asleep. He turns the pillow and pulls the blanket over his head, but the sun seeps in through the thin wool fabric, and he can hear Olya's TV tweeting downstairs. He tries to breathe, tries to count. He has to call a cab for Olya's four o'clock appointment at Magee-Womens. His car is in the shop until next Tuesday. He is thinking about this now. About cabs and how they are sometimes unreliable. Also about the bus schedule he needs to check for later, when it's time to go to work.

At half past ten, Seryozha gives up and slogs downstairs. The lack of sleep gives him a wobbly, hungover feeling—diffused headache, weakness in the stomach. On the living-room couch, Olya is watching soap operas and napping during commercial breaks. Her head is wrapped in a turban she's made for herself, because, she said, all the wigs they had seen were obscene and expensive. She thinks the turban makes her look like a collective-farm girl, but Seryozha disagrees. It is a nice turban. Besides, collective-farm girls wear kerchiefs.

Seryozha fixes the fleece blanket over Olya's feet.

"You go back to bed," she tells him. "Checking on me again?"

"Couldn't sleep," he says and goes to collect the mail.

He comes back with two bills, cable and electric, and immediately sits down to write checks. This is what Seryozha does in the morning when he cannot sleep. When there are no bills left, he goes over bank statements and sorts through receipts, adding them up, anticipating the next credit-card balance. From her couch, Olya jokes that he should get trained in accounting. He says he is too old to get trained in anything. He tries not to show how fidgety he's become in the four months since her cancer came back. The numbers help. The numbers keep his mind in order, his hands occupied. He records balances in a special notebook, his handwriting round and sturdy.

"Hey, bookkeeper," says Olya. "Have we saved enough for California yet?"

The doorbell at Seryozha Rodkin's house has a harsh and unpleasant ring. At eleven A.M. it jolts Olya out of her sleepy reverie over a series of baby food commercials. "Who's that?" she says and places her hand on her chest where her left breast used to be.

Seryozha goes to check. It can be anybody, thinks Seryozha. A postman with another package from Alex in San Diego. An activist with a petition. A neighbor who wants to park in their driveway. A thief? A murderer? Those are the least of Seryozha's worries. He stands on tiptoes and tries to see through the diamonds of insulated glass.

Outside, Kostya Kogan waits with a suitcase, shifting his feet, kicking at the doorstep, trying to peer into the window.

"It's Kostya Kogan," Seryozha reports to Olya.

"Send him away," she says.

Seryozha opens the door and looks at Kostya and the suitcase.

"So it's true? You and the Sinitsa woman?"

Kostya shrugs, sways uncertainly. "You know me, Seryozha. Marina's everything to me."

"You need a place to stay?"

He shakes his head. "I'm moving in with . . ." He makes exuberant hand gestures, like he can't remember the name.

"Sinitsa?"

"Yeah."

Olya comes out of the living room, her fleece blanket wrapped over her shoulders like a cape. Kostya bounces toward her: "Hey, Olya! How're you doing, Olya?!"

She says, "I was just going upstairs."

By eleven thirty the fickle October sun manages to warm up the sprawling apartment of Alyosha Kamyshinskiy. The rooms fill with the low rumble of domestic noises: The tea kettle gurgles; the dog, stretched on the sunlit kitchen floor, sighs in her sleep; hesitant, muffled music starts up in one of the bedrooms. And on the other side of the bathroom door, there is the lazy dripping of the water. Alyosha Kamyshinskiy wants to take a shower.

"Is it possible to use the bathroom in this house?"

He knocks, and leans his ear against the bathroom door.

"I'm talking to you, Tatyana."

"You always need the bathroom," says Tatyana. "You always need something. Can I have any privacy in this house?"

"I'll show you privacy." Alyosha's voice stiffens meanly, and he bangs on the door with his fist.

"You come and go," says Tatyana. "You don't tell us. How should we know when you come and when you go and when you need the bathroom? We live here, too."

"And the rent?" Alyosha shouts. "Who's paying the rent?"

"The unemployment office?" Zoyka, his older daughter, calls out from her room.

Zoyka's door is locked; she's been on the phone for the last thirty minutes, and Alyosha needs to use the phone. He knocks on Zoyka's door, and the dog wakes up and scuttles from the kitchen, barking. The dog has a thing about doors.

"Is it possible to use the phone in this house?"

Zoyka doesn't answer, and Tatyana doesn't answer, but the dog attacks Alyosha's ankles and bursts into spasms of hard, wheezy cries.

"To hell with you all," says Alyosha. He pulls a blue Windbreaker over his T-shirt, still wet in places from his run. He'll find himself a pay phone. They'll cry, they'll beg him, they'll regret this later. He reaches for the front door, and the trembling dog, its pink and black gums furious and bared, lunges at his feet.

"What's happening to Kamyshinskiy?" says Kostya Kogan. It's almost noon, and Seryozha is making organic lunch for Olya. She is cooped up in the bedroom upstairs and won't come down. Seryozha knows it's because of Kostya. But Kostya won't go away. He's taken a day off on account of his leaving Marina, and now the poor slob doesn't know what to do with himself. Why don't you go to your woman?

Seryozha wants to ask him, but he doesn't have the heart. Instead, Seryozha's making scrambled tofu on veggie pita.

"You want some?" says Seryozha.

Kostya shakes his head. He says he wants scotch. And a cigarette. But Seryozha tells him to relax.

"Kamyshinskiy runs," explains Seryozha. "I always see him running."

"I know," says Kostya. "Plays tennis, too. I saw him with a racket. He was wearing shorts."

"Can you blame him? The man wants to live healthy."

"The man wants to die healthy," Kostya answers grimly and makes a spitting sound. "You know he's getting out. Now that Irina's gone..."

Seryozha winces. He doesn't like to think of Irina's being gone. They had the same diagnosis at the beginning, Irina Kamyshinskaya and his Olya. "Don't gossip," he says.

"It's not gossip, it's a fact," Kostya says. "Tonight he's flying to Chicago. He says it's for an interview."

"So, good for him."

"There are no interviews on Saturdays."

"What do you want from me, Kostya? You want some scrambled tofu—have some. You want the Sinitsa woman, then go to her. What do you want me to say?"

"Nothing," says Kostya. "Nothing. All I'm saying, we don't know shit about Kamyshinskiy."

Alyosha Kamyshinskiy finds a pay phone in the lobby of Poli's. By twelve thirty the ladies from the nearby retirement community have arrived in pastel trousers and tailored peacoats. They give Alyosha funny looks—is it because he hasn't showered? Alyosha tries to ignore the ladies; he dials the number, waits to be connected. It's a disgrace that a man can't make a phone call from his own home.

"Galochka?" he says into the phone. "Is it you?"

"Of course it's me, silly. Who did you expect?" The voice on the phone is measured, slightly mocking. Galya Razumovskaya is twenty-seven. She lives in Chicago, teaches American history to undergraduates, writes her Ph.D. dissertation.

"I wanted to tell you about my flight. It's at nine forty-five. US Air."

"I know," she says. "I have it written down."

He imagines Galya in her room, in the apartment she shares with Hilda, another graduate student. Galya's room is tidy, with pink and white checkered curtains and a pink bedspread. He is picturing her on the bed, studying, a pair of small, wire-rimmed glasses perched on her straight little nose. She is shy about the glasses, refuses to wear them when Alyosha is around. The phone is wedged between her shoulder and ear. She is underlining something in a textbook, her mouth half opened, her girlishly thick lower lip . . .

"Are you sure this is wise, Alyosha? You visiting again so soon?"

"Galochka, my fledgling, please don't worry."

"All right," she says.

A miracle. No one ever says *all right* to Alyosha, everybody argues, only Galochka agrees. They could get a nice apartment in Chicago, a two-bedroom apartment. One room will be Galochka's office; she will spend her days reading history books, writing her dissertation. Alyosha will get a job, and she won't have to teach anymore—teaching makes her tired. In the evening she'll make him dinner and tell him about the smart things she's read that day. Together they'll go to see art movies at Galochka's university. Galochka likes art movies. Or maybe it's Zoyka who likes them. They are the same age, Galochka and Zoyka; they used to be in school together in Leningrad, and Galochka came over after school sometimes, an intelligent, mature girl—a little on the heavy side—with thoughtful brown eyes. Alyosha noticed her even then, but they met—really met—six months ago in

Chicago, by accident, when Alyosha was attending the wedding of his second cousin.

"Bring along your jacket," says Galochka. "The weather is changing."

She is so thoughtful, so sensible. He will bring his jacket. He wants to bring her so many things: soft, silky things; French perfume in a carton box with that fragile scent that makes him think of April and snowdrops. But he is afraid of these small frivolities—he is a serious man with grown-up children; Galochka doesn't expect this from him. So instead he is bringing her a slim book of poetry by Igor Severyanin, his guilty pleasure. *Pineapples in champagne! Pineapples in champagne! So extraordinarily delicious, so sparkly and piquant.*

"Do you miss me?" he says. "Do you miss me, baby?"

"I will see you at the airport, silly. Nine forty-five."

Kostya Kogan roams on Murray Avenue, hauling along his suitcase. It's after one o'clock, past his lunchtime, and he has forgotten his paper bag lunch at Seryozha's. The Sinitsa woman is waiting for Kostya in the small apartment in Greenfield, on a small street behind the old Giant Eagle, and Kostya will go to her eventually. Of course he'll go. But it's not time yet.

They call her the Sinitsa woman; they make it sound dirty. Sinitsa is her last name. It means a kind of bird. She used to dance with a snake at the Moscow Nights, the Russian restaurant, which opened two autumns ago and went bankrupt in less than a year. She came on stage in the scant trappings of a belly dancer. There were spangles in her makeup, and the snake lay over her naked shoulders like a shawl. That was how Kostya first saw her. A tall, light-haired woman, with plump arms and a white, round belly. "Enough to hold on to?" Borya Rivkin used to joke. He owns a jewelry store on Murray.

When the Moscow Nights closed, Sinitsa got a job as a cashier at the Edgewood Kmart. She's like everybody else now: speaks crummy

English, buys oranges on sale. At home, she is soft and unfocused, forgetting her appointments, misplacing her keys. Kostya scolds and soothes and cajoles her, and she yields, foolish and pliable in his hands.

Borya Rivkin's store is on the other side of Murray. It's called the Malachite Box. Kostya crosses the street, squints against the window. Inside, Rivkin, starch-collared and courtly, is circling around an American customer, showing off his good English, adjusting the mirror in front of her. Kostya wants to go in, wants to say, Hello, Rivkin! What's new in Rivkin's life? But Rivkin might only nod, look down at the counter.

They have loyalty to Marina, and Kostya can understand that. It almost makes him happy, because she needs it and because he wants what's best for her. It's not the first time that Kostya is leaving, but Marina never told anyone before. Loyalty is good, thinks Kostya. But why can't they have a little loyalty to him, too? They have loyalty to everyone, especially Kamyshinskiy. Kamyshinskiy with his soulful eyes, with small poetry books stashed in his coat pocket. They think he is a saint. But Kostya knows Kamyshinskiy's scheming; there's something cowardly in Kamyshinskiy's soulful eyes.

Alyosha Kamyshinskiy comes home and begins to pack. He packs an electric razor, three pairs of underwear, an extra sweater. In the kitchen Zoyka and Tatyana are arguing in muted voices, which means it's about him. There's the smell of something cooking in the kitchen, possibly chicken soup. Maybe they are feeling guilty.

They drift into Alyosha's room, hang by the door, quiet and unobtrusive at first, like shadows. They watch him as he folds his pajama bottoms.

"Going somewhere?" says Tatyana.

"Chicago. For an interview."

"Where's your suit?" Zoyka comes closer and looks into his bag.

"My suit?" he says.

Zoyka senses his hesitation and bristles with power. They both do, Zoyka and Tatyana.

"Your interview suit."

"I was going to wear it. It wrinkles easily."

"Your interview is on a Saturday?" Tatyana drawls uncertainly. Everything about Tatyana is uncertain. She makes no money, but wears nice clothes (long chenille sweaters; black pants tucked into tall, velvety boots). Alyosha doesn't know where the clothes come from. He doesn't ask, and Tatyana never volunteers.

"Maybe if you stayed in college, you'd know more about interviews."

Talking about college is the quickest way to get rid of Tatyana. She plucks at the plaited bracelet of her Seiko watch, and her face turns wistful with the thoughts of better places. It's the look she gets before bolting for the rest of the day.

"Zoyka," she says, "you wash the dishes."

"It's your turn," says Zoyka.

"Zoyka, please. I'm late. A person is waiting."

"Who?"

"It's not important," Tatyana says. "A date."

"It's one thirty in the afternoon," says Zoyka. "I want to know who's waiting for you at one thirty in the afternoon."

"You don't know him," Tatyana says too quickly, and her cheeks turn the color of brick.

"Dad, tell her! I'm not doing the dishes."

Alyosha cringes. "Can't you two resolve this between yourselves?"

Alyosha doesn't like to get involved. Girl stuff, he calls it. A young man who used to call for Zoyka is now calling for Tatyana. Tatyana is rarely home. Sometimes Alyosha has to take a message. Other times it must be Zoyka who answers the phone, brittle and unhappy Zoyka, who is looking more and more like her mother. But what can Alyosha do?

"Why can't you be mature about this?" says Tatyana.

Alyosha wishes she had stayed in school. He barely remembers the young man's name. Girl stuff, thinks Alyosha. Hasn't he fed them, educated them, stuck around through his own wretchedness so they could have a stable childhood? Hasn't he, in the end, brought them to America? The girl stuff turns Alyosha's stomach, but he can't be responsible, can't afford to interfere.

"I want you to clean this pigsty," he says. "And I don't care which one of you does it."

Zoyka pitches her eyebrows like two poisonous exclamation marks, her mother's facial expression.

"Clean the goddamn place!" yells Alyosha. "How many times must I tell you!"

When they leave, he goes to look for his interview suit. It's in the back of his closet, a black suit, appropriate for funerals, anniversaries, and job interviews. Should he wear it? He feels the stiffness, the dusty smell of naphthalene. The suit requires a shirt, a tie, a pair of black shoes that need polishing. Alyosha would have to pack his jeans and sneakers. Also another sweater. He might need a larger bag.

He leaves the suit hanging in the back of the closet. Stupid comedy, he mutters. The girls have figured it out anyway.

At two thirty, Olya is coming down the stairs, rubbing special antibacterial lotion on her hands and her elbows. She says the treatments have made her skin dry and cracked. The house now always smells of her lotion, the strange mix of fruit, medicine, and cleaning solution. When Seryozha leaves the house, the smell clings to his shirt.

"Are you ready, old lady?" Seryozha comes over, takes her hand, reaches for a kiss. They have a four o'clock appointment at the Magee-Womens.

"Is he gone?" says Olya. She's looking around for Kostya.

"Do you see him?"

"Don't let him come here again."

She's lost weight since the operation, and her face is now thinner. She puts on extra makeup before leaving the house. The spots of blush. The pink of lipstick. She goes crazy on mascara, and her eyes in the thicket of black lashes are big, tough, and frightened.

"He's our friend," reasons Seryozha. "We can't turn our backs on Kostya."

"He's the one who's turned his back," says Olya. "He's made his choice. We have to cut him off."

Seryozha pulls her coat from the closet, but Olya shakes her head and says it is too warm, she wants her leather jacket. Seryozha has checked the weather channel and the little thermometer outside the living room window, but he doesn't argue, he never argues, he does what Olya says.

"Remember in the English class?" says Olya. "Marina, Kostya, Borya Rivkin, Kamyshinskiy . . . Kostya isn't worth the soles of Kamyshinskiy's shoes. That poor man, the way he used to fuss over Irina."

Seryozha wonders if he should tell her what he knows about Kamyshinskiy.

She says, "They were the best. The cutest couple."

"Come on! We were the cutest!" He hugs her quickly. "We *are* the best."

He decides he shouldn't tell her. She will only get upset.

"We'll have him over sometime," says Seryozha, "Kamyshinskiy and the girls."

Olya's face sharpens and pales behind the protective pink of her makeup.

"Not now. Maybe when I'm feeling better."

Seryozha looks at her. "No rush."

She ties a silk scarf around her neck, and Seryozha says he has to see about the cab.

"Let's take a bus," she pleads with him. "We've got plenty of time."

Seryozha hesitates.

"Seryozha, please!" says Olya. "I need fresh air. I need a walk."

Passing by Café 61C, Kostya Kogan has a sudden, inexplicable urge to go home. His home, Marina's home. Just for one more day. He will tell Marina that he got locked out, that he's lost the keys to his new place. He will tell her the suitcase was heavy. It is tempting. Kostya leans against the low iron fence that separates the little side-walk tables from the foot traffic and thinks.

Marina will come home around six, six thirty if she stops by the Giant Eagle on her way. She will put her keys on the shelf, hang her handbag on the hat-and-coatrack, every motion exact and automatic. In the dark her face will seem arid with fatigue. Maybe she'll pause before the mirror, her back to the living room, the tight, braced-up back. The kids are clamoring upstairs—at least three hours before their bedtime—and she can't crumple yet. Instead, she'll touch her hair, tweak her lips; she'll pinch herself together. Then in the mirror, she'll notice Kostya in the living-room armchair, with the suitcase at his feet. And for a moment she will think that he came back, that he has changed his mind.

Somebody coughs behind Kostya, on the other side of the low iron fence, and then a voice—a young and forward voice, wavering around the edges—asks him, "Can you give me a light?"

Kostya turns and sees Tatyana, Kamyshinskiy's younger daughter, sitting at an outdoor table alone, twirling a cigarette in her fingers.

"I don't smoke," says Kostya.

He walks around the little fence and sits across from Tatyana. She is lean and languid, and her eyes are hidden behind shades. Her hair is brown and shiny with reddish streaks. It's cut bluntly just above her shoulders and in the front it's long, hiding half her face. That's how she is, Tatyana, she hides. And twirls, twirls that unlit cigarette in her fingers.

"How's your father?" Kostya asks her, because it's the right thing to ask and because she is his friend's daughter.

"My father is a dog," says Tatyana. "How are *you*, Kostya?"

She uses the polite form of *you*, but it doesn't sound formal; it sounds shy and a little flirty. And then there's the way she pronounces his name, *Kostya*, softly, tentatively, like she's trying it out. Kostya is younger than her father, seven or ten years younger. He has seen her with younger men and with older ones, too. She is always there, at Café 61C, smoking and reading and drinking coffee. Sometimes there are those men. And now there's Kostya.

"My father is moving to Chicago soon. Did you know? He will live with his new girlfriend, who's twenty-seven. They'll have babies."

"I'm sorry," says Kostya.

"Don't be. I'm glad he's going. I only wish he'd done it sooner. You have no idea what it was like living with him and my mother. Fortunately, *she* is gone."

"You don't mean it," mumbles Kostya.

"You think this is some shitty kind of grief? God, they hated each other. They hated me and Zoyka, too. Because of us, they were stuck together. That was noble or something. To be stuck. Somebody must have told them that. Or else they'd read it in some shitty parenting magazine."

"Listen," says Kostya, "your father is my friend . . ."

"You don't need to counsel me, Kostya. I like you. Do you like me? Did you know my father's girlfriend is twenty-seven? Did you know she went to school with Zoyka? It's like fucking your own daughter, right? How old is your new girlfriend, Kostya? Will you have many babies with her?"

She is almost shouting at him now, and the people at the other tables begin to notice. Kostya delicately coughs. Tatyana stops abruptly, stares at the table, drops her cigarette, then picks it up again.

She says, "I'm sorry. It's not your fault."

She is suddenly looking small and flat. She keeps her head down, her face hidden again by that slack, luminous hair, and Kostya thinks she might be crying. He is afraid to reach over; it's too intimate a gesture. A hug would be too intimate, too, given the circumstances. Instead, Kostya takes the unlit cigarette from Tatyana's restless, hopeless fingers. He goes inside the coffee shop and gets her matches. Back at the table, he lights the cigarette and hands it to her.

She says, "Thanks."

"Can I have one?" says Kostya.

She gives him a cigarette. They sit across from each other and smoke.

"You're a good man, Kostya," Tatyana tells him, using the polite form of *you*.

Seryozha and Olya miss the bus. First they miss the one that stops at the corner of Phillips and Murray, in front of the hardware store. It shows up early and passes by without pausing—no potential passengers in sight. Seryozha and Olya see it as they round the corner.

"See? Unreliable," says Seryozha. "Cabs and buses, all unreliable, but buses especially so."

They walk to the other bus stop. It's a long walk, and part of it is uphill. Several times Olya asks if they can stop. Just for a moment, she says. Seryozha regrets listening to her, regrets not getting a cab. It's windy, and Olya's silk scarf does nothing to protect her throat. Lately with all the treatments, Olya has become susceptible to respiratory infections. She is gasping, and Seryozha feels he's torturing her.

Seryozha did not want to come to America. The children went ahead, but Seryozha, who had a job with a security clearance, said no way. They had an apartment in a durable old building near the Voykovskaya metro station; they had a car and a garden plot, and Seryozha said he hadn't been working for nothing. He said that if Olya wanted to go, the door was open, she could have a divorce. It happened one morning, after weeks of Olya tormenting him with America. He said it in a hard, icy voice and went off to work, and it must have seemed odd, because normally he was reasonable, almost meek, and Olya was the one lording it over the household. After that, Olya began writing letters—too many letters—and recording the minutiae of their life on audiocassettes. She marked the days between the monthly calls from Pittsburgh—where the children lived— marked them with a pen, on the calendar in the kitchen. And how could Seryozha know that in less than a year she would get sick?

The other bus stop is at the corner of Forbes and Murray, by the Episcopal church. Seryozha and Olya are still a block away when they see two buses cross at the light, stop briefly, disappear.

"What? Now they go in packs?" says Seryozha.

By the time they get to the bus stop, it is three thirty and they have missed all the buses.

"Now what?" Olya asks, almost happily. Seryozha suspects she's been wanting to miss her appointment.

"We can't miss it," he says. "I won't have you miss it."

He tries to flag a cab, but there are no cabs around. He flags every car. That's what they did in Russia: When they couldn't catch a taxi, they caught a private car. But here private drivers don't stop, don't care about earning extra dollars.

"Maybe we should go home," says Olya. "Reschedule for later?"

But just then, a car stops, a red Corsica, and Alyosha Kamyshin-skiy rolls down his window and asks if they need a lift.

"Are you going to—"

"Yes," says Kamyshinskiy. "Get in." He knows where they are going.

It is quiet in Kamyshinskiy's car. He doesn't have tapes, doesn't play the radio. Seryozha sits next to Alyosha, and Olya is in the back-seat, next to a large duffel bag. It's the kind of bag you take on a weekend trip, the kind you carry with you on an airplane. Olya ad-justs her turban. Nobody asks any questions.

"How are the girls?" asks Olya. They are passing by Carnegie Mel-lon University, and Seryozha points at the new construction site. Those rich bastards, says Seryozha. They're building and building. Kamyshinskiy nods—the girls are doing fine.

Just after they turn from Bellfield onto Fifth Avenue, they hit a small traffic jam. Olya fidgets in the backseat. "How is the job situa-tion?" Seryozha asks Alyosha. Kamyshinskiy shrugs and doesn't men-tion Chicago. He checks the rearview mirror, catches Olya's face, switches into another lane. He is quicker than the buses; he doesn't need to make stops.

Olya shouldn't worry; Alyosha knows where he is going; he's been there many times before. They drive some more and turn where they are supposed to turn, and then there's a building with the fractured facade—jagged lines, squares of glass, the entrance shaped into a jut-ting corner—Magee-Womens Hospital.

Olya and Seryozha go inside, but Alyosha doesn't leave immediately. He is sitting in the car and watching the glass entrance, a wheelchair left on the sidewalk, the doors sliding back and forth, a corner of the vestibule barely visible. He didn't think he'd ever come here again. It was a year ago, but it doesn't feel like a year.

He says, The girls are fine. They don't do shit around the house, and Tatyana has dropped out of the university, but otherwise, they are fine.

He says, I have a job interview in Chicago.

She doesn't believe him. She never believes him. He can tell by her face, indifferent, shrunken, the color of wax.

She says, Who are you trying to fool?

He says, I might get married again.

She laughs: That poor little girl? Appliqué, blotting paper, math homework. Didn't she used to have a gerbil?

Alyosha remembers that he mustn't argue. They've had all of their arguments already. She was in pain, delirious on morphine. She was unlucky all her life. Wrong husband, talentless children, mediocre jobs, not enough money. Never enough money. And then . . . to come to America, the dream of all dreams, and to lose it all on the American hospital bed.

He says, I have to catch my flight.

She says, What are you waiting for? Go. You will move to Chicago to live with the girl, and Tatyana will live with the boy she has stolen from Zoyka. You'll stick Zoyka with the old, crazy dog, and you know how few apartments take dogs. That terrible, expensive apartment. But you know Zoyka: She will stay in there, alone. She will have nightmares. You will help her with the money at first, but eventually she'll have to get a job, something with typing, entering numbers into a spreadsheet. She won't like the people there—too provincial, small-minded, she'll say. She won't like the job or the room. She'll develop an allergy to the carpeting. I've always had allergies. Maybe that's how it starts. Bad genes, weak immune system, not enough sunlight. Something simple: an allergy, a nosebleed, a lump.

It's not my fault, says Alyosha Kamyshinskiy. She *is* twenty-seven. I can't stay around forever.

But who will be around to take care of Zoyka?

———

By seven o'clock the streets are dark and wet. The neon signs light up above the shop windows, reflected in the puddles. The green sign of the Barnes & Noble, where Zoyka Kamyshinskaya is looking for self-help books on love. The red sign of the West Coast Video, where Tatyana is renting a movie. The orange sign of the Burger King in Greenfield, where Kostya Kogan is smoking outside, just a couple of blocks away from the little apartment where Sinitsa is waiting for him.

And miles away, at the Pittsburgh International Airport, Alyosha Kamyshinskiy is waiting for his plane to Chicago, trying to lose himself in the thin volume of poems by Igor Severyanin: *Pineapples in champagne! Pineapples in champagne! I turn the tragedy of life into a reverie-farce.*

"Kamyshinskiy is in love," says Olya.

They are walking slowly from the bus stop, counting the puddles.

"You knew?" Seryozha is surprised. "Gray in his beard; devil in his ribs. Are you upset?"

"No," she says. "And Kostya left Marina. What is America doing to us, Seryozha?"

"It's not America. It's them. America just gave them space. Remember how we all used to live? Those apartments, those square meters, nothing to rent, nowhere to move? Remember the coupons for soap and sugar? Dear guests, you can either wash your hands with soap—"

"—or drink your tea with sugar," says Olya.

She is quiet for a while.

"Take me to California, Seryozha. I want to see the kids."

He says, yes, once the treatments are over, and the doctor permits.

But she is still uneasy, he can tell from the way she doesn't lean on him, from the tension in her wrist.

"I'm not leaving you, if that's what you're worried about," he says. "Look at me, Seryozha."

"You're not getting rid of me so easily. And if you meet a handsome clerk at the Kmart, well, tough, I don't want to hear about it. Even if he can dance with a snake."

Olya softly smiles, as if to herself, as if she is not convinced completely. But she lets her sleeve cling to Seryozha's sleeve. They don't have to talk about Kamyshinskiy yet.

"You knew this about me, Olya."

They are counting puddles. On a night like this, in the dark, you can pretend that this is a big city. Traffic swishes by. The footsteps are impersonal and quick. On a night like this you can pretend nothing has happened yet. Olya squeezes Seryozha's hand. It's just the two of them in the rainbow of fluorescent shops, in the round dance of streetlights. Many years ago.

LYDIA PEELLE

University of Virginia

Shadow on a Weary Land

It was Frank James, not Jesse, who buried the treasure in Brown's Ridge. This is what the Musician tells me as he pulls the metal detector out the back of his pickup and slings it over his shoulder. We find a deer path through the woods behind his cabin and take the back way up the ridge. The Musician breaks through low branches and lopes up the steep loose ground. *But Frank didn't have half as much dough,* I say, out of breath when we get to the top. To the south, the Nashville skyline crouches on the horizon like a stalking animal. *But he was smarter,* the Musician grins. *He planned ahead. For future generations,* I say. *Exactly,* the Musician says, tapping the end of his nose.

Life in Brown's Ridge is like this: at night, the howl of the coyotes can split you in two. In the morning the sun is slow to rise over the spine of the ridge, and starlings and wild turkeys pick their way across the dark fields and into the trees. The woods hold pockets of cool air in the summer, and warm air in the winter, and walking through them you tend to look over your shoulder, thinking something is following you. When the coyotes come by, Greenup Bird lifts his old head and howls, overcome by something ancient inside him. On the steepest parts of the ridge grow oaks and hickories over three hundred years old, saved from generations of loggers by their inaccessibility. Up there I have seen bald eagles, bucks with antlers like coatracks. In the valley below, Katy Creek rushes south to the Cumberland. Brown's Ridge Pike runs beside it, all the way to Kentucky. Out there on the horizon, Nashville seems to be hundreds of miles away. Not many people live here: less people than cows, less people than copperheads, coyotes, possums. They call it Brown's Ridge after Kaspar Brown, the first man killed by Indians here. No one knows exactly, but that was sometime around 1799.

The Musician and I have lived here since 1985, and never before has there been any talk of treasure. I can't believe that no one has thought to look for it yet, in the same way I can't believe that the Nashville developers have only now discovered Brown's Ridge. When Joe Guy's father bought his farm in 1935, the James brothers had only been gone fifty years. There were people around who remembered passing them on the road, seeing them at the horse races, smiling to their wives. It's a wonder that it never occurred to Joe Guy to look for some sort of a treasure buried somewhere on his thousand-acre tract. Or to anyone else, for that matter: the families in the trailers on the other side of the ridge, the dairy farmers, the kids in grubby T-shirts who miss the school bus day after day. Lacy, the pretty young waitress at the Meat 'n' Three, talks every once in a while about striking it rich in the new state lottery, buying a plane ticket to New York. Even Preacher Jubal Cain would not be above scratching around in the dirt for a few thousand dollars' worth of gold. So why are we the first? The Musician tells me, *None of them would have even known where to look.* The woods are quiet, the hot hush of late summer as it turns into fall. *Have you got a map?* I ask him. *Don't need one,* he says, handing me a shovel. *I got Steve.*

Since he showed up on the Musician's doorstep last winter, Steve has claimed to have a direct line to the spirit of Jesse James. He is quick to point out that it is not Jesse's ghost, that he is not among us. The first time Jesse spoke to him, Steve was lying on the Musician's floor, and he sat up and said, *Holy shit, the Lord speaketh,* and Jesse said, *No, man, listen, it's Jesse James.* Last week, over an after-dinner joint, Steve told the Musician that Jesse said that his brother's treasure was buried somewhere along the ridgeline. *Can Jesse be any more specific?* the Musician asked, taking a hit. *No, man,* Steve said, exhaling a cloud of smoke. *I don't want to bug him.* Steve believes the end of the world is coming any time now. *As in the book of Revelation?* I ask him. *Fuck Revelation,* he says. *I'm talking Old Testament here. Isaiah, man. He saw it all.* He keeps the book of Isaiah tucked in his coat pocket, torn from a bible he stole out of a church. The pages are held together with duct tape. When I first met Steve, I thought he was a homeless guy the Musician had taken in, like a stray cat, but then he pulled a fancy cell phone from a holster on his belt and took a call from his girl in California. *She's got the vision,* he says, pointing between his eyes. *She's got it better than me.* Every Sunday, at the Brown's Ridge Baptist Church, Jubal Cain preaches Jesus' love. Outside the church is a sign that says: HOT OUTSIDE? WE'VE GOT PRAYER CONDITIONING! And beneath that it says, YOU ARE WELCOME. COME AS YOU ARE. When Preacher Jubal slows his Oldsmobile at the stop sign by my house and I happen to be outside, he looks long and hard but does not wave. I've never set foot inside Brown's Ridge Baptist, and neither has Steve. Steve's cell phone ring plays "Dixie." He uses the pages of Revelation to roll his joints.

None of us can claim to belong here. The Musician and I came to Nashville in the seventies, him for the drugs and the music, me just for the drugs. We got to be friends, or at least were always showing up at the same parties. He was young and knew the good-looking girls. I was forty years old, just getting started on the heavy stuff. When the scene vibed out in the eighties, we both decided to move to Brown's Ridge. Way out to the country, we thought back then. Steve's from California or Nevada, or somewhere, no one really knows. I always thought Lacy was born here, but it turns out she moved up with her momma from South Carolina when she was a few years old. Preacher Jubal Cain is from Bowling Green, Kentucky. Joe Guy's daddy, when he bought the farm, moved down from Paradise Ridge, a good twenty miles to the north. Frank and Jesse James came from Missouri via Muscle Shoals, Alabama. Brown, before he was pierced through the heart with an arrow, was a Yankee from Philadelphia, forging his way south to find a better life for his family. The only person I know who is actually from Brown's Ridge is Joe Guy Jr., born the year we moved here, in the upstairs bedroom of his daddy's big white house, but he cut out of here two years ago and no one's heard from him since.

The metal detector that the Musician bought is cheap and unreliable. There is no depth setting and for the first few days he wastes hours digging up beer cans and pop tabs that lie just beneath the leaf litter. Every morning he knocks on my door and me and Greenup Bird go with him up the ridge. Steve comes, too, and we all help dig. The Musician points to a spot and I go at it with a short-handled spade, Greenup goes at it with his claws and teeth, dirt spraying out behind him through his back legs. Since the stroke, my left arm shakes so bad that it's difficult to control any tool. I get tired easy and have to sit down. Greenup's namesake was the victim of the first peacetime bank robbery in this country, which went down in Liberty, Missouri, in 1866. I live by the creek in a house that J. D. Howard, a local grain dealer known to be a gambler, built in 1879. The house has fifteen-foot-high ceilings and a fireplace in every room. Across the Pike is the field where J. D. Howard kept his horse, an exceptionally fine animal for a man of his humble profession. On weekdays developers trawl through Brown's Ridge in their Hummers, wider than one lane of the road. They pull over to ask us directions, looking down at us through mirrored sunglasses, and we point them the wrong way. I found Greenup Bird on the Pike two years ago, half starved and half dead, a cross between a God-knows-what and a Lord-have-mercy. He's got one blue eye and one black, a coat that feels like a wire brush. As the Musician says, he is one plug-ugly dog. We make a good pair, him and me.

The Musician once played bass for a famous band. He's been all over the world and he's got luggage stuffed in every closet in the cabin. He's got stories, whether you choose to believe them or not. He's played to a crowd of twenty thousand in Berlin, slept with a one-armed Haitian girl in the back of a Spanish club. The Musician's given name is Randy Spaulding, but when he started touring he had it legally changed to Lex Spark. He's got good days and bad days, and when I go to see him I usually know which one it is before I'm halfway up his mud-rutted drive. On bad days he stays inside the dark musty cabin, tending to his regret like it's a pot on the stove. On good days he is electric with plans, plans you wouldn't think he had in him, like searching for Frank James's treasure. He built the little cabin himself, back when we first moved out here, using wood he salvaged from an old amusement park. The kitchen counter is the door of the ticket booth. Three years ago, it was the Musician who broke into my house, dragged me out of a puddle of piss and shit, and drove me to the hospital, where after three days in a coma they told me I was a very lucky man. He hasn't been able to get session work in Nashville for years. The bass leans against his kitchen counter like a woman trying to catch a bartender's eye. He won't touch it. I imagine he doesn't play music anymore for the same reason I don't do drugs anymore: You can only push up to the edge so many times before you realize the one thing on the other side is your own mortality, with no one waiting there to keep your grave clean.

It's impossible to prove, but most people would agree that it was Jesse James, alias J. D. Howard, who shot Greenup Bird at that bank in Missouri, committing one of the first crimes of a lifetime of infamy. It was more than ten years before he moved to Brown's Ridge and changed his name, built his high-ceilinged house and tried to live the life of an honest man. Frank James, when he arrived soon after with his wife and young son, took the name of B. J. Woodson and rented a farm along the creek. Joe Guy's thousand-acre farm, the biggest tract in the entire county, was sold quietly this summer, in the middle of June. Just before Labor Day, when the work crews started rolling in, Preacher Jubal Cain watched the surveyor's tape go up and said, *Whosoever will, let him come. A time of prosperity is here.* We dig deep holes along the ridgeline, some because of a sign from the metal detector, some because Steve rolls his eyes back in his head and points, some for no reason at all. As we dig we call out to each other through the trees: *You got anything? Nothing, man. You? Nothing.*

My mind, before I ruined it, was a beautiful thing. As an old man I can say this without vanity or pride. Its brilliance was like the light of late day over Joe Guy's back field, but now the light is gone. What's left are the scraps, held together with wire and string. Nothing has grown back in the ruts of the drugs. I used to be an inventor. I've sold dozens of patents for things you use every day. I like to think I've made life easier for people, better. Some nights I think I can feel

Jesse's boot steps if I lean off my mattress and press my fingers to the floor, but it is only the rumble of the trucks coming down the Pike. Living in a place like this, you'd think it would be easy to start believing in ghosts. But I am haunted by something more real than ghosts. Behind the Minute Mart, on a scrubby lot where the gas trucks turn around, two perfect rows of daffodils come up year after year, just wide enough to line the drive of a farmhouse of which there is no longer a trace. Whoever planted those daffodils, a woman, I picture, in a homemade dress, did it decades ago, without any thought whatsoever of me. The Musician drives me into town to collect my Social Security checks and buy new boots, and I hold my left arm down with my right to keep it from jerking out and hitting the gearshift. Every once in a while, I'll speak a whole sentence backward, and the woman at the bank will smile at me with false patience, like I'm a little boy. We used to go to the honky-tonks on Saturday nights to tell stories about the old days and complain about the music, but we don't go out at night anymore, because the headlights on the Musician's truck quit. He's working part-time laying tile, his fingernails caked with grout. Days are rough for a self-employed tradesman, what with all the cheap labor the contractors can scare up. The Musician looks down at his boots, the steel toes showing through big holes in the worn-out leather. He sighs and says, *It's a tough row to hoe.*

Steve won't touch the metal detector. He thinks it is a blasphemy. He says that God will disconnect his line to Jesse if he gets too greedy. *If you ask, you shall receive,* he tells us, and many days when we go out digging he stays behind at the cabin, leaning back on the porch steps with a joint. *Jesse might want to get in touch with me,* he says. *You two go on ahead.* When we come back in the afternoon he is curled up snoring in a patch of sun. We've happened on a cobalt blue medicine bottle, which the Musician is certain we can sell at an antique shop in town. We've found a lug nut, an old snarl of baling wire, eighteen broken Coke bottles. We found a hornet's nest, a hollow tree that the Musician climbed inside of and looked all the way up to the sky. We found an old shoe, a ladder, a cracker tin, but still no treasure. *Jesse's not sure yet if he really wants you to find it,* Steve says when we wake him with the toes of our boots. *Well, tell Jesse to make up his mind,* the Musician says. *We haven't got much time.* At dusk I walk Greenup Bird through the hay fields of Joe Guy's farm, letting him scare up rabbits and bark at the deer. I find a dead raccoon hanging from its neck in the crook of a beech tree. I wonder how many more times we'll walk through the field: five more mornings, ten. I tell the raccoon: *You're lucky to get out now.* I rub out surveying marks spray-painted on the grass with my heel.

One morning in mid-September we think we've hit the jackpot. After an insistent sign from Jesse, Steve starts in on a level stretch of the hillside, alongside the grade of an old logging road. A foot and a half down his shovel strikes metal, and we all rush over to him, Greenup panting, slapping our legs with his tail. With his hands in the air the Musician circumscribes the size of Confederate bills, bars of solid gold. The shovel twangs encouragingly. But when we dig it up it turns out to be a sheet of rusted tin hinged to a spiraled copper pipe from an old still. The Musician slumps his shoulders for a moment, then gets back to work. He's tall and lanky and loose the way an upright bass player should be. He eats and eats but stays skinny as a whip. He feeds me and Steve in the cabin most nights, frying hamburgers when he's got work, boiling potatoes when he doesn't. Steve chucks the pipe downhill. In the teens, the ridge had more bootleggers than any other place in the county: so wild and steep, yet so close to town. They kept little fox dens at the foot of trees where they sometimes spent the night. They pinned photos of Betty Grable to the sycamores and ate the lunches their wives packed them in tin pails, throwing the chicken bones over their shoulders. The ones without women sometimes moved out here for good, squatting on unclaimed land in tar paper shacks. In the deepest hollers we find the last of these places, long abandoned by the gangs of teenage boys who once used them as clubhouses. Behind their graffiti and karate posters, the walls are insulated with layers of newspaper from the 1950s. We peel them off and read the ads for land auctions and farm liquidations, and I think about how this cashing in on the country is not any kind of new thing.

In 1969 Brown's Ridge damn near went. Joe Guy's father saw the development going on in the rest of the county and made up his mind to sell. He found someone in Clarksville who would buy his herd of Holsteins, mapped out roads, and even had sewer lines put into the front field. The caps are still out there: Sometimes I trip over them when Greenup and I walk at sunset, or Joe Guy's mower catches a blade and from my bedroom I hear the scrape of metal against metal. In the spring of that year, Joe Guy's father stood at the edge of the field with a notary public, a man from a development company, and blueprints for two- and three-bedroom brick ranch houses spread out on the hood of his Cadillac. He was all set to sign the final papers when he had a heart attack and dropped right where he stood, into the ditch on the side of the road. The pen fell out of his hand. The man from the development company said it was as if he had been struck by lightning. *Almost like an act of God,* he would tell people for the rest of his life. The farm and all the land, as drawn up in the will, went to the sole heir, Joe Guy, and Joe refused to sell. He bought the cows back from the man up in Clarksville and put them right back out in the pasture, kept on farming for the next thirty years. But now Joe is older than his father was when he dropped into the weeds that day, and he's got visions of Florida dancing in his eyes, clean fingernails, sleeping late.

Some days, if either of us has some money, the Musician and I get lunch down at the Meat 'n' Three. Lacy pours our coffee and sings along to the country video station on the TV. She holds her check pad up to her mouth and whispers not to order the fish. *The cat done licked it,* she says. The Musician eats fried chicken with okra, cottage cheese, pinto beans. I eat corn bread and a biscuit and take my rainbow of pills. Lacy's young enough to be the Musician's daughter, my granddaughter. She wears a wide black belt low on her hips, jeans, bright blue eye shadow. She's got the body of a 1950s movie star. The Musician watches her carefully as she moves around the room. Most days, she'll sit down with us while we eat, stealing a french fry or a potato chip from the Musician's plate, snapping her fluorescent gum. But these days the place is packed with developers up from Nashville, spreading out topo maps on the tables and picking the pork out of their turnip greens. Joe Guy comes in with a pretty lady in panty hose and a suit. They sit at the counter and go over a brochure of computer-generated images of big brick houses. *We're going to call it Apple Orchard Acres,* she tells him, and he rubs his hands together and nods. Lacy brings his sweet tea and asks if he's heard from Joe Jr. He only smiles and winks at her. His brand-new F-350 is parked outside the restaurant, the engine ticking. *Wouldn't you do it, too?* the Musician asks, when he sees me looking. *Wouldn't you do the same, for a couple million dollars?* What would I do with two million dollars? Buy back the land. Save it for the coyote, the heron, the possum, the bobcat, the kestrel, the broad-winged hawk.

Since my stroke, this is what I have come to know: The path to enlightenment is free of all desire. The doctors say it has something to do with a drop in my testosterone levels, but I feel it is something greater. I look at the world with a new, pure love. The graders rumble down the Pike and pull into Joe Guy's front fields, laying down the first roads. There are three phases of development planned, 188 houses total, with talk of a golf course. The smaller dairy farmers in town, when they hear about it, start to reassess their mortgages, talk to their wives. Steve doesn't want me and the Musician to get left behind at the second coming. He prays for us to find Jesus. But I don't need to. *I've found love without him,* I say. I look for other answers, other explanations. I read whatever I can get my hands on. Every mammal on earth, I've read, from mouse to man to mammoth, goes through roughly the same number of heartbeats in a lifetime. When I tell this to Steve, he says, *If that's not proof of God, then I sure as hell don't know what is.*

We dig up a mule shoe, six square-headed nails, a milking pail, a barrette. We find an old Maytag washer, rusted parts all tumbled down the hillside like spilled guts. I have a certain respect for folks who chucked their garbage out their back doors. When I was lying unconscious in the hospital, the Musician came into my house and cleaned out as much junk as he could, the boxes of old syringes, the rank buckets of piss. When I relearned how to talk, the first thing I said was, *Thank you.* Jesse James and a member of his posse, a man named Bill Ryan, alias Tom Hill, drank beer and ate canned oysters at the saloon that once stood on the site of the Minute Mart, which keeps its security lights on all day and all night, too. We stop to buy Cokes and cellophane-wrapped miniature chess pies, which keep us going until midnight. The kids who hang out there whisper when we come in. I hear them say, *There goes one crazy motherfucker,* and it's hard to tell whether they're talking about Steve with his apocalypse eyes, the Musician with his filthy jeans and busted boots, or me with my shaking hands and my slurred speech.

People driving down the Pike stop in front of my house to take pictures of the historical marker, and they cross the yard to look at the well, which Jesse James supposedly dug. I watch and wonder what they would say if they could see inside. Stacks of magazines from the eighties, old food, stuff even the Musician was too scared to touch when he cleaned the place out, a smell of piss hanging on the shades, which I keep drawn tight. Members of the Nashville ladies' garden club come and tend the outside of the house, watering the rose-bushes, trimming back the boxwood. Greenup Bird puts his paws on the windowsill and barks his head off at them. But I don't mind all the people. I remind myself that, though I've almost paid off the mortgage, this house doesn't really belong to me. I am no more than a squatter, only passing through. A few years ago, the ladies put a pine log wishing well on top of Jesse James's deep dank well, a hanging basket full of fake flowers, like something out of a miniature golf course. Steve gets work south of the city and leaves, promising the Musician that he'll give us a call on his cell if he hears from Jesse. The Musician comes down the road and knocks on the door, looking for clues. Frank's house burned in 1909, but the Musician reasons that maybe he left something at Jesse's place, a hint, a tiny bag of gold. *Think we could get down that well?* he asks. He eyes the living-room fireplace suspiciously and runs his finger along the mortar between the bricks. *Do you really think we'll find it?* I ask him. He straightens up, pushes his hand through his wild long hair. He looks at me, more serious than I've seen him in years. *For future generations. We need to find it,* he says.

At the start of October Steve returns, unannounced, to sleep on the Musician's floor. In the middle of the night he gets word from Jesse that he hasn't been remembering correctly. *Frank didn't put it up on the ridge,* Steve reports to us. *He buried it in one of the fields near his house.* The farm that Frank rented was sprawling, huge, hundreds of acres along the creek. It took him days to plow, even with a team of good mules, even with a half-dozen hired hands. We abandon the ridgeline and come down into the valley. We start out from east to west with no regard for fences, property lines, NO HUNTING OR TRES-PASSING signs. We dig wherever Steve or the metal detector tells us to, in farmers' cow fields, in people's backyards. We dig through shale and limestone filled with crinoid fragments and brachiopods, the fos-silized skeletons of creatures who inhabited Brown's Ridge five hun-dred million years ago, when we all would have been standing at the bottom of a shallow salty sea. We scare up a half-clothed teenage couple who spook out of the pawpaw like deer. I find an arrowhead, perfectly fluted. When the white man first came, the Indians would lure him into the woods by imitating animal sounds: at night, a fox or an owl, during the day, a squirrel, horse bells. Kaspar Brown was stalking what he believed to be a rutting buck the day that he was ambushed on the steepest part of the ridge.

Joe Guy stands in the gold light of his back field in late October, shading his eyes with one hand. The cows, some of them the great-granddaughters of his father's herd, the ones he bought back in 1969, have all been trucked to Alabama. The first roads have been roughly graded. A bobcat that he has watched all its life will spend a few weeks cowering under the construction foreman's trailer until it streaks out of the pasture and into the hills. The sadness I feel when I see the backhoes moving in is much bigger than me. It seems to shadow the land with heavy wings. At the Meat 'n' Three, Lacy leans over the toilet in the back and throws up before her breakfast shift, holding her hair at the nape of her neck. Joe Guy comes in for one last breakfast, trying to fill a creeping emptiness. *At least the house will stay in the family,* he mutters, hunched at the counter over his coffee and eggs. When Lacy hears this she pauses, her heart pounding, stooped over the bleach bucket with a dripping rag.

B. J. Woodson and J. D. Howard used to ride their horses down the Pike and across the river on Saturdays, taking the Hyde's River Ferry and kicking up dust. Just across the Cumberland, in a floodplain at the bend of the river, was the racetrack where they used to spend their hours, Frank always anxious to get back to the farm, Jesse always convincing him to stay longer. The flat alluvial deposits of the land, the silt and fine-grained sand, made it an ideal place to run horses. Seventy years later, it made it the obvious spot to build the Cumberland County airport, and when they built the runways they dug up hundreds of horseshoes and coins. When the airport moved out to the interstate in the eighties, the floodplain became the Metro-Center Mall, a movie theater, vast parking lots, elaborate fountains. Since it went bankrupt a few years ago it's been all but abandoned, save for one former shoe store at the back, facing the river, that has been converted to the State Democratic Headquarters, some interns and a couple of laptops, without even a prayer. You can see it from the top of the ridge, this white elephant, and if you know how to look you can see the palimpsest of the land clearly, the story written on top of story written on top of rubble and bone.

Sometimes I don't know where Steve gets it from. He takes things he hears here and there and cobbles them all together into one unified theory of Armageddon. He pushes his greasy black hair from his face, rolls a joint, takes Isaiah from his pocket. *The earth is utterly broken down,* he reads. *The earth is moved exceedingly. It shall reel to and fro like a drunkard.* If this is true, we ask him, why is he bothering to dig for buried treasure? *If we strike it rich,* he says, *I can buy my girl a Greyhound ticket out from Cali. Get a fuck before the end of the world.* The Musician rolls his eyes behind Steve's back. We have spent long hours debating the existence of this girl. If you spend enough time with Steve, it is hard to keep track of what is true. I do know this: I haven't believed in God since the 1960s. These days I'm not sure what I believe in at all, save the law of the conservation of matter, which means everything is made of what came before, the shrapnel of the big bang runs through my veins, the dinosaurs, the mammoths, the cells of the bones and shit of every man, woman, or cockroach that walked this earth before me.

Years ago we held huge parties up at the Musician's cabin. We'd roast a pig, plug in the amps, invite loads of music industry people who would drive out from the city, get trashed out of their skulls, and wake up in the morning next to a stranger on the cabin floor. Back then there was no Minute Mart, and people brought beer and liquor in huge metal coolers, not to mention sheets of acid, coke, all the heroin you could ask for. The Musician slept with second-rate country singers and girls just off the Greyhound from Huntsville or Tuscaloosa, headed for Music Row. I would lock myself in the bathroom with a producer or two and try to slip free of my mind. When my veins started to fall apart, I shot up between my toes. After the stroke, I realized that the world is much bigger than I'd ever before imagined, and that it will close up seamlessly on my absence, like water over a sinking stone. This is the most important thing I know. Walking with Greenup Bird one morning along the creek, I saw him shove his nose into a tangle of thorns. He pulled it out, looked up at me with a startled face, then opened his mouth, and a tiny sparrow flew out from between his teeth and disappeared into the trees.

November comes, and the woods get gray. The leaves crumple into fists. On his good days, the Musician is talking in ten-year plans— stocks, mutual funds. *When we find the treasure,* he says, *I'm gonna get*

me one of them mutual funds. On his bad days, he leaves the metal detector hanging on a hook near the door, drinks himself to sleep in the
cabin. I have no idea what he suddenly needs all this money for, and
I worry that he's planning on leaving town. Steve's friend's cousin
gives him a quart jar of peach-flavored moonshine, and he passes it
on to the Musician. Steve quit drinking when he found religion, and
he knows I won't touch the stuff now. The Musician will do anything
that's handed to him. The moonshine is colored with Kool-Aid and
he wakes up on his couch with pink drool stains like fangs at the corners of his mouth. Sometime in the night, Joe Guy Jr. comes back to
Brown's Ridge. He drives down the Pike in a new Ford truck, just
like his father's, and brings a tape measure to plan how he will furnish
the big house, which is already adrift in a choppy sea of broken
ground. Lacy wakes up when she hears the distant sound of the
truck's big engine and knows, deep in her blood, that it is him. The
Musician, when he hears about Joe Jr.'s return the next morning at
the Minute Mart, doesn't yet have any reason to think twice about it.

Frank James loved Brown's Ridge because he could do an honest
day's work here. He could spend ten hours behind the plow and have
nothing to hide when he fell exhausted into bed next to his wife. He
stopped cussing and joined the church. He befriended the Nashville
policemen. *Frank was always the levelheaded one,* Steve says. *Jesse tells
me that all those years on the road, his brother was really just along for
the ride.* Just before he leaves for Florida, we run into Joe Guy at the
Minute Mart, buying bread and milk. *I seen you boys out there in the
field,* he says, not unkindly. *What are y'all doing out there?* The Musician looks down at the dull steel toe of his boot. *Not your worry now,
is it?* he says, taking a swig from a forty in a brown paper sack. Joe
nods his head. It is not his fault, not really. He's just a tired old man.
I think I know how he feels.

———

Joe Guy isn't long gone by the time Phase One of Apple Orchard Acres is up. One day it's just a handful of foundations and the next the first families are moving in, black middle-class families from the city, bringing boxes of appliances and purebred dogs. The yards are still open sores of fill dirt and truck ruts. The new families plant spindly dogwood trees next to the broad stumps of the hackberries, tie them to a stake with string. They install aboveground pools along the creek line and put out poison meat for the coyotes. I lock up Greenup Bird at home and go out with a garbage bag to collect as much of it as I can, then burn it in the woodstove. The streets of the development are named after apples, part of the orchard theme. Gala Court, Macintosh Way, Granny Smith Drive. *I didn't know that Joe Guy ever had apple trees here,* the Musician says. He didn't. He had Holsteins, and before that it was a tobacco field, and before that, who knows, a Shawnee hunting camp, a battleground in some long forgotten war. *Well, what do names mean, anyway?* the Musician asks. Fred Profitt built a road up his holler in 1957 and we still call it Fred Profitt Way. When the city came around to put up street signs, Jim Harnell named the road up to his place Schlitz Lane. Hyde's Ferry Road dead-ends at the river, and most people don't think to wonder why. Last year I gave Lacy a dog I found on the Pike, a big scary boxer that she feels safer coming home to. She gave me directions to her house when I went to drop him off, up on Bear Hollow Road, where in 1873 a man named Zeb Mansker shot and killed a black bear, then covered its hide in salt and left it in his cow pasture for his cows to lick and rasp clean of flesh. *It's the third house on the left,* she told me, *if you don't count the trailers.*

No one in Brown's Ridge, as far as I know, remembers the girl for whom Katy Creek is named, but I like to think of her, a plain dark-eyed girl with a temper, and secrets. Downstream, where the water widens before emptying into the big brown Cumberland, there's a one-lane bridge over a stretch that's deep enough to swim in. In the summer the kids jump off the bridge, hollering and whistling. They all know it's okay to jump off the west side of the bridge, but not the east. Rumor has it there's a Pinto rusting underwater just to the east, and you could slice your foot off, or impale yourself, or worse. It's wisdom that's been passed down through years and years among the kids: *Not there,* they tell the younger ones, *there's a Pinto down there, not there. That's where the Pinto is, the Pinto, the Pinto.* The kids at this point probably have no idea that a Pinto's a kind of car, but then again, the kid who drove it off the bridge twenty-five years ago probably had no idea that a pinto's a kind of horse.

In December two things happen: Brown's Ridge Baptist paves a brand-new parking area, and Lacy's baby starts to show. Every Sunday, more and more people file through the doors of the church, in search of salvation. Preacher Jubal rubs his hands together and says, *You are all welcome,* then looks around and pauses, struck by the fact that he's never seen a black face in the congregation before. After the service he walks to the Meat 'n' Three and orders coffee and a slice of pecan pie. *Why don't I see a nice girl like you in church?* he asks Lacy. Then to no one in particular, *She'll make a good mother. Even to a bastard child.* Joe Guy Jr. eats supper there every night. He eats with his eyes on Lacy, measuring her the way he is measuring the new furniture he will buy for his father's house. She hums and with her thumb checks to see if the soup in the Crock-Pot is hot. When she was sixteen, Joe Jr. took Lacy up to one of the shacks on the ridge side and laid her down on the yellowed newspaper and broken glass. In that moment on the ridge, Lacy gritted her teeth and saw clearly what her life was meant to be. Joe Jr. will live in his father's old house, strange among the new brick mansions, and drive every day to Nashville to his new job at a used car lot. For the past two years, in the dark of her bedroom at night, Lacy has silently moved her lips and wished for his return, the closest she has ever come to praying.

Every night, the coyotes come closer and closer to my house, spooked by the activity in the fields. Soon there will be nowhere left for them to go. The developers gas up their SUVs at the Minute Mart, toss coffee cups into the road. The electric company comes out and trims all the trees along the power lines and birds fly into the air as the branches fall. I hear that there are two new developments in the works, one along the creek, one for the field across from my house, the one where Jesse kept his horse. The electric company comes back and cuts many of the trees down, replaces all the power lines with bigger, thicker wires. The town holds a zoning meeting at the Meat 'n' Three about the development on the creek, and the only people who show up are the people from Phase One of Apple Orchard Acres and me. I stand in the back, holding my left arm behind my back to keep it from shaking, and the women pull their little children away from me and stare. For some reason I think they will fight the commissioner, point out the floodplain, the pollution, the water table, but instead, all the talk is about mailboxes. They are concerned that the prices of the new houses are too low, that they will attract the wrong kind of people. *We worked too hard for this,* a woman with a baby on her hip stands up to say. They settle on bricked mailboxes and cul de sacs, things that will make the new development look a little classier. I step out the back door to quiet the scream in my head. What about the herons? What about the coyote, the bobcat, the turtles? My heart aches for the turtles of Brown's Ridge. They've been around, unchanged, for 250 million years. I know they'll be here longer than any of us, long enough to see the creek turn into a Wal-Mart parking lot, the ridge cut in two for an on-ramp to some superhighway. Still they won't leave, because this is their home, and turtles never leave their home range. Each one of them trudges along the same paths for more than a hundred years, even if someone builds an in-ground swimming pool in the middle, even if someone builds a road straight across. Some will make it a month or a even a couple of years, miraculously dodging cars and dogs and children, before they are crushed beneath the tire of a late model sedan, a country song so loud on the radio that the driver doesn't even hear the crunch.

Steve reads from Isaiah as we hike past the new houses, heading to the edge of the creek. *The streams shall be turned into pitch, and the dust into brimstone, and the land shall become burning pitch. For it is the day of the Lord's vengeance.* The Musician turns around and says, *Oh, shut up. I've got more important things to worry about.* Something I know that Steve doesn't: The Musician is going to be a father. He's forty-nine years old and has never dreamed of this. When we pass, the dogs in the new yards throw themselves against the ends of their chains. The houses are enormous, windows piled on windows, pink brick. Every single family that has moved into Apple Orchard Acres has been black, a fact that neither Joe Guy or any of the developers could have predicted. *Haven't those people been fighting all these years to get out of the country?* Jubal Cain asked the crowd at the Meat 'n' Three. *Why do they want to come back?* The Musician can't get any work laying tile, even in the new houses. The detail work has all been subcontracted out to Mexicans who come up from Nolensville Pike in the backs of crowded pickups. *Look right here,* Steve says, jabbing at the pages of Isaiah. *Strangers shall stand and feed your flocks, and the sons of the alien shall be your plowmen and your vine-keepers. It's all in here,* he says. He shakes the Musician's arm. *Are you sure you should take that all so literally?* the Musician asks him. He's been talking about playing music again, going back out on the road, calling some old friends. Anything to make a little money. He hasn't had work for weeks and we are all living on dried beans and peanut butter. But no new band is going to hire a fifty-year-old bass player, even if he has played with Clint Black and George Strait. When he finally told me about his child, we were up on the ridge, digging through the sandy soil. *Why didn't you tell me when we started?* I asked him. He was smiling like a sphinx. *Didn't want you to think I was crazy,* he said. He doesn't realize it may be one of the least crazy ideas he's ever had, that his kid's future might lie buried somewhere in Brown's Ridge.

The black families keep coming, moving out from Jefferson Street and Charlotte Avenue. They want a half-acre yard, a three-car garage, no more screaming neighbors. The first night they spend in their new houses, the smell of fresh paint curling their noses, they hold each other and vow to lose twenty pounds, to argue less. Preacher Jubal sits in the Meat 'n' Three and says to the four or five men eating there, *Now wait a minute, brothers, is this how we want our town to grow?* Lacy gets so big that she can't bend over to wipe the tables, so she leans over and wipes them behind her back. She sits down with us, blows her bangs up from her forehead. *You boys been up to much?* she asks. In her face it's plain that she's quit expecting anything from the Musician. *Not much,* he says, eyes on her belly, grinning. When he finds the treasure, he's going to come for her at work and take her in his arms, tell her he can give her and the baby anything they need. Until then, he's not letting on to anything. He wants it to be a surprise. While we drink coffee, the Musician leafs through a *Pennysaver,* and among the ads for grave plots and truck caps he finds one for a new metal detector, state of the art, an LCD display, $500, OBO. *No,* I say. *Yes!* he says, slapping his hand down on the table. Surveyors' stakes go up in the field across from my house. We find orange tape around the hackberry trees, which can mean only one thing. *Good god,* the Musician says. *It's all going.* He takes off his hat and rakes back his hair. *They're coming out here for the same reason we did, aren't they?* I nod my head yes. *For peace.*

Steve disappears for three days, then comes up to the cabin to tell us we are close. He had a dream that told him so. *It's right under our noses,* he says. All day long, the Musician has been calling friends looking for loans, and he's flat out on the couch, exhausted, his eyes bloodshot and glazed. *Really?* he says halfheartedly, but still feels moved to sit up and crack a beer. Greenup Bird lies in the corner with his head on his paws and follows us with his eyes. *My girl's comin' out,* Steve says. *I talked to her just last night. She says the end may come sooner than we think.* He puffs a joint, examines the glowing tip, hands it to the Musician. *I think it's gonna come on real slow,* he says. *Then hit like an atom bomb.* He smacks his hands together. Lacy parks behind the Minute Mart with Joe Jr., who is making wild promises with his hand between her legs. *But he's not yours,* Lacy tells him, for the hundredth time, but he doesn't care. He looks into her tired eyes and feels not love, but a flutter of anticipation, which for him is close enough to it.

Jesse James liked it well enough here, but he was always anxious to get back to traveling. Frank loved this place, and would have stayed forever, if he could. He loved the life of B. J. Woodson, simple, honest, repetitious. *I don't know how he did it, settled down like that after a life on the road,* the Musician says. *I could never do that.* Frank and Jesse and their band, all living in the area under assumed names, met at twilight at the saloon, drinking beer and watching the hills light up with the setting sun. All through the spring, without anyone knowing it, Lacy and the Musician were walking up into the back pastures of Joe Guy's farm, making love on a blanket and afterward picking seed ticks off one another, laughing. He told her stories of his travels, meeting David Bowie and Jerry Garcia, playing with George Jones, and she listened with her afternoon eyes half closed and probably wished she knew him back in the day, when he was twenty years younger. On the coldest day in January, the Musician drives past the Meat 'n' Three and sees the big Ford parked outside. He slows and sees the two of them through the steamed plate-glass door, Joe Jr. leaning across a table, Lacy's chair pushed back to make room for her enormous belly. Without thinking he cuts the engine and pulls over to watch them, his fingernails gouging deep crescents in the steering wheel.

The next morning I look out my window and the stakes in the field across the Pike are gone, vanished, and the field looks exactly as it did before, exactly as it has for the past few hundred years, the starlings rising and falling over it like breaths, the trees' shadows spreading out around its edges. Greenup Bird and I take a slow walk around the perimeter and hear deer footsteps in the water of the creek. For an hour or so, I think that it may be spared. Then in the late morning I hear a thunderous thud and I look out the window to see an army of earthmovers. The house shakes. Greenup howls and scratches his nails along the wood floors. My coffee shudders in its mug. I take a deep breath and try to be fluid, like the creek. In the evening the Musician comes down, knocks on the door all wild-eyed. *Time's up,* he says. *We got to get in there before they do.* We strap on headlamps and start to dig, not waiting for Steve to show up. We go haphazardly, without even the metal detector, the Musician throwing shovelfuls of soil over his shoulder like a madman. As we dig, Lacy is sitting with Joe Jr. on the wide bench seat of his Ford, eating a bucket of fried chicken. The grease makes the baby turn somersaults. *Feel,* she says to Joe Jr. and puts his hand on her belly. He looks into her eyes and says, *We'll name him Joe Guy the Third.*

All through the cold night the Musician digs. He is now only casting about, digging a foot here, a few inches there, trying to sniff
it out. Greenup Bird whines and follows him, nosing at each hole
when he leaves it. *Dig, Greenup, dig!* he shouts. Greenup whines and
scrapes at the holes with his claws, tags jingling. I huddle in my
jacket and doze on and off. When I wake I know where they are by
the white clouds of their breath. The Musician digs until morning,
leaving craters behind him, cursing Frank and Jesse James. He drops
to his knees alongside Greenup and digs with his hands, his fingernails bloody. Still he finds nothing. His son or daughter, like all babies in the womb, turns its head away from the light when Lacy sits
down in the weak January sun to smoke her first cigarette of the day.
A possum hit on the side of Brown's Ridge Pike slowly decays, picked
at by crows and ants, until it is just a spine like a zipper, nothing
more. Steve's girlfriend calls to tell him it's too late, she's not coming,
not unless he comes up with the money. The Musician goes to the
Meat 'n' Three before they open for breakfast and kneels in front of
Lacy, begging her to wait. *Trust me,* he says. *I will give you and this
baby everything you need.*

We keep digging. There is nothing else for us to do. The houses will
go up fast, concrete foundations that are bound to shift in this floodplain soil, some drywall and some fake brick siding, and just like it
happened at Joe Guy's, in a few weeks, a month, there will be a row
of houses where there was none before, lined up along the Pike like
pigs at a trough. The creek will continue to flood, every spring, and
people will wake up to find their backyards full of crawdads and cat-
fish. There will be streetlights, turning lanes, stoplights. In time
people will want a Chili's. They will want a Sonic, a Jack in the Box,
an AutoZone, a Piggly Wiggly, a Ruby Tuesday's. A McDonald's will

go up at the crossroads, and the Meat 'n' Three will close. A bobcat's den will be bulldozed away for a store that sells hair extensions and curling irons. The coyotes will root through Dumpsters for a few years before they are run off to the north, howling as they go. *Lo,* Steve says, clutching the book of Isaiah, *there will be burning instead of beauty. Ruby Tuesday,* the Musician says, resting on his shovel for a moment, the haze in his mind parting. *Isn't that a song?*

If I squint at the field I can almost picture it all now. If I squint harder, I can see the Indians making a dugout canoe down by the creek, burning trees to clear space for their crops, and before that, the dire wolves, the saber-toothed tigers, the ferns and giant trees, before that, the vast immutable sea. *With the Lord stood three angels,* Steve reads, *each with six wings. With two they covered their faces, and with two their feet, and with two they did fly. And they cried to one another, holy, holy, holy, is the Lord, the whole earth is full of his glory,* raising his voice to compete with the growl of the engines of the bulldozers.

Everything changes. Even in Brown's Ridge. Of course I know. Bill Ryan will sit alone in the saloon and talk revolution too loud, not knowing that Jack Earthman, a Nashville sheriff, is sitting next to him and listening carefully as he eats a boiled egg and drinks a beer. After he is arrested, J. D. Howard and B. J. Woodson will gather up their families and leave in the night, never to return. Jesse will be shot and killed a year later, in Missouri, and Frank will grow old selling tours of their childhood home for a quarter. Lacy will be terrified of motherhood and for months will sit and stare at her child, a boy, not knowing what to do. Jubal Cain's heart will tar over with hate until it kills him, and the bulldozers will move steadily up the steepest ridge side. *It is with a sense of despair,* said Frank James, *that I drive away from our little home and again become a wanderer.* The Musician stays up all night with a bottle cradled against his chest, watching tapes of his old days on tour, keeping the volume muted, so he cannot hear the applause. Greenup Bird will outlive me, and will end up in the Nashville pound, where no one will want to adopt him. After two weeks in a cage he'll be euthanized, his body thrown in the city incinerator, and his ashes will fall on the Cumberland River like snow. The houses go up, they keep going up, and for now we stay one step ahead of them, digging. The Musician still hasn't lost hope. *The time is at hand,* Steve reads from the book of Revelation, leaning his shovel against his hip and rolling a joint for the end of the world. *Fear not, for I am the first and the last, he that lives and he who has died. Which is, and which was, and which is to come.*

YIYUN LI

University of Iowa

PERSIMMONS

April comes and April goes, and May, and June, all passing by without shedding a drop of rain. The sky has been a blue desert since spring. The sun rises every morning, a bright white disk growing larger and hotter each day. Cicadas drawl halfheartedly in the trees. The reservoir outside the village has shrunken into a bathtub for the boys, peeing at each other in the waist-deep water. Two girls, four or five, stand by the main road, their bare arms waving like desperate wings of baby birds as they chant to the motionless air, "Come the east wind. Come the west wind. Come the east-west-north-south wind and cool my armpits."

Now that July has only to move its hind foot out the door in a matter of days, we have started to wish, instead of rain, that no rain will fall and the drought would last till the end of the harvest season. Peasants as we are, and worrying about the grainless autumn as we are, the drought has, to our surprise, brought a languid satisfaction to our lives. Every day, from morning till evening, we sit under the old pagoda tree, smoking our pipes and moving our bodies only when the tree's shade threatens to leave us to the full spotlight of the sunshine. Our women are scratching their heads to come up with decent meals for us at home. The rice from last year will be running out soon, and before that, our women's hair will be thinning from too much scratching until they will all go bald, but this, like all the minor tragedies in the world, has stopped bothering us. We sit and smoke until our daily bags of tobacco leaves run out. We stuff grass roots and half-dead leaves into the bags, and when they run out, we smoke dust.

"Heaven's punishment, this drought," someone, one of us, finally speaks after a long period of silent smoking.

"Yes, too many deaths."

"In that case, Heaven will never be happy again. People always die."

"And we'll never get a drop of rain."

"Suits me well. I'm tired of farming anyway."

"Yeah, right. Heaven comes to spank you, and you hurry up to bare your butts and say, come and scratch me, I've got an itch here."

"It's called optimism, better than crying and begging for pardon."

"A soft persimmon is what you are. I would just grab His pants and spank Him back."

"Whoa, a hero we've got here."

"Why not?"

"Because we were born soft persimmons. Seen any hero coming out of a persimmon?"

"Lao Da."

"Lao Da? They popped his brain like a watermelon."

Lao Da was one of us. He should have been sitting here with us, smoking and waiting for his turn to speak out a line or two, to agree, or to contradict. When night falls, he would, like all of us, walk home and dote on his son, dripping drops of rice wine from his chopsticks to the boy's mouth. Lao Da would never have bragged about being a hero, a man like him, who knew his place between the sky and the earth. But the thing is, Lao Da was executed before this drought began. On New Year's Eve, he went into the county seat and shot seventeen people, fourteen men and three women, in seventeen different houses, sixteen of them dead on the spot and the seventeenth lived only to see half a day of the new year.

"If you were born a soft persimmon, you'd better stay one." Someone says the comforting old wisdom.

"Persimmons are not born soft."

"But they are valued for their softness."

"Their ripeness."

"What then if we stay soft and ripened?"

"Heaven will squeeze us until He gets tired of squeezing."

"He may even start to like us because we are so much fun for Him."

"We'll just have our skins left by then."

"Better than having no skins."

"Better than having a bullet pop your brain."

"Better than having no son to inherit your name."

Silent for a moment, we all relish the fact that we are alive, with boys to carry on our family names. Last year at this time, Lao Da's son was one of the boys, five years old, running behind older boys like all small kids do, picking up the cicadas that the older boys shot down with their sling guns, adding dry twigs and dead leaves to the fire that was lit up to roast the bodies, waiting for his share of a burned cicada or two.

"Lao Da's son died a bad one."

"As if there is a good way to die!"

"Those seventeen, weren't theirs good? Fast and painless."

"But in the city, they said those seventeen all died badly."

"Mercilessly murdered—wasn't that how they put it in the news-papers?"

"But that's true. They were murdered."

"True, but in the city, they wouldn't say the boy died badly. They didn't even mention Lao Da's son."

"Of course they wouldn't. Who would want to hear about a mur-derer's son? A dead son, not to mention."

"Even if they had written about him, what could they have said?"

"Drowned in a swimming accident, that's what was written in his death certificate."

"And accidents happen every day, they would say."

"The boy's death wasn't worth a story."

The seventeen men and women's stories, however, were read aloud to us at Lao Da's trial, their enlarged pictures looking down at us from the top of the stage of a theater, a makeshift courthouse to con-tain the audience. We no longer remember their names, but some of the faces, a woman in heavy makeup that looked like a girl we were all obsessed with when we were young, a man with a sinister mole just below his left eye, another man with a pair of caterpillar-like eye-brows, these faces have stuck with us ever since. So have a few of the stories. A man who had been ice-swimming for twenty years and had never been ill for one day of his adult life. A mother of a teenage girl who had died earlier that year from leukemia. An official and his young secretary, who, as we heard from rumors, had been having an affair, but in the read-aloud stories, they were both the dear husband and wife to their spouses. The stories went on, and after a while we dozed off. What was the point of telling these dead people's stories to us? Lao Da had no chance of getting away. He turned himself in to the police, knowing he would get a death sentence. Why not spare those relatives the embarrassment of wailing in the court? Besides, no story was read aloud about Lao Da. He was an atrocious criminal was all that was said about him.

"Think about it: Lao Da was the only one who died a good death."

"A worthy one."

"Got enough companions for the trip to the next world."

"Got us into trouble, too."

"It wasn't his mistake. Heaven would've found another reason to squeeze us."

"True. Lao Da was just an excuse."

"Maybe—I have been thinking—maybe Heaven is angry not because of Lao Da, but for him?"

"How?"

"I heard from my grandpa, who heard from his grandpa, that there was this woman who was beheaded as a murderer, and for three years after her execution, no drop of rain fell to the area."

"I heard that from my grandpa, too. Heaven was avenging the woman."

"But she was wronged. She did not kill her husband."

"True."

Lao Da was not wronged. You killed seventeen people and you had to pay with your life. Even Lao Da nodded in agreement when the judge read the sentence. He bowed to the judge and then to the guards when he was escorted off the stage. "I'm leaving one step earlier," he said. "Will be waiting for you on the other side." The guards, the judge, and the officials on and off the stage, they all tried to turn their eyes away from Lao Da, but he was persistent in his farewell. "Come over soon. Don't let me wait for too long," he said. We never expected Lao Da to have such a sense of humor. We grinned at him and he grinned back, but for a short moment only, as the judge waved for two more guards to push him to the backstage before he had time to give out too many invitations.

"Lao Da was a man."

"Spanked the Heaven."

"But who's got the upper hand now?"

"It means nothing to Lao Da now. He had his moment."

"But it matters to us. We are punished for those who were wronged to death."

"Who?"

"Those seventeen."

"Not the wife of the cuckold, I hope."

"Certainly not. She deserved it."

"That woman was smaller than a toenail of Lao Da's wife."

"That woman was cheaper than a fart of Lao Da's wife."

"True."

"Good woman Lao Da had as a wife."

"Worthy of his life."

We nod, and all think about Lao Da's wife, secretly comparing her with our own women. Lao Da's wife worked like a man in the field and behaved like a woman at home. She was plump, and healthy, and never made a sound when Lao Da beat her for good or bad reasons, or for no reason at all. Our wives are not as perfect. If they are not too thin they are too fat. If they are diligent, they do not leave us alone, nagging us for our laziness. They scream when beaten; even worse, sometimes they fight back.

"That good woman deserved better luck."

"She deserved another son."

"But her tubes were tied."

"The poor woman would've lived if not for the Birth Control Office."

"A group of pests they are, aren't they?"

The Birth Control Office had been after Lao Da and his wife when they had not reported to the office after their firstborn. *One child per family,* they brushed in big red words on Lao Da's house. *Only pigs and dogs give birth to more than one child,* they wrote. But Lao Da and his woman never gave up. They played hide-and-seek with the Birth Control Office, hiding in different relatives' places when the woman's belly was growing big. After three daughters and a big debt for the fines, they finally had a son. The day the boy turned a hundred days old, Lao Da killed a goat and two suckling pigs for a banquet; afterward, the wife was sent to the clinic to have her tubes triumphantly tied.

"What's the point of living if she could not bear another son for Lao Da? What's the use of a hen if it doesn't lay eggs?"

"True."

"But that woman, she was something."

"Wasn't she?"

We exchange looks of awe, all knowing that our own women would never have had the courage to do what Lao Da's wife did. Our women would have screamed and begged when we faced no other choices but divorcing them for a fertile belly, but Lao Da's wife, she never acted like an ordinary woman. When we, along with Lao Da, dived into the reservoir to look for the body of Lao Da's son, she drank all the pesticide she could lay her hands on, six bottles in a row, and lay down in bed. Six bottles of pesticide with that strength could cut her into pieces, but she did not make a single sound, her jaws clenched, waiting for death.

"An extraordinary woman."

"Maybe Heaven is angry on her behalf."

"She was not wronged by anybody."

"But her soul was let down."

"By whom?"

"Lao Da."

"Lao Da avenged her, and their son."

"Was it what she wanted?"

"What did she want?"

"Listen, she was making room for a new wife, so Lao Da could have more sons. She didn't poison herself just to make Lao Da lose his mind and carry out some stupid plan to shoot seventeen people. Think about it. Lao Da got everything wrong."

"Her death could have borne more fruits."

"That's true. Now she died for nothing."

"And Lao Da, too."

"And those seventeen."

"And the three daughters, orphaned for nothing."

We shake our heads, thinking about the three girls, their screaming and crying piercing our eardrums when the county officials grabbed their arms and pushed them into the Jeep. They were sent to different orphanages in three counties, bad seeds of a cold-blooded killer. Lao Da should have listened to us and drowned them right after they were born, sparing their troubles of living in pain.

"Lao Da could have done better."

"Reckless man."

We could have made a wiser choice than Lao Da. We would have let the dead be buried and gone on living, finding a new wife to bear a new son, working our backs bent to feed the wife and the children. There would be the pain, naturally, of waking up to the humiliation of being a soft persimmon, but humiliation does not kill a man. Nothing beats clinging to this life. Death ferries us nowhere.

"One man's mistake can capsize a whole ship of people."

"True."

"Death of a son is far from the biggest tragedy."

"Death of anybody shouldn't be an excuse to lose one's mind."

"But Lao Da had the right to seek justice for his boy."

"Justice? What kind of justice is there for us?"

"If one kills, one has to pay with his life. Nothing's wrong with the old rule. The man who killed Lao Da's son should have been punished."

"He was punished all right. The first one Lao Da shot that night, wasn't he?"

"Two shots in the brain. Two shots in the heart."

"In front of his woman."

"Well done it was."

"Couldn't be better."

"When I heard the news, I felt I had just downed a full pot of sorghum wine."

"It beats the best wine out there."

"See, that's what justice is."

"True. One can never run away from justice's palm."

"You just have to wait for the time."

"Heaven sees, doesn't He?"

"But if He does see, why are we punished? What kind of justice is this?"

"I've told you: there is no justice for us persimmons."

"If you kill one person, you are a murderer. If you kill a lot, you are a hero."

"Lao Da killed seventeen."

"Not quite enough."

"If you've made a point, you are a hero. If you've failed to make a point, you are nothing."

"What's the point to make?"

"There should be an order for everyone to follow."

"A dreamer is what you are, asking for the impossible."

"We all asked for that at the riot, but it didn't get us anywhere."

"That was because we gave up."

"Bullshit. What's the point fighting for a dead boy?"

"True."

"What's the point risking our lives for a nonexistent order?"

"True."

We all nod, eager to shoo away the tiny doubt that circles us like a persistent fly. Of course we did what we could—after the boy was found in the water, we marched together with his little body to the county seat, asking for justice. Hoes and spades and axes and our fists and throats we all brought with us, but when the government sent the troop of the armed police into our direction, we decided to go back home. Violence will not solve your problem, we said to Lao Da. Go to the court and sue the man; follow what the law says, we told Lao Da.

"Maybe we shouldn't have put the seed in Lao Da's mind to sue the man."

"Had I been him, I would have done the same."

"The same what? Going around the city and asking justice for his son's death? His son was drowned in a swimming accident—black words on white page in his death certificate."

"The other boys told a different story."

"Why would the court want to listen to the story?"

We sit and smoke and wait for someone to answer the question. A group of boys is returning to the village from the reservoir, all dripping wet. Lao Da's boy would never have been drowned if there had been a drought last year. We don't worry about our sons this year, even the youngest ones who cannot swim well. But last year was a different story. Last year's reservoir was deep enough to kill Lao Da's son.

"But don't you think the officials made some mistakes, too? What if they gave Lao Da some money to shut him up?"

"What if they put that man in jail, even for a month or two?"

"Isn't that a smart idea? Or, pretend to put the man in jail?"

"Yes, just tell Lao Da the man got his punishment."

"At least treat Lao Da a little better."

"Would have saved themselves."

"But how could they have known? They thought Lao Da was a soft persimmon."

"Squeezed him enough for fun."

"Squeezed a murderer out of it."

"Lao Da was the last one you would think to snap like that."

"Amazing how much one could take and then all of a sudden he broke."

"True."

"But back to my point, what's the good losing one's mind over a dead son and a dead wife?"

"Easier said than done."

"True. How many times did we tell him to stop pursuing the man?"

"Sometimes a man sets his mind on an idea, and he becomes a hunting dog, only seeing one thing."

"And now we are punished for his stupidity."

We shake our heads, sorry for Lao Da, more so for ourselves. Lao Da should have listened to us. Instead, he was writing down the names and addresses of those officials who had treated him like a dog. How long he had been preparing for the killing we do not know. He had the patience to wait for half a year until New Year's Eve, the best time to carry out a massive murder, when all the people were staying home for the year-end banquet.

"At least we have to give Lao Da the credit for carrying out his plan thoroughly."

"He had a brain when it came to revenge."

"And those seventeen dead souls. Think about how shocked they were when they saw Lao Da that night."

"I hope they had time to regret what they had done to Lao Da."

"I hope their family begged Lao Da for them as Lao Da had begged them for his boy."

"You'd never know what could come from a soft persimmon."

"I hope they were taught a lesson."

"They're dead."

"Then someone else's taught the lesson."

"Quiet! Be careful someone from the county hears you."

"So hot they won't be here."

"The reservoir is not deep enough for them now."

"The reservoir is really the cause of all these bad things. Think about the labors we put into the reservoir."

We nod and sigh. A few years ago, we put all our free time into building the reservoir, hoping to end our days of relying on Heaven's mood for the rain. The reservoir soon became an entertaining site for the county officials. In summer afternoons, they came in Jeeps, swimming in our water, fishing our fishes. The man was one of the judges— but what indeed was his line of work we never got to know, as we call everybody working in the county court *judge*. That judge and his companions came, all drunk before they went into the water. Something Lao Da's son said, a joke maybe, or just a nickname he gave to the judge, made him angry. He picked up Lao Da's son and threw him into the deeper water of the reservoir. A big splash the other boys remembered. They cried, begged, but the judges all said it would teach the little bastard a lesson. The boys sent the fastest one among them to run for help. Lao Da's son was found later that night, his eyelids, lips, fingers, toes, and penis all eaten into bad shapes by the feasting fish.

"Remember, Lao Da was one of those who really pushed for the reservoir."

"He worked his back bent for it."

"The poor man didn't know what he was sweating for."

"None of us knows."

"At least we don't have to sweat this summer."

"Of course, you don't sweat waiting for death."

"Death? No, not that bad."

"Not that bad? Let me ask you—what will we feed our women and kids in the winter?"

"Whatever is left from the autumn."

"Nothing will be left."

"Then feed them our cows and horses."

"Then what?"

"Then we'll all go to the county and become beggars."

"It's illegal to beg."

"I don't care."

"If you want to do something illegal, why be a beggar and be spat at by everybody? I would go to the county and request to be fed."

"How?"

"With my fist and my ax."

"Don't talk big. We were there once with our fists and our axes."

"But that was for the dead boy. This time it'll be for our own sons."

"Do you think it'll work?"

"You have to try."

"Nonsense. If it works, it would have worked last time. Lao Da wouldn't have had to kill and we wouldn't have to be punished."

Nobody talks. The sun has slowly hauled itself to the southwest sky. The cicadas stop their chanting, but before we have time to enjoy the silence, they pick up the old tune again. Some of us draw and puff imaginary smokes from our pipes that are no longer lit; others pick up dry twigs from the ground, sketching in the dust fat clouds, heavy with rain.

M. O. WALSH

University of Mississippi

THE FREDDIES

Frederick the Third slept in a house of mannequins, half dead himself until the phone rang. His mother had to whisper. "Look, Freddy," she said. "Don't come. I just wanted you to know." Then she hung up. The news, of course, was that his grandfather Frederick the First was dead, a massive coronary on the ninth hole of the Colonial Golf and Tennis Club.

Freddy dropped the receiver and rolled off the couch. Then he stumbled to the bathroom and pissed blood. He had kidney stones again, and this particular batch moved through him like broken china. Freddy thought about cleaning the rust-colored spots that dotted the rim of the toilet, as well as wiping the pink runners that dribbled the side of the bowl, but then remembered that Clara, his reason for cleaning, had left him. Just that morning, in fact. In the pouring rain, maybe.

Freddy sat on the side of his bathtub and attempted to cry, not only over the loss of Frederick the First, but also over his newly re-membered split with Clara the Fourth. If there was any appropriate time for tears, Freddy figured, this was it. But before any water could come, it's likely that Freddy found shelter in the abundance of his grief, in the consoling thought that no one person could possibly mourn two such simultaneous and tsunamic losses in any proper way. So, Freddy wondered, why try? What did he have to give, anyway? Drops of salt from his eyes? What does that change? What did they do in places like Asia for grief? Fall on their swords? Eat their own bowels with chopsticks? Something like that was needed here, because Frederick the First was the rock. Frederick the First was the glue.

And so the last time Freddy cried seemed ridiculous to him now: a fishing hook through the web of his palm. He wondered how the act of crying could possibly serve as the exit for both the orbital pains in his heart and the barb in his hand. It seemed unjust. This thought quieted Freddy, and soon the obligation of it all turned heavy and distant. He sat there stone-faced. And here I imagine him grabbing the shower curtain for balance and the whole thing crashing down on his head.

So Freddy threw the curtain off his shoulders. "Don't come?" he said. "They tell *me* don't come? Don't come for Frederick the First?"

Freddy then stood up from the bathtub, full of a new and lam-poonish energy. He ran down the hall like a kid to a swimming pool. He hit the bedroom door with his shoulder and tripped onto his own unmade bed. He buried his face deep in the comforter. "Clara!" he yelled into the feathers. And then let's say the room became silent, except for the sound of thrown pillows sliding off the nightstand.

Thirty-five years old, Freddy was four times married and soon to be four times divorced. He eased off the edge of the bed and pulled the sheets down with him, wrapping them around his head. He stared at the full-length mirror Clara dressed in front of every day and, through a film of pain pills and mirror dust, Freddy saw in his reflection a shepherd.

"Listen, everyone," Freddy said. "The good man is dead. Tell the flock. Lower the flag."

With the expanse of his forehead and gobble neck hidden, Freddy would look young and clean. So he pulled the fabric tight around his face and crawled toward the mirror. "ClaraBell," he said. "Frederick the First is gone! The good man is deader than denim. And they tell me not to come."

Freddy felt these words intensely, especially since his wife was a seamstress. And the fact that it was her phrase about denim leaking from his mouth when he spoke of his grandfather multiplied his anguish in invisible ways. Because he had meant what he said about the good man, no matter whose words he used. As soon as they passed from his lips, however, Freddy's face resumed its sleepy-still posture. This was a fierce bother to him, that his features could lie blank in the wake of legitimate sadness, so he squinted his eyes to say it again.

"He's dead, Clara-britches. Gone." He held a frown for a second and then relaxed, his face back to nothing. He tried this several times. "Hell," he said.

Freddy breathed heavy toward the mirror. He made crying noises like a baby. *Waa,* he said. *Waa.* Then he fell asleep on the floor.

Three and a half divorces, one miscarried child, and two bouts with AA notwithstanding, his grandfather's death was the first thing Freddy had felt deep in his guts since he kissed his first wife-to-be, Shelly Fremont, through a chain-link fence in the eighth grade. So it is likely that he dreamed about her on the floor that day.

Of course he would go.

Freddy had nothing to wear to a funeral but found all sorts of khaki pants Clara had brought home to hem. He put on the pair that came the closest to fitting and grabbed two neckties of his own. He threw blue socks into a suitcase with some dress shoes and put a button-down shirt over his shoulder. Then he went to the kitchen and gathered his pills. Freddy ate two more white ones for pain and did what any good grandson would do. He thought of his grandmother and searched for reasons she should live from here out.

What had it been, sixty-three years of marriage? What was that party he hadn't been invited to? What had his grandfather said on the phone?

"I had no idea you weren't coming, Freddy. Your sister did all the invitations. It was a surprise party. Sixty (-one? -two? -three?) years, can you believe it? I spoke to her about all this mess," he said. "I'm trying. But you know how she can be."

How many years ago was that? And where was Freddy when he called? What house? What wife? Regardless, Freddy remembered the call, and he remembered the sound of his grandfather's voice. The man had the voice of a giant, the voice of a bull.

"You know we love you, Freddy," he said. "You know I don't care for broken relations."

This was a man who should never be buried. A man who completely forgave. A man who lit up old black-and-white photos. He was perhaps more than that, even, a full cargo of traits too difficult to catalog. And so, to Freddy, his grandfather became a man who looked not dissimilar to the mannequin in his kitchen, dressed in a seersucker suit that Clara had yet to alter. The hard jaw was there, the stiff chest. Everything was similar except the hands that, on the mannequin, looked unable.

Freddy grabbed this mannequin by the waist and hauled him out to his car. He placed him in the passenger seat. And after three trips back inside the house to collect his keys, suitcase, and five beers,

Freddy drove to Jackson, Tennessee, the place it seemed everyone but him now lived.

On the drive, Freddy and the mannequin did not speak. Instead, Freddy reasoned that his grandmother would appreciate this gesture, this gift. He recalled that it was never the conversation of his past wives that he missed when they were gone. Instead it was the hump of a body under the sheets, the quiet closing of a door so as not to wake them. It was having two burgers on the grill instead of one. And, although he knew the mannequin itself could never reason, Freddy thought it looked comfortable in its seat, still standing in the place of something.

They arrived in Jackson at dusk. Freddy pulled up to the town house his grandparents lived in. Cars were parked alongside the road. It was pouring rain, so Freddy turned off his wipers and finished the last of his beer. He saw his sister's husband's car, a tall blue SUV with a faded Republican bumper sticker. This was not good.

It was this man's sister who was Freddy's second wife, the woman who miscarried the child and stopped drinking. The one who forced Freddy's first bout with AA. The one who involved the police. The one who became best friends with Freddy's sister, and the one Freddy left on the day she found Jesus.

Had it all gotten so complicated? I imagine when Freddy thought of it, he didn't think so. To him, this ex-wife was a woman he could barely remember, an anecdote he found no reason to tell. But Freddy's sister Shirley was of a different persuasion. She was made of scissors, and had long since cut the ties of her brother's belonging.

The garage door of the town house opened and a young man stepped out. Freddy watched him from the car. The kid stood in the garage and lit a cigarette; he was no more than fifteen, sixteen, seventeen years of age. He blew smoke out into the rain.

Who was this kid? Freddy wondered. What did he know about mourning Frederick the First? Freddy thought about his cousins but couldn't place any so young. He thought maybe his grandparents had adopted this boy, to show him the golf courses of America. This is the type of people they were.

The kid spotted Freddy in his car and waved, then shouted something back at the house. Shirley appeared in the doorway and threw Freddy a look that was terminal. Then she went back inside.

"Here we go," Freddy said and unbuckled the mannequin. He got out in the rain and slid its body through the driver's-side door. The town house was on a hill, and as Freddy ran up the slick driveway he fell. The mannequin tumbled down the concrete and into the street, its head in the rush of drain water.

Freddy picked it up and started back toward the house as Ronald Hutchins, Shirley's husband, bolted out of the door. He told the kid to go inside and unbuttoned both of his shirt cuffs. That's how bad it had gotten. He charged toward Freddy in the rain.

"You shit-eating bastard," he said, and went to punch Freddy in the face. This was a difficult thing to do on the driveway, though, and Ronald's foot slipped from underneath him. He opened his fist in a panic and, instead of landing one on Freddy's jaw, only grabbed hold of his T-shirt. All three of them fell and Ronald got the worst of it. Freddy landed on top of him, dug his knee into the man's crotch, and rode him back down to the sewer. The mannequin smacked the ground hard and slid to a stop. The kid blew smoke from his nose because, at that age, he thought everything was beneath him.

Freddy got up and saw that his khakis were ripped at the knee. Ronald lay in the water, holding on tight to his privates. "Jesus, Ronald," Freddy said. "This isn't about us here at all. I told you a thousand times I was sorry! Tell your sister to call me or something. Look what you did to my pants!"

The kid threw his cigarette into the yard. "Uncle Freddy?" he said.

Freddy dragged the mannequin into the garage and wiped the water from his own eyebrows. The kid pulled a small camera from his pocket and snapped a picture of him doing this. His pose was the kind seen in tabloids, the guarded face of a celebrity on trial, the yeti peeking out from the woods. And with that picture, Freddy's existence, or at least this moment of it, became indisputable and permanent for the boy.

"Shit," the kid said. "*It lives!* I mean, I always kind of thought they were making you up."

That this young man was Nat Hutchins was probably no easy blow to Freddy. He had seen this kid born. This was his nephew, his godson. But Freddy remembered him only as a circumcised penis, a hungover 8:00 A.M. baptism. Had it been that long? Could Freddy only be in his thirties, then? At what point did he become a ghost to his family, I wonder?

Freddy didn't answer the boy but leaned the mannequin against his grandfather's new Buick, parked in the same spot he remembered the old one. He straightened the mannequin's sport coat and tried wringing the water from its sleeves.

Ronald rolled around in the street. He yelled that Freddy was some "piece of work."

"Want your uncle's advice?" Freddy asked. "Your father is the Olympics of asshole."

"Tell me about it," the kid said. "You should smell his farts. It's like he's rotten inside."

Freddy slapped at the pants of the mannequin and straightened him up, embracing him like a brother.

"You have any beer?" the kid asked.

"In the car," Freddy said and headed into the house.

The kitchen was swarming with people, all quiet, none of whom

Freddy recognized at first. He stood on the floor mat and wiped his feet. He heard someone say, "Christ."

Shirley came at him from the crowd, snapping her claws like a sea creature. "Where's Ronald?" she said. "What did you do?"

Freddy spotted his mother by the sink, washing out an empty coffeepot.

"Honey," she said. "I thought I told you not to come."

"You called him?" Shirley yelled. "I can't believe you called him!"

"Shirley," his mother said.

"Where's Grandma?" Freddy asked.

People made a path through the kitchen, and Freddy saw his grandmother at the table. She had her head in her hands and two stacks of paper in front of her. As he walked toward her, Shirley grabbed the arm of the mannequin.

"Don't you dare!" she yelled and jerked hard on the mannequin's wrist. But the replacement grandpa was strong and Freddy just yanked it away.

"Have some respect!" Freddy said. "What did *you* bring? I don't see you with anything."

Shirley pulled at her hair and ran outside to get Ronald.

When Freddy reached the kitchen counter, the pain of his stones roared back to him. He bent over and toppled some snack trays. Someone asked if he was all right, if maybe they should call 911. Then Freddy held up a finger to calm them, and made his way to the dining room table.

Despite all the time he had spent alone in the car, Freddy hadn't thought of what to say when he actually got there, of how awkward the exchange between him and his grandmother might be. Now it seemed littered with complications. He sat the mannequin down on the chair and knelt beside his grandmother. He shut his eyes. But instead of crafting tender words, Freddy, I imagine, could only think of the pain, now scraping a path through his kidneys and bladder. And by the time Freddy could focus, his mother was standing there, too, rubbing the shoulders of a widow. He heard her say his name. He heard someone else diagnose him with appendicitis. He tried to block out each of these noises, every other voice but his conscience, and said the first thing that came to his mind.

"I brought this for you," Freddy said. "I know it's kind of wet."

Freddy's grandmother wiped his head with her handkerchief. She combed his hair with her nails. "I remember when you used to take the train here," she said. "After your father left, and your mother moved down to Memphis."

Freddy remembered this, too. He would walk through the train to the snack car. He would order a ham and cheese sandwich and they would give him silver packets of mayonnaise, with pictures of old-time cabooses.

"And Frederick would tell you that joke about molasses," she said. "Right when you got off the train. Remember? I'd get so upset with him for telling you those dirty jokes. Doesn't that seem silly now? But you always got so tickled. I know that you loved him so much, Freddy. I know this is hard for you, too."

"Mole asses," Freddy whispered.

"That's the one," his grandmother said, and Freddy put his head in her lap. He heard his mother begin to sob.

Just then, Ronald Hutchins came in through the doorway.

"I'm calling the cops," he said. "You could have done permanent damage!"

Shirley was right behind him. "Get out of here, Freddy!" she said. "Nobody wants you here."

"Shirley," his mother said.

"It's true isn't it? Even you told him not to come!"

"Shirley!"

"It's just like Ronald says. You are some piece of work, Freddy. You know that? Some pathetic piece of work!" She walked up behind Freddy and poked him in the back. "And take this goddamned thing, too," she said, and pushed fake Frederick out of his chair.

"Honey," his mother told Freddy, "maybe you *should* go. Just until things settle down. We can see you tomorrow at the funeral. Just until things settle down."

"He's *not* coming," Shirley said. "It's a disgrace."

A bunch of people in the kitchen said, "Shirley!" but Freddy couldn't stand to hear that name once more. And it still has for me a hissing-sharp edge to it, the name *Shirley,* because this was a woman who never once gave in. Her unforgiving nature came from a place no one knew and rendered her ugly, eventually gashing spaces between her and her husband, and between her and her son, providing material for many other stories than this one.

So Freddy got to his feet and dug his knuckles into the small of his back.

"Go!" Shirley said.

Freddy picked up the mannequin by its armpits. "Just let me know if you want this," he told his grandmother. "I thought maybe it would be something to sleep with. I don't know, someone to cook for. I thought the jaw looked just like him."

His grandmother studied the mannequin's jaw and pressed at her cheek with the handkerchief. "We both thought the world of you, Freddy," she said. "We tried to call. You know we did. Let us see you tomorrow, okay? Let us get you cleaned up."

Shirley pinched Freddy's side. "Don't even bother," she said.

Ronald yelled into the phone, "We have a trespasser in the house! A goddamned intruder!"

Freddy edged his way through the crowded kitchen and took his fake grandfather with him. The last voice he heard upon leaving was a stranger's, a woman's: "Now, who was that man again?"

When Freddy got outside, his nephew was still in the garage. "You've got the right idea," he said, and asked the kid for a smoke.

"There wasn't any beer in your car," the kid said, and shook a cigarette out of his pack. "I got soaked."

"Sorry," Freddy said, and adjusted the mannequin on his hip. "You're just going to have to give me a break on this one. I mean it's Clara, it's your mother. Maybe it's just women in general. You know anything about that?"

"Well, I know it's kind of creepy," the kid said. "Lugging a wooden person around. Maybe you should bring it to the funeral, though. I love to see my mom get pissed."

"So I guess you heard all that in there?"

"I can imagine," the boy said.

Freddy let the kid light his cigarette and stared into the rain. At this point, he probably knew that there was no way he could show up tomorrow, despite what his grandmother had said, and despite what she felt when she said it. Because what would he even wear now, anyway? Now that those pants that never fit had been ripped? And what would it be like later, the moment the funeral ended? Would he caravan back to the house? Would he follow these people back home? Or would he let cars get between them in traffic and slip off on an exit to Georgia? Freddy would do the latter. And so his mourning, he figured, would have to come soon, and take place while those he loved slept. So Freddy decided to go to the body himself, and asked the kid where it was.

"Just look for the place with headstones," Nat said. "It's next to the Long John Silver's."

Freddy took another long drag off his cigarette and looked his nephew all over. He had large veins that ran along the side of his neck, and a silver ring that pierced the top of his ear. He looked strong but wet, and water dripped from the elbow of his sleeve.

"I'm sorry you didn't get to know your great-grandfather," Freddy told him. "He really was a hell of a man. The type of man we should all be."

"I knew him," the kid said. "We live right down the road."

Upon hearing this, Freddy had to fight back a playground form of jealousy. After all, this kid probably had known his grandfather better than he had. He might even have seen him that morning, cleaning his sand wedge and backing his cart out of the shed. But to say that Freddy became impossibly jealous would be wrong. Maybe with his first three wives, whom he'd fled from, and maybe with this last one, who had fled from him. But Freddy wasn't impossible in this moment, no matter what people say, because, unlike his sister, Freddy found no strength in hating. Instead, he saw in his nephew an ally, a believer.

"See, *you* know what I'm talking about!" Freddy said. "You want to get out of here? You want to come with me? Go see the old man one last time?"

The kid lifted up his pant leg. He showed Freddy an electronic bracelet on his ankle. It weighed exactly two and three-quarters pounds. "House arrest," the kid said. "I ran a buddy's car into a lake."

"Ouch," Freddy said, and again rubbed the small of his back. "I guess we're both a bit friendly with trouble."

"You're not all that scary," the kid said. Now he wishes he'd said more to his uncle.

It's easy to imagine Freddy's drive to the funeral home as misguided at best. Freddy stopped to buy beer. Freddy stopped to hold his testicles. Freddy stopped to dig pills out of his glove compartment and Freddy stopped to ask directions.

When he finally got to the home it was closed, and the rain had not let up a bit. He told the mannequin to stay in the car, that he would be fine by himself, and then lurched to the only door he saw.

A heavyset man answered. He had bags, like pools of ink, under his eyes. A Chihuahua barked in the background, and the man hushed it with only a look. Freddy doubled over in pain.

"No vacancies," the man said.

Freddy couldn't even look up.

"It's an old mortuary joke. Sorry."

"You have a man named Frederick Little in there," Freddy said. "He was a great man."

"There are no great men in here," the undertaker said. "Just dead ones."

"I don't think you understand," Freddy said. "My grandfather! Not like you and me. He really was!"

Freddy meant to explain, but a wave of numbness overtook him. Not the good kind either, he realized, not the kind he had lived on for years. This one carried a dark consistency of purpose, and crept upward from his fingertips.

"Listen," the undertaker said. "You'd be surprised how many people come here just like you, in the rain. But, trust me, there's nobody special in here. In fact, this is the only place where everyone's the same."

"You don't understand," Freddy said.

"I don't? Well, what did this man of yours do?" he asked. "Was he kind? Was he brave? Did he tell you jokes? Did he give you butterscotch candies? Did he drag three children through a jungle after accidentally killing their mother? Is your grandfather greater than that?

That's what someone else's grandfather did. You want me to dig him up so you can see him? There's nothing great about him now."

Freddy got on his knees and crawled toward the doorjamb, as if trying to slip past the guard. The undertaker put his foot on his shoulder to stop him, like Saint Peter at the gates. "You'll be here soon enough," he said.

"You're a monster," Freddy said, and drooled a bit on the welcome mat.

"I think maybe you have a lot of monsters," the man said. "I think maybe what you should do is go back to your car. You've got someone inside of it waiting for you. I can see them. That's who you should go to. That's who you should touch. I don't know why people insist on touching the dead, anyway. They fix their hair, rub their cold hands. And this is after they've paid me to do it. I think they imagine themselves dead when they touch them. Maybe that's the real kick."

Freddy placed his palms on the pavement and felt the ground as a thing becoming dear to him, another thing to dream in, another thing to inhabit.

"Listen," the man said. "I'm not trying to be smart, but there's no reason to coat this with sugar. It's late. You feel like it's over. Maybe it is. Because if there's one thing I've learned it's that tomorrow there will be more of them, men twice the height of your grandfather. Children, too. Because people are dying right now, you see, right now as we speak. There goes another one. See? And another. Maybe that was a doctor. Maybe there goes the cure for everything. So go to your wife or whoever. You'll get enough of me in the morning."

The man closed the door on Freddy, but not out of viciousness. I imagine he *had* seen men like Freddy before, women, too, and he recognized that look in their eyes, the look of idiots wanting meaning from death. So when they finally came to rest on his table, it's likely he took pleasure in erasing the look from their faces.

Freddy tried to bang on the door again, but found himself nowhere near it. So Freddy cried onto the pavement. He vomited on the lawn by the sidewalk. Then Freddy slept for good in the rain.

Meanwhile, his fake grandfather sat slumped in the passenger seat, the engine still running. And I have to wonder what it was thinking, even though I know dead wood cannot think. Was the mannequin only amazed by the outcome of a day that had started so calmly in their kitchen? Did it feel anything at all for this man? Were there senses of loss, pity, rot? Or was it able to see through the rain, the way a body relaxes when it dies? The way stones just spill out from the bladder and nestle in the cup of white cotton? And would it carry the mark of that evening, when finally returned to Clara or placed in a department store window? Would Clara ask it for answers, and beg to know if she was to blame? If so, how could it resist the temptation to say *Yes, Clara!* if only you could have stayed one more day, one more week, one more year? Could it not say *Yes, Clara! Yes, Shirley! Yes, Mother and Ronald and Nat!* How could this fake man not answer at all, I wonder? If only to say, *Yes, I remember, that day in the car, when I felt so ashamed of my hands.*

But they tell me this is the wrong type of thinking. They say this is the thinking of blame, and why I have all the troubles I do. Because I am on my third wife now, you see, and I haven't spoken to my parents in years. And my wife and I are seeing this hotshot marriage counselor, and I have crept up to the age of my uncle. They need to know what kind of person I am, my wife says, so they can tell me why I turned out like I did.

This week they had me bring in photos from my childhood, and said it would get to the roots. So I am looking at that snapshot from the garage now, the one with my soaking wet uncle. And I think they may be right, because it's a funny thing about pictures, the way you notice new things in the background. With this one, I notice a re-flection in the glass of the Buick. It is me with my stupid flash cam-era. It is me just standing there, watching. It is me not doing a thing.

But you are getting ahead of yourself! my wife tells me. Just describe *who it is* in the picture. Just look at them. Imagine them. Speak of them.

Don't pretend that they are speaking for you.

VIET THANH NGUYEN

Fine Arts Work Center in Provincetown

A CORRECT LIFE

Liem's plan was to walk calmly past the waiting crowd after he dis-
embarked, but instead he found himself hesitating at the gate, scanning the strange faces anxiously. In one hand he held his duffel bag,
and in the other he clutched the form given to him by Mrs. Lindemulder, the woman with horn-rimmed glasses from the refugee service. When she had seen him off at the San Diego airport, she'd told
him his sponsor, Parrish Coyne, would be waiting in San Francisco.
The flight was only his second trip by air, and he'd passed it crum-
pling and uncrumpling an empty pretzel bag, until his seatmate
asked him if he would please stop. American etiquette confused him,
for sometimes Americans could be very polite, and at other times
rather rude, jostling by him as they did now in their rush to disem-
bark. The lingering pressure in his ears bewildered him further, making it hard for him to understand the PA system's distorted English.
He was wondering if he was missing something important when he

spotted the man who must be Parrish Coyne, standing near the back of the crowd and holding up a hand-lettered placard with MR. LIEM printed neatly on it in red. The sight nearly overwhelmed Liem with relief and gratitude, for no one had ever called him "mister" before.

Parrish Coyne was middle-aged and, except for his gray ponytail, distinguished-looking, his deep-set green eyes resting above a thin, straight nose. He wore a brown fedora and a black leather jacket, unbuttoned over a generous belly. After Liem shyly approached him, but before Liem could say a word, he said Liem's name twice. "Li-am, I presume?" Parrish spoke in an English accent as he clasped Liem's hand and mispronounced his name, using two syllables instead of one. "Li-am, is it?"

"Yes," Liem said, guessing that his foreignness was evident to all. "That is me." He meant to correct Parrish's pronunciation, but before he could do so, Parrish unexpectedly hugged him, leaving him to pat the man's shoulder awkwardly, aware of other people watching them and wondering, no doubt, about their relationship. Then Parrish stepped back and gripped his shoulders, staring at him with an intensity that made Liem self-conscious, unaccustomed as he was to being the object of such scrutiny.

"To be honest," Parrish announced at last, "I didn't expect you to be so pretty."

"Really?" Liem kept smiling and said no more. He wasn't sure he'd heard right, but he'd learned to bide his time in situations like this, sticking to monosyllables, until the course of a conversation clarified matters.

"Stop it," the young man next to Parrish said, also in an English accent. "You're embarrassing him." Just then the pressure in Liem's eardrums popped, and the muffled sounds of the terminal swelled to normal volume and clarity.

"This is Marcus Chan," Parrish said, "my good friend."

Marcus appeared to be in his midtwenties, only a few years older than Liem, who'd turned eighteen over the summer. If Marcus's smile seemed a little disdainful as he offered his hand, Liem could hardly blame him, for compared to Marcus, he was sorely lacking in just about every regard. Even the yellowness of his teeth was more evident next to the whiteness of Marcus's. With body erect and head tilted back, Marcus had the posture of someone expecting an inheritance, while Liem's sense of debt caused him to walk with eyes downcast, as if searching for pennies. Since he was shorter than both Marcus and Parrish, he was forced to look up as he said, "I am very happy to meet you." Out of sheer nervousness, Marcus's hand still gripped in his, he added, "San Francisco number one."

"That's lovely." Marcus gently let go of his hand. "What's number two then?"

"Hush." Parrish frowned. "Why not be helpful and take Liem's bag?"

With Marcus carrying the duffel bag and trailing behind, Parrish guided Liem through the terminal, hand on elbow. "It must seem very overwhelming to you," Parrish said, waving in a way that took in the crowds, the terminal, and presumably all of San Francisco. "I can only imagine how strange this all appears. Coming from England to here was hardly culture shock for me."

Liem glanced over his shoulder at Marcus. "You come from England, too?"

"Hong Kong," Marcus said. "You could say I'm an honorary Englishman."

"In any case," Parrish said, squeezing Liem's elbow and bending his head to speak more confidentially in Liem's ear, "you must have had an awful time of it."

"No, not very bad." Liem spoke with nonchalance, even though the prospect of rehearsing his story one more time flooded him with dread. In the four months since he'd fled Sài Gòn, he'd been asked for his story again and again, by sailors, marines, and social workers, their questions becoming all too predictable. What was it like? How do you feel? Isn't it all so *sad*? Sometimes he told the curious that what had happened was a long story, which only compelled them to ask for a shorter version. It was this edited account that he offered as Marcus drove the car through the parking garage, into the streets, and onto the freeway. Casting himself as just one more anonymous young refugee, he recounted a drama that began with leaving his parents in Long Xuyên last summer, continued with his work in a so-called tea bar in Sài Gòn, and climaxed with the end of the war. Even this brief version tired him, and as he spoke he leaned his forehead against the window, watching the orderly traffic on the wide highway.

"So," he said. "Now I am here."

Parrish sighed from the front seat of the sedan. "That war wasn't just a tragedy," he said, "but a farce." Marcus made a noise in his throat that might have been an assent before he turned up the volume on the radio a few notches. A woman was uttering an encomium to a brand of furniture polish, something to bring out the luster without using a duster. "You'll find the weather here to be cold and gray, even though it's September," Marcus said. "In the winter it will rain. Not exactly the monsoon, but you'll get used to it." As he drove, he pointed to passing landmarks, the standouts in Liem's memory being Candlestick Park with its formidable walls, and the choppy, marbled waters of the bay.

Then, as traffic from another freeway merged with theirs and the car slowed down, Parrish lowered the volume on the radio and said, "There's something you need to know about Marcus and myself."

A white passenger van, accelerating on the right, blocked Liem's view of the bay. He turned from the window to meet Parrish's gaze. "Yes?"

"We're a couple," Parrish announced.

Out of the corner of Liem's eye, he saw the white van edging forward, past the shrinking blot of moisture left by his forehead on the window. "In the romantic sense," Parrish added. Liem decided that "in the romantic sense" must be an idiomatic expression, the kind Mrs. Lindemulder had said Americans used often, like "you're killing me" and "he drives me up the wall." In idiomatic English, a male couple in the romantic sense must simply mean very close friends, and he smiled politely until he saw Marcus staring at him in the rearview mirror, the gaze sending a nervous tremor through his gut.

"Okay," Liem said. "Wow."

"I hope you're not too shocked."

"No, no." The small hairs on his arms and on the back of his neck stiffened as they'd done before whenever another boy, deliberately or by chance, had brushed his elbow, sometimes his knee, while they walked hand in hand or sat on park benches with their arms slung over each other's shoulders, watching traffic and girls pass by. "I am liberal."

"Then I hope you'll stay with us."

"And open-minded," he added. In truth he had no other refuge but Parrish's hospitality, just as there was nowhere else for him to go at the end of the day in Sài Gòn but a crowded room of single men and boys, restless on reed mats as they tried to sleep while breathing air humidified with the odor of bodies worked hard. "Do not worry."

"Good," Marcus said, turning up the volume again, the way one of the boys would around midnight, on Liem's transistor radio, when everyone knew but wouldn't say that sleep was impossible. Liem's eyes were closed by then, but he couldn't help seeing the faces of men he knew casually or had watched in the tea bar, even those of his own roommates. In the darkness, he heard the rustle of mosquito netting as the others masturbated also. The next morning, everyone looked at each other blankly, and nobody spoke of what had occurred the previous evening, as if it were an atrocity in the jungle better left buried.

He thought he'd forgotten about those nights, had run away from them at last. Now he wondered if the evidence still existed in the lines of his palms. He rubbed his hands uneasily on his jeans as they drove through a neighborhood with bustling sidewalks, trafficked by people of several colors. They were mostly whites and Mexicans, along with some blacks and a scattering of Chinese, none of whom looked twice at the signs in the store windows or the graffiti on the walls, written in a language he'd never seen before: *Peluquería, Chuy es maricón, Ritmo Latino, Dentista, Iglesia de Cristo, Viva La Raza!*

After turning onto a street lined with parked cars jammed fender-to-fender, Marcus swung the sedan nose-down into the sloping driveway of a narrow two-story house, upon whose scarlet door was hung, strangely enough, a portrait of the Virgin Mary. "We're home," Parrish said. Later Liem would learn that Parrish was an ambivalent Catholic, that the district they lived in was the Mission, and that the name for the house's architectural style was Victorian, but today all he noticed was its color.

"Purple?" he said, never having seen a home painted in this fashion before.

Parrish chuckled and opened his door. "Close," he said. "It's mauve."

Mrs. Lindemulder had squeezed Liem's shoulder in the San Diego airport and warned him that in San Francisco the people tended to be unique, an implication he hadn't understood at the time. Every day for the first few weeks in Parrish's house, Liem wanted to phone Mrs. Lindemulder and tell her she'd made a huge mistake, but Parrish's generosity shamed him from doing so. Instead, he stood in front of the mirror each morning and told himself there was nobody to fear, except himself. He'd silently said the same thing last year, at summer's end in 1974, when he bid farewell to his parents at the bus station in Long Xuyên. He hadn't complained about being dispatched alone to Sài Gòn, several hours north, where he'd be the family's lifeline. As the eldest son, he had duties, and he was used to working, having done so since leaving school at the age of twelve to shine the boots of American soldiers.

He'd known them since he was eight, when he began picking through their garbage dumps for tin and cardboard, well-worn *Playboy* magazines, and unopened C rations. The GIs taught him the rudiments of English, enough for him to find a job years later in Sài Gòn, sweeping the floor of a tea bar on Tu Do Street where the girls pawned themselves for dollars. With persistence, he sandpapered the two discourses of junkyard and whorehouse into a more usable kind of English, one good enough to understand the rumor passed from one foreign journalist to another in the spring of 1975. Thousands would be slaughtered if the city fell to the Communists.

In April, when rockets and mortars began exploding on the outskirts of the city, the rumor seemed about to come true. Although he hadn't planned on kicking, shoving, and clawing his way aboard a river barge, he found himself doing so one morning after he saw a black cloud of smoke over the airport, burning on the horizon, lit up by enemy shellfire. A month later he was in Camp Pendleton, San Diego, waiting for sponsorship. He and the other refugees had been rescued by a Seventh Fleet destroyer in the South China Sea and taken to a makeshift Marine Corps camp at Guam, and then flown to California. As he lay on his cot and listened to children playing hide-and-seek in the alleys between the tents, he tried to forget the people who clutched for air as they fell into the river, some knocked down in the scramble, others shot in the back by desperate soldiers

clearing a way for their own escape. He tried to forget what he'd discovered, how little other lives mattered to him when his own was at
stake.

None of this was mentioned in the airmail he posted to his parents, soon after coming to Parrish's house. It was his second letter
home. In June, at Camp Pendleton, he'd dispatched his first airmail
care of the resettlement agency. In both cases, assuming no letter
would go unread by the Communists, he wrote only of where he
lived and how to get in touch with him. He was afraid of endanger-
ing his family by marking them as relatives of someone who'd fled,
but he was even more afraid the letters might never make it home at
all. The only time his family's fate wasn't on his mind was during
those few seconds after he woke up, in a warm bed under three blankets, remembering dreams in which he spoke perfect English. Then
he opened his eyes to see a faint blue glow filtered through foggy
windows, the murky and wavering shimmer reminding him where
he was, in a distant city, a foreign place where even the quality of
light differed from the tropical glare he'd always known.

Downstairs, he would find Parrish and Marcus eating breakfast
and discussing the local news, international politics, or the latest
film. They bickered often, usually in a bantering way, about whether
or not they should vote for Jimmy Carter or Gerald Ford, or whether
Ford's would-be assassin, a San Francisco woman, should get life or
death.

When they began arguing seriously in front of him, he knew he
was becoming a part of their household. Sometimes the fights
seemed to occur for no reason, as happened one morning in October
after Parrish asked about the date of Marcus's final exams. "Why
don't you take them for me?" Marcus snapped before stalking out of
the kitchen. Parrish waited until Marcus had run up the stairs before

he leaned over to Liem and said, "It's the terrible twos. The second year's the hardest."

"Oh, yes?" Liem nodded his head even though he was uncertain, once again, about what Parrish meant. "I see you both yell many times."

"Even though he's older, he's not as mature as you," Parrish said. He stirred his coffee, his spoon making figure eights instead of circles. "He hasn't seen the things you or I have. Of course, when I was his age, I was spoiled and a little lazy, too. But I'm better now. My ancestors made their money from means of which I'm ashamed, but there's no reason why I can't put my own to some good use. Is there?"

"No?"

"No," Parrish said. Liem understood he was one of the good uses for the money Parrish had earned in two decades as a corporate accountant, a job he'd given up a few years before to work in environmental protection. Although Parrish refused to let Liem pay rent, Liem had found a job anyway. The week after his arrival, he'd wandered through downtown until he came across a liquor store in the heart of the Tenderloin, on the corner of Taylor and Turk. HELP WANTED was scrawled in soap on the window next to SE HABLA ESPAÑOL. The book he carried in his pocket, *Everyday Dialogues in English,* had no scenarios featuring the duo patrolling the corner outside the store, so he said nothing as he brushed by the shivering prostitute with pimples in her cleavage, who dismissed him at a look, and the transvestite with hairy forearms, who did not.

His shift ran from eight in the morning to eight in the evening, six days a week, Thursday his day off. He swept the floor and stocked the shelves, cleaned the toilet and wiped the windows, tended the register and then repeated the routine. During downtime, he read his book, hoping for clues on how to talk with Marcus and Parrish, but finding little of use in chapters like "Juan Gonzalez Visits New York City and Has to Ask His Way Around," or "An Englishman and an American Attend a Football Game." At the end of his shift, he dragged two garbage bags to a Dumpster down an alley where people with questionable histories urinated and vomited when it was dark, and sometimes when it wasn't. No matter how much he scrubbed his hands afterward, he sensed they'd never really be clean. The grease and garbage he dealt in had worked their way into his calluses so deeply that he imagined he was forever leaving his fingerprints everywhere.

By the time he returned to the Victorian, Parrish and Marcus had already finished dinner, and he ate leftovers in the kitchen while they watched television. As soon as he was done, he retreated upstairs, where he showered off the day's sweat and tried not to think of Marcus's lean, pale body. The endless hot water left him pliant and calm, and it was in this relaxed state of mind that he opened the door of the bathroom one evening after his shower, wrapped only in a towel, to encounter Marcus padding down the hallway. They faced each other in silence before both stepped to the same side. Then they both stepped to the other side, feet shuffling so awkwardly that the laugh track from the sitcom Parrish was watching downstairs, audible even on the landing, seemed to be directed at them.

"Excuse me," Liem said finally. He could feel a sheen of perspiration on his back, sweat from the heat of the long shower. "May I pass?"

Marcus shrugged, his eyes flickering once over Liem's body before he bowed slightly, in a mocking fashion, and said, "Yes, you may."

Liem hurried past Marcus and into his room. As soon as he shut the door, he leaned against it, ear pressed to wood, but another burst of canned laughter from downstairs made it impossible to hear Marcus's footsteps fading down the hallway.

———

On an overcast Thursday morning in mid-November, Marcus and Liem drove Parrish to the airport. He was spending the weekend in Washington, at a conference on nuclear power's threat to the environment. As the wind beat against the windows, Parrish explained how the government buried its spent plutonium and uranium in the desert, where it poisoned land and threatened lives for millennia. "And mostly poor lives at that," Parrish said. "Just think of it as a gigantic minefield in our backyard." Marcus drummed his fingers on the steering wheel as he drove, but Parrish gave no sign of noticing. On the curb at the airport, his suitcase at his feet, he kissed Marcus good-bye and hugged Liem. "See you Sunday night," Parrish said before shutting the passenger door behind Liem. Liem was waving through the window, and Parrish was waving back, when Marcus accelerated into traffic without so much as a glance over his shoulder.

"When's he going to stop trying to save the world?" Marcus demanded. "It's getting to be a bore."

Liem buckled his seat belt. "But Parrish is a good person."

"There's a reason why saints are martyred. Nobody can stand them."

They rode in an unbroken silence for the next quarter of an hour, until they neared the center of the city. There, the sight of a bakery truck entering the freeway from Army Street made Liem ask, "Are you hungry? I am hungry."

"Don't say I *am* hungry, say *I'm* hungry. You have to learn how to use contractions if you want to speak like a native. Move your lips and tongue like this, see?"

"I'm hungry. Are you?"

The restaurant Marcus chose in Chinatown was on Jackson Street and nearly the size of a ballroom, with pillars of dark cherrywood and tasseled red lanterns hanging from the ceiling. Even on a Thursday morning it was noisy and bustling; waitresses in smocks pushed carts up and down the aisles and bow-tied waiters hurried from table to table, checks and pots of tea in hand. They sat by a window overlooking Jackson Street, the sight of Asian crowds comforting to Liem. As the train of carts rolled by, Marcus picked and rejected expertly from the offerings, ordering in Cantonese and explaining in English as the varieties of dim sum were heaped before them in a daunting display, including shu mei, dumplings of minced pork and scallions, long-stemmed Chinese broccoli, and sliced roasted pork with candied skin the color of watermelon seeds. "Parrish won't touch those," Marcus said approvingly as he watched Liem suck the dimpled skin off a chicken's foot, leaving only the twiggy bones.

After the waiter swept away the dishes, they sat quietly with a tin pot of chrysanthemum tea between them. Liem rolled the bottom of his teacup in a circle around a grease stain on the tablecloth before he asked Marcus about his family, something Marcus had never discussed in front of him. All Liem knew about Marcus was that he'd lived in Hong Kong until he was eighteen, that he was enrolled in business administration at San Francisco State but hardly ever went there, and that he worked out at the gym daily. His father, Marcus said with a snort, was an executive at a rubber company who had sent him to study overseas, expecting he would eventually return to help run the business. But three years ago a spiteful ex-lover had mailed his father one of Marcus's love letters, with candid pictures tucked into the folds. "Very candid pictures," Marcus said darkly. After that, his father had disowned him, and now Parrish paid his expenses. "Can you imagine anything worse?" Marcus concluded.

Liem wasn't sure whether Marcus was referring to the lover's betrayal, the father's plans, or Parrish's money. What he really wanted to know was what "candid" meant, but when Marcus only sipped his tea, not seeming to expect an answer, Liem spoke instead about his own family, all farmers, hawkers, and draftees. Nobody had ever traveled very far from Long Xuyên, unless he was drafted by the army. Liem was the family's first explorer, and perhaps that was the reason his parents had been so anxious at the bus station in Long Xuyên, one of the few moments of his past he recalled with any clarity. The patch of unshaded dirt and cement was crowded with passengers ready to board, holding cartons tied with twine and keeping close watch on their pigs and chickens, shuffling in wire cages. As the heat rose in waves, the odor of human sweat and animal dung, thickened by the dust, rose with it.

"We raised you well," his father said, unable to look him in the eye with his own bluish gray ones, hazy from cataracts. "I know you won't lose yourself in the city."

"I won't," Liem promised. "You can depend on me." He heard the driver shouting for passengers to board as his mother ran her hands up and down his arms and patted his chest, as if frisking him, before she squeezed a small wad of bills into his pocket. "Take care of yourself," she said. Around her mouth, deep wrinkles appeared to be stitches sewing her lips together. "I won't be able to anymore." He hadn't said he loved her, or his father, before he left. He'd been too distracted by his desperation to get on the bus, for without a seat he'd have to stand shoulder-to-shoulder in the aisle, or else risk his life riding on the roof all the way to Sài Gòn.

"How could you know what was going to happen?" Marcus leaned forward. "You're not a fortune-teller. Anyway, that's all in the past. You can't dwell on it. The best way to help them now is to help yourself."

"Yeah," he said, even though this was, to him, a very American way of thinking.

"The point is, what do you want to be?"

"To be?"

"In the future. What do you want to do with yourself?"

No one had ever asked Liem such a question, and Liem rarely asked it of himself. He was content with his job at the liquor store, especially when he compared his fate to that of his friends back home. The underage ones, like him, had become bar sweeps or houseboys for Americans, while the older, luckier ones dodged army service, becoming thieves or pimps or rich men's servants. Unlucky ones got drafted, and very unlucky ones came home not at all, or if they did, returned as beggars who laid their stumps on the side of the road.

Marcus was watching him expectantly. The idea of saying he wanted to be a doctor or a lawyer or a policeman was utterly ludicrous, but the desire to appear noble in Marcus's eyes, and maybe his own, seized him.

"I want to be good," he said at last.

"Well." Marcus glanced at the bill. "Don't we all."

The next day at the liquor store, Liem counted seconds with sweeps of his broom and rings of the register, his shift threatening never to end when only yesterday he'd hoped the day would run on forever. After he'd paid for the dim sum, almost throwing Marcus to the ground as they wrestled for the check, they had browsed the curio shops of Chinatown together, then driven to Treasure Island to see the Golden Gate Bridge, winding up by dusk in a Market Street theater, where they sat knee-to-knee watching *One Flew Over the Cuckoo's Nest.* Later, eating sushi at a Japanese restaurant on Sutter in Japantown, neither mentioned the contact. They talked instead about Jack Nicholson, whose films Liem had never seen before, and Western Europe, which Liem had never visited, and the varieties of sushi, which Liem had never eaten before. In short, Marcus did most of the talking, and that was fine with Liem.

Talking with Marcus was easy, because all Liem had to do was ask questions. Marcus, however, rarely asked him anything, and during those moments when Liem ran out of inquiries, silence ensued, and the hum of the car or the chatter of the other diners became uncomfortably noticeable. Neither spoke of Parrish, not even when they returned to the Victorian and Marcus opened one of Parrish's bottles of red wine, a Napa Valley pinot noir. Never having drunk wine before, Liem woke up the next morning feeling as if the corkscrew had been driven into his forehead. He could barely crawl out of bed and to the bathroom, where, as he brushed his teeth, he vaguely remembered Marcus helping him up the stairs and easing him into bed. Seeing no sign of Marcus before he went to work, he concluded Marcus was sleeping in.

When he returned to the Victorian in the evening, he found Marcus watching television in the living room, clad in his bathrobe and with his hair mussed. "A letter came for you today," Marcus said, switching off the television with the remote control. On the coffee table was a battered blue airmail marked by unmistakable handwriting, the pen marks so forceful they almost cut through the thin envelope. Liem's father had written back to his first note, because the airmail was addressed to him at Camp Pendleton, Block 35, Tent 27B, and had been forwarded by the resettlement agency in San Diego.

"Aren't you going to open it?" Marcus said.

"No," he muttered. "I don't think so." He rubbed the envelope between his fingers, unable to explain how he'd dreaded the letter's arrival as much as he'd yearned for it. Once he opened the letter, his life would change again, and perhaps he wanted it to stay the same. Summoning all his will, he laid the airmail on the coffee table again and sat down next to Marcus on the couch, where together they stared at the blue envelope as if it were an anonymous letter slipped under an adulterer's door.

"They think we've got a Western disease," Marcus said. "Or so my father says."

"We?" Liem said. "What Western disease?"

"Don't think I don't know."

Liem kept his eyes on the letter, certain his father had written no more than what needed to be said: *make money and send it home, take care and be good.* The message would be underlined once and then once more, leaving him to guess at anything too dangerous to be said in his father's bare vocabulary. But whereas his father had never sought to find new words, Liem was the opposite. He looked up at Marcus and asked the question he'd wanted to since yesterday.

"What does candid mean?"

"Candid?" Marcus said. "Yeah, right. Candid. It means being caught by surprise, like in a photograph or a film, when someone takes your picture and you're not looking. Or it means someone who's frank. Who's honest and direct."

Liem took a deep breath. "I want to be candid."

"I'd like to be candid."

"Shut up," Liem said, putting his hand on Marcus's knee.

Afterward, he sensed things might not have gone well. First, their clothes didn't come off as smoothly as he expected, because all of a sudden the buttons and zippers were smaller than he knew them to be, and his fingers larger and clumsier. His rhythm seemed to be off, too. Sometimes in his eagerness he moved too fast, and to make up for it, or because he was embarrassed, he went too slow, throwing them out of sync and causing him to apologize repeatedly for an elbow here, or a knee there, until Marcus said, "Stop saying you're sorry and just enjoy yourself, for heaven's sake." So he did his best to relax and give himself up to the experience. Later, his arm thrown over Marcus's body, facing his back, Liem wasn't surprised to discover how little he remembered. His habit of forgetting was too deeply ingrained, as if he passed his life perpetually walking backward through a desert, sweeping away his footprints, leaving him with only scattered recollections of rough lips pressed against his, and the comfort of a man's muscular weight.

"I love you," he said.

Marcus did not roll over or look behind him, did not say "I love you" in return, and, indeed, said nothing at all. The ticking of Parrish's antique grandfather clock grew louder and louder with each second, and by the time the patter of rain on the roof was distinct, Liem was fumbling awkwardly with his underwear.

"Can you just wait a minute?" Marcus said, turning around and hooking one leg over Liem's body. "Don't you think you're overreacting?"

"No," Liem said, trying to unpry, without success, Marcus's leg, honed by countless hours on the treadmill and the squat machine. "I need to go to the bathroom, please."

"You just got caught by surprise. Sooner or later you'll figure out love's just a reflex action some of us have." Marcus stroked Liem's hand. "A week from now you're not even going to know why you told me that."

"Okay," he said, not sure whether he wanted to believe Marcus or not. "Sure."

"You know what else is in your future?"

"Do not—don't tell me."

"A year from now you'll be the one hearing other men say they love you," Marcus said. "They'll say you're too pretty to be alone."

Marcus pulled him closer, and, as the rain continued to fall, they held each other. Outside a car began honking repeatedly, a sound Liem knew by now to mean that someone, double-parked, was blocking the narrow street in front of the house. Then all was quiet but for the clock, and he thought Marcus might have dozed off until Marcus stirred and said, "Aren't you going to read the letter?"

He'd forgotten about the airmail, but now that Marcus had mentioned it, he felt it glowing in the darkened living room, bearing on its blue face the oil of his father's touch, and perhaps his mother's, too, the airmail the only thing he owned that truly mattered.

"I never read it to you."

"I *will never* read it to you. That's the future tense."

"*I'll* never read you the letter."

"Now you're being petty. Don't read it to me, then."

"But I *will* tell you what *I'll* write."

"Only if you want to," Marcus said, yawning.

Until this moment, Liem hadn't thought about what he would write to his father and mother once their letter had arrived. So he improvised, beginning with how the tone would be as important as the content. His letter, he said, would be a report from an exotic city, one with a Spanish name, famous for cable cars, Alcatraz Island, and the Golden Gate Bridge. He would include postcards of the tourist sights, and he'd mention how funny it was to live in a city where people who weren't even Asian knew about the autumn festival. When enormous crowds in Chinatown celebrated the lunar new year, he'd be there, throwing firecrackers at the feet of a dancing lion, hoping his family was doing the same. The crunch of burned firecrackers under his feet would remind him of his boyhood at home, and the letter he'd write would remind him of times when the family gathered around his father as he read, aloud, the occasional note from a distant relative. At the end, Liem would tell them not to worry about him, because, he'd write, *I'm working hard to save money, I'm even making friends. And we live in a mauve house.*

He heard the steady rise and fall of Marcus's breathing, and, afraid Marcus was fading into sleep, he couldn't stop himself from asking the other question he'd wanted to ask since the previous day.

"Tell me something," he said. Marcus's eyes fluttered and opened. "Am I good?"

A light drizzle tapped against the windows, the sound of Friday night on a rainy day. "Yes," Marcus said, closing his eyes once more. "You were very good."

This much, at least, he could write home about.

After Marcus fell asleep, Liem slid out of bed and went to the bathroom, where he stood under a spray of hot water for so long he nearly fainted from the heat and steam. He had his pants on and was combing his hair when the phone rang in the living room.

"I just wanted to see how you two were doing," Parrish said, loud and cheerful, as if he'd been out drinking.

"Just fine," Liem said, eyeing the letter on the coffee table. "Nothing special." He didn't like speaking on the phone, where body language was no help in making himself understood, and he kept the conversation short. Parrish didn't seem to mind, and said good night just as boisterously as he'd said hello.

Liem sat down on the couch and opened the letter carefully. When he unfolded the single sheet of onionskin paper, translucent in the light, he recognized once again his father's script, awkward and loopy, as hard for him to decipher as it was for his father to write.

September 20, 1975

Dear son,

We got your airmail yesterday. Everyone's so happy to know you're alive and well. We're all fine. This summer, your uncles and cousins were reeducated with the other enlisted puppet soldiers. The Party forgave their crimes. Your uncles were so grateful, they donated their houses to the revolution. Our lives are more joyful now that your uncles, your cousins, and their wives and children are living with us in our house. The cadres tell us that we will erase the past and rebuild our glorious country!

When you have time, send us the news from America. It must be more sinful even than Sài Gòn, so remember what the cadres say. The revolutionary man must live a civil, healthy, correct life! We all think of you often. Your mother misses you, and sends you her love. So do I.

Your Father

After he read the letter a second time, he folded it, slid it back into its envelope, and let it lie inert on the coffee table. Restless, he stood up and walked over to the bay window overlooking the street and the sidewalks, empty this late in the evening. The light in the room had turned the window into a mirror, superimposing his likeness over the landscape outside. When he raised his hand, his reflection raised his hand, and when he touched his face, the reflection did the same, and when he traced the curve of his cheek and the line of his jaw, so, too, did the mirror image. Why, then, did he not recognize himself? And why did he see right through himself to the dark street outside?

Raindrops on the glass dappled the reflection of his face. He waited at the streaky window for several minutes until he saw a sign of life, two men striding quickly down the street, shoulders occasionally brushing and hands deep in the pockets of their jackets. Their heads, ducked down low against the drizzle, were bent toward each other at a slight angle as each listened to what the other was saying. At one time he would have thought the two men could only be friends. Now he saw they could easily be lovers.

As they passed under a streetlamp, one of them said something that made the other laugh, his head tilting back so that his unremarkable face was illuminated for a second. The man's eyes turned to Liem at that instant, and Liem, realizing he was quite visible from the street, wondered what kind of figure he cut, bare-chested and arms akimbo, his hair slicked back. Suddenly the man raised his hand, as if to say hello. When his partner looked toward the window as well, Liem waved in return, and for a moment there were only the three of them, sharing a fleeting moment of camaraderie. Then the men passed by, and long after they had vanished into the shadows he was still standing with his hand pressed to the window, wondering if someone, behind blinds and curtains, might be watching.

CAIMEEN GARRETT

Florida State University

THE TEMPERATE FAMILY

To: D. Stokely
Black River Falls, Wisconsin   Sunday, July 2nd, 1876

Dear Sir:—Your letter of the 22nd ultimo is to hand. I have enclosed a photograph and full description of my son.

I regret that you are still unable to obtain a picture of the child in question. In your last letter you expressed frustration that I did not immediately travel to see the boy. Lest I seem indifferent, let me explain. Over the past two years more than five hundred cases have been brought to my attention; had I given myself over to hope each time, I should have landed in Friends' Asylum long ago. Also, you will forgive my misgivings about anyone recognizing a child from a woodcut. Bear in mind that of the scores of children I have personally seen—and ruled out—most were brought to my notice by people who, like yourself, believed the child to be "an exact likeness, the very image" of my son.

Your ambiguity over eye color also troubles me. In your first letter you thought the eyes blue, but in the second deemed them closer to brown. Charley's eyes are brown and could never be taken for anything else. Since most blonds do have blue or gray eyes, this has been a very useful way for us to rule boys out by post or wire, thus avoiding pointless trips. Still, we have learned that people are often unreliable in this regard. Men often have difficulty discerning different shades, so I suggest you get a woman's opinion; we have found them to be more accurate.

I also want to add that it is not uncommon for lost and abandoned children to call themselves "Charley Ross," nor is yours the only case of a child registered under that name in an orphan asylum. I visited such a child at the Detroit Home for the Friendless, and I also learned of another child at a public institution in Albany.

I am currently traveling to investigate another child, but I expect to be back in Philadelphia by July 6th or 7th. Based on everything you have told me, I do not believe the child to be my son; however, if you do obtain a photograph, please send it, as that would definitively resolve the matter.

I thank you for the interest you have taken in our case.

Respectfully yours,
C. K. Ross

To: L. Murdock
Thomasville, Georgia   Sunday, July 2nd, 1876

Dear Sir:—Your favor of the 14th of June only arrived a few days ago, just as I was leaving town, or else I should have replied earlier.

The tintype of the child you enclosed is indeed poor, as you indicated, yet it is detailed enough for me to say that he does not appear to be my son. The cowlick is on the wrong side, the ears are too prominent, and the shape of the face is quite different. Some of the child's statements are incorrect—the prayer is not the one our children recite, and Charley has no brother Albert. Some things are true: Uncle Joe is our neighbor, and his mother's favorite horse was Polly. However, both these facts are in the Pinkerton circulars. Even so, I cannot explain the child's comment about our tree "with chickens in it" and his habit of throwing things at them. A few months before Charley's disappearance, a flock of chickens took up residence in one of our pine trees, and the children used to pelt them with stones. No one but our family, or someone very close, would know about this; for this reason, I want to investigate this child further.

This is my suggestion: If you are able to take the boy to the nearest telegraph office, we can conduct a detailed interview by wire. I am currently in Vermont, but will be home within the week; if this plan suits you, we can arrange it then.

Thank you for your kind interest in our case.

Respectfully yours,
C. K. Ross

To: P. Jones
Bergin's Point, New Jersey   Sunday, July 2nd, 1876

Dear Madam:—I must confess my ignorance in regard to the science of Mesmerism, yet I fail to see how it might aid the recovery of my son. Naturally I am desirous to learn more before committing myself to any investigation or experiment. I am particularly curious to know what would be expected on my behalf.

Respectfully yours,
C. K. Ross

To: J. W. Baillet
Aylesford, Nova Scotia   Sunday, July 2nd, 1876

Dear Sir:—Your favor of the 26th ultimo is to hand, and also the letter of a few days' earlier date.

   While I acknowledge your point, that a young child, particularly
one subject to rough treatment, may greatly change in appearance,
the boy you describe cannot be my son. Charley's eyes are most definitely brown, as are those of his six older siblings. With respect to the
physician you consulted, I must tell you that I have spoken with several oculists, all of whom agree that the iris does not change in color,
nor is there any means of effecting such a change in order to disguise
a child.

   Thank you for the interest you have taken in our case.

                                              Respectfully yours,
                                                      C. K. Ross

To: James Wilson
Atlas Hotel, Philadelphia   Sunday, July 2nd, 1876

My Dear Sir:—I have posted this to the hotel you mentioned in your
last letter—I hope it finds you there. I had intended to be in Philadelphia for Independence Day, but was called away on a matter of
some urgency. I was not keen to journey to Brush's Mills without
more promising evidence, but there are some interesting details that
match a man we have been searching for. The fellow is itinerant in
his habits, and likely to flee, so I thought it best to go immediately.

   I will be home in a few days; it would please me greatly if you and
your family would call on us. Mrs. Ross is anxious to meet the
gentleman who made such effort to help us. I know you are eager to
visit the Centennial Exposition, but this week the crowds will be at

their worst. I must caution you, the Centennial is an overwhelming affair. Through experience I have discovered this ratio: For every day at the Centennial, one must spend two additional days recovering from the event. It is particularly taxing for ladies. Mrs. Ross, who has long been out of health, did visit once, but only in a rolling chair. They rent for sixty cents an hour—four fifty for the day—which seems less unreasonable after a few hours in the July heat. Another pleasant option is the Sawyer Observatory—the glass elevator climbs nearly two hundred feet, giving a view of the entire grounds. Unless you have gone up in a balloon—and I have not—you have never soared so high in your life!

Also, don't believe everything the newspapers print. With my travel I read out-of-town papers almost as often as the *Inquirer,* and I have noticed that the farther one gets from Philadelphia the more sensational the stories about the Exposition are. Granted, my opinion of newspapers in general is very low; even the so-called respectable papers have little scruple about printing the most vicious rumors and innuendo. Still, I can only imagine what fanciful tales about the Exposition you may have read in Germany. The worst humbugs I've seen are the stories about "Centennial Fever"; hysterical warnings to avoid Philadelphia water, nay, even to refrain from breathing too deeply within city limits! One paper suggested chewing bits of leather or shingle nails to relieve thirst. Considering the hot weather, this is dangerous, not to mention unnecessary, advice. "Centennial Fever" is nothing more than the consequence of too much sun, exertion, and indulgence.

You may have heard of the Shantyville, also called Dinkytown, which has sprung up on the outskirts of the Exposition. Though food and drink are reportedly much cheaper there, I would avoid it; what you save on lemonade and sausages you may spend later on sulphur tonic and Plantation Bitters. From what I hear, Shantyville's fare is as harmful to the stomach as its attractions are to the morals. Thankfully I do not speak from experience. If your children are as desperate as mine to see the man-eating Feejees, you might remind them of our zoological gardens in Fairmount Park, still the only attraction of its kind in the country. Conjure up visions of the bear pits and Jennie the elephant and your children will forget all about the Wild Men of Borneo and the five-legged pig.

I am writing this letter from St. Albans, Vermont, where I have boarded for the night. My journey began two days ago, on a midnight train to New York, followed by an eight A.M. train on the Hudson Railroad, which lasted nearly twenty-four hours, leaving me in St. Albans just as day was breaking. Unfortunately, no trains being run on Sunday, I am obliged to stay here until tomorrow morning. Though the journey has been tiring, I am anxious to reach Brush's Mills; the man I'm looking for, being fearful of arrest, may bolt before I arrive, taking the child in question with him. Still, St. Albans is a lovely place to be waylaid: I walked around the town all afternoon, happy to feel the sun after thirty hours in railway coaches. Even now, sitting at the writing desk in my room, I can still make out in the fading twilight the handsome row of stores on the street below—the harness and tobacco shops, the livery stable, the blacksmith and the milliner.

The rest of the day I used for catching up on my correspondence, which consumes a great deal of my time. Very few of the letters I receive contain any useful information: Most are humbugs and schemes. I had a doubtful letter from a prisoner in Ithaca, which I forwarded to his warden—I receive many letters from convicts—and a letter from a Londoner claiming Charley is with a band of Gypsies near Bradford. He suggested I pose as a tramp and infiltrate every Gypsy group I find. I did respond to a ridiculous letter about Mesmerism, only because it came from a New Jersey neighborhood the police have long been suspicious of. A few letters were more promising, though I don't hold out much hope.

Tomorrow the last leg of my journey begins: ninety miles to Brush's Mills, a small village four miles south of the Canadian border. Just over a month ago, in late May, I received a letter from a lady reporting that a stranger had arrived in their village, accompanied by a little boy about six, who did not resemble the man in the least. The child was described as nervous, shy, yet well-mannered, with hazel eyes and light hair cut close, but likely to curl if longer. The man, ugly, cruel, and heavily scarred, claimed to be a clock tinker, and had visited several houses, telling conflicting stories at each. He mentioned my son's disappearance repeatedly, said many people believed his son to be Charley Ross, and insisted that he'd scarcely avoided arrest more than once.

For two years I have followed every promising lead no matter the physical distance, and, as you well know, my search has not been confined to this country, massive though it is. Charley Ross has been found in all thirty-seven states, in the Indian Territory, ten times in Canada alone, in England and Scotland, in Nova Scotia, in Cuba, and, of course, in Germany. I've discovered that people are quick to suspect any Gypsy or stranger of doubtful character with a child in tow. Even so, some details about this clock tinker suggest that he might be a particular associate of the kidnappers, a man the police had heard was in Vermont or Canada. I sent a photograph of this man to my correspondent, asking her to study it closely. Three days later a telegram proclaimed it an exact likeness. I should have liked to have seen a picture myself before undertaking such a journey, but any attempt would have alerted the man to my interest.

I must confess, there is some relief not to be in Philadelphia this week. Under happier conditions there is no place I'd rather be on Independence Day. My family has a proud history there: My great-uncle George Ross was among the signers of the Declaration, and Betsy Ross's home has always attracted visitors, even before the Centennial. But yesterday, July first, the two-year anniversary of Charley's disappearance passed, and I find the signs of celebration unbearable.

No matter where I am Tuesday, even trains cannot outrun the illuminations that will flower the sky. Fireworks—that reminder of how Douglas and Mosher lured my two youngest boys into their buggy. I picture Walter in the cigar shop, twenty-five cents to spend, unaware that the wagon, the men, and his four-year-old brother are gone. He was found alone, crying on a Kensington street corner, a paper sack of crackers in his hand. For myself, I think of that evening, returning from work with a cartload of seashore sand to fire the crackers into, which I had promised the boys that very morning. They were desperate for fireworks, but I insisted on sand for safety. How misplaced my fears were; in those days the worst danger I dreamed of was fire.

The fourth of July was another harrowing day: That first monstrous letter reached me at the police station, its motive overwhelming me with horror. This unnatural offense, child-stealing to extort money, was so appalling that a roomful of policemen were struck speechless. The act was so unknown in this country that no existing laws had foreseen it. The irony does not escape me, that the burden I've borne these last two years should announce itself on Independence Day.

It still moves me to think of your efforts in investigating the "Würzburg child." I have been aided by the U.S. Consulates in several countries besides Germany—England, Scotland, Belgium—and all the people they employ impressed me with their generosity, but none so much as you. The lengths you went to trace the child, your cleverness in contriving to get a photograph, your diligence in making certain the boy was not my Charley. In a small box I keep a stack of all the photographs and tintypes I have received. Of all the "lost boys," only two or three likenesses affect me, one being that of the Würzburg child, for though clearly not my son, there is a resemblance—the broad forehead, the fullness of the cheeks, his shy yet appealing expression. Did you ever discover anything more about your little waif? Has the family remained in Wurzburg, or did they return to the U.S.? I agree that the story the child's adoptive guardian gave is quite fantastic. I don't know which part is more incredible: that he would undertake to travel from San Francisco to Bavaria to return an illegitimate child left at his house, or that any grandparents would not open their arms to such a precious child. Also, I agree with you that such a fine child must have a higher parentage than a Bavarian servant girl.

I have written more than I intended—four sides of foolscap—but on this subject I am prone to ramble. My candle is fast guttering away, so I will close by wishing you and your wife a lovely visit, and I will contact you upon my return home.

With the warmest regards,

Christian Ross

To: W. H. Leib

Quincy, Illinois   Tuesday, July 4, 1876

Dear Professor Leib:—I hope this letter finds you well, but I know that this time of year is as wretched for you as it is for me. Since receiving your fliers I have distributed them on all my travels—at railroad depots, ferry stops, and livery stables—and on my most recent trip—from which I am just now returning—I was reminded that your own cruel anniversary recently passed. As of three days ago my Charley has been gone two years. It is unimaginable, yet you have suffered more than twice as long. Five years! It is too painful for me to contemplate. I suspect you would tell me it gets no easier.

You may come across a newspaper account of my journey before this letter reaches you, but any item in an out-of-town paper will be brief and, likely, unreliable. Please know, of course, that if I had any urgent information about your dear Freddie, I would wire straight away. I cannot see even the slightest connection to your case, but since you believe that the miscreants who took your boy have New England ties, I will describe my experience in full, and let you determine its relevance.

You must forgive me for writing in pencil; I am so often on trains that I must put the time to use. Though it feels like days ago, it was only yesterday morning that I arrived in Brush's Mills, where I was received by Mr. Bray, the husband of my correspondent. Mr. Bray was a young man, thirty at most, a broad-brimmed hat set back on his head, clean-shaven except for an imperial under his lower lip. He was quiet, taciturn even, looking straight ahead as he answered my questions, as if addressing the bay mare he was driving. He had little to tell anyway, since he hadn't seen the child himself. I did not mind the silence, as his home was only five miles from the station. The horse seemed hardly jaded from the heat and scampered along, pulling the wagon, an old falling-top buggy, at a good clip, at least eight miles an hour.

I was less impressed by Mrs. Bray; she was a pleasant enough woman, charmingly plump in her blue linen dress, a lunatic fringe highlighting her eyes, but she was a bit overeager. A neighbor woman was also in the parlor, perhaps to help with dinner or the children who were scattered about—two little girls cutting up an old copy of *Appleton's*, a little boy of two, and an infant asleep in a basket. After a simple dinner of cold ham, boiled beef, and corn bread, I leaned back in my chair and asked Mrs. Bray why she thought the boy was my Charley.

Mrs. Bray dabbed at the corners of her mouth with her napkin. "I knew as soon as I saw the boy—he was too well-bred to belong to that brute. Even though the child was dirty, and his hair horribly shorn, he was very well-mannered."

"Yes," the neighbor woman added, dandling the little boy on her knee. "And shy like it hurt to look at you, putting his arm across his head when forced to speak."

A spark of hope flamed up, but I snuffed it out just as quickly. This was indeed a habit of Charley's, but it had been noted on one of the Pinkerton circulars. After parleying like this a bit more, it came out that while Mrs. Bray herself had not seen a flier, the neighbor, Amelia, had. I asked where the clock tinker had gone after leaving them.

"To our closest neighbors, the Wylies," Mrs. Bray replied.

I thought the neighbor would stay back with the children, but instead the entire lot of us, babe in arms included, tramped a quarter mile to the next house. The Wylies were even more adamant that the boy had to be Charley. They said the clock tinker had not treated the boy like a son, but like a burden he would be glad to be rid of. He had asked directions to a boardinghouse. Meanwhile, word of my visit had rippled through the community, and by the time we reached the boardinghouse we had been joined by a large group of villagers.

At the boardinghouse the elderly proprietress said that, yes, the stranger and his boy had stayed with her two Saturdays before. The man had talked of Canada, and mentioned some boxes that would soon arrive in Châteaugay that he was anxious to get hold of. The village was twenty-four miles away; the train from St. Albans had stopped there shortly before my own stop. Several villagers wanted to search the countryside for the pair, but I thought it best that I head to Châteaugay alone.

Before I left, the old lady touched my sleeve. "Mr. Ross, I was alone with the boy, we talked for nearly an hour, and he can't be yours. He is too old, and not fair at all."

I thanked the woman, and said that I, too, thought the game not worth the candle, yet I had traveled so far that I was determined to see things through to the end. At the Châteaugay station I was directed to the closest hotel. The innkeeper immediately recognized the pair I described.

"That man certainly was here. He was drunk, and made a terrible disturbance. He insisted on fixing our clock, though it worked fine, and promptly broke it. He then threw a fit, smashing a chair and a lamp. How we escaped a fire, I'll never know. They gave him ten days in prison, though he should have gotten more."

I asked about the boy and the boxes, and the innkeeper began to leaf through the hotel register.

"Here it is," he said, marking an entry with an ink-stained finger. "George Poole and Charley Ross." The innkeeper looked up from the register. "He told me to put the boy down that way. It was a joke; he said the local children were teasing his son. Right now, the boy is staying with the constable's family; I just saw him there a few days ago. Poole's boxes finally came, and I took them out to the constable's house myself. A bit of a bother, but I didn't want that man back here for any reason." The innkeeper turned to a calendar on the wall. "Poole's time should be up soon. Let's see," he said, walking his fingers along the dates. "Today. He should get out of jail today."

The innkeeper graciously offered to drive me out to see the boy. As we converged upon the house I saw four boys playing quoits. The innkeeper brought his horses to a halt, and pointed out the tallest boy, who was running to fetch the rope coil.

"That's him there."

Even from our distance of fifty feet I could see that the boy was certainly eight years of age, taller and more robust than my own Walter.

"That boy looks nothing like any picture of my son," I said, unable to keep my voice from going sharp. "My son was still in dresses when he was taken. That boy is two or three years older than he would be. If people had just used a little judgment, I could have been spared this whole ordeal."

Still, I approached the child. His borrowed clothes, too short at the wrist and ankle, made him seem even larger. I noted his sallow complexion, blunt nose, and close-set green eyes—nothing in his aspect suggested Charley in any way. He told me that his name was Willie Poole and that he was from Canada.

You need not wonder if this could have been your Freddie—for the boy might have been as old as ten years of age—for what happened next removed all doubt of his identity. On our way back to town the innkeeper and I met the boy's father. He was walking from the opposite direction, bareheaded and disheveled. He had a roughly trimmed mustache, and his sun-reddened face was pitted with smallpox, but even so the resemblance between him and the boy was plain. As we questioned him about the hotel registry the clock tinker became increasingly distressed. When he learned who I was, he truly had the fantods; he gripped a carriage wheel, and I thought he might swoon. After calming him and offering some water, he confessed that he had been drunk and had no memory of checking into the hotel; however, he was sure he had done such a thing, as children had been calling his son Charley Ross ever since they arrived in the area, and the clock tinker had begun to follow suit as a joke.

"You must never use my son's name again," I said, helping the man to his feet. "You don't understand the difficulty this sort of thing causes me."

With that settled, we resumed our drive. I was quite excited and could not resist giving my companion an earful all the way back to town.

"You would not believe how many similar cases I have had. Not only is it a common nickname, but it is becoming popular as a given name as well. And lost children of all ages identify themselves to police as Charley Ross. Some do it in the hope of better treatment, but others seem to think that all stray infants are called Charley Ross. Why, I was told two children from Kensington, a brother and sister, had become lost, and when an officer asked their names the little boy said 'Charley Ross,' and the sister added, 'I'm Charley Ross, too.'"

I have many more stories like this, more than I could tell in that short carriage ride. Here is a story I didn't tell him, about a little boy found in Frankford, just outside Philadelphia, in the early months of this ordeal. When I arrived a crowd had gathered around the boy, and though he did resemble Charley, with his golden curls and sweetly serious face, it was not him. I had a difficult time convincing the crowd, for they had decided that a lisp explained the boy's claim that his name was "Charley Loss." As I took the streetcar back to Germantown, I could not refrain from mumbling the name over and over to myself: Charley Loss, Charley Loss, Charley Loss.

So you can see why the notoriety of our case has been a mixed blessing. Why have we gotten so much attention? As you say, it is true that I'm fortunate to have powerful friends, including our mayor, but about myself you are mistaken; I am not nearly so prominent a citizen as you believe, nor my wealth so great, even before the '73 panic crippled my business. The reason is simply this: It was clear from the start that Charley had been abducted. Not only had a witness, my son Walter, also been taken and released, but the kidnappers' letters made it plain: This was a new crime. In your own case, even you believed at first that Freddie had suffered a tragic accident. But even in our situation, interest faded after a few months, and Charley might have been forgotten if not for the kidnappers' untimely deaths. No dime novel would hazard such a preposterous plot: the suspected kidnappers shot in an unrelated burglary, Douglas's deathbed confession. He said, Yes, it's true, we took Charley Ross. Mosher knows where the child is. Told Mosher was dead, Douglas's last words were that Charley was safe and would be returned home within a few days.

Why, minutes from death, should he lie? What earthly laws could touch him then? Everything he said corresponded with the ransom letters. From the start they had warned us that the boy was boarded with people ignorant of his identity, and in the event of their death or arrest we would never discover him. Was it so unbelievable that Mosher would keep the child's whereabouts from his accomplice? The police didn't think so; experience had made Mosher cautious, and years before Douglas had betrayed several friends to gain his own freedom.

At that time I was convalescing at my mother's home in Middletown. The strain of the previous months had taken its toll—the constant suspense, the repeated threats to "annihilate" my son, not to mention a malarial fever from the swamps of New Jersey, and the many slanders on our domestic life—and for several weeks my family despaired of my life. Yet by that fateful December day, I had already begun to rally, and we had such renewed hope; we thought Charley would be home for Christmas. He was hidden in some remote rural corner, on some unsuspecting farm or tenement, and so we saturated the country with fliers and circulars, convinced that eventually we would flush him out of his hole. Of course, that was eighteen months ago, but with every false lead I remind myself of this: I just have to find the right boy once.

I have heard of no other child taken for ransom, and this is some comfort. No one can conceive of what my family's sacrifice has cost us—no one except you, who suffers as we do. For I know that if we had paid the ransom, Charley would have been returned to us long ago. But if I had rewarded the crime, a dangerous precedent would have been set—surely other criminals would have followed suit, and no child would be safe. How could I put my own needs before the public's?

You asked in your letter if I'd seen any other boys who I thought had been stolen. Only once, and of course you know about that boy, Henry Lachmueller. I hope that case gives you as much solace as it does me. When I met Henry, I saw that he was not my son, yet I also felt sure that unlike many of the poor waifs I see, this boy had indeed been taken. Despite his disfigurement, the dyed hair, the acid-scarred face—and I must tell you, it was far worse than the newspaper illustrations suggested—I knew this boy was of gentle breeding. A few days later his father, intrigued by the newspaper accounts, traveled from St. Louis, Missouri, to Chester, Illinois, and recognized his son, lost three years before.

But that was the only boy who I was sure had been stolen. It has been shocking to discover how many children are in the wrong hands. There are an astonishing number of lost or abandoned children, not to mention the more fortunate ones in charitable institutions. I don't know why so many children are astray—I think the war must have something to do with it, but that cannot explain it entirely.

I am sorry to stop so abruptly, but the conductor has just announced that we will soon be stopping in Rutland. This will be my first opportunity all day to stretch my legs and get a little refreshment. I will contact you again if I learn anything that might benefit your case, and I will keep you and your family in my prayers.

With warm regards,
Christian Ross

To: Bridget Ross
Middletown, Pennsylvania   Tuesday Evening, July 4th, 1876

Dearest Sister:—It may surprise you to receive such a letter from me, but my emotions must find some outlet, and no other is afforded me. It is nearly midnight, my railcar almost empty, and I am quite alone. This evening I had the most unsettling experience.

Just before our stop in Rutland, Vermont, the train conductor, who knows my identity, told me there was a traveling circus showing a wax figure of Charley. Since we had a three-hour stopover, I decided to take a look. First, to work up an appetite, I took a stroll up the main thoroughfare, then dined at a tavern with a patio so I could continue to take the air. Children were everywhere, waving balloons and penny flags, cracking peanuts, and gnawing on red, white, and blue popcorn balls. It was a festive display, though modest in comparison to what takes place in Philadelphia.

Most people seemed headed toward the circus—many more of the upper class than I would have expected. Great crowds milled between the three tents. I passed the first tent, for performers and live animals, and the second, where charioteers raced blindfolded, and entered the third. Inside, two dozen wagons circled the perimeter. These wagons were much like cages, with walls on three sides, and on their front sides, flap doors that could be folded back like hinged boxes. A net web was strung across the lower half of each cage to keep visitors from pressing too close. I began to proceed clockwise, following the orbit of the crowd. There were two attractions per wagon, a dividing curtain between, and sometimes there was a clear connection between the figures—Voltaire and Rousseau, Moses in the bulrushes next to David with his slingshot. But other wagons made no sense at all: the wild boy of Aveyron alongside Lord Byron in Greek dress, the Flowery Land Pirates hard by Marat in his bath. Another wagon made neighbors of Cleopatra and the lycanthrope of Düsseldorf.

The display was where I'd suspected: the farthermost point from the entrance, where the crowd was thickest. At first I couldn't see the right side of the cage, where I took Charley to be. People were clustered so close that I dared not push my way through, but instead waited in front of the first tableau in the cage, a scene of true wretchedness: a horrid-looking man with a menacing brow, a glass in his hand, and a bottle poking out of his pocket. On a narrow cot lay a shriveled old man, clearly the drunkard's dying father. A slattern slumped on a kitchen chair, staring into an empty cupboard. Two children, dirty and barefoot, huddled in the corner, and a half-naked infant squalled on the floor, an empty bottle just beyond its grasp. The walls of the cage were dressed to look like a hovel. Poverty and misery, unanswered longings were carved into their faces, though in the man of the house there was also something sinister. In the last two years I have witnessed too many genuine scenes of this kind; that such squalor exists is bad enough, why must it be depicted? I would have ignored that display completely, had I not been waiting to see the other side.

I caught a glimpse of pale peach wallpaper and a fake bronze wall sconce, and then a moment later I was in front of the right display, which resembled a parlor. There were several figures, but the closest, most prominent one was that of Charley. Dressed in a brown linen suit, he was perched on a small step stool, one arm steadying himself on the table beside him. He seemed about to speak to a little girl seated on the other side of the table. The figure was very handsome, and his hair was flaxen like Charley's, but with none of its luster, and instead of curling it hung straight. The features were sharp, the face thin. Do you remember how round his face was? Still babyish, all curves—forehead, temple, cheek, chin—each feature flowing into the next. How full Charley's cheeks were! Perhaps they are not so full now; if not, I hope it is from maturity, not want and privation. Should I catalog the other differences? As I stood there bitterly, I could not stop from making a mental checklist. The figure's mouth was wrong, wider but thin-lipped, and the chin smooth and un-dimpled. Charley's forehead is higher and broader, and his eyebrows much lighter, so faint that I could only see them when he was in my arms. The eyes, at least, were brown, but there was nothing of Charley in them—dull, empty, unseeing. And the expression! Bridget, I wish you could have seen it—a pious, sad look, entirely unlike Charley's, an expression unknown to him; in fact, I don't believe any child ever possessed such a pensive, beatific look—the saintly expression children assume only in biblical illustrations. All in all, this figure represented Charley in only the most superficial manner. His appearance may have been altered in so many ways—his golden curls cut and dyed, his skin darkened by stain or sun, or scarred by acid or harsh experience. He might be changed in so many shallow ways, yet that was all this wax figure reflected; there was nothing of Charley's essence in it, nothing real or true that anyone might recognize.

The other figures in the tableau I examined more casually. The little girl, who seemed Marian's age, looked like neither her nor Sophia, though strangely it did remind me of Aunt Margaret, that daguerreotype Mother has of her in the foyer. None of Charley's older brothers were there, not even Walter, which was a surprise; instead there was a mystery toddler cavorting on a hobbyhorse. As for my

wife, the mother's hair was dark like Sarah's, but upswept in a complicated way, and she wore an arsenic green silk dress, a voguish frock,
like something copied out of *Godey's Lady's Book,* much more fashion-
able and ornate than anything you've ever seen Sarah wear. The face
was handsome yet sad, and looked nothing like my wife. And then
there was The Father, seated at the table, a small smile as he glanced
up from his newspaper and studied his happy family. Bridget, how
you would have howled if you had seen it! It was remarkable how unlike me it was. The father was tall and well-built, much more robust
than myself, with thick black hair, and clean-shaven except for a large
mustache. His complexion was ruddy, and he had a nose seen only on
antique coins. I know you are laughing now. And he was young, too!
In the prime of life, no more than thirty-five; but even twenty years
ago I looked nothing like him. You can imagine how ridiculous it was.
As I stood facing him I thought that none of the other patrons would
ever suspect that this wiry, middle-aged man, his hairline advancing
by the minute, was staring at his wax double.

I began to feel that I had lingered too long; there was still a crowd
impatient to see the display, so I moved back to observe their reac-
tions. I noticed a plaque, signed by the circus proprietor, affixed to
the top of the wagon.

The Ross Family
I will give to anyone who will restore to me
the lost child, Charley Brewster Ross, or who
will give me any information which will lead
to his recovery, the sum of $2,000.

I don't know why the wax Charley bothered me so much. All the
other lost boys, they were not my son, however much they might
wish it. Peel back the layers of lies and fantasy, and each one of those

boys had a true identity and history, no matter how much they might want to abandon it. But this wax figure was not my Charley, yet it was also no other. Standing there, watching the crowd, I had the feeling that this figure was changing him somehow, in small, insidious ways, and with every person who gaped at him and studied his little face, the real Charley became more and more lost.

A gentleman with two small children took turns lifting them up.

"That's Charley Ross," the father said. "He was playing in front of his house when two bad men stole him away. He still hasn't been found."

The children's mother shifted to get a better view. "If I ever laid eyes on that child, I should know him in an instant," she said, great conviction in her voice. "Isn't he the image of his father?"

I overheard many similar remarks, and when I could bear no more I set out to find the circus owner. Before I walked away, the crowd parted briefly and I caught sight of the wax father, his smug, lordly manner, and I thought what a fool he was.

The doorkeeper pointed the proprietor out, and I approached him and complimented him on his exhibits. I then asked him if it was true that he had a wax figure of Charley Ross.

"Oh, yes," he said, and pointed toward the wagon. "We have the entire family. It's our most popular attraction, as you can see, and it doesn't cost me a cent."

I then asked him if it was a good likeness, to which he nodded, and led me over to the display. He said it had been modeled after a photograph, which with a little prodding he admitted getting from the Ross family themselves! You can imagine my surprise. Apparently his family lives a stone's throw away from us, and he has been to our home several times! I pretended to be impressed.

"So the rest of the family, they're accurate, too?"

Oh, yes, he insisted. The crowd in front of the display had dispersed, and the tent had begun to empty. I could keep up the charade no more. I looked from the wax father to the circus proprietor.

"Sir, do I look like that father in the cage?"

The man looked confused and shook his head slowly.

"Well, I must, sir," I said, "since I am Charley Ross's father." With that I showed him the photograph I always keep in my breast pocket. The man took the picture from me and studied it hard, looking as if he wished to disappear into it. I was surprised to feel a flutter of sympathy for him. But the proprietor quickly recovered, and began pumping both my hands, telling me how much his heart went out to me, and how he believed his exhibit was a great boon to our case, and that he hoped that he might someday have the opportunity to pay the reward to someone.

In regard to the wax figure, he said that he'd gotten the photograph from our mayor, and that Smith's circus had a figure from the same mold. I explained that while the figure was very attractive, it didn't look anything like my son, and I couldn't imagine anyone identifying him from it.

"What about the brown linen suit?" he said. "I had a dressmaker run it up special, so it would be exactly right."

"Yes," I said, "it is very like it. The costume is completely accurate, though it is also the only thing that has surely changed." I was feeling quite defeated, and ready to leave, when I asked how he happened to come by the rest of the Ross family.

The proprietor stepped closer to me. "Well, it's not something I'd want to advertise, Mr. Ross." He spoke in a low, conspiratorial tone. "That wagon used to contain the 'Temperate Family' and the 'Intemperate Family.' They were separated by that same curtain," he said, gesturing to the velvet drape, "and the point was to show the contrast.

Anyway, when we got Charley, we left the intemperate family alone, turned the temperate family into 'The Ross Family,' and stuck Charley in front. We thought it made a pretty good arrangement."

This confession startled me, and I reconsidered both sides of the display. I had taken them to be two separate things, but now I realized they made up one awful whole.

The circus was empty by then, and the workers were closing up for the night, pulling down the wagon doors and locking them up. I asked the proprietor if I might stay and look for a few minutes more. Of course, he said, repeating his expressions of sympathy, and then he added that when I did find Charley I must let him exhibit him, and he would pay me a thousand dollars a week for thirty weeks or more. I thanked him for his concern and said that my only focus was finding my boy, nothing more.

Alone, I studied the wagon, paying more attention to the left side, the intemperate side. The squalor of the scene, which I thought merely unseemly before, now reeked of menace. Charley might be in a situation much the same; he might be like that ragged infant on the floor, or that pinched urchin with the matted hair. I looked at the drunkard hunched over his table, desperation in his face. At such depths of misery a man might consider any evil. And over there was Charley, my innocent, unaware of what lurked behind that cheap curtain. For the first time I noticed a little straw hat resting on the table. It was the hat Charley was wearing when he disappeared, found weeks later in Trenton on the side of the road. And then I understood this exhibit: This was The Moment Before. Look at that fatuous buffoon of a father, that proud fool, never dreaming his greatest treasure will be snatched from under his nose. There was the resemblance I hadn't seen earlier. I was that wax father; he was me before. Before Charley was stolen I thought of myself in so many lights—businessman, husband, father, citizen. Now all lights have been doused except one: I am only Charley Ross's father. I had not thought about myself being different before, as being two separate men, but there it was. If I met my former self on the street what would I possibly have to say to him? He would be as foreign and strange as this wax figure before me now.

Have you ever noticed how some wax tableaux transcend their individual characters—there is an affinity between them—while others are nothing but a jumble, a miscellany of disparate figures? I saw the latter in the waxen Ross Family, that paragon of temperance and nobility. Looking at that pathetic clan, virtue did not seem like anything to aspire to. I saw a family frozen and imprisoned by virtue, forever on display. A terrible knowledge hung over them; only I knew what it had cost.

When Sarah and I agreed not to pay the ransom, not to compound the crime, I thought our sacrifice was temporary. Our suffering was unbearable and overwhelming, yet we consented to prolong it, to delay Charley's return, for the sake of the common good. These were the terms I clung to—*prolonged, delayed*—and even my worst fears assumed some resolution. I did not imagine that someday my prayers would not exclusively seek a happy ending, but any ending at all. I did not understand that some sacrifices are forever.

I don't know how closely you followed the accounts of Westervelt's trial in the paper, but one reporter said of me: "his eyes have a darting, roving quality." I thought I had no vanity, but the observation stung—it had the force of a truth previously unseen.

It does no good to regret now; that path leads only to madness. You understand that I have never expressed any doubt to Sarah. I have never said that I wish we had paid the ransom right away— damn the police and the newspapers and the public uproar. The police: If the fiends realize no money is coming, they'll give up and set the boy free. The newspapers: If the ransom is paid, all our children will be vulnerable. There was so much pressure not to bargain with criminals that I was too ashamed to be selfish. I tried to be both a good father and a good citizen—everyone expected it of me. Everyone, that is, except the kidnappers. They were the only ones who expected me to be only a father. Perhaps that was their mistake. It was certainly mine. I should have acted only as a father, because now that is all I am. It is strange, but now that he is gone, I am much more Charley Ross's father than I ever was before.

Did my sacrifice make a difference? Did the failure of those two river thieves give other villains pause? I'd like to believe that, but in my heart I know otherwise. The next monster to steal a child will have no trouble with the ransom. All he will have to say is "Think of Christian Ross." I am the lesson here. No other father will face the same dilemma I did. They won't agonize a whit over civic duty. Parents hear of me and hold their children close, and vow in my place they'd pay the ransom quick, justice be damned. Look, they will say, at poor Christian Ross, that haunted man with the roving, darting eyes—he searched and searched the rest of his life.

Well, I could go on forever, but what good would it do? Thank you for letting me confide in you. I will probably tell Sarah about the circus, but I won't burden her with too many details. I want to thank you again for your visit last month. It was a great comfort to me whenever I was away to think of you with Sarah.

Your Loving Brother,
Christian

FATIMA RASHID

University of Central Florida

SYRA

On the plane, flying toward a country he's turned his back on for twenty years, Khalid remembers what he has never really forgotten. He remembers how he left Paposhnagar at nineteen, with the stink of fish radiating from his hands and hair, and his nose and lips bleeding from the blows of his mother's fists. "Go die like a *ghoons* in the gutter," she screamed. Her hair, prematurely gray, swung about her face as she hurled at him first books, then plates, porcelain flowers, a footstool—whatever came to her hand. His father and brothers tried to quiet her. *Don't curse your own son. A mother's words strike like an arrow.* But the words and fists flew nonetheless. "No one needs a piece of misery like you. *Dafa hojaw.* You've been nothing but trouble since you were born."

And trouble was his middle name, Khalid told his wife, Shagufta, years later, when they were newlyweds, when Abdullah floated inside Shagufta's womb, multiplying by millions of cells each minute.

"I fell off roofs, dived off a cliff once and almost drowned," Khalid said. "Once I tried to clean this stray cat with gasoline and she caught fire." He spun his tales with a storyteller's instinct, molding them into escapades worth laughing about. And so Shagufta laughed about the twelve stitches on his scalp, the broken ankle, the motorcycle accidents, a grade school teacher who had threatened to resign unless he was expelled.

He had never told Shagufta the real reason he left home, of course. That knowledge he kept tucked inside him, like a broken tooth wrapped in a dirty handkerchief. He let Shagufta assume he'd come to America for the reason all *desi* illegals did: money. Money to send back for siblings' educations, debts, a better house, sisters' weddings. In a survey of *desi*s, sisters' weddings would no doubt top the list, Khalid thinks.

But Khalid has no sister to worry about. Not anymore. When he backed away from his mother and stalked out of their whitewashed concrete home, it was her words, not necessity, that drove him. "Did you hear what I said? I'll bury you with her. You, your future, your fishing rods—"

He slammed the door behind him. He didn't imagine then that twenty years would pass before he would see his mother again. He didn't think further than the end of the street, or maybe a friend's house, or the *chai-wala's* at Paposh Plaza. Boys from respectable families didn't leave. Not if they married, not if they won the lottery. So Khalid imagined he'd slink home at nightfall, avoid his mother for a while. Then one day, he'd clutch her feet and beg her to forgive him. All things blew over, he thought.

But as he plowed down the street all those years ago, his father ran after him, kicking up a plume of dust. He grabbed Khalid's shirt and brought him to a standstill. Khalid watched as his father struggled for breath, leaning heavily against Nazar the Tailor's dusty maroon Toyota. Age had ambushed him. That morning his father had left the house humming *Iqbal,* reeking of Brut cologne, a lunch tin stuffed with *paratas* swinging from his hand. Now his skin sagged, and so did he. When Khalid pictures that day across the distance of time, he sees himself, a lanky boy all elbows and jeans, facing his saggy-skinned father on the sunbaked road. He wills his father to grab that boy by the nape of the neck and drag him home.

But his father straightened and pulled a bundle of ill-stacked faded rupees out of his *khameez* pocket. "It's not your fault," he offered, holding out the money.

Khalid froze. His father thought he was leaving, and that knowledge jarred Khalid more than his mother's fists. A few lines from his father's favorite book, *Idioms and Quotations,* rambled through Khalid's mind. *Some storms are best left unweathered. A road once walked can never be untraveled.*

"Three *lakh,*" his father said. "It's your brother's college tuition. You can pay it back when you get to America."

America, the land of milk and honey. Where the streets glimmered gold, the stars shone during daytime. And Khalid had begged to go, hadn't he? Begged and nagged his parents since he'd finished Intermediate. So many boys had gone ahead, and the dollars they wired back showed in the cars their families drove and the hoity-toity way they spoke.

But being *sent* away was another thing entirely, even if it was to America.

Later, when Khalid told Shagufta he entered the United States on foot across the Mexican border, she didn't believe him.

"That's crazy," she said, lying behind him, one leg slung over his, on the *multani* coverlet in their moonlit bedroom. Her skin stretched, bluish, across her stomach, and Abdullah kicked through it, drumming Khalid's back. "*Desi*s don't do that. I mean, why didn't you just buy a fake visa?" She knew all about fake visas, having arrived in the United States on one herself. But unlike Khalid, Shagufta had immigrated at the age of four, with her parents and several siblings, so her English didn't suffer from a *desi* accent like his.

"I thought that's what I was getting, a U.S. visa," Khalid said, "and the next thing I knew, I was on a plane to Mexico." He gave her the impression that he was a naive teenager, hoodwinked by crooked men. The truth was, his father's three *lakh* bought nothing better than a Mexican crossing.

But when his father held out those rupees, they appeared enough to accomplish anything. Or perhaps on a day like that, nothing. Khalid didn't whoop like an idiot or shake hands with every man he knew, or jump on his Honda 125 and take off to celebrate at The Pink Panther with his friends. A day earlier, he might have. But the world was twisted as if in a distorted dream, like life viewed through a shard of glass. He stunk of fish and seawater, Khalid suddenly realized, and something else, harder to pinpoint and define. His little sister, Syra, lay lifeless at home on the drawing room couch, the turquoise of her jumper running and staining the white brocade. And his father was crying, head bent under the beaming sun, holding out a bundle of faded cash.

The money repelled Khalid. It frightened him like a snake rising out of water. But he pocketed it and walked away. In one quick motion, just like that. "You don't have to go," his father shouted after him. The words, hollow yet desperate, followed Khalid all the way to America.

And now they follow him back. Khalid slumps in his seat, remembering. Two caplets of Benadryl fog his brain as he reluctantly races toward the country he abandoned twenty years earlier. The mood in the airplane is strangely festive. Khalid's fellow passengers—all men, all deportees—joke and compare jail times. Six months, three and one-half, eight. They pace the aisles restlessly, banging Khalid's elbow this way and that. They pick apart personal histories. *You used Bhai Wajahat, that dhokay baz? I heard his visas weren't worth the price of the ink he used to print them. I was okay till this registration shit started up. They put me in solitary. With a name like mine, you might as well pin "Osama's brother" on my back. Man, I mortgaged my arms and legs, even my parents, to get to America.*

America, the land of milk and honey. The land that swallows people whole. Transforms them into thin voices lurching over bad phone lines, and then belches them out at random.

And what did these particular men pine for while mired in the quicksand of America? Khalid listens as they recount lists of favorite haunts and foods. Chicken Jalfrezi at The Pink Panther, one says. Agha's mango shakes. Kite flying and camel rides at Clifton Beach. The *adhan* waking them for morning prayers.

"They have the *adhan* on loudspeaker in Queens, too," interjects Khalid. "At the mosque on 168th." The other men ignore him. Nothing positive about America on *this* flight. Besides, they've entered a new discussion now: family. Yes, family is what they missed most. Tears pop into their eyes at the mention of family. Some, like Khalid, haven't set eyes on their parents and siblings for decades.

Maybe, one young man ventures, deportation is a kick in the ass from God. *Go home to your parents, you* nadans, *before they die. Give them your time, not your money.* Several others nod fervently. Yes, the INS has done them a big favor, plucked them from a bog of mindless labor and flung them back where they belong—Allah be praised—into the bosoms of their families.

My family, Khalid starts to say, is in New York. But the thought of Shagufta, left alone in Queens with a mountain of legal bills, their son, and a pregnancy to worry about, silences him. She sounded frightened when he spoke to her before boarding the plane this morning. She kept telling him—or maybe herself—not to worry. A month, she said, two at the most. She'd sell the house and join Khalid in Karachi before he knew it. And then she cried, whether for him or for herself he couldn't tell. And he imagined her slumped over the kitchen counter, her short choppy hair slicked back from the shower, shaggy robe folded over her already swollen belly.

Where is she right now, Khalid wonders. In their sage green bedroom, packing, or perhaps across the hallway, curled up next to Abdullah on his race-car bed. She's been sleeping there even though the bed is uncomfortable. She wants Abdullah to get rid of it. "You're a big boy now," Khalid remembers her saying. "No second grader sleeps on a toddler bed." But Abdullah loves that bed. Before Khalid's arrest, when Shagufta left the two alone sometimes—while she and her sisters shopped at Indian boutiques in Jackson Heights—Khalid and Abdullah perched on the bed, side by side. They pretended they were at the Grand Prix, racing head to head, flying around the track at two hundred miles per hour. Abdullah always let Khalid win. "Because anyway," he said, "I'm going to win a real Grand Prix when I grow up, Baba." Khalid nodded. He nodded although the idea of his son racing—or riding a motorcycle, or even a roller coaster—made Khalid want to pick up his box of tools and build a padded world where his son would always be safe.

Now the thought of that son walking alone to school in Queens floats heavily in Khalid's chest. He presses the air hostess's idea of a pillow into his stomach. A month is too long, he thinks, two an eternity. Fatherhood has taught him many things. That your own child's diapers are rarely as disgusting as another's. That it is possible to survive a sixteen-hour shift laying roofs after a sleepless night. That spoiling a child is easier than unspoiling one. That love can crush your heart as well as fill it.

But diapers and sleepless nights cannot teach a man everything, even about fatherhood. Four months of INS detention—four months deprived of Abdullah—opened to Khalid the darker side of parenthood and offered him a glimpse of what his mother felt. What he did to her that day when he returned from fishing at Kimarhi with a brown-legged body dangling out of a turquoise jumper. Syra, but not *really* Syra, because Syra had drifted out of reach somewhere between the child-sized fishes of Kimarhi and the nets that lie in wait for them.

Gone though she is, Syra's presence has colored every word Khalid has exchanged with his mother for the past twenty years. Before his arrest, before he complied with the INS registration order for all Pakistani males and was detained, Khalid dutifully phoned Karachi every week from his home in Queens. He pretended, as did his parents, that he'd abandoned Paposhnagar for the reason other men do. "I wired Habib Bank the money last Tuesday, but you know how slow they are."

And in recent years, his father replied, "You've earned enough, Khalid. Come home. I'll lose my mind or the rest of my hair, listening to your mother jabber about you day and night."

Did she really, Khalid wondered. Now that his mother finally chimed in through the speakerphone, after years of brief, stilted *Salaams,* she spoke of little more than dollar-exchange rates, Eid festivals, and impending monsoons and the swarms of crickets that swept in with them. Then she asked for Shagufta, or Abdullah, her *chand ka tukra,* her little slice of the moon, she called him. And she always went silent when Khalid's father imparted his standard farewell. "Let us know when you'll be here. We've added another floor, so tell Shagufta not to worry about privacy."

"It's not privacy I'm worried about," Shagufta told Khalid once. She lounged on a bar stool at the kitchen counter, her eyes watering from the onions Khalid sliced. Sunday was his day to cook, and the calls invariably occurred on Sunday. "Once I go, I can't come back. I can't ever see my parents again. Do you have any idea how scary that is?"

"What do you think?" Khalid said. He banged about pots and lids, peeled ginger with unnecessary force, slicing away thick layers of flesh along with the skin. "Do you have any idea how long it's been since I've seen *my* parents?" He swiped the ginger peels into his palm and tossed them into the garbage. "But I guess the world revolves around you, doesn't it?"

Shagufta hopped off her stool. "I don't know how you can take it," she said. She began to crush garlic, the act an apology in itself. "I'd go crazy."

Khalid maintained his sullen expression as he sprinkled coriander and cumin into the simmering curry. The upper hand was hard to come by in this household, and he didn't mean to relinquish it just yet. But the truth was, his family was like an old album locked in a file cabinet. Almost forgotten. Hidden away—or kept at bay—in the recesses of his mind.

Because America had grown on Khalid by then. Or perhaps he'd grown out of himself in America. He'd left behind the old Khalid, the-boy-who-had-drowned-his-sister. Shed him like a skin somewhere along those four miles of Mexican dirt, before crawling through the neatly snipped fence and into America. So it was the new Khalid—self-assured family man, proud owner of a house in Jamaica Estates, Queens, and a roof-laying business—who scowled at his wife to let her know the discussion was over.

"You take it because you have to," he said. "Besides, why do you need to make a big deal out of everything? You know we're not going anywhere."

But he had been wrong, hadn't he? And now, on the plane, the new Khalid chomps peanuts and jokes with the other men while the old one raps on the door of his consciousness, trying to slip back into being. *No one needs a piece of misery like you. I'll bury you with her. You, your future, your fishing rods.*

Those words mean nothing now, Khalid reminds himself. His father's constant nagging is proof of that. "We're teetering into our graves here, Khalid. Your mother cries all day about how she'll die without seeing her youngest again."

But he's not really the youngest, Khalid wants to remind his father. Syra is. That tiny surly-eyed creature with the precocious tongue, the flower of her parents' old age. At the age of five, she'd shouldered the responsibility of waking her seven older brothers for breakfast. She dragged them out of bed at six, even on Fridays. Their only day off, they begged. The sun, barely up, crawled in from between the curtains, lighting up the tired green walls. Khalid and his brothers slumped around the *dastarkhan*. They yawned and grumbled while Syra, apron sweeping her feet like a sari, served them cold tea.

"Ammi-jan," they teased her, "how about some eggs, too? And *paratay* if you don't mind."

"I mind, I mind," she scowled, mimicking their mother perfectly. "Just be good boys and drink your tea." She made sure they drank the evil-tasting thick brown liquid that swirled in their cups like muddy water.

If Syra had lived, she might be a mother herself now. She might be waiting down there at Karachi International with Khalid's parents and brothers, her own children milling about her. They'd be waiting to greet him, and he'd step off the plane a different man, definitely different. Still a deportee, sucked clean and spat out like a peach pit, but ready to meet his mother's eyes without fear of what he'd find.

It amazes him how much he fears her now, when as a child he feared nothing. If anything, his mother feared him. She feared his tendency to swing from balconies and aggravate older boys. She feared his swims at Hawk's Bay where the waves were the size of killer whales. And she feared the phone calls from irate relatives, neighbors, and schoolteachers.

"What did he do now?" she asked each time, her face paling at the mention of his name. She slapped him in the presence of school principals, promising she'd straighten him out. She threatened to disown him when she found out he drag raced his Honda 125 on the Super-Highway, weaving between the traffic that traveled in no apparent order. And once, while shopping at Paposhnagar Bazaar, she heard reports of a boy crushed beneath a truck and, convinced it was Khalid, scoured every hospital in the area. She returned home sunken-eyed, hair awry, and found him in the drawing room, playing Ludo. She froze. Stood still for a while, just inside the lime green double doors, watching him, saying nothing. Then she flew into the room and swatted his head as if he had done something wrong.

Those double doors are no longer lime green, Khalid notices when he alights from his brother's Datsun. His brother—the one who picked him up at the airport—is no longer a stubbly jawed, broad-shouldered boy. And Paposh is nothing like Khalid remembers. Yet it is the same. The *dhobi*-shop at Chandi Chawk, full of clean clothes waiting for their owners; Nazar's Tailor Shop, except Nazar's former apprentice is the one cutting cloth with the swift strokes of oversized scissors; the convenience store—once a stall—across from Khalid's childhood house. And the house itself has sprouted two floors. To Khalid, it appears burdened, as if his old home holds someone else's on its back. Children—his brothers', no doubt—cluster at the barred windows. They shout excitedly when they catch sight of him, and Abdullah springs to Khalid's mind, the image of his son flowing into him like a tidal wave, washing away the kernel of happiness bouncing around in his chest since he stepped off the plane.

Still, when the children, followed by Khalid's parents, stream out of the house a few moments later and surround Khalid, he manages to smile and tuck the standard hundred-rupee notes into their hands. Though this is his first time back, he knows what is expected of the relative-from-America: money sprinkled about, the suitcase full of toys and gifts, bolts of cloth from Jamaica Avenue, plastic bottles of honey and olive oil, cell phones and cameras, tubes of toothpaste, a dressed-up account of his occupation in the United States, humility befitting a son of Paposhnagar. This last is meant to be demonstrated through the placement of the bulging suitcase before his mother to show that, despite the fact that he is now married, she remains the authority over all that he is, all that he owns.

But Khalid has brought none of that—no wife, no toys from which the MADE IN CHINA stickers have been carefully peeled, no bulging suitcase. Nothing to support a performance of the obedient son untainted by America. So it is another kind of performance Khalid and his mother offer their family. They embrace. Khalid's father shines with relief. But Khalid senses the tension in his mother's arms, the stiffness in his own, the valley that stretches between them, carved by a tiny child in a turquoise jumper.

The day Khalid left Paposhnagar, so long ago that it now seems a dream, the turquoise of his sister's jumper bled onto the white brocade of the only sofa in the drawing room. Now three sofas, none of them white brocade, line the walls, and the drawing room is twice the size it used to be, vast enough to accommodate the entire family. Two nights after Khalid's arrival, they all sit cross-legged in a giant rectangle around the *dastarkhan,* plates and glasses lined up before them as if at a banquet. Steel fans vibrate overhead. Any moment now, Khalid thinks, one might break free from its base and shear off the remaining hair on his head. Like Khalid, his brothers are curly haired and half bald. His parents appear faded, dried-up, like henna-topped raisins, dressed in cotton. Khalid tries not to dwell on the women and children. They remind him of Shagufta and Abdullah.

"When is your wife coming?" Khalid's mother hands him a plate piled with *murgh cholay.* She tucks a *roti* into his hand. "I bought some clothes for Abdullah." Their eyes meet for a moment, then slide past each other as they've done for two days.

Khalid's father slaps him on the back. "You see how women are, Khalid? She's been crying for you all this time. And now that you're here, she's moved on to Abdullah."

"Probably next month," Khalid says. He eats slowly, tearing pieces of *roti* and wrapping them around the chicken and peas with unnecessary concentration. He feels awkward, unnatural, like a bus driver in a boardroom. And his parents notice, he thinks. His father insisted on driving him around Karachi today, to the homes of his old friends, who embraced Khalid and pumped his hand, then within minutes revealed themselves to be strangers. Since his arrival, his mother has drifted behind him through the house, wearing a long white *chador* and an awkward smile, trying too hard.

How about nihari *for dinner tomorrow? Or maybe you want to go to The Kabana. Show me those pictures of Abdullah again. Why are you sitting here alone? Is that why we all live together? So people can sit around alone?*

But the night after he arrived, when he came down for a drink of water, Khalid found *her* alone. Tucked into a corner of the living room, the furniture looming over her in the dark. The smell of her tobacco *paan* wafted up to where he halted on the stairs. She didn't notice him, and he retreated quickly, not wanting her to. He knew where she was. Lost. Sucked willingly or not into the memories he's brought back with him.

"She's too *chulbuli* to be on a boat," his mother said when Khalid suggested Syra go fishing with him. "She moves around too much." She buttoned her *burkha* and twisted her thick hair into a braid. She was only forty-seven then, but cords of gray wound through the braid, and deep grooves lined her forehead. Most likely from worry over him, Khalid thinks now.

But back then, as he watched her push out the door, her oversized purse weighing down her petite frame, a stab of annoyance shot through Khalid. He'd promised to let Syra tag along if she let him sleep late. And now she crawled under their parents' old four-poster bed, singing "Rub a Dub Dub," searching for her boots.

Khalid cleared his throat. "Ammi said you can't go." It didn't come out as matter-of-fact as he'd hoped. A disheveled, cobwebby Syra emerged from under the bed, her bottom lip sticking out. Her thick bob waved in all directions. "I'm *going*," she said. She tugged on her boots and pulled a boat-shaped pin from her pocket. She carefully fastened it to her turquoise jumper. "I'm going," she repeated, "or you're a liar."

Only one person ever called him a liar after that. Shagufta—a few months after their marriage, when she learned he didn't have a green card. And because she, a woman whose family had lied about their illegal status as well, had no right to call him anything, Khalid slammed a hole into their dining room wall, barely feeling the impact on his fist.

But when his sister called him a liar, years before Khalid even dreamed of Shagufta, Khalid scooped her up. He spun around the surly-eyed angel his mother had conceived at the age of forty-one, fourteen years after her youngest son was born. Abort, her friends had advised. The pregnancy endangered her health, they said, and the family's image. People tittered behind your back when you went around—at that age—advertising your bedroom activity on your belly.

After Syra's birth, those same friends called Syra an unexpected gift from God. A blessing, the flower of her parents' old age.

The problem with such flowers was that they rooted themselves so deep, you couldn't bear to see them wilt. So Khalid plopped down in the drawing room, pulling Syra to the floor with him. He pushed a video into the VCR. "Let's wait until Ammi gets home," he said. "Remember you wanted to watch Bhai-jan's wedding?" He winked at his brother's wife and she shook her head. *This isn't going to work, Khalid.*

She was right. The moment Khalid slipped out the door, Syra screamed and stumbled after him. "You lied, you lied." She grabbed the front of his T-shirt, her boat-shaped pin bumping against his jeans, and bawled until he picked her up.

"I'll take you some other time," he said. But she twisted his shirt into her eyes and his heart twisted as well. His friends, waiting for him in their rust-colored pickup, honked and yelled, *Hurry up, Khalid.*

And he'd like to say now that he hesitated. That he considered staying home for Syra's sake, forfeiting his fishing jaunt with his friends. He'd even like to say that once they'd reached Kimarhi, once their boat floated far from shore in the murky yellow green water—everything a tangle of lines, hooks, busy fingers, and bait—that his arms and his eyes never left Syra. Not for a moment.

That day branded him: DON'T TRUST THIS MAN. He never told Shagufta about Syra. Still, she hovered whenever he held Abdullah. *Watch out for his arm. My god, Khalid, stop it, you'll make him throw up. Don't swing him like that, do you want his elbow to come out?* And when Abdullah got older, started kindergarten, Shagufta claimed Khalid indulged Abdullah too much. Abdullah was too young for remote-controlled cars, she said, and too old to crawl into their bed at night.

"You don't know how to say no," she said. Which wasn't true because Khalid did say no, to a backyard pool, horse-riding lessons, school trips to the beach.

But some things weren't worth saying no to.

"Can I tell everyone you're an alien?" Abdullah asked once. Who could say no to a question like that? And then Abdullah went around swearing on the Quran—complained his teacher at Al-Huda Academy—that his father had descended from the sky. When a classmate called him a liar, Abdullah punched him in the stomach.

"He's turning out just like you," Shagufta told Khalid. She confined Abdullah to his room and confiscated his TV and Nintendo. "An alien? You're teaching him to lie. What were you thinking?" As if Khalid could have predicted what happened. But by then, Shagufta viewed Khalid through the lens of the stories he'd told her. "Do you think you're still a kid in Karachi, terrorizing your teachers, doing God knows what, thinking nothing of the consequences?" she'd say.

He knew more about consequences, he could've told Shagufta, than she ever would.

The next day, Khalid requested permission to speak to Abdullah's class. He took along his expired Pakistani passport and Abdullah's American one and explained to the class why he was an alien. An illegal alien. Descended to earth in an airplane, not a spaceship, but an alien nevertheless.

Here in Karachi, Khalid is not an alien, but Karachi is alien to him. He aches for the familiarity of New York, Crown Fried Chickens dotting almost every corner, city buses shouldering their way up

Hillside. He continuously calculates time differences, imagining Sha-gufta and Abdullah about their daily routines. Curled up together on Abdullah's bed, raking the leaves that must carpet their lawn by now, Shagufta showering, Abdullah playing Nintendo in his room when he should be doing homework.

At times, the images leap so intensely into his consciousness that Khalid believes Paposhnagar is a dream. He inhabits his parents' home like a stranger, a guest or a ghost. He makes small talk with his brothers. He avoids his mother without meaning to. He breakfasts before she does, picks up a magazine if she enters the room. To es-cape, if only for a short while, he paces the road between his home and Paposhnagar Bazaar, or the beach at Clifton. Occasionally, Khalid's father walks with him, but the silences stretch like taut rub-ber bands. Sometimes Khalid drives to Sadar and scouts possible lo-cations for the electronics store he plans to open. Almost every day, he calls Shagufta. Over and over she says, "After the baby is born."

"You think they don't have doctors here?" Khalid says.

"It's a third world country," she answers. "My parents think I'll die or something."

Is your mother dead? Khalid is tempted to ask her. *Is mine? Between them, they turned out thirteen children in Karachi, didn't they?* But he fears angering Shagufta, so he holds his tongue, pushes a hot pickled mango into his mouth to stifle the words. "After the baby, then," he says when he can speak. "But at least call me every day."

"Khalid, you're not thinking straight." Shagufta's voice seeps im-patience. "Do you have any idea how expensive that'll get?"

He has an answer for that one, too. Phone cards. Some as cheap as fifteen cents a minute. Times have changed, he tells Shagufta, his anger finally pushing through. This isn't 1984, or even 1994. Back then, calls to Karachi burned four dollars a minute. The only inexpensive option was to ride the subway to Grand Central Station in Manhattan and stand in line, holding out a twenty-dollar bill, until some black guy in a leather jacket dialed you a connection to Karachi using a stolen credit card.

When you chose the wrong route into America, the crooked path never righted itself. Still, Khalid's mode of entry outshone others' in one way: It made a good story. He didn't even have to embellish it.

An hour before daybreak, Bhai Wajahat's men picked up Khalid at his motel in Mexico and plunked him down four miles south of the U.S. border. He peered around him at the shadow-filled terrain, the shrubs cloaked in darkness. Fear rose like bile in his stomach. "Are you kidding?" he said. *Shut up and listen,* he was told. Bhai Wajahat's men ran through a list of landmarks, drilled precise instructions into his head.

Here, you're on your own. Don't make noise. Lie flat on the ground if you see anything move. When—and if—you cross the border, don't dawdle. Go straight to Maria's Bed and Breakfast. And run. Run like you mean it.

So Khalid ran like he meant it. Those four miles, dodging shrubs and imagined sentries in the half darkness, brambles snagging his ankles, he sprinted like a madman. Like a world-class runner, he told Shagufta once. Heart banging, lungs constricting, as if one moment of hesitation, one look back might allow everything he'd left behind to overtake him.

When he glimpsed the border—a wall of wire rising out of the darkness—relief sizzled through Khalid like lightning. There ahead of him lay the land of milk and honey, where new lives bloomed from the wreckage of old ones washed ashore. That instant, that first glimpse of U.S. soil, was the happiest moment of his life. Terrible, excruciatingly terrible with the threat of discovery and disappoint-ment, yet *aching* with profound promise.

After he crawled across the border, Khalid ran until he reached town. Then he slicked back his hair with sweat and followed the mental map provided him by Bhai Wajahat's men. He found Maria's Bed and Breakfast (a surprisingly clean establishment manned by a shockingly masculine Maria). A room, a suit, and another list awaited him there.

Don't leave your room for three days. Sleep as much as you can. Got to rest, it'll scrape that illegal look off your face.

On the fourth day, Khalid shaved and Maria gave him a haircut. He donned his snazzy new suit, stuck a local newspaper under his arm—*so you look like you belong,* the list advised—and caught a taxi into the heart of Texas.

And that, Khalid thinks, should have been that. But life has a way of turning the page when you least expect it. Khalid learned this long ago when he looked up from the monstrous, slippery, scaly fish he'd just wrestled in and realized that Syra was gone. As if she'd risen from the plank she sat on, stepped off the boat, and walked away over the yellow green water.

How long had he looked away?

The sky, Khalid surprises himself by recalling, spilled like a jug of aqua paint into the horizon that day. *Sit still,* he told Syra. Her turquoise jumper stuck to her in the heat. Sweat glistened on her forehead and fuzzy upper lip. She leaned over the side of the boat, trying to touch the water, and she talked too much.

Are there snakes in there? How come the water's so yellow? Can I fish, too?

"Shut her up, *yaar,*" his friends said. "Did you have to bring her along?"

And then, without warning, Khalid's fishing rod leaped from his hand and he scrambled for it. And when he looked up again, there was no turquoise jumper, no Syra.

"Where's Syra?" he yelled, the fish spilling from his arms.

His friends, startled, jerked about, peering into the corners of the boat. Khalid dived into the water. His breath fizzed around him like a hopeless prayer. Where to look? Which way to go? He burrowed— lungs exploding—halfway into the bowels of Kimarhi before he saw her, before he glimpsed the turquoise jumper drifting near a bed of seaweed below. And when he burst to the surface, he pulled Syra with him.

Who knew CPR in those days? Khalid and his friends thumped Syra's back. They pumped her chest. Held her nose and breathed into her mouth. Screamed and lashed out at each other. Sobbed. Rowed back to shore. They pulled the oars swiftly, frantically, though they should have known that time no longer mattered.

But now, waiting for Shagufta and Abdullah, time matters more than anything to Khalid. And time in Karachi lives as languid an existence as the city's inhabitants. Days saunter by on stunted legs. Khalid's store is up and running, pulling in a decent income. He whiles away his time there, driving home later than he needs to. He dreads his mother's watchful eyes, her insistence on speaking constantly of Abdullah, her attentiveness during his calls to Shagufta. He dreads the inevitable question that follows—*Are they coming yet?*—and when he shakes his head, the expression, that ghost of the what-has-he-done-now? look that flows into her features before she turns away. So he calls Shagufta less and less. By his fourth month in Karachi, he calls her twice a week instead of every day. Then once a week, and finally, stubbornly, not at all.

It is Shagufta who finally calls late one evening. Khalid tucks the phone between his shoulder and ear. He is alone on the third floor, hunched on the saffron-colored carpet, busy assembling a crib for the room his children will share. He drops the screwdriver when Shagufta says, "Here, listen to this." Then he hears a baby cry.

"What do you want to name her?" Shagufta asks.

"Syra." Before Khalid can pluck the name back out of the air and swallow it, Shagufta latches onto it. Nice and short, she says. Easy for Americans to pronounce.

A cold fist spreads open inside Khalid's chest.

"When are you coming?" The question is quick, almost reckless.

Shagufta is silent for a moment. "When things get a little less hectic," she offers, and Khalid detects the lie in her voice.

"You *are* coming, aren't you?" His anger surges ahead of his words.

"Give me a break, Khalid." Shagufta sounds angry, but also uncertain. "I'm in a hospital bed here. What do you want me to do, kill myself getting there?"

Khalid wants to plunge his hand through the phone line, through that invisible winding tunnel of shuttled words, and kill her himself. "I'm asking you a straight question, Shagufta."

This time the silence stretches longer. When Shagufta speaks, her tone is subdued. "All I know about Karachi is what you've told me. And I don't know, Khalid. I just don't know if we can depend on you."

"Is that so?" He wants to say more, much more, but footsteps sound on the stairs and Khalid knows from avoiding her these past months that they belong to his mother. When she sees his face, she stops at the door to the room, one hand braced against the doorframe.

"Is something wrong?" she asks. Khalid shakes his head. On the other end of the line, Shagufta talks faster and faster.

"We can use Web cams." A tremor runs through her words. "And pictures, I promise. And when they're older, I'll send them to visit, because they're citizens. Are you listening to me, Khalid?"

He nods as if she can see him, but he's really gone. Evaporated from the room. Rematerialized somewhere just south of the U.S. border. Then he's crawling back into his old skin, the skin he shed as he ran toward the land of milk and honey.

He places the phone softly onto the cradle. His mother follows him downstairs to the kitchen. Watches him as he gulps down a glass of water. "Is something wrong?" she asks again.

"No," Khalid says. *No one needs a piece of misery like you.* He closes his eyes and he's back in Kimarhi, plunging through the yellow green water, searching for the turquoise jumper. He places the glass in the sink. He doesn't tell his mother about the baby. If he does, the next thing she'll ask is the baby's name. And "Syra" is not a name Khalid's lips can form in the presence of his mother.

It is finally his mother who voices the name some days later, drops it into the conversation as casually as a lump of sugar into her tea. She has cornered Khalid as she often does on his return from work. They're seated in the kitchen, watching rain pour into the dark courtyard, going through photographs of Khalid's life in America. Khalid's mother hands him a snapshot of Abdullah.

"Abdullah looks a bit like Syra in this one," she says. She stares Khalid straight in the eye as if daring him to look away. Khalid nods slowly, though it isn't true. Abdullah looks nothing like Syra and they both know it.

"I'm sorry," his mother says after a moment, her words barely audible. "I wanted you to come home, but not this way."

Several seconds tick by on the sunflower-shaped wall clock before Khalid understands what she means. *A mother's words strike like an arrow.*

On her face she wears the what-has-he-done-now? look that has tormented Khalid for months, reminding him of everything he was and everything he'll ever be. But that look, Khalid suddenly knows, is not for him. It has been pointing at *her,* asking what-have-I-done?

"No, no." Khalid clutches his mother's hand. "Every man shoulders his own destiny." He's quoting his father's book of idioms, he realizes, pulling words off a page he read twenty years ago. And he cries, crushing his mother's hand in his own.

KEVIN A. GONZÁLEZ

University of Wisconsin-Madison

WAKE

It's New Year's Day and I'm on my godfather's Dusky doing five thousand RPM on the North Sound of Virgin Gorda with a mechanic named Michael Jackson at the helm. He's shoved the twin Evinrude controls all the way down on the console, and I keep trying to sip my beer, but it spills all over my face until there is nothing but dead wind left inside the bottle. A boomerang-shaped key glides past our starboard, and scattered marinas dot the port side, with their schools of masts rasping the sky, and the unrelenting logos of petroleum empires stenciled against the green backdrop of the mountains. The other night, my father mistook the orange Gulf sign at Leverick Bay for a full moon. He was drunk and wearing sunglasses, and hitting on a young bartender from St. Kitts.

"Look at that moon, Bertha." He pointed with his entire arm. "It's as full as I am with lust for you."

"Who Bertha, mon?" she said. The *t* cut through the name like a razor. In the Islands, they swallow their contractions and say *mon* instead of *man*. If Batman lived here, for example, he be Batmon. "I not Bertha, mon. I Martha. And that no moon, mon. That the gas dock."

This week, I've visited every marina in the North Sound—Biras Creek, Saba Rock, Leverick Bay, The Bitter End—and learned the name of nearly every bartender therein. Back in my mother's apartment in Puerto Rico, a stack of college applications lies untouched on my bed, though I suspect she may have already begun to fill them out for me, unwavering as she is in her determination to see me go to college. This is a test run: If Michael Jackson says the engines are tiptop, I could be home tomorrow. He's zigzagging the boat to avoid cracking any of the moorings that peek out like turtle shells throughout the Sound. We're spilling a heavy wake at the anchored motor yachts and the dinghies that loll a few yards behind them as if tied to leashes. The waves look like carpets being unrolled for royalty, and the crew of a bobbing trawler is screaming at us to slow down, but Michael Jackson doesn't care. He's got a big paycheck coming if the Evinrudes hold up, and it looks like they will. He starts singing "Billie Jean" and moonwalking in place, but he never lets go of the wheel, and the twin controls pressed down to the console never come up. The oval edge of his belly prods out from under his T-shirt, and the wind rips into his Afro, vacuuming the lyrics into the Dusky's foam trail. It is almost noon, and we're flying past The Bitter End as if we're deliverymen late for a funeral with a cabin full of flowers.

Ten days ago, no one believed me when I announced the boat had sunk. I was coming down the hill from our hotel room, and saw a tilted bimini top in the slip where we'd docked the night before, but no boat beneath it. The ropes were still tied to the pier, but the pleats had ripped off the gunwale and lay floating above the Dusky, almost motionless, with the other ends of the ropes still lassoed around them. Floating, too, were the white seat cushions that were always loose because their buttons had rusted, the zip-up bottle holders from Tortola, the empty Medalla cans we'd thrown on the deck during the trip, the free jug of Pusser's Rum we got when we gassed up at Sopper's Hole, a quarter-full bottle of Pennzoil, and, surprisingly, even the Igloo, full of salt water and beer. There was a block of ice hovering like a cadaver, melting away, changing shapes. A round lifesaver was sunk halfway, tilted at a perfect ninety-degree angle, as if half its insides were rotten. The tanks were leaking gasoline, which pooled within the seawater, and it looked like the boat had been bleeding rainbows.

My father and Yasser were sitting at a table next to the bar at The Lighthouse. Yasser was eating breakfast and my father was drinking a Cuba libre, which meant he'd already drunk two or three screwdrivers and, perhaps, a preceding Cuba libre as well. He'd gotten up before seven that morning and he'd flicked on all the lights in the room and raised the volume on the television as high as it would go, just to get back at me for eating his sandwich. Our first port of call, fifty-seven miles east of Fajardo, is always Crown Bay in St. Thomas, where they make my father's favorite roast beef. Yasser and I always eat ours on the spot, but my father safeguards his. He wraps the cellophaned sandwich in a grocery bag and tucks it in the Igloo and, at night, takes it to the hotel room, and then he puts it back in the Igloo the next morning. This goes on for days, and he never eats the damn thing. Yasser and I had stayed up late the night before, and by the time the bars closed, there was nothing to eat but my father's sandwich. Yasser didn't want any, because it had three-day-old mayo and he didn't trust it, but I tore into it. When my father realized what I was doing, he jumped out of bed and began gnashing his teeth, screaming that his sandwich was sacred. He demanded I give him what was left, which was most of it, and he sat on the edge of the bed and ate the whole thing. The whites of his eyes blared like neon lights in the dark. He was still breathing heavily when I fell asleep. "I will never, ever, ever forgive you," he said.

"The boat sank," I said.

My father just sipped his drink.

Yasser spoke without taking his eye off his plate. "Hey," he said. "Do you want to eat crabs tonight? Because if you do, the chef said you have to order them now."

"Fuck the crabs," I said. "The boat sank. It sank!"

They both grinned and looked up at me, as if expecting a lame punch line.

"Fine," I said, and pulled out a chair. "It didn't sink."

We kneeled on the pier and looked down at the boat, trapped beneath the gaudy film of diluted gas. Even the bimini top had gone under by then, and the empty beer cans had begun to drift.

"I just saw it when I came down the hill, like half an hour ago," Yasser said. "It looked fine. What the hell do I do now, Hector?"

"Well," my father said, "you get it out."

"How?"

"With a lift bag. Hire someone to do it, then find a mechanic. I'll be right back." He hobbled away, and I knew he was going back to the bar, because that's where he goes whenever he says he'll be right back. Yasser and I went to the marina office. The dockmaster was a middle-aged British blond with leathery hands and a handheld marine radio latched onto her belt. We told her our twenty-five-foot fish-around cuddy-cabin Dusky with twin 150 horsepower Evinrude outboards had just sunk in slip B17. She didn't seem impressed.

"So, lady," Yasser said. "How you get it out?" His English is terrible.

"Lift bags," she said. "Underwater Safaris has them. But that's the easy part. What you need is a mechanic on the spot when they lift it, and maybe he'll be able to salvage your engines."

"Where you get mechanics?" Yasser said.

"There's only two outboard mechanics on the island. One's at Biras, the other's at Bitter End."

"What is their name?"

"Bozo and Michael Jackson."

"Can I use your phone?"

"I'll call," she said, flipping through her Rolodex. "I'll say it's an emergency. Which one should I call?"

"Both," Yasser said.

"They don't like each other."

Yasser shrugged. "Call which one you want." He leaned on her desk and pouted his lips. "What you do today for dinner?" he said.

She looked up from the Rolodex and studied his face. "Excuse me?" she said.

"I will like to thank you for your help, sweetheart," Yasser said, "with crabs."

"I'll be right back," I said.

The bar at The Lighthouse is shaped like a sailboat, and my father was sitting at the bow. He was the only customer, and he was already drinking a Dewar's and soda. This is how he does it: a Stoli screwdriver or two when he gets up, then it's on to Cuba libres until the Coca-Cola gets too sweet, and, finally, scotch for the rest of the day. He can drink an entire bottle, but I've never seen him stumble or vomit or make a scene. And he never eats: especially in the Islands, because by the time he's ready for dinner all the restaurants have closed.

He was talking to the bartender and, before I sat down, she reached into a cooler and pulled out a Heineken, opened it, and set it on top of the bar. My father dragged out the stool next to his and patted it. "Update me," he said.

"Yasser's trying to fuck the dockmaster," I said. "But she's not into him."

He smirked. "Well, I've been finding out a lot of things." This meant he'd just bombarded the bartender with a bunch of questions and was getting ready to relay the information. "The Virgin Gorda Carnival starts tonight," he said, and sipped his drink. "Some reggae bands from Jamaica are playing, but it's in Spanish Town, so we need to rent a car, because the taxis will kill us. There's some guy named Speedy who rents Jeeps, and Martha here is getting ahold of him for us."

I looked at the bartender, who was slicing lemons, and took a sip of the Heineken. "Well, the dive shop here has lift bags, so they're going to get the boat out, and they're trying to find a mechanic."

"The fucking bilge pump," my father said. "I told him before we left. You heard me, I told him to check it. There's a little Ping-Pong ball sensor in there that sets off the pump when the water level gets high, I told him to check it. I bet you anything the Ping-Pong ball was rotten and it didn't float. He has no idea what he's doing, you know."

My father sold the boat to Yasser when he was getting divorced from my mother. He'd bought it in Florida after winning a big case in '87, and the day after, he came home, put frying oil in the burner to make some french fries, fell asleep, and burned down our apartment. My mother pleaded with him to return the boat because they needed the money to rebuild, but he didn't return it, and they never got along after that.

Yasser doesn't have a feel for the boat, nor does he take care of it the way my father did when it was his. All the fenders are partially deflated, and the ropes don't match in length or color. He's afraid to take the boat out unless my father is with him, yet he insists on maneuvering it, though he always smashes it into docks, and he skitters all over the marinas before he's able to plant it in a slip. My father and I call the boat "Baryshnikov" since all it does is prance around like a ballet dancer when Yasser's at the helm. He doesn't even know how to talk on the VHS and his sense of direction is nonexistent. Whenever we arrive at an island, he walks up to the first person he sees and says, "Excuse me, where are we?" just to piss off my father, since my father knows the names of all the Islands and knows exactly where we are at all times. After the divorce was final, my father tried to buy the boat back from Yasser for what he'd sold it to him for, but Yasser wouldn't sell.

"What did he say to the dockmaster?" my father asked.

"That he wants to give her crabs, sweetheart."

"No. But, did he complain at all? He knows the marina is liable. We'll sue when we get back home." My father always talks about doing things he never gets around to doing. He often threatens to write letters to the *San Juan Star,* the slender English-language newspaper that nobody reads, in response to things that bother him, but he never does. I've heard him say, for example, "I was driving to Old San Juan, and you wouldn't believe how run-down that huge fountain in front of the Capitolio is, it doesn't even have water in it," or, "I hate all these people who build $100,000 homes on government land in Piñones, they're goddamn rich and they're squatting," and he always caps it off with, "I'm going to write a letter to the *San Juan Star.*" I like to tease him about it.

"I mean," my father continued, "Yasser's paying for the marina's services. They're supposed to have someone on duty, watching the boats, making sure no one breaks into them, that they don't sink. Think about it: Baryshnikov sank in the middle of the morning. There should have been someone watching. It's neglectful."

"Definitely," I said. "You should write a letter to the *San Juan Star.*"

"Fuck off, Tito," he said. He took a little tube of Orajel out of his shirt pocket, squeezed some onto his finger, and rubbed it inside his mouth. He'd had a toothache since we left. "Hey, did you see those two girls over there, having lunch? They're your age."

They were sitting outside, right across one of the arcs that divided the indoor and the outdoor parts of the restaurant, and they had temp Rasta tattoos on their lower backs. They were obviously from the States, and, like most white girls do when they come to the Islands, they'd gotten sunburns and braids. "If I was your age, I'd be over there buying them a drink right now, before one of these dirty Island guys gets to them. Look at their tattoos," my father said. "They're looking to get laid."

"Well, I got Camille at home," I said, knowing well that my father knew I had a girlfriend.

We've been together for six months. She didn't want me to come on this trip.

"You're too young to be faithful," he said. "Here, take the card and go buy them one of those frozen drinks those girls go crazy for." He handed me my grandfather's MasterCard. The three of us have the same first and last name. My grandfather is at the Presbyterian Hospital in San Juan—yellow, dying.

"Maybe later," I said.

"They won't be here later," he said. "Come on, don't be a pussy. As your dad, I order you to go talk to the two little sluts over there."

"You're not my dad," I said. It was a joke we had, which started with a card I'd given him for Father's Day. It said: *Anyone can be a father, but it takes a special one to be a dad.* My father told me he wasn't a special one. He said that serial rapists, ax murderers, military dictators, all kinds of horrible people could be fathers: It was just a biological accident. *Dad* had more to do with being there to watch the son grow up. My father's father had not been a dad, and neither had mine, so it was something we had in common. We were both, also, only children.

"Fair enough," he said. He looked at the girls again. "As your lawyer, I advise you to go buy frozen daiquiris for the two little sluts sitting at that table." A month earlier, my father had gotten me off the hook from a DUI because he was old poker buddies with the circuit judge who was on duty that night.

"You're not my lawyer," I said. "You're still disbarred." This was true: Because my father had not tried a case in years, he had stopped paying his Bar Association membership fee, and they had revoked his license. He has been living off my grandfather's MasterCard and the money my mom paid him when she bought his half of the apartment.

"Either you go over there and buy those girls a drink, or I'll go over there and buy them a drink and tell them every little thing you don't want them to know about you," he said, and started to get up. I knew he would: He never bluffs, and he loves to embarrass me in public. He's not shy, and he can be the most charming man in the world when he makes an effort. I ripped the MasterCard from his hand and pushed out of my stool.

Picking up girls in the Islands is a breeze: All you have to do is be straightforward and confident, and avoid flowering shit up. I walked over to their table with the MasterCard in one hand and my beer in the other, leaned on one of the green plastic chairs, and said, "Hi, girls. I'm Antonio, and I'd like to buy you a round of daiquiris." I exaggerated my accent, but spoke eloquently. They looked at each other and giggled, and I sat down before they said anything because I knew I was in. It's a simple thing: What girl who is not yet old enough to drink in her own country is going to refuse a free frozen drink on a tropical island?

They were sisters: one of them my age, the other a freshman at Columbia. They were from Maryland, and they were staying on a chartered sailboat with their family. I was Antonio, a parasailing instructor from San Juan, who was headed to Yale, early admission, in the fall. It's a thing we do when we come to the Islands: Yasser is always Augusto, my father is always Ramón, and I'm always Antonio. Sometimes, in the mornings, when we set off for the next island, women wave from piers, or from the decks of cruise ships, or from chartered motor yachts, yelling "Augusto!" or "Ramón!" My father and godfather grin at each other and say, "Gee, I wonder who she's calling to?" and we speed off into the open sea.

The girls had a strawberry daiquiri each, and we flirted and made plans to meet the next day. They told me the name of their sailboat, a fifty-foot Beneteau, and pointed to where it was moored. There was a plastic seat cushion from Yasser's boat drifting toward it, and, from where we sat, it looked like a dead stingray, belly-up on the water. I told them I'd be around the bar for the next few days, gave them each a peck on the cheek as they left, and returned to my father.

"Give me the card," he said. "Speedy's come through for us." I handed him the card and he forwarded it to the bartender. My father always finds somebody else to run his errands. "So, what they packing?"

"A fifty-footer, Moorings charter, bareboat." Bareboat meant they had chartered it without a captain. "I guess the father knows how to sail."

"You pick up their lunch tab?"

"No," I said.

"You're not my son," he said. "You have no class. No wonder you never get laid." He shook his head. "Where'd they moor?"

"Out there," I pointed. "It's called *Uhuru*."

At this, Yasser walked into The Lighthouse, stood behind us, and put a hand on my left shoulder and the other on my father's right one. "So, Hector," he said. "You want to buy the boat now? It's officially for sale."

My father spun his neck to look at Yasser and chuckled. "Any luck?" he said.

"Well, they're lifting it up pretty soon, charging a fortune. I left messages for the only two mechanics to come. Bozo and Michael Jackson, can you believe that shit? This place is a circus."

"No. I meant, any luck with the dockmaster?"

"Ah? No. She has nice lift bags, but she knows my real name," he said. "I figure we'll be here for a few days, at least. I called Monica and told her to fly down. She might come tomorrow." Monica is Yasser's girlfriend. She's over twenty years younger than he is, and she works for American Eagle, so she flies free. My father says it fucks up our trips when she's around, since Yasser cannot be Augusto.

"Well, while you've been out there doing nothing," my father said, "we've been finding out all sorts of things, and we have great news. The Carnival starts tonight, it's in Spanish Town, and we have a Jeep. And Tito's got two rich teenage gringas with braided hair and tattoos who will be joining us."

"You do?" Yasser's eyes lit up.

"No," I said, and sipped my beer. "The tattoos are fake. Where's the phone? I need to call home."

Virgin Gorda is only about a hundred miles upwind from Puerto Rico, but calling long distance is a pain in the ass, because the operators are incomprehensible. It took fifteen minutes to place a collect call to my mother, who was upset instead of sympathetic.

"What do you mean the boat sank?" she said. "What did you do to it?"

"Me? Nothing," I said. "It sank. It just sank."

"Well, you're still coming home in a week, right? That'll give you four days to fill out your applications. Did you start writing your essay yet?"

"Don't worry, there's plenty of time."

"Have you called your grandfather?" she asked. "He's not well, Tito. You shouldn't have left. It's so irresponsible of you and your father to just take off like that, when your grandfather is so sick. I don't know how your father could just—"

"Okay," I interrupted. "Listen, this call is costing you a fortune. We'll be back in a week, if not before, okay? I've got to go help them get the boat out. *Bendición.*"

She sighed. *"Que Dios te bendiga, mijito."*

The applications on my bed are all for Ivy League schools that I won't get into. Colleges have been bombarding me with mail for the last year, all because I got a high score on the PSAT. If my GPA was over 3.5, I would be a National Merit Scholar, but I've coasted along with a middling 2.9. The application for the University of Puerto Rico, where I want to go, is not due until February. Both of my parents, as well as Camille and my college counselor, think I should go to college in the States, so I've decided to apply to the impossible ones. Camille really is headed to Yale, early admission. People in school have no idea why I'm with her, or, rather, why she's with me, because we have nothing in common. While she's conducting National Honor Society meetings on Friday mornings before school, I'm out in my friend Bondy's station wagon, getting high and listening to Israel Vibration. While she's representing Canada or Finland or Djibouti at Model UN on weekends, I'm sitting on the bench for the basketball team, sweating away a hangover. In school, while she's raising her hand to recite integrals in her AP Calc class, I'm sitting in the back row of algebra, writing notebook after notebook full of poems to give her, which is something that nobody else knows. I couldn't believe she refused to accept the charges when I called.

The divers from Underwater Safaris lifted the boat in less than an hour. The hardest part was sliding the yellow lift bag under the keel, but once they started emptying scuba tanks into the valve, the boat rose like a bubble. They used an electronic pump to drain the water that remained inside. Yasser and I dried the anchor and battery hatches with a hand pump, and we sprayed WD-40 on everything. My father sat on top of the Igloo on the dock, nursing a scotch in a plastic cup, yelling out instructions and tossing us beers when we asked. Underwater Safaris brought a machine from Spanish Town to siphon the watered-down gas from the tanks. They left the inflated lift bag under the hull of the boat to make sure it didn't sink again, and Baryshnikov looked as if someone had tried to wrap a yellow ribbon around it but came up short. Then, the mechanics showed up, at the same time, and we could hear them arguing as they made their way to slip B17.

"Who the owner of this boat?" one of them demanded, and Yasser stepped forth, extended his hand, and shook both of theirs. They introduced themselves: Bozo, Michael Jackson. They both had bristly beards and were the same height, but Bozo was thin and Michael Jackson wasn't.

Michael Jackson pointed at Bozo. "What you doing calling this fool, mon?" he said to Yasser. "He don't know what he do. I the best mechanic here."

"No way, mon," Bozo said. "You don't listen to him, Captain. I seen him burn down a engine. A 200 Mercury, mon. I seen him burn it down over Gun Creek."

Yasser smiled. "Okay, which is better one of you two?" His English really is terrible.

"I tell you, Captain," Bozo said. "This man here, he crazy. He think he Michael Jackson, mon, King of Pop. Let me look your engines. You got no time to waste." He took a step toward the boat.

"I ain't burn down no engine, mon," Michael Jackson said. "This fool just jealous 'cause I hook up with his girl at Maddogs. He a clown. He ain't shit." He poked Bozo in the shoulder.

"You don't fucking touch me, mon," Bozo said, and shoved Michael Jackson with both hands. Michael Jackson lost his balance and fell into the water, and his head barely missed the platform of the Hatteras docked on the other side of Baryshnikov. The water splashed up on the pier, and my father got wet, which rarely happens on these trips, since he's always in the bar.

We all looked at Bozo without saying anything: me, my father, Yasser, and the two divers from Underwater Safaris. "Shit, mon," Bozo said, and he picked up his toolbox and scampered down the dock.

"I fucking kill you, mon," Michael Jackson said, his head poking out of the water like a buoy. He propelled himself onto the platform of the Hatteras and stood on it. "Come back here, fool."

Yasser smiled. "Well, Mr. Michael," he said. "You get my job. No burn down no engines, okay?"

"I'll be right back," my father said.

The road in Virgin Gorda is like a roller-coaster track. The island, if you look at an aerial map, looks like a dumbbell: One of the ends is the North Sound, the other is Spanish Town, the capital. The thin middle is all hills. Yasser and my father made me drive the Jeep and risk the foreign-country DUI. I'm young, they always say, and, while Yasser has his political post to worry about, my father simply cannot drive because of his bad eyesight. Michael Jackson was able to start one of the engines on the spot, after putting in new fuses, but the other needed a part that had to be sent for. My father used the MasterCard to rent the Century Tree Villa, which had a private pool overlooking Leverick Bay, right by the marina. There was a three-night minimum, and we figured that a mechanic who thinks he's Michael Jackson would take at least that long to fix a boat. Plus, my father said, it was Carnival weekend, so we might as well spend three days in Virgin Gorda regardless, before going on to Anegada, our next port of call.

We parked in a lot full of cars, across the street from a huge tent that had thousands of people inside it. Inside the tent, there were long parallel tables full of artwork and T-shirts and food and drink vendors, and once we passed all that and came out on the other side, there was a patch of grass with bars and game booths on either side, and a stage on which a reggae band was playing. We went to get a drink at one of the makeshift bars: a tall metal table, behind which were two bartenders, several coolers, and about a dozen bottles on a smaller table. The bartenders kept all the money in their pockets. My father ordered two scotches, for him and me, and Yasser ordered a Finlandia on the rocks, which meant the crowd had energized him. He started talking to a very tall local girl with a gap-toothed smile. My father drifted to the next table, where they were playing some sort of game, and I knew he wouldn't be able to resist gambling for long. I started walking toward the stage. Everyone had a plastic cup or a glass bottle in their hand, and they were all smoking cigarettes or weed or both. I still couldn't believe Camille hadn't accepted the charges when I called. Someone spilled beer on my sandals, and it trickled between my toes. Someone was calling someone else's name, and it took me a few seconds to realize it was mine.

"Antonio! Antonio!" One of the sailboat sisters, the youngest one, ran up and put her arms around me. "What's going on?" she said. "What you doing here?"

"Waiting for you." I smiled and ran my fingers through my hair.

"We begged, and our dad actually let us take a cab from the marina." She said this as if it were some sort of unprecedented event. "Ohmigod, we just had these shots at one of these bars over there. Liquor forty-three, you ever tried it? It's like orange NyQuil with a kick. I can get you one, they don't card."

"I'm good. I got a drink." I raised my cup and jiggled it lightly. The ice cubes hit the plastic sides. She looked at it, surprised.

"What is it? Can I try it?"

The older sister came up behind me and whispered something indecipherable in my ear, and then backed up to look at me. "So, you know where we can get some?" she asked.

"What?" I said. The little sister took a sip of my scotch and made a sour face.

"Weed!" the older one said, leaning into me. "Do you know anyone here?"

"Yeah," I said. "How much?" She took a hundred-dollar bill out of her purse, bent it twice, and handed it to me. I gave it back.

"Stay here," I said.

In the Islands, a dime bag costs six bucks, and the stuff is better than in Puerto Rico. I had only smoked it twice, with a bartender from Tortola named Zeus, in the back of a bar where women took off their tops and signed them, then left them tied to the wooden rafters on the ceiling. At the Carnival, I just asked the first guy I saw with a joint in his hand.

"That dude over there," he pointed. "Camouflage hat. He Speedy. He hook you up good."

Speedy didn't ask any questions. I gave him $12 and he gave me two bags and some papers. "Thanks for the Jeep, mon," I said.

"Yeah, the Jeep," he said, as I walked away. "That kid so fucked up. He call the spliff the Jeep." The people around him burst out laughing.

The Ivy League sister rolled and sparked the first one, and we passed it around, watching the band play a Bob Marley cover. Both girls danced only from the hips up. The younger sister was in front of me, and I kept glancing at the temp tattoo on her lower back. It looked like two dolphins sixty-nining in yellow, red, and green. After the joint burned to a roach, the Ivy League sister went to find a bathroom, and the younger one began to lean her back against me. I put my arms around her waist. She turned her neck and looked at me with her lips parted, so I went in for a kiss, and she kissed back. She kept leaning into me, and I kept my arms tight around her waist, and our upper bodies danced. "Don't say nothing to my sister," she said, pressing up against me.

When the older one returned, she hugged us both and complained about having to piss in a Porta Potti that was full of flies and stunk like shit while some old dudes watched her. I loosened my grip on the little one, because if there ever was a mood-stopper, I'd just heard it. "Now I'm ready for another drink," the older one said. "What about you guys?"

"Sure," I said. "What you girls want? I got it."

"A beer," the younger one said. "And a shot. That forty-three NyQuil liquor thing."

"I'll come with you," the Ivy Leaguer said. And, to her sister, "We'll be right back, don't go anywhere." She grabbed my hand and pulled.

As we walked to one of the bars, I saw my father, still sitting at the game table, throw both his hands up in the air as if he'd just lost a bet. There was a small crowd gathered around him, nothing unusual. Yasser was nowhere to be found, not that I was looking. The girl and I stood in line to order drinks.

"I'm having such an awesome time," she said. "Are you?"

"Yeah," I said.

"Hey, you know what 'Uhuru' means in English?"

"Freedom," I said. I'd seen Black Uhuru in concert with Bondy. "Why?"

"You wanna make out?" she said, and laughed, and made eye contact.

When the younger sister found us, she yanked the older one's braids so hard that her lower teeth scraped my tongue and cut into my lip. "What the fuck are you doing, you bitch?" the Ivy Leaguer yelled. I thought, briefly, about Camille: the way she slides her hair back on her head using only her pinky, ring, and middle fingers. All the locals stopped what they were doing to laugh at the two white girls going at it. The younger one turned around and began to run away. The older one didn't even look back at me. She just ran after her sister, cursing. I stood still for a second, until they disappeared into the crowd, then turned to face the bartender and ordered two more scotches.

I brought my father a refill and stood behind him while he played the game. I could see, as I approached, that he was down. It was a complicated game, and it took me a few minutes to understand what was going on. The player got three Ping-Pong balls for $10 and had to toss them onto a board with holes in it, and each hole had a set number of points, and you had to get to a hundred. You could buy an extra ball for $5 if you didn't get to a hundred with the first three. The first toss usually earned you at least fifty points, and so it seemed that reaching a hundred would be a sure thing. But then, the points added up very slowly—you got two points, five points, half a point with every toss—so you had to buy extra balls. Finally, after you reached a hundred, you had to play a game of five-card stud. There was a sign behind the booth that said, in big red letters: FOUR OF A KIND WINS $1,000. I'm certain that's never happened. My father got a pair of queens and won a five-dollar bill, which was a quarter of what he'd spent trying to get to a hundred points. He got up from the table.

"It's a scam," he said, as if I hadn't figured that out myself. "They let you win your first hand, then they take you to the bank."

"No shit. You should've at least kept one of the Ping-Pong balls for the bilge pump thing. Why the hell did you play? You know those things are scams."

"No, it should be illegal. There should be some kind of commission regulating these games, you know. I'm an idiot who has money to throw away, but there are other people. They see that sign that says you could win a thousand and they get sucked in by it, and it's impossible to win."

"I know," I said. "You should write a letter to the *San Juan Star.*"

He chuckled and put his arm around me. We began walking toward another bar, and we saw Yasser in the crowd. He had his arm around the tall gap-toothed girl, and they were talking to an older couple.

"Augusto!" my father called out to him, and he motioned for us to come over.

"Yes, where have you gone?" Yasser said. He turned to speak to the girl and the couple. "This is the best man, of course, Ramón. And this is the wedding planner, Antonio.

"And this!" Yasser said to us, "This is the beautiful Wanda! We have been getting engaged tonight!"

My father and I looked at each other and grinned. Wanda had an Adam's apple.

"And these!" Yasser continued, "are Wanda's much wonderful very great parents! Mr. and Ms. King, like the royalty! The royalty of

Virgin Gorda! They keep giving me their daughter's hand for married. I have told them you are very good friends with Mr. Speedy, Ramón, yes? He is the cousin of Wanda. You will be best man, yes?"

The parents shot us a suspicious look. My father shook both their hands. "Yes, of course. Speedy and I are good friends. Good friends for a long time." He stopped to look at his watch. "Will you excuse us? We'll be right back."

The Bath and Turtle was more comfortable and less crowded than the makeshift bars at the Carnival. My father was having another scotch, and I had a mellow buzz, so I'd switched back to beer. It stung every time I sipped it, because the sisters had cut my lip. My father and I had walked right past a closed jewelry store on the way to the bar, and my father stopped by the window to look at the watches, like he always does when we come to the Islands.

"Next trip, I'm getting that Submariner with the blue dial," he said. "I miss that watch." He used to have one, and he told everyone it was stolen at gunpoint. Once, drunk, in a rare moment of vulnerability, he told me the truth. He was in Boston, arguing a case in the appeals court, and after the case was over, he'd met a woman in the lobby of the Four Seasons, and he took her to his room. The next morning, when he woke up, the woman was gone, and so was the watch. The door was cracked open, and there was a fresh turd floating in the toilet. He called it the time he traded a Rolex for a piece of shit. When he returned to Puerto Rico, he had to make up a story for my mother.

"Why don't you just get it on this trip?" I said. "Get it over now."

"No, not yet." He looked at his Casio. It was just after 2:00 A.M. "When I get the Pateks, I'm giving you one, you know. As soon as you pass the bar exam. I don't need both of them." My grandfather has two Patek Philippes, which I have only seen once, in the wall safe of his mansion. I honestly don't see the point of walking around with something so expensive on your wrist. My grandfather has pancreatic cancer, and it's too late for surgery. They put him in the hospital the day before we left. "I don't want it," I said. "You can wear one on each arm if you want. It doesn't matter to me." When my father was my age, my grandfather told him if he studied law, he'd set him up with a good job at his firm. After he passed the bar, my grandfather gave him a clerk job and paid him $300 a month. "I'm not going to law school," I said.

"Well, you don't know that yet, Tito," my father said. "You're almost as smart as me. Maybe someday you'll even be smarter. If only you got off your ass every once in a while."

"Hey, it's the genes, mon," I said. "Ain't got much to look forward to, mon."

"So," my father began, "you think your grandfather—"

At that moment, three men with black stockings over their heads, wielding Uzis, rushed in and told everyone to shut the fuck up and get the fuck down. One of them stood by the door, one of them jumped over the bar, and the last one opened fire at the ceiling, and everyone in the place got on the ground, except my father, who didn't move. The one by the door kept yelling to the one behind the bar to hurry up, but he was having problems opening the cash register, so he unplugged it, picked it up, and took off running with it down the beach. The other two followed. It happened in less than a minute. Everyone got up and left without paying.

Because it was such a good night for bar business on the Island, I guess the Bath and Turtle wanted to make up for what it lost, so it stayed open. My father and I stayed in our spots, though we were instantly sober from the rush of adrenaline. I looked at the zinc roof and studied the small arrangement of bullet holes, shaped like a seven. My father stared at the top shelf. "You ever had Blue Label?" he said.

"Yeah," I said. "Every Tuesday, after polo."

He ordered us both a drink, not a hint of humor.

"Mom says I shouldn't have come on this trip," I said. "Well, that *we* shouldn't have come."

"She's probably right." He took a sip of Blue Label, but he didn't react to it. "But I don't want to be there. You know your grandfather will find a way to fuck with me, even with a tube stuck down his throat." When my parents got divorced, my father needed a loan to buy my mother's half of the apartment, and my grandfather, instead of lending him the money, asked him to move into the mansion with him, to return to his childhood bed.

"It's good," I said, holding up my glass.

"It's all he ever drank," my father said. My grandfather always lived in the mansion he'd inherited from his mother, who had always thought my grandmother—my father's mother—was unworthy. The only thing my grandmother ever wanted was a house of her own, but my grandfather never gave her one. In the sixties, he had a Cuban mistress, and he bought her a condo in Miami. The mistress killed herself in the condo. "Well, here. Let's drink to him."

Our glasses met and we drank. "Hey, maybe you'll become born again," I said. "Like Mom."

"Nothing like three big black men with Uzis to put it all in perspective," he said.

As we were leaving, a white-haired Englishman walked right up to us. "Excuse me," he said, very properly, to my father. "We think we have the assailants trapped under a house. Would you be so kind as to come with us? We want to drive them out, and we need you to guard the north lawn of the property, in case they happen to come your way."

My father looked at me for a second, then back at the Englishman. "Excuse me?" he said. "You're telling me that there are three men with automatic weapons trapped under a house, and that you want *me* to stand guard, in case they *happen* to come my way? These men have Uzis, and what do I have?" He pulled the little tube of Orajel out of his shirt pocket. "I have this little tube of Orajel. What should I do when they come at me? Orajel them to death? I don't think so. I'd rather have another drink."

The Englishman stormed out. We finished our drinks and went looking for Augusto and his groom-to-be.

The crowd at the Carnival had dwindled, and, instead of a band, loud recorded music poured out of the speakers. Yasser was sitting at one of the makeshift bars, drinking vodka on the rocks, his arm around Wanda's waist. All of the ice in his drink had melted, and it had slightly overflowed onto the metallic surface.

He got up from the stool when he saw us. "Ramón! Antonio! Have you heard? Terrorists! Terrorists with Uzis have taken Virgin Gorda." Word of the holdup had apparently gotten out, but neither my father nor I were willing to explain any of it to Yasser, not at that point. "I'm happy you are not shot. Good health for everybody!"

My father leaned discreetly into Yasser. "You're engaged to a man," he whispered. "A man dressed as a woman."

"No?" Yasser said, looking at Wanda. He leaned over and grabbed her crotch. Well, *his* crotch. Wanda jumped out of his stool and spilled his drink. "Yes," Yasser said. "Yes, let's go."

On our way across the undulating road, Yasser kept asking where we were and what had happened. I was laughing, but still shaking. My father, on the passenger seat, asked how I was doing.

"I sure as hell could eat a sacred roast beef sandwich right now," I told him.

"You know, you're still not forgiven for that," he said.

"Can somebody please tell me what has happened?" Yasser yelled.

Soon after we returned to the villa, someone began knocking on the door. My father and I were lying in bed, watching TV. Yasser was in the other room, sprawled on a king-sized bed, which he would share with Monica during the coming week. The knocking began to sound more like punching. My father answered the door, and I heard my other name being called, so I peeked out of the bedroom, in my boxers.

"You Antonio?" a white, middle-aged man wanted to know.

"Who the hell are you?" I said, snootily.

The man took a step into the house. He held up a bunch of flowers. He threw them onto the tiles. Some of the petals broke off. He pointed at the wrecked bouquet. "What the fuck is the meaning of this? Who do you think you are?"

"Antonio," my father said. "I think this man is coming on to you. Should I leave you two alone?"

"You stay out of this," the man said.

"Is this a joke?" I said, to both of them.

My father put his hands in his pockets. He took a deep breath and looked at the man. Then, he looked at me. "Antonio," he said. "I think I'm going to leave. This man clearly wants a taste of what you gave those two girls. I hope they didn't wear you out, it looks like he could go all night." I had not told him anything about what happened with the sisters at the Carnival. I had no idea what was going on, but my father's words pushed the man over the edge. He charged me, arms extended face-high. I jumped over the living room sofa, opened the sliding door, and ran half a lap around the pool in the yard. The man stopped and stood at the opposite end of the pool, knees bent, ready to take off again.

"What the fuck do you want?" I said.

"I'm gonna kick your ass, you little Puerto Rican shit."

"What for, man? What the fuck did I do to you?"

"What the fuck did you do to my girls?" he said. "That's the fucking question here."

My father walked up behind the man. Yasser had gotten up, and was standing behind my father. "Look," my father said. "It was just some innocent, friendly flowers. What's the big deal? He's just a kid. You want to know the truth? He didn't even send them. I did. I sent them for him."

The man ignored him. "Tell me," he yelled. "What the fuck did you do?"

"Sir," Yasser said. "Sir, please, please go. This boy is not good. You give him much too stress for his sick, sick heart." My father and Yasser had to be at least fifteen years older than him.

"Bullshit." The man started around the pool, toward me, but my father tripped him up and he fell. I had begun to run in the opposite direction. My father kicked the man hard on the side. Yasser kicked him, too.

"That's my kid," my father said. "Don't fuck with my kid. He didn't touch your girls, you dumb fuck. You hear me. He didn't fucking touch them. You touch him and I'll kill you. You understand? Get the fuck out."

The man got up slowly. He looked at me. "You stay the fuck away from them," he said. My father and Yasser grabbed him by the arms and walked him to the door. I followed far behind. I went to pick up the flowers, and noticed a note buried among the rough stems:

> Dear Uhuru Girls:
> It was wonderful to meet you both
> Kisses, Antonio
> PS: Century Tree Villa, up the hill

"You're an asshole," I told my father, after the man had limped away.

"What?" he said. "It was a nice gesture. Classy. It's not my fault the guy was a redneck, you know. I'm just trying to help you get laid."

"Well, fucking don't. Okay?" I turned back into the room, clutching the note. I lay in bed, and read it again. It was beautiful cursive. What got me: the two little sails in the middle of "Kisses," the three little cups in "Uhuru." The way that, like a reckless suicide note, it had no final period.

Monica came the next day, and Yasser calmed down, and my father and I went drinking around the North Sound. We did not return to the Carnival, nor did anyone come looking for us. Eight days passed before we finally got the part Michael Jackson needed to fix the engine. We drove to the airport at least ten times, waiting for the package to come on a flight from Puerto Rico, but not once did it occur to us to buy a ticket and get the hell out of there. The man in the Hatteras next to Baryshnikov told us, one night, that he'd surprised some skinny nigger with a beard fucking around with our gas tanks—that's how he said it. The gas-siphoning machine had to be brought back from Spanish Town, and Michael Jackson kept saying, between songs, that he was going to kill Bozo. My father bought five Ping-Pong bilge pump sensor balls, had them gift wrapped at the same place where he'd bought the flowers, and gave them to Yasser as a gift. The masked assailants were caught after holding up a bar in Saint Martin, several hundred miles southwest. They were pulling jobs all over the Caribbean. I have sat, drunk, each night, with a new notebook, writing poems for Camille. I want to give her everything when I come home. The first night my father saw me doing this, he asked what I was writing.

"Your eulogy," I said, and he never asked again.

This week, the days have flowed into the nighttime without us noticing, except for yesterday, when we sat at Biras Creek, drinking champagne, toasting to a new year, watching the hazardous hills bleed the sun until there was no glow echoing off the Sound. Though we've cruised from bar to bar in water taxis, downing blended malts and overtipping on a card that doesn't belong to us, the immediacy of disaster has kept us sober. We have not called anyone and there is no way to reach us: This is an island with two ends that look like giant wings, but what little is between them is tied to the bottom of the ocean.

The boat's keel digs into the water like a blade. Michael Jackson gives me a nod and looks back at the wake the boat is tracking. He asks if I want to bring Baryshnikov in, and I dock it on the first try. My father and Yasser are waiting by the slip, and Michael Jackson throws them the lines.

"Everything good?" Yasser asks.

"No problem, mon," Michael Jackson says.

"Everything good, Tito?" Yasser looks at me.

"Perfect," I say.

Yasser has just dropped Monica off at the airport. My father has returned the key to the villa and left Speedy's Jeep in care of the bartender. I have left both engines on. While Yasser writes Michael Jackson a check, my father and I load our things onto the boat. The Evinrudes purr like resuscitated beasts.

After we've unknotted the pleats and pushed off, and after we've zigzagged past the moored sailboats in the bay, and after we've each opened a beer, Yasser points the bow toward the channel between Prickly Pear and Mosquito Island.

"Anegada, here we come!" he yells, over the wind. Anegada is the sharpest edge of the Bermuda Triangle. It is bound by the famous horseshoe reef on all sides, and its highest elevation is only twelve feet above sea level, so you can't see it until you're right on top of it.

My father looks at me. His eyes are flooded, as if his eyeballs, too, have sunk. How could he not love his father?

I put my hand on Yasser's shoulder. "That's enough" is all I have to say. He looks at me, then at my father, and he understands, and turns the wheel the other way.

Our wake looks like the tail of a cloud: shaking everything up from underneath, unsettling the plane of the surface. The wind, this time, is on our backs, and the waves are pushing the boat down the Sir Francis Drake Channel, trying to hurry us home.

ANNE DE MARCKEN

Vermont College of Union Institute & University

ASHES

Fifty-two years ago the sun was shining. Louise and Dan made love somewhere along here in the wide-open on a blanket borrowed from the cottage where they spent their honeymoon. It had been brazen, like skinny-dipping. Exposed. She remembers feeling both small and vast, and as if some part of her—an arm, a leg—might come loose and drift up into the sky. They had been rushed and nervous and de-lighted with themselves, and had known even then that however fleeting the experience, it was emblematic. As she would know two years later the moment they conceived Thomas, she knew then that they had conceived the mythic kernel of their marriage. An idea of themselves that would sustain them through tedious years. An idea that Dan retreated to in his last days.

Louise wishes the tide were all the way out, as it was then. Red-dening green spartina hummocks softened the edge of the wide, shal-low Willapa Bay. Herons far out in the oyster beds took an eternity to unfold each leg. Now, what she remembers is mostly submerged. The ponderous blues of water and distant hills and cloud-heavy sky threaten to blot out the way she saw it with Dan.

If everything can't be the same as it was fifty-two years ago, she'd like the tide a little farther up, which at least would bring the water to where she stands at the dike so that she could dip her fingers through its glassy surface. She doesn't have the hour to wait for the tide to come in; she told the kids she would meet them at the inn with time to spare for a drink before the graveside ceremony. Dan would tell them to go to hell, start the funeral without him, and then he'd sit down on this rock to wait for the moon to drag the bay up to him. That's how he thought. Not afraid of grandiosity. Perfectly comfortable talking about himself in the same breath as the moon. Happy to let people wait—*it's their own choice,* he would say.

Geraldine and Thomas have taken up positions on either side of the inn's stone fireplace and are exchanging remarks without exactly addressing one another. Louise sees that they will never outgrow their sibling rivalry.

"Wood is fine for ambience," says Thomas, looking peevishly at his scotch as if he has discovered lipstick on the edge of his glass, "but who has time to spend a month every fall splitting and stacking enough to get you through the winter?" And then he winks at Kay, his wife, who is sitting in an armchair beside him emanating uncomfortable blankness.

"Well, Thomas," says Geraldine, gripping the mantel and bracing her foot against the hearth as if she were stretching her hamstrings in preparation for a run, "I like to think Al and I have got our priorities straight. Beauty matters to us. 'Ambience' as you say." She glances over her shoulder at her husband, Al, who smiles and chuckles good-naturedly as if listening to a different conversation.

"I thought she was some kind of environmentalist," Thomas says to Al. "You know they don't even allow woodstoves in new houses at the lake anymore. Too polluting."

"You know what?" says Geraldine, swatting away Al's hand as he reaches to soothe her. "All I said was I liked the fireplace. I said, 'Isn't this fireplace welcoming?' Just because I live in L.A. doesn't mean I'm superficial."

Listening to her children bicker, Louise is irritated with Dan for dying, for forcing them into this room together, for bringing her back here to relive a memory from more than fifty years ago. It feels insistent and sentimental and it exasperates her. Worse, if he were here, he wouldn't be any more bothered by this petty strife than he is now. In fact, the ridiculously heavy brass urn containing his ashes, which Geraldine has placed in the middle of the coffee table as if it were a bouquet of lilies, is exactly as unconcerned and self-satisfied as Dan would have been.

Recently Louise has been feeling sexually aroused and it has made her impatient. She doesn't like the idea of herself, an old woman, masturbating, but a week ago after turning off the light, she stuffed Dan's pillow between her legs and squeezed her thighs together until she came. She has done this every night since, even while staying here at the inn with her grown children in rooms nearby. She thinks that when she has an orgasm, she must look more as if she is having a stroke.

Louise sighs without realizing it. Everyone turns to look at her. "Is it time?" she asks.

"I'm sorry, Mother," Thomas says. He knocks back the last of his scotch.

"Well, it's her own fault," says Geraldine. "We all count on you to make us seem better than we are." She crosses the room, scoops Dan's urn into the crook of her arm like a football, and kisses Louise on the top of her head with as much affection as a bus passenger depositing her fare.

The next day, as he and Kay are leaving, Thomas says from the window of their rental car, "You know, Mother, Geraldine is right about one thing, anyway. We know you'll retouch the truth. You're going to write about this, aren't you? Then we'll be able to remember it just the way Father would have liked. I'm sure that was part of his plan."

His plan. A three-day funeral complete with mandatory family reunion, formal grave-marking ceremony, and solitary ash scattering scheduled to coincide with their anniversary. They had to wait more than five months so the timing would be right. Dan's death had been a long time coming, and he tended to its details much the same way he tended to his scalp when, early in his thirties, he began to bald. Not obsessively, but fondly, dotingly, with a certain advance nostalgia and essential denial. During his last months, Louise had humored him. Lying beside him on the bed where he was tucked in under an extra comforter, she listened and took notes. She indulged his speculations about the meaning of the falcons that came to nest on the cornice outside their bedroom window. When he was dead, the notes came to seem like the published version of something she herself had written. They were formal and closed to revision, if not particularly well edited.

The crunch of gravel underneath the car's tires as Thomas and Kay pull out of the inn's driveway is familiar and comforting to Louise. She stands there, not watching them go, but instead looking at her shadow. It is slender in the slanting morning light. She is surprised by a sudden recollection of her youth. Until five years ago, her youth was not a thing she experienced as separate from herself, but now it has come apart from her, like a label that has soaked off.

She remembers what it was like to stand outside of the house they rented during the first year she and Dan were married: She walked out to get the paper wearing her slippers and her housecoat and felt the newness of being a wife. Dan liked to have sex in the morning, and sometimes afterward she wouldn't brush her hair right away, because she liked to look like a woman who had just been made love to by her husband.

Geraldine drags her rolling suitcase across the gravel. It resists her like a terrified dog. Louise thinks her daughter looks good for her age, thin and not so tan as she was for a while. She's letting the gray in her hair show; her age makes her fitness that much more impressive. "Are you sure you're all right here by yourself, Mother? You know you don't have to do this exactly the way he wanted. Al and I could stay another day." Even as she says this, Geraldine heaves her suitcase into the back of their SUV.

"I'm sure," says Louise. Unfortunately, since Geraldine shared some of her and Al's marital troubles last winter, Louise has been unable to get rid of the image of the two of them beating each other with giant foam bats in their therapist's office. It has combined with the memory of an article she read about infantilism, and she pictures them wearing diapers as they pummel one another ineffectually.

Al comes along with three more suitcases and stops in front of her. "Louise," he says, "Geraldine and I want you to come for Christmas."

"Al," Geraldine scolds, giving his name three syllables (A-a-l), "that's not a nice invitation. Mother, we'd love to have you. I know you want to have Christmas at home, but since Father isn't going to be there, if you change your mind, Al and I and the kids have nice traditions."

She has such a strange way of talking. Louise wonders where that comes from. *Since Father isn't going to be there.* As if he's somewhere else this Christmas, like the year he was in Korea and she and the kids stayed with the Neffs at their place in Vermont.

Nice traditions.

Louise hugs them both good-bye and waves as they pull away. She goes back inside to wait out the day. The tide will not be right until six o'clock, so she plans to do some writing. She already knows that the essay she will write about the experience of scattering Dan's ashes has a place at *Home & Hearth*. She has been a regular contributor to the magazine since the seventies. Her work appears elsewhere, but Louise and Vivian Lang have an understanding that *H&H* gets first crack at the really personal stuff. Louise doesn't mind. Her *H&H* fans are rock solid. She can count on them for good holiday sales of her collections. They have followed her through marriage, child rearing, the passing of her parents, through Dan's illness, and now into her mourning. She imagines that someday they will accompany her to death's door: She pictures herself there on the dark threshold with an entourage of well-groomed women in various shades of beige and pink. She gets letters from the daughters and granddaughters of women who wrote to her thirty years ago. They all say the same thing, that her essays help them face life with optimism and gratitude. They use virtually the same words, with adjustments for psychological and spiritual fads: "uplifting," "validating," "life-affirming." These are the sort of quotes that her publisher pulls for the dust jackets of her books to go along with the various photographs of her that have been used over the years. In each she is smiling and in some recognizably homey setting: at a kitchen table, in front of a fireplace, on a front porch. Not their actual kitchen table or fireplace. They've never had a porch, not even a balcony. She has lived in the same apartment building in San Francisco for more than thirty years, the entire length of her publishing career. Of course,

she's never pretended in her writing that she lives in a suburban setting, but the image *plays well with her readership*. She doesn't feel cyn-
ical about this. She defers to her publisher and thinks about it no
further—it is not her part of the business.

Arlene, the innkeeper, has been nice enough to arrange for a desk
to be put in her room. "Happy to accommodate." On the telephone,
when Louise was making plans, Arlene told her that they often
hosted writers. "In fact," said Arlene, "you will have esteemed company during your stay. Jackson Elliott will be in room nine. Perhaps
you know his novels? He's working on something new. Mr. Elliott
likes room nine because of the soaking tub." When she was introduced to Jackson Elliott the first evening of her stay, Louise attempted to suppress the image of his naked bulk, bright red as a
boiled lobster, stuffed into a barrel-like hot tub. She had not read
anything of his, but she could not help associating the man with a
style of book jacket that relied primarily on red, gold, and black and
whose title was in smaller font than the author's name.

Louise is in room two. She has a view of the bay. By the time she
sits down to write, the sun is too high to lend emotional dimension
to the landscape, and the trees and grasses and tide flats are ordinary
looking. Beautiful, but not heartrending. The tide is far out, but has
even farther to go. Another two hours before it turns. Then another
six to wait for it to turn again so that she can stand on the shore
where she once stood with Dan, and pour his ashes ceremoniously,
but without witnesses, into the ebbing sea, per his instructions. She
tries to imagine making a similar request of Dan, or of the kids, and
it makes her shake her head. The movement startles her.

She has realized for some time that Dan was in the habit of co-
opting her writing for documentation of his personal dramas. This
maudlin funerary extravaganza is in part a grandstand. A way to be
immortalized. Even, she thinks, a way of summing up her career, of

taking her with him to the grave, to the sea. She tolerated Dan's arrogance, his insecurity. It must have been difficult at times to be the subject of her career, a character in the dramatized version of their marriage.

He was, she thinks, faithful and devoted. He remembered every anniversary, even this one. He was an indulgent father. But she knows her audience, and she knows that they don't really care about Dan. They will want to know how it was for *her*; they will be relieved when she writes to tell them about how it was to come home afterward to an empty apartment. They will wonder whether she can fall in love again—they will want for her what they want for themselves, and what they see as possible once she has done it. She might have to take a cruise somewhere, go on a couple dates, or perhaps something more imaginative—a year abroad, a new house. They will want for her, and for themselves, an adventure of humble proportions, a divertissement.

The key to her success has been the modesty of her readers' expectations. She is not gifted, but people can't relate to genius. And people don't want earth-shattering happiness, either. They want safety. They want things to be nice. They don't want to know that she is sexually frustrated at the age of seventy-two. That is not safe or nice.

She makes notes on yesterday's grave-marking ceremony for the piece she'll submit to *H&H*. She remembers clearly. She paid attention. Noted details. She thought about the article during the ceremony. Thought about how it ought to be about the deathless quality of commitment. About the love that issues from love, the many lives and relationships that are generated by a marriage. But she couldn't settle on a suitable image. Nothing seemed to reflect anything. Things were just themselves: the weather, the kids, cars passing on the road, crows, sound of the distant ocean, pale sky, tall trees, fake hyacinths, fake dahlias, little plastic American flags flapping in the breeze, fenced-off family plots, the smell of turned earth, the priest's unfortunate cough, the same readings that were recited at her father's funeral, Geraldine's pink umbrella.

And no suitable metaphor presents itself now in the view from her window. Louise's mind wanders out along the shining tidal tributaries; a swift flock of shorebirds lifts, shimmers white, then turns and disappears.

She thinks of burying her father and remembers feeling lost and exposed and deeply alone as she stood beside his grave. A cold, suffocating, nighttime, night*mare* feeling. As if she were standing inside the dark cavern of her own chest, surrounded by the deafening wallop of her own heart. With her mother, seven years later, it was different. An emotional surge filled her from head to toe. She felt peaceful and buoyant, as if she actually were floating inches above the mown grass. When she hears people talk about ecstatic experiences, she turns to this memory to reawaken her understanding of what they mean.

But yesterday, beside Dan's grave—or his grave *marker*, or, rather, his plaque, because his body was not placed beneath it and so it doesn't *mark* anything—she felt nothing. Not sad, not relieved. Neither was she objective, though. She was unable to reflect meaningfully on the event or her own condition. At one point during the ceremony, she became aware of a voice in her head, her voice the way it might sound under the covers, repeating over and over lines from the Wallace Stevens poem "Thirteen Ways of Looking at a Blackbird." And she thought, *I think those are actually starlings, not blackbirds,* for nearby there was a young birch alive with birds. *"O young men of Haddam,"* said the voice in her head—or was it *"thin men"*? *"O thin men of Haddam, / Why do you..."* but she couldn't put the poem together.

Louise decides to take a walk, perhaps find a place to eat lunch. She puts on an extra sweater, and a scarf, and a canvas beach hat, and waves good-bye to Arlene as she leaves the fenced-in yard of the bed-and-breakfast.

Louise is a woman who still wears skirts, even on days like this when the air is not particularly warm and the sunlight a chilly gray through high overcast. Her calves are still shapely, her ankles not swollen by edema. She is grateful to her legs for holding their own against varicose veins.

She thinks she looks *handsome,* the word her mother used to describe attractive women over fifty. She has made an effort not to become quaint or dear in her old age. She has steered away from cardigans and small prints and has incorporated articles of Dan's wardrobe into her own: this hat she has on, his silk handkerchiefs, his Pendletons. She likes skirts with pockets. She wears dark blue canvas sneakers. She only wears pearls with diamonds. She doesn't paint her fingernails, but she does wear lipstick—an out-of-fashion pink for daytime, and dark red after five.

She heads toward the ocean beach, away from the bay, turning south and west through blocks of vacation homes and run-down rentals, until yards dense with untended rhododendrons and overgrown grass begin to struggle against the dry creep of sand and the roots and needles of shore pines, finally giving way utterly where the dunes crest and swell away down to the long, gray edge of the western world. The Pacific is not frothy today. Its kelpy waves curl in and crash without fanfare. She goes close to the edge of the surf where the sand is wet and hardpacked. The impression of uniformity that the beach gives from a distance falls apart up close. Little deltas fan out from the shards of broken clam and crab shells and sand dollars that litter the beach. Pebbles and small feathers part the retreating waves and form complex, argyle patterns of feldspar and fool's gold.

It feels good to walk. Louise breathes in and out deeply and finds that she is smiling. She feels mildly elated. She has gotten free of Dan's agenda. She keeps her eyes open for an unbroken shell, a worthy beach treasure, something to serve as a good metaphor. She picks up a piece of driftwood and tries to see something in it. Could be a sea serpent. She tosses it out into the shallow waves. *Keep nothing.*

Up ahead, sitting on a hulking, silvered tree trunk, there is a man. He is smoking a pipe. Louise smells the smoke, a smell she loves. As she nears, she sees that it is Jackson Elliott from room nine. She thinks it won't work to pretend she hasn't seen him, but perhaps she can get off with a well-timed friendly wave. But no, he is beckoning to her. She waves, pretending not to understand the meaning of his gesture. He grows more energetic and even pats the log next to him, indicating—she can hardly believe it—that he means for her to come sit next to him.

"A Woman in a Skirt on the Beach," he announces as she extends her hand to him. He turns her hand in his and kisses the back of it. His lips are moist, the O-shaped bristle of his mustache and beard vaguely obscene.

She resists the urge to wipe the back of her hand: She puts her hands in her pockets, instead.

"Sit with me, madam."

She thinks, *He must have forgotten my name.*

"Well," she says, doing her best to substitute a tone of feminine fluster for the feeling of distaste that he inspires, "thank you, Mr. Elliott." She sits noncommittally, poised for departure. "What a nice spot you've found for yourself," she says. She feels very small sitting next to him.

"Never know what the Pacific will provide," he says, suddenly keen-eyed and farseeing. "The ocean giveth and the ocean taketh away."

"Indeed," says Louise, not too dryly, she hopes.

They sit quietly for a minute. Jackson Elliott broods. Louise enjoys the smoke from his pipe. She wonders what it would be like to make love to a man his size. There must be logistical issues. Alarmed by the warm pulse of arousal she feels at the thought of his naked mass pressing down on her, she says quickly, "What are you working on? I mean, Arlene led me to believe you had a project you came to work on. I hope I'm not being indiscreet."

"But what is indiscretion among friends?" he asks and nudges her with his thick, tweedy elbow. "A novel," he says. "A big, burly rottweiler of a book. It might be gentle by nature, but it's a beast, no question. I thought it had me. I felt its teeth near my vital artery."

"My," says Louise. "What's it about?"

"Life!" he barks. "And death."

"Mmm," she says. "Weighty subjects."

"Mm," he says, and clamps down on his pipe.

"I came here to scatter my husband's ashes," she says, maybe because she is bothered by his arrogance and wants him to feel ashamed of himself for talking about life and death so casually, maybe because she has needed to say it out loud, and have it heard. The line comes back to her. *O thin men of Haddam, / Why do you imagine golden birds?*

"How long were you married?" Jackson Elliott asks.

"Fifty-two years, today actually. It's our anniversary," she says, and laughs a little. "Imagine! It sounds like such a long time. What did we do for all those years? I feel I have to account for it somehow." She is about to cry.

"Those were your children staying here?" he asks.

"Yes," she says, getting a hold of herself. "Geraldine and Thomas. And their people, their spouses, Al and Kay. Their kids are grown.

Busy. Kay's a scientist. I don't know why that matters. Geraldine is a housewife. Thomas publishes the weekly in their town. None of them is happy. But it doesn't seem to bother them."

"And Al?" he asks.

"Al?" she says.

"What does Al do?"

"I don't really know," she says. She looks out at the waves. A mile out, beyond the break there are fishing boats. Louise hopes for a whale or a seal or a shark's fin, but there are only gulls. "You're kind to listen," she says. "I'm sorry to go on."

"Have you had lunch?" Elliott asks. "There's a shack just over the dunes there, where they serve manna disguised as clam chowder. Would you care to join me?"

Of course he offers her his arm, so she is obliged to insert her hand through its sturdy crook. Louise imagines that they look like Babar the Elephant King and the Old Lady.

"When Geraldine was a child," Louise says, "she had a stuffed Babar who wore a green felt suit. You remind me of him." It is not a flattering comparison, and she surprises herself with her lack of concern for his feelings. It is a relief.

He laughs.

"If you pulled a cord, the toy said something simple in French." She uses a deep, Frenchman's voice, *"'Bonjour, je m'appelle Babar.' 'Comment ça va, aujourd'hui?' 'Je t'aime.'"* They laugh together at this and make their way up the beach and through the dunes.

"Je m'appelle Babar!" he bellows. *"Il fait beau! J'ai faim! Nous allons déjeuner!"*

By the time they return to the inn, it is nearly three o'clock. Louise has enjoyed herself and has enjoyed Jackson Elliott. She now calls him Jacks. "Thank you, Jacks," she says on her way into her room.

She thinks he must be something like Geraldine and Al's harmless foam bats. She will take a nap before it is time to go to the bay with Dan's ashes. There is more than enough time to lie down for an hour or so, have tea, and drive out to the point for the ebbing tide.

The brass urn is sitting on her dressing table. She has already looked inside. The ashes are in a sealed bag, like a Ziploc. They are not uniform, not even as fine as portland cement. There are chips of bone that neither the cancer nor the furnace could reduce. Probably his teeth are in there. This might be an apt metaphor. Morbid, but eloquent—Dan's ashes as lumpy and irreducible as their marriage. Dense and gray and strangely weightless. At the crematorium, they warned her that getting any ash in her eyes or in her lungs could cause serious damage and that she should choose a calm day. So far, the weather has cooperated.

She lies down and pulls up the quilt. Louise loves to nap. To lie under covers with her clothes on. To have her eyes closed when it is light. She loves the irresponsible, irresistible luxury of sleep during the day.

She dreams that she is pregnant. Although she is due to give birth at any moment (she feels it could happen here in this strange house with the flooded pantry and the unhealthy houseplants) she is barely showing. She is relieved, but vaguely disappointed when Geraldine doesn't recognize the bulge of her sweater. She keeps smoothing her hand over her belly, again and again, enjoying the slight swell. She feels very well, very fit. She thinks she could go for a long run, or swim laps, but the doctors have told her that at her age, it is best to take it easy. She has to pee, but has on a leotard that she doesn't want to take off with all these people around. Now the baby wants to nurse even though it is still inside of her, so she goes into the pantry for privacy and, balancing on two floating boards, lets it crawl inside the leotard up to her breast. The feeling of its mouth on her nipple arouses her and she pushes the baby back down. It starts to cry and she is afraid that people will hear it. She really has to pee now, but can't take off the leotard without revealing the baby.

A knock at her door wakes Louise. It is dark. She realizes immediately that she has overslept. Another knock. "Just a minute," she says. She has to use the toilet. "I'll be right there." She feels sweaty and weak from sleep, clumsy as she makes her way to the bathroom in the dark. She turns on the light and the electric brightness of the white tile is blinding. She squints at her wristwatch. It is already past seven o'clock. How could she possibly have slept for four hours? She closes her eyes and sits on the toilet. Peeing is unsatisfying, an endless thin trickle. The coolness of the tiled room clears her head. Her eyes adjust.

She goes to the door of her room. Jackson Elliott stands there with his pipe in one hand and two glasses of scotch in the other. His eyes resolutely and chivalrously settle on her face after just a quick inspection of her rumpled clothes, her pillow-flattened hair. She is sure that her eyes are puffy, that her lipstick has bled into the fine wrinkles that radiate from her mouth. "Mr. Elliott," she says.

"Madam," he says. "I've disturbed your rest."

"It's a good thing you did," she says. "Thank you. But I'm in a hurry now. Is there something you needed?"

"Only the pleasure of your company," he says, advancing a half step. "I'm prohibited from enjoying an evening pipe indoors, and I wonder if I could entice you to join me in temporary exile."

"Most kind," she says, keeping her hand on the doorknob, "but as I said, I am in a hurry. I've overslept. You'll please excuse me?"

"Oh, but... May I take a rain check?"

"I have an early flight tomorrow."

"So brief," he says.

"Yes," she says, and closes the door.

The fog has come in. It is almost heavy enough to be called rain, but instead of falling the fine drops mill around in the air. Louise needs her windshield wipers as she slowly follows the dim beams of her headlights along the narrow strip of road out to the end of the peninsula. She has never liked driving at night, but it is worse in the last few years. She leans in close over the steering wheel. A small animal shambles along the white line, a possum or a raccoon. She swerves unnecessarily. Her heart races and her skin goes clammy. The canvas book bag that holds Dan's urn flops over onto its side in the passenger's seat.

As she pulls onto the rutted dirt road leading out to the point Dan and she discovered as newlyweds, the fog presses even more thickly against the car. She switches the headlights between high and low to try to see better, but either way the halogen brightness is more blinding than illuminating. She turns off the headlights and creeps forward using only her parking lights. She can see the fog-heavy grasses on the side of the road. She can see bright bits of oyster shell embedded in the muddy ruts like the bits of bone in Dan's ashes. There is no landmark to tell her when she has gone far enough, or that she has gone too far. She stops the car.

The night sky is blotted out by fog. There is no sign of the moon. No stars. Louise stands in the yellow glow of the parking lights. She can hear the water, the splash and cartoonish quack of a duck, it is hard to tell how far off. She calculates: The tide was high at five o'clock, was probably slack for half an hour, and has by now been ebbing for at least two hours. Louise thinks she will have to walk well out into the bay grass before she comes to open water. If she can find one of the little sloughs that cut through the reeds, she might not have to wade into the mud.

She gets the book bag, heavy with Dan's urn, and the cheap aluminum flashlight Arlene lent her. Afraid she won't be able to find her way back, she leaves the car's lights on and heads into the tall grasses at the edge of the road. She comes to the dike and has to walk along it for what seems like several yards before finding a way up onto the overgrown jumble of boulders. Once on top of the wide breakwater, she has to go farther to find a way down the other side. She looks back in the direction from which she came and finds she cannot see the beacon of the car over the embankment.

She switches the book bag from one shoulder to the other, alternating the ache of the urn's weight. She heads away from the shore, steps cautiously on matted succulents and flattened reeds, alert for sudden drop-offs and hidden sinkholes. A killdeer bursts out from under her sneakers, its wings a frantic bright commotion, then disappears, whistling alarm, from her flashlight's narrow field.

She comes to an edge, a curving, reed-carpeted shelf that drops down a foot or more and runs in either direction. She follows it for a while, hoping it will loop out into the bay, but it does not seem to bring her any closer to the water. She thinks that fifteen more minutes must have passed and the tide has gone out that much more. This time she looks at her watch so that she can keep track. 7:40.

She hears a splash close by—a bird diving, or an otter. She steps down off the shelf. The spartina comes above her knees and reaches up her skirt with smooth, curving blades. Her feet sink down; she feels dampness begin to seep through her sneakers, but her footing is fairly solid; the mud does not suck at her shoes. She moves cautiously in the direction of the splash, though she can't be sure whether she is going the right way. The memory of it seems to repeat like an echo, ricocheting all around. The darkness is insistent, clinging. She just needs to get to a finger of open water. She only needs an entry to the sea for Dan's ashes.

Louise hears something approaching. She is unsure whether it comes over water or land. She squats down in the reeds, suddenly afraid of getting caught. By the sheriff. By an oysterman. She sees herself with her hands up in the air, trapped in the humiliating glare of a spotlight. It sounds like tires on wet pavement, but there is no pavement nearby, unless she has wandered as far back as the county road. Then she thinks it is the wind. But it is the rain. It is the sound of fine rain falling on the wide blades of spartina. It reaches her. She feels she might start to cry; this might be too much.

She takes the canvas bag from her shoulder. She considers whether she can just leave Dan here. She sets the flashlight down on a sedge hummock; its beam has grown weak and yellow. She takes the urn out of the bag and sets it on the sodden ground. It leans to one side, held upright by the reeds. She removes the top of the urn and opens the Baggie containing Dan's ashes: If she leaves it like this, will the ashes be carried away when the tide returns? They seem light, but really they must be heavier than water. Without surface tension to support them, surely they wouldn't float. Drops of rain plop into the ash with little puffs. She imagines the urn as a miniature brass cement mixer, Dan a gritty paste. Her *H&H* fans wouldn't go for that at all.

First this makes her laugh out loud, then she is overwhelmed by irritation. *What,* she thinks, *is a seventy-two-year-old woman doing in a salt marsh in a rainstorm in the pitch dark?* Then she puts her face in her hands and cries. She cries for several minutes.

There is no image. She looks down at the urn, at Dan's bone-flecked ashes. Then she says it aloud. "There is no image." Her voice is startling, like a voice raised in a library. "There is no suitable image," she says, looking up into the night. The rain is coming down more heavily, a breeze has begun to stir, and the fog has thinned slightly. Louise sees a light. A red light. The riding light of a boat? It blinks on and off unsteadily. Now there are two. Buoys?

She hurries to zip up the Baggie, fumbles with the urn's lid, gets it back into the canvas book bag. She pushes herself to her feet. Hoists the bag to her shoulder. She hurries into the dark, keeping an eye on the red lights, watching her step as well as she can with the dim beam from her flashlight, feeling her way along. Her shoes are soaked and muddy and so are her legs up to her knees. She feels heavy and slow. She is back up on higher ground, then drops down again. She loses sight of the lights. She stops, her breathing heavy. The rain is really coming down now. She waits for the lights to reappear. She imagines the boat has swung around with the breeze, concealing its lights from view. She waits. Waits. They are gone. She listens for the water. The rain is too loud now. She thinks there is nothing for it but to continue. The ground begins to rise. There are rocks. And blackberry vines. It takes a few seconds for Louise to recognize the breakwater. The details and mass of what she is looking at reorder themselves and fall into place, into meaning. Suddenly locating herself in the darkness is oddly disorienting. It makes her dizzy, as though she has vertigo.

She tears her hands on the thorny vines as she scrambles up the low embankment. There is her car on the other side, its taillights clear now that the fog has lifted, their red bulbs flickering as the tall roadside grasses shift and bend. She has come around in a circle.

She picks her way down the tumbled boulders and leans against the car, dropping the urn in its bag to the puddled rut at her feet. She stays there for a few minutes without really thinking anything. Catching her breath. Relieved that she has not had a heart attack. She looks at the muddy book bag.

"Dan?" she says, as if she is testing to see whether he is asleep. "Dan," she says. "I think I am going to leave you here," she says. "Right here." The sound of the rain falling is delicate, intimate. She heaves herself forward and with great effort lifts the book bag. "I think it wouldn't have been like you imagined it anyway," she says, going around to the front of the car. "I don't think you would ever have made it to the sea." She squats down in the glow of the amber parking lights and takes the urn from the book bag. She unscrews the lid and pulls out the Baggie of Dan's ashes. "I'm not convinced this is all of you anyway," she says. "Seems like the same amount that we got back from the vet when Dimby died." She smiles. "Where are you, Dan?" She opens the Baggie and pours the ashes into the rutted road. They darken and settle. *"Je t'aime,"* Louise says in her Babar voice.

She puts the urn back in the book bag and gets into the car. She is soaked through, shivering. She drives slowly back to the inn, watching for animals, running the heater full blast. When she gets out of the car, she can smell Jackson Elliott's pipe. She considers her appearance. Her sneakers squelch as she crosses the gravel drive. When she reaches the brick walk, she pauses to take them off. His voice—pompous, but somehow welcome and welcoming—comes from the gazebo across the lawn. "Have you been swimming with your clothes on?"

"Caught," she says.

"Only thing more shocking than skinny-dipping," he says.

She waves in the direction of his voice and lets herself inside.

ROBERT LIDDELL

University of Houston

WHATEVER HAPPENED TO SÉBASTIEN GROSJEAN?

"It's a fine day for tennis," Win said. He was wearing linen slacks and a pair of Cole Haan loafers with no socks. I knew they were Cole Haans because he'd told me. "I adore Cole Haans," he said, as though they were a pair of soft leather kittens. "Like sex on the feet." We were cruising in his Boxster down San Felipe. The car was small and close to the ground and I could feel the grade of the road beneath us. Win drove with a drink in his right hand, shifting gears with the heel of his hand whenever he felt the need to jolt us through a closing portal in the traffic. Ice rattled against the Styrofoam wall of his cup.

"Federer is playing," he said. "He's Swedish."

"Does he still live there?"

"God no, man!" He glared at me. "None of them live in Sweden because of the taxes. Taxes in Sweden are outrageous. Like sixty percent. But it doesn't matter because he's really Swiss."

"Why'd you tell me he's Swedish?"

"He's Swedish," he said, "because they say he's Swedish."

Win had called me at the beginning of the week and asked if I'd fly down to Houston and visit him for the weekend and maybe check out the tournament. I'd spoken to Lauren for the last time the week before, and being anywhere but where I was seemed like a great idea, so I agreed. On the plane that Friday I'd been thinking about something my father once said to me: All men lose their hearts eventually. He was lying in a hospital bed at the time, with another arterial blockage, but that's not what he meant.

"We have to pick up the girls," Win said, as though I knew already that there were girls, just not that they'd need to be picked up. This irritated me and I started to say something, but stopped myself. He cut through a side street and we sped by an assortment of Easter-colored mansions: pinks, blues, and yellows. Most of the houses were brick.

Win continued to talk tennis at me; the players' histories, their injuries. Federer's opponent was from Lyon. He'd torn a hip flexor three years earlier in Paris at the French Open, and had not been the same since.

"It's tragic," Win said at a light. He pressed a button, then lit a cigarette while the top rolled back and the sunlight crawled up our laps. "Absolutely tragic. In the second week! For a Becker or an Agassi, it's just a disappointment; they have opportunities. A player like Grosjean gets one crack at a major—maybe. So much has to go right. The draw, the surface. The body. He could have won it really. But the hip gave and that was the end of it. The entire country went into mourning." I assumed he meant France. "Of course, no one here will remember that."

When the car started forward, Win's fine black hair, just long enough to suggest impertinence, whipped in the wind. We crossed a major street and passed several sets of two-story apartment buildings with gates and stairways of black iron. A store on one corner sold wire frames in the shapes of animals. The frames were filled with fertilizer and you grew jasmine vines around them. Win told me how fine Vickie was.

"You could grow jasmine all over this girl, Jack."

I still saw pieces of Lauren: the thin silver cuff she wore on the back of her left ear; her smooth legs over the length of our couch (her feet tucked under my thigh to keep her toes warm); the plastic amber daisies she used to clip her bangs aside; her eyes catching mine in the mirror when I stepped out of the shower. I remembered her foot in my hand, the slender white curve of the arch, and my teeth soft against the back of her ankle. And later, my finger tracing the lines of her face while she slept. I could remember things she'd said to me, phrases she used, even words she liked. *Solace. Illusion.* But I couldn't hear her voice.

And I shouldn't have called her. I called her up and everything I had to say was wrong, but I said it anyway, and she listened and I kept on talking and when I finished, she didn't say anything, so I began to say things for her, and then for me again as well, and she just listened until there was nothing left.

"Pathetic," Win said outside Vickie's apartment. He knocked on the door. "Their clothes will be inadequate. They'll be dressed up, I swear, but it'll be faux Chloé and faux Gucci. You shouldn't say anything about it."

Vickie wasn't answering. I looked around the courtyard. She lived in one of those overnight stucco jobs marketed to whatever they call yuppies now; the kind with its own fitness center, weekend mixers, and a conference room reservable with advance notice. The landscape was cramped and themeish. In the courtyard was a small pool shaped roughly like the lower two-thirds of a snowman and surrounded by palm trees and large dark lava rocks.

"Who's Chloé?" I said. The palms looked ridiculous.

"Of London." He knocked again. "Just take fashion off the table altogether, okay? If anything needs to be said, I'll say it. But under no circumstances will I say anything at all."

It was just after eleven o'clock, already hot enough that my shirt was sticking to my back. There was supposed to be a front coming in late in the day, but there was no sign of it.

The sky was so blue it hurt.

Win opened the door himself and entered. "Men in the house," he announced. "Jesus, doesn't a girl answer her door anymore?" I waited on the breezeway a moment, but Win motioned for me to follow. The room smelled like perfume and candles, like the apartment of a woman I didn't know. Vickie and her friend were sitting on a pair of stools in front of a kitchen bar. I didn't know who was who. When they saw Win, they smiled at him like a couple of teenagers.

"Win, baby!" the woman on the left cried. Her eyes were a sharp brown and she wore a short white skirt and tank top with a pale yellow blouse tied at the waist. She slipped off her stool and skied across the carpet in platform sandals. She hugged Win, who spun her around and set her down in front of me. Her toes were bare and polished.

"Vicks, this is Jack," he said.

"We were just talking about you," said Vickie. Since I'd heard her name for the first time twenty minutes earlier, I was of the opinion she was lying. "This is Sandra," she said. The second girl approached. She had straight blond hair to her shoulders and wore a strapless sundress that trickled down her figure like blue honey. She was gorgeous. They were both gorgeous.

"I've heard so much about you," she said to me.

"Then," I answered, "I guess the only decent thing for me to do is leave." They all laughed a little too hard and I knew Win had told them about Lauren.

Both of their outfits were fantastic and I found myself relieved that Win had been mistaken. Not that I cared one way or the other about fashion etiquette. I just wanted him to be wrong.

"You'll have to follow us," Win said to me, taking Vickie's arm. "I'm in the Box." Box was his pet name for the Porsche.

"We'll take my car," Sandra said. "But I don't know the way to the club, so don't lose us."

In the car Sandra asked me how I knew Win.

"We were at Duke together," I said. "You?"

"I don't really know him, except through Vickie. I've been out with them a couple of times. He's tough to get a read on." I couldn't argue with that. It had taken me a long time to understand his particular brand of sincerity. I first met Win in our third semester at Duke. We had an instructor, a man named Wizzenhand, who held a theory that all literature was reducible to the confrontation of fear. The first day of class he asked each of us to tell him what it was we feared most. The majority of answers were predictable: rape; a plane crash; failing out of school. I don't remember mine. But when it was Win's turn, he leaned back and rested his arm over the back of his chair and said, "My greatest fear is that I'll never give my best to anything." People laughed at that. Win laughed with them. They believed he was joking.

Win performed his standard magic act on the road, vanishing through holes in traffic that Sandra couldn't possibly get through in her Honda. We lost them once, but managed to catch sight of them again when he made a turn, Vickie waving back at us helplessly.

Sandra said she was an editor for a magazine and told me its name, and I said I thought I'd heard of it even though I was sure I hadn't. I told her I lived in Chicago and was a trader and didn't want to be a trader, but the money was good and it was a question of how long I could stand it. She'd been to Chicago and thought the El was wretched. I told her after a while you don't think about it.

Then there was the time when no one says anything.

"Do you know how his father is?" she asked finally.

"Not good," I said. "It's metastasized to the spine. They told Win he'd have to take him home next week. They can't do anything. They're surprised it's gone on this long."

"Has he talked to you about it?"

"No," I said. I laughed and she looked at me. I pointed at the slippery black Porsche ahead of us and said, "It's just not something he would do."

We arrived at the club, which was at the end of a long boulevard of plantation-style homes. You half expected to see slaves working in the lawns. Cars were parked for blocks along the surrounding streets, and people walked in small clusters along the sidewalks toward the entrance. Win drove right up to the gate and spoke to a guard. The guard leaned down and listened to Win, then shook his head. Win began gesturing with his hands, pointing back to us and then at the guard, and his head moved like he was agitated. Then he shoved the car into gear, screeched his tires, and shot the Porsche straight into the club.

Sandra pulled up to the guard and said, "We're with him," and I wondered if that was the best thing to say. The guard explained that because her car had no sticker, we'd have to park on the street. Sandra said, "He has our tickets and we don't know where to go," but the guard told her, "I'm sorry, you'll have to turn around now." Sandra said, "What are we supposed to do then?" and I said, "It's okay. We'll turn around." This surprised her because she hadn't finished with him, but she gave it up.

The club was nearly a mile away from where we parked, and Sandra was annoyed, but the houses were beautiful with deep quiet lawns and most of the walk was in the shade of wealthy oaks. A pair of twin ponies grazed on the lawn of the last house before the club. We stood and watched for a moment.

"Aren't they worried they'll run off?" she asked. There was no fence.

"I guess not," I said. "But I'm not sure it's legal to keep them in the city like this."

She grinned at me. "I know they're not worried about that."

We walked to the entrance of the club. When we saw the guard again Sandra traded eyes with him, but after we passed she said, "I suppose he didn't have a choice."

We followed the flow of people across the grounds, which were interspersed with rows of pink azaleas. The stadium was a small, tastefully green structure at the back of the club in front of a golf course. As we neared it, the noise of the crowd rose.

Vickie was waiting for us at the end of a long gallery between the stadium and the clubhouse where everyone collected before the match.

"I'm so sorry," she said. "Did you have to park far?"

I let Sandra field this question.

"It was fine," she said. "Jack and I had a decent walk in."

"It's amazing you found the club at all. Win drives like such a spaz. He's at Will Call now."

We stood and watched the people. Everywhere were kisses and hats and light-colored suits. Alcohol, linen, bow ties. It was the Sunlight Costume Ball. A white billboard announced the 63RD ANNUAL RIVER OAKS TENNIS INTERNATIONAL in large black letters, along with the players' names and scores from all the matches up to the final. Under each match was the amount of money at stake for that round. The winner of the final would receive fifty thousand.

Win showed up with the tickets and a fresh drink in each hand. He handed one of the drinks to Vickie and licked a small spill off his wrist.

"Jesus, Vicks," he said, surveying the girls, "your outfits are atrocious! They'll accuse me of running a bordello."

"What a thing to say!" Vickie slapped him hard on the shoulder and the jolt spilled his drink again.

A splash of frozen pink liquid hit the front of his shirt. He wiped at it with his free hand. "Jesus' baby sister!" he said. "We're a fine disgrace. I'll be barred from the grounds."

"Is he always this obnoxious?" Sandra asked.

"Audacity," he said, "is the seed of aristocracy, my dear. Care for a drink?"

He took us through a gate into an enclosure reserved for members of the club. People lounged in white iron chairs at round tables under white umbrellas. Women dressed like parrots gave orders to waiters in white jackets. A row of tent stands offered food of various nationalities. There was the green lawn and a pale wall and the clean blue gleam of a pool. And the feeling you did not belong.

Win and Vickie ran off to get our drinks. I felt someone grab my arm, and it was Sandra, and she said, "My god, will you look at these clothes?"

When she grabbed me, she startled me, and my foot slipped off the sidewalk and into a deep puddle where the lawn intersected the pavement.

"I'm so sorry," she said, clutching my forearm with both her hands. I pulled my foot out and my right shoe was coated in mud. Next to me was an orange cone indicating not to step there.

"It's okay," I told her. I felt cold water seeping into my sock. I tried to wipe the mud off on the grass, but there was too much of it. Sandra found some paper napkins and I limped over to an empty chair and began wiping at my shoe.

"I hope they're not ruined."

"Just the one," I said. She looked down at me fearfully, then realized I wasn't serious. "Really, it looks better than the clean one."

It wasn't long before I had wiped the mud evenly across the surface of my shoe and was holding a wad of sopped napkins. There was nowhere to put them.

"Let's just leave it," Sandra said. "One of the waiters will pick it up." But I felt awkward about it, so she wandered with me through the crowd of gorgeous people, in search of a garbage receptacle. My foot was cold now, and squished conspicuously with every other step. There were no receptacles, but we found Win and Vickie at the front of the drink line.

Win couldn't stop laughing about it. "I can't leave you anywhere," he said. Sandra said, "It was my fault, Win. For god's sake," but he just kept on laughing, and it was funny, and Vickie saw that it was funny, and then all of us were laughing except Sandra, who still felt bad, until she looked down again at my shoes, and then she said, "It's still not funny. I feel terrible," but she was laughing when she said it.

Win signed for our drinks at the bar, and we headed to our seats. I was still holding the napkins, and Win told me to hand them to a waiter. I said no, I'd find a garbage can somewhere, but he called one of the waiters over and instructed him to take care of the napkins for me. The waiter took them from me, and when I thanked him, he said, "You're welcome, sir," but he looked less than pleased about it.

"He pegged you as a guest," Win said. "No self-respecting member would've thanked him."

We walked back through the gallery to the stadium, and an usher took our tickets and escorted us to Win's father's box, which was designated by a sign that read Winfred H. Maddox III. Every box had a sign like that, most of them suffixed with a Jr. or roman numerals. I sat with Sandra in front of Vickie and Win.

The court was a dirty baked orange. The players had taken their sides already and were warming up. You could hear the clay crunch under their feet as they moved about the court and stepped into each shot. Federer was the younger player, with a nest of long blond hair that whipped like a horse's tail when he swung his racket. His body was lean, arrogant, and unbattered. Grosjean was more reserved than Federer. His short black hair and dark eyes gave him a melancholy appearance, but his movements were light and deliberate.

The stadium seated around four thousand, most of them still in the gallery. Their noise filtered up through the green boards under our feet. The boxes were nearly empty.

"They'll stay that way until the second set," Win said.

"What about the match?" I asked.

"They're not here for the match, Jack. The match is here for them."

He explained that the court was made to look like French clay, but was actually crushed limestone. "They dye it to make it look like the real thing. But the French is a redder surface. It's made of brick dust, so it's a finer grain. This stuff is gravel and plays a lot faster even though they scrape the top layer off."

"Who do you think will win?" Vickie asked.

"Federer is too strong. Grosjean is a smart player, and he can make it close. But he can't win."

"And how do you know that?" Sandra asked.

"It's a matter of realities." He told them about the injury. I kept looking at the stain on his shirt, wondering why it didn't look ridiculous. "A year ago even, Grosjean might've beaten him. But Federer is stronger now, and Grosjean is only older. He can't win. The leg will prevent it."

"Well," Sandra said, "I hope he proves you wrong."

"Yes," Vickie said. "We should cheer for Grosjean."

"We'll all cheer for Grosjean," Win said. "How 'bout it, Jack? *Vive la France?*"

"I'm game."

The tennis was well played. Grosjean was overmatched at the start, and Federer took an early lead. His shots were strong and heavy and he kept the points short.

"His game is power," Win said. "Power's the first weapon they learn, but it's the weakest. Grosjean will adjust if he wants to."

The crowd was distracted. People talked and moved about during play and I waited for the umpire to say something, but the tournament was merely an exhibition and didn't count toward the players' rankings. There was a staged quality to it all, the feeling that the people had come to watch each other more than the tennis. We sat in Win's father's box under permanent shade and watched the players slide on the orange clay. Even in the shade it was hot and there was no breeze to relieve us. Win and I took turns buying fresh rounds of drinks. He told me to go back to the members' bar and just sign his name and number on the ticket, but instead I dragged the obscenity of my shoe to the concession stand in the public gallery and paid with cash. We played a game to see who could return with the most exotic drink. Win beat me every time because the concession stand didn't have a full bar. His trump card was a cloudy concoction known as planter's punch.

"What the hell is in this?" I asked him.

"Motor oil."

The general public sat on the far side of the court on a temporary grandstand with no awning. They sweated and burned in the heat, and the sun's light reflected off their sunglasses and annoyed us. We chatted between points. I heard several people refer to Federer as "the Swede." When I showed up with four margaritas, Win took a long sip and then said, "Christ, man, show some imagination. The Amish drink margaritas!"

After Federer won the first set, Win took Vickie to find food, and I was left alone with Sandra. I enjoyed being around her, but I sometimes had to remind myself who was sitting next to me. Every time my attention fell to the match or to Win, I'd forget, and when she spoke or laughed at something, it was always a surprise to me that it was Sandra. She became the girl who was not Lauren.

She said to me, "Your friend is vicious."

"Yes. More to himself than anyone."

"Do you suppose he's right?" she asked. "About the match, I mean."

"I don't know," I said. "Probably."

"He says ugly things."

"Sometimes."

"I'm not sure I like him."

"You should tell him."

"Be serious!"

"He'd tell you."

She laughed. It felt good to make a woman laugh again. I tucked my unclean shoe under the chair.

"I'm sorry about what you're, you know . . . going through."

"I'd rather not talk about it."

"I realize. I just knew you knew Win told me, and I didn't want to pretend."

"Thanks," I said.

What can I say about Lauren? Once, I spent a weekend with her in Massachusetts. We stayed in a cabin suite at a small inn on the Cape. In the daytime, we drove from town to town, stopping every so often to stretch and catch the flavor of a place. The towns were old and you could walk the length of each in minutes. The shops and restaurants occupied houses strung along main streets, and we walked among the people and didn't worry because there was no one to find, nowhere to be getting to, and it was all of the moment. We went inside the stores, but didn't buy anything. Sometimes, I pretended to be distracted by a painting for sale or a title in a shop that sold used books, and I let her walk ahead of me so I could watch her. People passed right next to her on the sidewalk and still missed it. Knowing her was like knowing a secret. She was beautiful and thin and what she loved was always simple: the walking, the sunlight, the cool raspy feel of the air so close to the sea. She loved the twists of the road and the view of the trees along its curves and the pale sky behind them. She had to point these out to me.

Win and Vickie returned with drinks and penne. The pasta came in little cardboard containers with stiff plastic forks. We were all hungry, and it was good to have food on the tongue and a sweet drink. We ate and watched the match.

A very old man with silver hair combed back in wet, greenish waves, and wearing a seersucker jacket, tapped Win on the shoulder.

"How's that father of yours?" he asked. He was a fat old man. It looked like it would take him half an hour to walk out of the stadium. Patches of white whiskers glistened on his pink jaw where he'd missed shaving that morning.

"They've got him on an epidural," Win said, standing up. "He's coming home Wednesday."

"What are they giving him?"

"Fentanyl. The morphine wasn't cutting it." There was a casualness of tone between them, as though they were discussing an old car with a failing transmission. "Of course, he doesn't want any of it. Or thinks he doesn't."

"Raising a bit of hell, is he?"

"Said he's only lending me these tickets."

"Well, see that you don't get comfortable, then." They laughed, and the old man shook Win's hand, then cut the laugh short and pulled Win close to his striped girth. He raised an eyebrow and stared hard at Win more with one eye than the other. "You give him my best now. Understand?"

"Absolutely," Win said. He was smiling.

The match went on during all of this.

The man clapped Win on the arm and shuffled toward the exit, clinging to the rail in the way of old men who can no longer find good footing. He offered a final piece of advice over his shoulder: "Hope your money's on the Swede."

Win sat back down and said, "I'm in the mood for a comeback."

The stadium had filled considerably by now, and the crowd settled its attention on the match. Federer was a grunter. He struck the ball with a certain brutality, as though he were angry it had been returned, and when he made contact, he expelled a hollow growl that covered the sound of his shot. Grosjean, though, was elegant. He was silent and effortless, and you heard the strings on his racket *fong* when they met the ball. There was a flare to his game, a fluid simplicity that drew me to him. The crowd, though, was mostly in favor of Federer. Win said this was because Federer had played at River Oaks before anyone knew him, and now that his name was beginning to be known, the crowd appreciated his willingness to return to their little tournament. "A few come back on their way down," Win said. "But it's rare."

Both players moved and placed the ball with precision, but Federer's game was founded on aggression, whereas Grosjean's seemed composed of a weary inevitability. It was the difference between dogma and philosophy.

In the second set Grosjean hit several terrific shots to keep the match close. The sun had fallen behind the awning and a broad shadow crept across the court. The players moved from shade to sunlight and back into shade again, and it was difficult to follow the ball as it passed through the changing light. The wind picked up. Grosjean seemed to handle the change in elements better than Federer, who lost a pair of long rallies with loose shots. Grosjean took the set with a backhand lob that caught Federer too close to net, sailed easily over his head, and clipped the back line behind him.

A segment of the audience rose and applauded. People whistled and yelled the players' names. Sandra stood up in front of Win and shouted a few cheers. There was a nervousness to things now, and for once the crowd seemed to lose sight of itself.

"He's decided to make it real," Win said.

But it was never real for Federer. The third set was brilliant tennis, but you could tell the Swede was holding back. There was a hollow look to his game, as though he were doing only what was necessary. Grosjean mixed the points well, varying the pace and spin of the ball. He made some amazing shots, and Federer let him. More than once, Federer hit a shot that seemed a certain winner, but the Frenchman tracked it down with a silent, graceful sprint and placed it delicately out of Federer's reach. With all the dramatics, it seemed as though Grosjean should be way ahead, but every time we checked the score it was even.

"He's favoring the leg," Win said.

We watched the next two points.

"He isn't," Vickie said. "I don't see a thing."

"I'm not seeing it either," I agreed.

"It's there," Win said. "You have to know what you're looking for."

"You know what I think?" Sandra said. I could feel it coming. "I think you're being an ass because you want him to fail." She turned and looked right at him.

He was unperturbed. Vickie placed a hand on his forearm and said, "Please be civil, Win."

"Of course, I'll be civil. We'll all be civil." He grinned at Sandra and then at me. "You have to appreciate honesty when you see it."

"You could at least take him seriously," Sandra said.

"I do," he said. "More seriously than you take him."

They stopped talking then and turned their attention back to the match, but none of us felt comfortable.

The points grew even longer. Each player had learned enough of the other's habits that it took more time to gain an advantage. The sun was fully behind us now, and all of the court in shade. In the distance, a bluff of dark clouds was sneaking toward us. The wind had stiffened, and I knew I was cold, but I had such a stiff buzz going I couldn't feel it. The girls were sitting on their hands to stay warm. I wanted to leave and get another round of drinks. I wanted to leave and just leave. But Grosjean was beautiful and authentic, and more than anything else at that moment, I wanted to see him win the match. I'd decided Federer was a powerful sham, and I wanted him to pay for it.

"There it is," Win said again, after Grosjean missed a forehand. "See? How he hit that shot off his back foot? He couldn't step into it." None of us answered him. We had all seen it. "It'll be over now."

A few minutes later, with Grosjean trailing by a game and trying to pull even, there was an extended rally. Federer controlled the point from one spot on the court. He moved Grosjean from side to side, slugging the ball at sharp angles. Grosjean ran in quick choppy steps. He slid his way into every shot, then scrambled to get back in position. He looped deep defensive strokes to keep Federer at bay, but he was forced to cover more of the court as the point wore on and you couldn't help looking for the leg to give. Then Federer struck a perfect ball, a quick dipping shot at such a severe angle there was no way Grosjean could reach it. But he ran anyway, with no regard for what is possible, and there was a strain in his voice as he stretched for the ball, the first sound we'd heard from him, and he reached the ball, *he reached it,* and laced a running forehand down the line. The crowd buzzed at the shock of it. Federer had no play because he hadn't believed he'd need one. He watched the ball sail past him and land flawlessly in the back corner of the court.

There was a beat of silence before the line judge called it long. People in the stands muttered at one another in confusion. Grosjean approached the net and asked the umpire to check the mark. The umpire got down from his chair and trotted to the area where the ball had landed. He said something to the line judge and the line judge stepped forward and pointed to a mark. The umpire examined the mark and confirmed the call that the ball had been out.

There were a few suspicious groans.

"That's not the mark," Win said. He was right: The linesman had selected a mark from earlier in the match. The umpire climbed back into his chair and announced the point in favor of Federer.

"That's not the mark!" Win shouted. There were murmurs of agreement. He stood up and stepped between my chair and Sandra's and leaned over the rail of the box. "It's the wrong mark, I said!"

Grosjean didn't protest. He took his place at the line for the next serve and waited for the noise to settle.

"Advantage Federer," the umpire said. "Players are ready."

"No one is ready," Win shouted, "until you correct the call!"

People began staring at Win, who showed no sign that he knew or cared. Grosjean tapped the ball against the ground with his racket.

Federer stood waiting to return service. Neither of the players looked in Win's direction. "Quiet, please," the umpire said. "Players are ready."

"The ball was good!" Win screamed. His face was calmer than his voice.

Someone in the crowd said, "Sit down, Maddox."

Vickie put her hand on his. Sandra and I stood up from our seats and backed away.

"Win, baby," Vickie said. "Let them play."

He pulled his hand away.

"The call was bogus!" he continued. She put her hands on his shoulder this time, and tried to whisper something in his ear, but Win shook her off and pointed at the umpire. "Ask anyone in this stadium if that's the mark," he said. "Ask him!" He pointed at Federer. "Ask your Swede there and I'll shut up."

"Ladies and gentlemen, please take your seats," the umpire said. And again, "Players are ready." There were some boos for Win now, and a few scattered comments—from, I supposed, people who knew him—that he should leave. I saw a policeman talking to the usher who had seated us. The umpire nodded and the cop came down the aisle toward us.

"Can't you see?" Win shouted. "Any of you? Can't you see what's happening here?" The umpire ignored him and waited for the cop. "The man is doing something genuine, goddamn it! And you've gone and wrecked it."

The policeman reached our box and looked at me and I stood up and said, "Win." I said it in such a way that he heard me. He turned and looked at me, at the cop, and at Vickie and Sandra, and at all the people staring at us. Then he smiled like it was all a joke.

"Officer," he said, pointing at me. "I'm glad you're here. This man's shoe is covered in mud. As you can see, that sort of thing isn't allowed in here."

The cop said to Win, "You'll need to come with me, please, sir."

Win slumped his shoulders in a posture of concession. His face took on an expression of terrible guilt. He raised a hand to his eyes and rubbed them with his thumb and forefinger, then looked directly at the cop and said, "I'm not going anywhere until that fucker corrects the call."

The cop said, "Sir, why don't you just come outside with me." The players had gathered at the net. They watched us blandly and talked with their hands over their mouths. The cop gave Vickie a look and we all stepped out of the box except Win. "Let's not have this get ugly now," the cop said.

"It was ugly before you arrived. Taking me out of here won't fix that."

"Just the same."

"Yes." Win smiled like he was pleased by what the cop told him. "I suppose it is." He stepped out of the box and gave the cop a friendly tap on the side of the arm. Then we all made our way down the aisle together under the watch of offended eyes.

They forced us to leave the club, and Win offered no more protest. He gave me the key to his house and vanished with Vickie in his little black Box, which was just as well because Sandra had had enough of him.

Sandra suggested we go to dinner. She took me to a small café, but neither of us was hungry and we drove right by the place. We sat in her car outside Win's house and talked, but I wasn't in a mood for it and she realized that, or possibly she had no interest. Or both. The weather had tamped out the day's remaining light and I told her she should try and beat the rain home. She thanked me for my company and I apologized for same. I got out of the car and said good night.

I stepped inside and removed my shoes by the door. The mud had dried in silky streaks and was beginning to flake. The house was dark and cool and empty, and the silence set me further into a mood. I went upstairs and took a long shower until steam filled the room and the mirrors were useless. I fell asleep on the bed with a brush in my hand, the towel still wrapped around my waist, as the first darts of rain hit the windows. I never heard Win come in.

When I woke it was still dark out. My flight was early, and we left the house at five. The air was fresh and wet, and the driveway glistened under the house lights. Win rattled on about his exploits with Vickie after the tournament.

"She despises me," he said. "That's a fine enough reason to marry anybody." I sat stunned and exhausted in the passenger seat and sipped my coffee with both hands as it quivered in the cup. The road was clear of cars, and it was a smooth black ride to the airport.

"It was good you came," he said. He stopped the car in a zone of red stripes in front of the terminal. "Learn not to take it all so hard. The score's all that matters."

We shook hands.

I said, "Wish your father good luck for me." Win would never have said this.

"There isn't any left, kid." Always a goddamn smile. I got out with my bag and the Porsche screeched away before I'd finished closing the door.

Inside, I bought a local paper and waited at the gate. The sports section had a small article on the tournament, and I saw that Federer had won 7–5 in the third set. The article said only that the match had been close.

I sat in the airport and watched people walk by, dragging baggage on their way to everywhere. I thought about Win's father, then Grosjean, likely still asleep in bed. Or maybe he went to his hotel, showered and packed, headed straight for another city. A new tournament. The next fat chance. And I wondered if he knew he was finished. Was it all just the same to him, or was he kidding himself? If he received a letter saying, *I'm sorry, dear boy, this will never be enough,* would he still walk on the court and offer his best? What kept him going? Was he waiting for the sound of a voice?

RYAN EFFGEN

George Mason University

THE INAPPROPRIATE BEHAVIOR OF OUR ALLEGED LOVED ONES

There's one in every family. I want to say it's usually the youngest. I want to say there's one in every family, and it's usually the youngest, and this—our private little disgrace—is merely our own version of the private little disgrace that every family attempts, more or less, to conceal. The youngest in our family is Miriam, who yesterday filed a domestic abuse charge on Kole, her boyfriend of four months. I was sitting in my kitchen with my wife and my brother, Eric, and we were discussing the appropriate course of action.

"I'm going to kill the motherfucker," Eric said with a shrug, as if the matter were out of his hands. Eric was born big, and he wrestled in college. He could do some damage.

"I could be wrong, but doesn't domestic abuse imply that they're living together? Is Miriam living with Craig?" Lynn, my wife, asked as delicately as she could. She was sitting on a chair and running her hands over her belly. She was very pregnant, practically overdue.

"Wait, what's this prick's name? Craig or Kole?" Eric asked.

"It's Kole," I said. "And they've been living together for a while, yes."

"Not anymore, they're not. His living days are over," Eric said.

"He's a son of a bitch, there's no question," I said. "But there's more to the story."

"No, there isn't." Eric took a long sip of his beer. "He hit your sister. That's all you need to know."

Eric had a point. He definitely had a point. But still, I was going to think this through. I wanted to sleep on it. Eric exploded when I said that.

"That's fucking perfect. When the shit hits the fan, you take a nap."

"I'm just saying we need to be rational," I said. I looked to Lynn for approval, and she gave me a little nod.

"Come on, mister psych professor—this is your chance to bust out some Hannibal Lecter shit on this guy," Eric said.

"Bust out some Hannibal Lecter shit," Lynn repeated slowly, raising her eyebrows.

I'm an adjunct, not a professor—a frequent mistake that I rarely correct. I spend most of my time in a lab, conditioning pigeons to respond to lights and pictures. Not exactly applicable to the situation at hand, but since Eric had brought it up I played that card. "You want to hear a behaviorist's take on this? Kole has exhibited deviant behavior. Miriam, somewhat miraculously, has done the correct thing by reporting this deviant behavior to the authorities. The authorities will apply measures of negative reinforcement in an attempt to shape Kole's behavior to an appropriate mode of conduct. Done deal."

"Are they going to take his pigeon food away?" Lynn said.

"I mean it," I said. "Miriam took it to the cops. That's that."

Eric exhaled loudly.

"Think about it, Eric. If you go down there and do something to him, what effect will it have? It'll make you feel better, but it won't help Miriam." I still call her Miriam, though for years she's gone by Mimi, which, phonetically, couldn't be any more appropriate.

Eric's beer can made an empty sound when he set it down. He gave me a disappointed look, turned his head away, and made a big display of walking out of the room. He stopped at our front door and turned to me.

"Let me tell you something. I promise you right here and now that if someone ever fucks with you, or fucks with Lynn, or fucks with Connor, I won't sleep on it. I'll kill the motherfucker."

Connor is the name we've picked. We saw his little unit on the ultrasound.

"Because we're family," Eric added. Then he left.

"Drive safe," Lynn called after him.

From our front window, I watched Eric climb into his Dodge Durango and drive off. I tossed his beer can in the recycling.

"So," Lynn said, "you said there was more to the story." She repositioned herself, straightening her back against the chair.

"Know why we could never remember if the new guy's name was Craig or Kole?"

"Oh."

"Yeah," I said. "I know it sounds terrible to say this about one's sibling, but it seems clear to me that she brought all of this on herself."

"Still—that's no excuse. Is she all right?"

"She was hysterical when she called. She was on the expressway, shouting something about Kole. I could only make out every third word. Then she says, 'Kole hit me.'"

Lynn sat up and retied her bathrobe.

"But you got her to take it to the police?"

"First I got her to pull over. You know how she drives. So she pulls over and she really starts talking. She told me too much, I think. Kole finds out about Craig. They're friends, or they were. Some other girl brought everyone up to speed. So Kole confronts Miriam. Miriam tries to laugh it off, and he hits her."

"That's horrible," Lynn said.

"When she was telling me all this, a cop pulled up to see why she was pulled over. So she gives him the entire story, too. She left the phone on; I heard all of it twice. She also told the cop too much, I think. But that's how they got involved."

"Do you think Eric's going to do something?" Lynn asked.

"Eric? He'll cool off," I said.

"If you say so."

She started to get up. I went over to help her.

"I got it, thanks," she said and walked slowly toward our bedroom.

I'm guessing that Lynn felt she couldn't say anything. We have a rule: Only I can trash my family, only she can trash her family. And we do plenty of trashing. We have several people in our lives that we can bring ourselves neither to love unconditionally nor to disregard entirely. So instead, we talk about them endlessly. This is how we typically spend the few hours of free time that we have together. We sit in the kitchen and we talk about the inappropriate behavior of our alleged loved ones. It's not always about Miriam. Sometimes it's about Lynn's father, who went on a business trip when Lynn was fifteen and never came back. A few months after we were married, she spotted him on Jay Leno, of all places. Leno was stopping people on the street, asking them if they knew what the phrase *magna cum laude* meant. Lynn's father thought it meant "with ice cream." Lynn will sometimes order a piece of strawberry rhubarb pie *magna cum laude*—we always laugh when she does it, but it's a joke that only she's allowed to make. Sometimes we talk about my father, who closed himself off after my mom died, who never left anybody, who hardly ever left the house, who hardly said a word. Sometimes we talk about Lynn's sister, Elizabeth, who's married to a cardiologist, and who refers to our house as "cute" when she comes over. And we talk about Eric, when he's not around, and how embarrassed we feel for his wife when he starts going off on racial issues, as he tends to do after a few drinks.

But it's Miriam who keeps supplying us with new material. Miriam who disappeared with the photographer at our wedding; we have only four pictures from our reception—two are of her. Miriam who, when caught shoplifting at Nordstrom, claimed to have a sick relative in another time zone—hence the second wristwatch on her arm. Miriam who is determined not to learn from her mistakes— who can't seem to comprehend that her actions have consequences.

Would it change Eric's take on things if he knew the whole story about Miriam and Kole and Craig? I don't think it would. *Because we're family.* Frankly, Eric doesn't think that much of Miriam. But it's instinctual, I suppose. Pigeons, to take an example that I'm forever taking, are extremely protective of their young. Both the mother and father sit on the eggs, both the mother and father produce pigeon milk—a sort of nutritious vomit that they pass into their babies' mouths. They don't let them leave the nest until they're full grown. This is the answer to a question my students frequently ask: *How come we never see any baby pigeons?*

That night I lay next to Lynn and looked at the mound of sheets that her belly made. *If anyone ever fucks with Connor*—I tried to imagine someone pushing around the little guy that we saw on the ultrasound. It seemed unlikely. But someone would fuck with him, eventually. Not for years, but it would happen. Someone will do something violent or humiliating to him. Was someone going to fuck with Connor? No question.

And what would I do about it? I had never been in a fight. Not a real one, anyway. Lying there next to my pregnant wife, I felt useless.

Her body was changing, she was carrying our child. Aside from the conception itself, I had hardly done anything for Connor worth mentioning. And even my small role in the conception was less than admirable. Lynn and I had been trying for a while, and something about deliberately trying to conceive made sex anticlimactic. On the night in question, amid thoughts of basal body temperature and cervical mucus, an image formed in my mind: Karmen Lindsey. Karmen is a student assistant at the lab. She's slightly smarter than the pigeons whose cages she cleans, but at the moment of passion I was struck with an image I had never considered—Karmen Lindsey, naked beneath her unbuttoned lab coat. In my fantasy she emerged from a thin haze of steam rising from various test tubes and beakers. My eyes panned downward from neck, to breasts, to crescent belly button, to respectably trimmed mons pubis, to thighs, to knees, until finally, inexplicably, they landed on a pair of pink Converse All Star high-tops. And thus Connor was conceived.

Lying there beside Lynn, I tried to imagine protecting Connor. I could hypothesize scenarios where I heroically came to his aid, but these were untested, worthless. Then I got to thinking about Miriam. Our alarm clock, which I kept sixteen minutes fast, read 2:32 A.M. I hadn't slept. I hadn't slept on it. And I decided I wasn't going to.

I can't say that I had anything specific in mind when I left our house. I was clear and alert. I used the turn signal when pulling out of our driveway. I kept it right at the speed limit, even when I got onto I-25 South, which I had pretty much to myself. I stayed in the slow lane, eyes front, hands on ten and two. My colleagues working in cognition would challenge me on this, but I can almost swear that I didn't have a single thought. It was something different. It was more like a continuous sense of appreciation. There was something satisfying about the symmetry of the white and yellow lines. Everything was clean. Everything tingled. As miles passed, I felt, without thinking it,

that there was no separation between the sparkling highway paint
and my headlights that reflected it and my retinas that received it. I
kept my eyes forward. I hardly blinked.

Then the gas light came on.

Most of the routine experiments that I re-create for the edification
of undergraduate psychology majors (99 percent of whom will end
up in sales or marketing) involve conditioning animals to respond to
the appearance of a picture or a light within their cages. I give frequent reminders that the lab is a controlled environment in which
you can discover cause-and-effect relationships without ambiguity;
the real world is messier. Nonetheless, the gas light appeared and I responded. Had this mission been premeditated, it would have occurred to me that the six-hour drive from Denver to Santa Fe would
inevitably involve a pit stop. Before I could develop any serious
running-out-of-gas-in-the-middle-of-nowhere scenarios, I passed a
PUEBLO 28 MILES sign.

I took the first exit and pulled into a combination Citgo/7-Eleven.
It was warm outside and there were loud crickets. I swiped my card
and filled up. Inside, the lady behind the counter was staring at a
small black-and-white TV that was probably intended to be part of a
security device but instead was playing *Happy Days*. I walked into the
shop right as the Fonz walked into Al's. A round of shrieks and applause followed the ding on the shop door. The lady looked me over
as if the timing were somehow presumptuous on my part.

A sign warning against the risk of BRAIN FREEZE! was hanging
above the Slurpee machine. I filled up the biggest cup they had with
Blue Shock Mountain Dew and then carefully paced the three tiny
aisles. Had the lady been watching me on the security camera rather
than watching the Cunninghams, I might have appeared to be brows-
ing. I wasn't. A combination of the fluorescent lights, the blasting
AC, and the squeaky floors put me in lab mode. I was observing. In

my office I have a three-by-five card with a B. F. Skinner quote: "The human species, like other species, is powerfully reinforced by sugar, salt, and sexual contact." They were evident everywhere in the store— Ho Hos, Ding-Dongs, Twinkies, Planters Peanuts, Chili-Cheese Fritos, Rold Gold Pretzels, blistered hot dogs, and *taquitos*—cylindrical tacos spinning on Teflon tubes. At the magazine rack, silicon-breasted girls appeared on the covers of *Maxim, Stuff, Penthouse,* and *Playboy.*

Then I spotted the word *pigeon*—it was one of a few captions on the cover of *Guns & Ammo.* "Clay Pigeon Championships in Baton Rouge." A lady looking through the scope of a rifle was on the cover. A sidebar article gave a brief history of clay pigeons, which began as an alternative to the nonclay variety. Every year the student paper at Denver criticizes the psych department for using animals in experiments. We even get the occasional protest. The task of writing up a response, outlining the history of animals in psychological tests— Pavlov and his dog, Thorndike and his cats, Skinner and his rats and pigeons—fell the way of most menial tasks: to me. I thought that a paragraph on some of the other uses of pigeons—namely, as target practice—would make our routine of messing with their heads seem less diabolical. So I brought the magazine and my Slurpee up to the counter.

"Is the Fonz taking care of business?" I asked.

She answered me without looking up. "Some mobster's trying to muscle in on Al's. The Fonz is the only one who'll stand up to him."

"He's the man," I said. The Fonz coolly snapped his fingers, ever in control of the situation. His clean, white T-shirt glowed on the black-and-white screen.

She rang me up.

When I got back on the highway I got to thinking about Miriam. She was seven when our mom died. I cried at the funeral. I knew that

I was sad, but I also remember feeling obligated. Eric wept with his mouth clamped shut; his face turned dark red as if he were holding his breath. Miriam just seemed distant. I remember that, while our grandma was talking to the three of us, Miriam stood up and crossed the room to the grand piano in the corner of the funeral parlor. She sat down at it, posed like a somber concert pianist, and played the first seven notes of "Old Time Rock and Roll"—*da-na-na-na-na-na-nuh*. It was the only thing she could play. She played it over and over as our aunts and uncles walked by the casket, until finally Aunt Eileen led her away as discreetly as she could. Then Miriam went to the dessert table, grabbed a tray of macaroons, and locked herself in the bathroom.

The following day someone from the funeral parlor called our house. Apparently they had found I HATE GOD written in child's handwriting in the registry. I later got it out of Miriam that our neighbor, Mrs. Shultz, had told her God was the cause of all things.

A famous experiment that I re-create for my students touches on the mental habit of connecting cause and effect: B. F. Skinner's "Superstition in the Pigeon." He originally performed it in 1947—ancient history, really, but it's always a surprise to my students. It goes like this: A pigeon is placed in a Skinner box, a small, confined cage free of distracting stimuli. A food hopper swings down at fixed intervals, allowing the pigeon to stuff its face until the hopper swings back out of reach. That's the setup. Here's what happens: Pigeons keep doing the last thing that they did before the food appeared. The students' job is to observe and record the pigeons' operant conditioning. *Glenda turns counterclockwise. Cromwell tucks his beak under his wing. Paco does this funky head-bob thing like he's listening to Sly and the Family Stone.* No matter what the repeated behavior is, the pigeon infers a causal relationship between its own actions and the appearance of the food—it thinks that shaking its tail, bobbing its head, etc., made the food appear.

I took a long sip from my Slurpee and was struck with a sudden, severe case of *telalgia*—more commonly known as brain freeze. Under different circumstances I might have described the sensation as being stabbed in the back of the head with an ice pick. But I think it was the copy of *Guns & Ammo* on the shotgun seat that had me thinking of a bullet. This sparked a few things. I began to think about how Santa Fe would go. I got an idea involving a long-distance rifle, like the lady on the cover of *Guns & Ammo*. I imagined the scene through a scope. It's bright out. Kole is in a parking lot walking out to his car. He's wearing sunglasses and spinning his key chain in his hand. The moment he steps into the crosshairs his body is jolted, his arms fly back, and he falls to the pavement. Three or four pigeons scatter into the air.

That was as far as I had gotten when I saw flashing red and blue lights ahead. An ambulance and a police car were stopped, blocking off the highway. I was the only other car there. There was an accident—a motorcycle was on its side, one of the handlebars bent upward, a mess of reflector plastic and bits of mirror scattered on the pavement. They had a man on a stretcher. I heard one of the cops say into his radio, "Rider had apparently lost control of the bike—" Most of his face was bandaged, one of his legs shook wildly, the other was still. The paramedics took their time rolling him into the ambulance. I lit a cigarette and waited. When they took him away, the cops set up flares around the bike and motioned me through.

The sky went from black to blue black as I crossed the state line. The mountains thinned out into patches of desert and as the sun slowly came up the rocks turned from purple to dark red. By the time I hit the Santa Fe city limits, it was light out. It occurred to me that

Kole wasn't going to be there. Not at Miriam's apartment, anyway. I figured Miriam would probably know where he was staying—at his own apartment if he had one, or with friends. Probably not with Craig.

I didn't know Miriam's address. Lynn and I had visited, but that had been months earlier, when Lynn was just beginning to show. I pulled into a Dunkin' Donuts, where I could see a pay phone and phone books through the window. My legs felt stiff and icy when I stepped out of the car. I found Miriam's address and wrote it down on a page that I had torn from *Guns & Ammo*. Her place was just a few blocks away; I found it no problem.

When I knocked, it was Kole who answered.

"Joshua?" he said.

"Oh," I said. "Are you Kole?"

He nodded. I hadn't actually seen Kole before. He was tall. Athletic, but not the grunting jock that I had been imagining. He needed a shave, but otherwise he looked clean-cut.

"I recognize you from your picture," Kole said. "Mimi's got pictures on the fridge. Why don't you come in?"

He held the door open.

"Where is she?" I asked.

"She just stepped out to pick up the Sunday paper. We both were up all night." He closed his eyes, shook his head for a moment, and gave me a searching look. "You're the one she called, right?"

"That's right, Kole," I said.

"Look, I'm sorry," he said. "Of course I'm sorry, but I mean— crap, I'm going to make a mess of this, I know. I haven't slept a wink and—" Then he looked over my shoulder out toward the parking lot. "Did you drive down here?"

"That's right, Kole," I said.

"You must have been up all night, too. Hey, why don't you come inside and sit down. I just put on some coffee. Miriam will be back in a minute. Come on." He waved me in.

We sat at the coffee table. Their ashtray was filled with half-finished cigarettes. The television was on with the sound turned low.

"Joshua, would you allow me to say a few things?"

"Let's hear it," I said.

"Well, for starters, I love Mimi. Really, I do. I don't have to tell you—"

"So why did you hit her?" I said. I took out a cigarette and set the pack on the counter. The magazine page came out with it. Kole gave me a surprised look.

"Wait, did you just pull out a picture of a gun?" he asked.

It was an advertisement for a Biakal .22 semiautomatic target pistol. The photo included a target—a blackened silhouette of a man with bullet holes in the face and neck.

"It's nothing. Just a scrap of paper I wrote Miriam's address on."

"So, what did you come down here for?"

I didn't say anything for a moment, but found myself focusing on the ad copy: *This gun is designed for one purpose: offhand target shooting.*

"You hit my sister," I said.

Kole stood up. And then I stood up.

"Um, I was just going to get the coffee." He pointed to the kitchen. "Do you still want some?"

"Oh. Yeah, sure." I sat back down.

Kole brought over two cups of coffee and a little Crate and Barrel–looking cream-and-sugar set. He stirred some sugar into his coffee and was silent for a long time.

"You know, I'm surprised you came all this way," Kole said.

"Are you?" I tipped my cigarette on the ashtray.

"Yes, I am," he said. "I understand that you told Mimi that she brought this on herself."

"Excuse me?"

"Yeah, she told me. She says that she called you and you told her that she'd brought this on herself."

I started to say something but I dropped it. I was suddenly exhausted. It all caught up to me at once. I kept my eye on Kole. He was fading, too. We sat there not saying anything. An infomercial for shrink-wrap came on the television. I eventually nodded off. I had one of those dreams that come from sleep deprivation. I fell right into full dream mode, in medias res, as it were. I was back in the kitchen with Lynn. It wasn't our kitchen; it was the one from my parents' old house in Indianapolis. Lynn was no longer pregnant, she was somehow younger—she was the girl that I sat next to in a sociology class but never spoke to until I ran into her in the bookstore and pretended to reprimand her for selling back her textbook. She was talking. I don't remember what she was saying. I just remember sitting in our old kitchen and feeling incredibly happy.

Kole must have dozed off, too, because when the door opened we both sat up, startled.

"Josh?" Miriam said, closing the door behind her, a fat newspaper under her arm. Her left eye was dark and swollen. In the dreamy instant of reawakening I saw her eye and thought of a plum, the word *plum* came to my mouth, I started to form the plosive *p*—and I heard her say, "What are you—" Then it felt as if in one single motion the little cream-and-sugar set was firmly in my hand and then it came swiftly cracking down on Kole.

This brings us up to the present. Some of the events in between then and now happened as I would have expected. Miriam screamed. Neighbors, aware of the recent activity at Miriam and Kole's apartment, called the police. The police, expecting to find a repeat incident, practically kicked down the door. My small gestures of compliance (hands in the air, lots of *Yes, officers*) didn't impress them.

Kole was in no shape to say whether or not he'd like to press charges, but I was told that bits of ceramic had to be removed prior to sutures. So I'm taking that to mean, "Yes, I believe I will be pressing charges." This was all to be expected. All subjects exhibited predictable behavior under the circumstances.

What I didn't expect was no answer at my house when I called. It was nine thirty in the morning by the time I got to use the phone. No one home at Eric's. I tried Miriam and Kole's—she must have gone with Kole. I tried my place again and got an answer. It was Eric.

"Why the hell are you in Santa Fe?" he shouted. Caller ID.

I started to tell him, but he cut me off right away.

"Lynn had the baby," he said.

"What?"

"Yeah, she's at the hospital—she had the baby at six this morning. The kid's fine. Where the fuck are you?"

"What?" I said again.

"Lynn woke up with contractions and panicked when you weren't there. She finally called me, and I flew over here and got her down to St. Joseph's just in time."

"Jesus, well, thank you. She's okay?"

"She's fine. And congratulations," Eric said. Then he added, "You stupid son of a bitch."

So, to the expenses that come with a new baby, we get to add bail money, which we sure as hell don't have. Eric is going to help us out in that regard. He's making the drive down here right now, actually. In the meantime, I'm waiting here, in one of the four holding cells down at the West Santa Fe Police Department. There's a shirtless man sleeping in the cell across from me. The other two are empty. My cell isn't so bad, as far as cages go. Since Eric won't be here until later this afternoon, they've actually brought me some lunch. The food even looks decent, but I don't feel like eating. I'll likely spend the next few hours staring at it and going over the events prior to its appearance. One thing happened. Then another thing happened. Given the lack of distracting stimuli, I will predictably infer a causal connection between the former and the latter.

Miriam is sitting in a hospital nearby. Nurses are asking about her eye; she's telling them that she's just waiting for someone. Miriam is twenty-five years old. She's no longer a young person I need to worry about. Lynn is lying in a hospital bed with our son in her arms. He's perhaps aware, at some level, that he's with his mother—though oblivious to the absence of his father. The world will slowly come into focus. He'll learn to recognize Lynn's voice first, and then mine. He'll hear this story eventually. Not for decades, perhaps not even until he has a child on the way, but it'll come up. *Oh, you didn't know?* This is one that he can always pull out whenever he and whoever are sitting around some futuristic kitchen talking of all things inappropriate. I won't be there to correct him on the details; it just doesn't work that way. But there's one thing that I hope he remembers to include: His uncle Eric, who didn't think very much of me at the time—and likely doesn't think that much of me at all—drove six hours to come spring me. Granted, he probably spent those six hours thinking about what a fuckup his brother is, and how he doesn't have the time or money to come bailing people out of jail. But he did it anyway. That would be worth mentioning, I think.

KEYA MITRA

University of Houston

POMPEII RECREATED

Their mother's body, submerged in water, is yet to be found, Rumu's brother tells her over the phone. All he knows is that her house in Calcutta, India, was destroyed during the flooding of the Ganges, and neighboring families now wade through contaminated water looking for bodies of parents, siblings, and children. Rumu looks down at her skirt as though it is somehow responsible for her mother's death. The inside of her mouth tastes like rust. Are you sure she's really gone? Rumu asks before she realizes how ridiculous it sounds, the idea that her mother is amphibious, capable of surviving underwater, and will leap back onto shore after growing tired of aquatic life.

Rumu begins listing adjectives, as she frequently does when she's nervous. Unbelievable. Devastating. I'll fly to Calcutta, Rumu says, and he stops her. There's a good chance the body won't be recovered at all, and she certainly should wait until the flooding stops. No need to make a trip all the way from Houston.

Rumu and her brother haven't spoken in five years, ever since she moved to the States and he settled in England shortly afterward. Neither one has the energy to fill the long, flat pauses between them.

Rumu lies still on the bed with the phone resting on her thighs after she hangs up. She hears her daughter Putul shuffling items around in the kitchen, signaling a desire for companionship. Rumu exhales and walks into the kitchen. "Hello, my sweet girl," she says. In this one aspect of parenting, she is a success—she can make anyone, person or pet, feel luminous.

Putul and Rumu cook spaghetti for dinner. Though she watched her mother cook often in India, Rumu never learned how to prepare Indian dishes on her own. She slaps the bottom of the jar of meat sauce with a rhythmic, persistent anger, as though spanking a child.

"Who was that?" Putul has recently turned thirteen, old enough to notice that her mother rarely speaks to her relatives abroad unless bad news is involved. Good news is left for e-mail.

"Your uncle," Rumu says, still beating the bottom of the jar with her palm. The sauce trickles out—slow and obstinate. She puts aside the meat sauce for a moment and searches for the perfect midpoint of the spaghetti noodles before snapping them in two.

"The Ganges River has flooded."

Putul visited the Ganges last year with her grandmother, her Dadi, who told her that the water in the river was considered pure and holy. When Putul took off her sandals and tried to dip her toes into the water, balancing one foot tenuously on the bank, Dadi stopped her.

"Don't do that to an old woman in a wheelchair," she said. "You may fall in, and I won't be able to save you. Anyway, this water is filthy. If you ingest it, it will probably kill you."

"But you said it's holy water."

"That doesn't make it clean," Dadi said. "If we stand here long enough, we'll see a rotting cow float by. People throw dead livestock in here all the time."

Putul stood beside her grandmother, waiting for a cow to drift by them. When the body failed to show, she felt betrayed, as though a promise had been broken.

"Is Dadi okay?" Putul asks now.

Rumu says nothing. Her back turned to Putul, she drops the broken noodles into the water, which now bubbles over the sides of the pot.

Putul picks up the abandoned bottle of sauce, turns it upside down, and shakes it over a bowl. Her mother's attempts to protect her from tragedy are transparent. Rumu burned a turkey in the oven when she told Putul, years ago, that her father had "gone away on vacation."

"What happened to Dadi?" Putul asks again, her voice loud. A lump of meaty red sauce falls on her leg and makes its gradual descent down her calf.

"Go clean yourself up in the bathroom," Rumu says, her voice sharp.

Putul's resentment breaks out like a rash over her body. She leaves the room with her hand cupped over her leg as though nursing a bleeding wound.

Putul's spill relieves Rumu. Over the years, she's come to depend on everyday anxieties to preoccupy her and keep her from thinking of her past. When she divorced Sunil, her husband of six years, her mother refused to speak to her for a year and a half. Rumu's father died around the time that she separated from Sunil, and her mother become a vacancy, a body for rent.

"A lifelong companion is nothing to throw away," her mother said.

"We can't carry on a conversation," Rumu tried to explain. "We are too different."

But then there were those intimate details that Rumu didn't feel comfortable relaying over e-mail or the phone. She'd frequently find the toilet seat lifted, with Sunil's pubic hairs stuck to the edges, and felt intruded upon, as though the bathroom had been opened to the public. When the baby started crying and they were both studying— he for his medical school exams and she for her English composition exams at Rice—he'd never glance up, forcing Rumu to go to Putul's aid each time.

She was uncomfortable with the way he posed as an Episcopalian, despite his Hindu upbringing, at the local YMCA where he lifted weights. Each week he posted prayer requests on the bulletin board in the gym without ever truly grasping the idea of prayer.

"Please pray for my wife, who doesn't know how to cook actual Indian meals," he wrote. Then, a few days later: "Please pray for my wife, who has stopped cooking altogether and has put on twenty pounds eating Snickers and cake."

Every time Rumu found a message, she tacked on her own prayer request underneath. "God, please show my husband that his habit of reading medical journals while urinating is inadvisable."

The bulletin board provided a forum for aggressive flirtation, an illicit message trading never referred to at home. At dinner, Rumu snuck glances at Sunil as he ate with his head bent over his food, his glasses so far down his nose that they threatened to fall onto the plate. When Rumu posted a particularly feisty message, he'd move closer to her in bed, his shoulder grazing hers. She'd shift closer, barely, waiting for his breathing to deepen. She held her own until his fingers kneaded the skin on her upper thigh. It seemed, at those times, that they were strangers engaged in a fleeting affair.

For a short time, the YMCA suspended use of the bulletin board

because members were "misusing the board to post domestic com-
plaints." Three weeks later, the board was back in commission, now
with prominent, yellow cutout letters above it reading "POST YOUR
KIND PRAYERS." The notes stopped. When a week passed without
Sunil posting a note, Rumu knew, somehow, that it was over, that
coyness had run its course.

When Sunil left, his eyes were naked and wet. He'd taken off his
glasses, and in his eyes she could see the fear of a child leaving home
to attend school for the first time. The fear of deserting all that was
comfortable and known, the fear of leaving his last human connection with India. She'd taken him into her arms and whispered: "You
are my only friend."

Before her mother lapsed into the silence that lasted for nearly two
years and permanently strained their relationship, she said to Rumu:
"There is nothing that could hurt me more than a broken family."

Sunil moved to California for his residency after the divorce, and
his only contact with his daughter consisted of notes accompanying
his monthly checks, as though he believed his donations could buy
intimacy with her. Putul rarely asked questions about her father. Her
mother's premature wrinkles, half-white head of hair, and beaten eyes
conveyed enough.

Rumu scrubs at a spot of sauce on the floor with a wet paper
towel, longer and harder than necessary.

Putul bathes after dinner. She holds her breath underwater and studies her legs, which are a corpselike white, with dusty hairs swaying in
the water like minuscule tentacles.

After her bath, she goes to her room and wraps herself in the comforter so that it covers her entire body—her toes, arms, neck, everything aside from her face, which she presses into a pillow. When she
visited India last summer, mosquito nets hung from the posts of her

bed at Dadi's house. They seemed impenetrable, a barrier from the rest of the house, the world. She read books for hours in bed, behind the mosquito nets, as rain and wind beat against the windows or heat engorged the rest of the house. The sky outside was moody, bipolar. Elated one moment, tormented the next. Sometimes Dadi sat inside the tentlike cover of the nets with Putul and sang Bengali hymns to put her to sleep. Putul never understood all the words but lost herself in the tireless repetition of her grandmother's voice. Through half-closed eyes she'd peek at her grandmother, who was clad in a plain white sari with rolls of stomach fat protruding from underneath her blouse.

A picture of Dadi rests on her dresser. Though she passes by it every day, she hasn't examined it closely in nearly a year. In it, Dadi stands by her mother, and Putul's face is a tiny blur behind them. Putul makes it a habit to steal her way into photographs. Only the smallest fragments of her are caught—a swirl of hair in the corner of the picture or a leg—but the idea of her body present in other people's photos and lives thrills her.

Rumu enters the room, and Putul sits up. "What happened to Dadi?" she asks.

Rumu lies on the bed next to her, feet vertical, toes pointed at the ceiling. She still wears her suit skirt and white, tailored shirt. She takes comfort in formality.

"I don't know, baby. Her house has been destroyed. No one has found her yet."

"What if she's drowned?"

Rumu doesn't respond right away. "Your father and I went to Pompeii before you were born. Did I ever tell you that?"

"No," Putul says impatiently.

His family had given them money so they could travel every two months. Rumu and Sunil's marriage was arranged, and they barely knew one another. His parents hoped that one of the honeymoons would arouse enough passion to last for the span of a marriage. Sunil wore a cowboy hat to Pompeii and amused himself by speaking in a Texan accent loud enough that others could hear. "Looka ere," he'd say. "We don't see nuthin' lak thess in Tex-ass."

Rumu was disgusted by his need to prove to everyone that he was an American—and not just an American but a *Texan*. Tuning him out, she absorbed the ruins on her own.

She continues, "A volcano called Vesuvius erupted, and the whole city was destroyed. Somehow, the bodies were preserved, and casts were made of the people fleeing the city. You can see the expressions on their faces, even the clothes clinging to their bodies."

"That's disgusting."

"But they'll always be seen," Rumu says. "I imagine Dadi underwater, in a city where everyone is preserved the way they want, and she's the loveliest she's ever been."

"Is she dead?" Putul asks. Her mother often uses metaphors to dodge the truth.

"Think about what I said," Rumu says, propping herself up. She leaves the room.

Putul lies awake all night until the gray light of dawn creeps in through her window, an unwelcome visitor. She imagines Dadi floating alongside the dead cows in the water and wonders whether the cows will be preserved along with her, whether their bodies will no longer be diseased, but pure at last.

Rumu spends the night arranging letters from her mother into piles on her bed. When Rumu first moved to America with Sunil, she wrote to her mother in Bengali. But Sunil stopped speaking Bengali altogether early in their marriage and always communicated with Putul in English despite Rumu's protests. "She'll never learn Bengali if you keep talking to her in English," she'd say. Eventually she gave up. She began writing her own letters in English. Her mother wrote back in the same language, but it was unfamiliar to her, so her letters consisted of short, garbled paragraphs. Dadi frequently confused words like *chicken* and *kitchen* when she wrote, and Putul grew up reading the letters and assuming that her grandmother's mind was as incoherent as her English.

Rumu's mother eventually started speaking to her again after the divorce, but her tone was still guarded, her sentences clipped. "Your relatives—they have no sympathy for divorce," she said once. "They would have nothing to do with you here. You cannot raise a child without a husband."

At the time, she wanted to remind her mother she herself had virtually raised Rumu and her siblings alone. She read stories in Bengali to put Rumu to sleep. While her husband was away at work, she taught Rumu math, and afterward let her write stories about a golden elephant named Kaka who lost his way in Calcutta. But the idea of a single parent was intolerable to her mother.

Putul needs a father, Rumu decides, a man unafraid of his Bengali heritage. Then perhaps she can return to India, her husband at her side as she visits relatives, and her family will become whole again. That night, she begins researching candidates for husband on the Internet.

At school the next day, Putul contemplates the idea of a body preserved in a cast. With her dark skin and huge pink glasses, she has accepted her place in her group of friends as an adviser, an observer in the world of flirtation and surreptitious crushes. She sits with her head sunken into her neck at her desk in the hope that James Delaney, who sits behind her, will stop tossing spitballs into her hair. Every day, she tries to remain as invisible as possible, outside the target range of taunts. In class, Putul daydreams about dying an honorable death. Perhaps kidnappers will arrive in the classroom and drag James Delaney out of his chair. They will threaten to throw him off a mountain into a sea. With humble steps, Putul will walk to the front of the classroom and extend her arms. "Take me instead," she'll say, and James Delaney will flash tortured, sorry eyes at her. Later, her body will be found, and the entire school will celebrate her sacrifice and mourn her lovely corpse. Her beautiful body, overlooked in life, will be venerated by all.

Her body will be a monument in the school courtyard, preserved in heavy white stone. James Delaney will approach it in tears, throwing his arms around the torso of the statue. Arms splayed, chin tilted upward, head thrown backward, Putul prepares for impending corpsehood until the teacher calls to her: "Poo-tool? Are you paying attention?" James Delaney promptly throws another spitball into her hair. She asks permission to use the restroom. On the toilet, she arches her rear as she urinates in an attempt to emulate grace in even the most primitive of postures. In case the city is annihilated instantly, destroyed by a bomb or meteor, she needs to look gorgeous and pure. Her grandmother has set the precedent.

Putul wears a black, formal dress with heels at dinner that evening. She wore the dress last year for Halloween when she posed as a witch. She angles her nose toward the wall as she eats so she misses her mouth altogether and jabs the fork into her chin. If she dies immediately, artists surveying her preserved corpse will muse, "Look at the angle of her face. The girl spent so much time contemplating the world that she had no use for food. Look at how she raises the fork to her chin, so deep in thought."

"Putul," Rumu says. "What on earth are you doing?"

"Nothing," Putul says.

Her mother wears a bright red salwar khamese. Thick gray eye shadow clumps around her eyes, and a blackish red lipstick dulls the natural glow of her lips. Her mother has never worn a salwar here, and she rarely wears makeup, even while teaching her English class at the University of Houston.

"Why are you dressed like that?" Putul asks.

"I'm meeting a friend," Rumu says, standing to place the dishes in the sink.

"What friend?" Putul persists. She follows her mother into the kitchen, her arms glued to her sides, a smile plastered to her face. "A friend from the university?"

"No," her mother says. She brushes crumbs off her blouse. There was a "friend" in the department six months ago, her only sexual liaison since the divorce. For the first time, she'd started to almost approach orgasm, which may have been why she ended it. Elation was inevitably followed by guilt. "I'll be back in a few hours, my beautiful girl. Go to bed after you've finished your homework."

After she hears her mother locking the door, Putul turns off the lights in her room and lies flat on her bed. Her shadow on the wall is amorphous. She closes her eyes. The kidnappers force her to bathe naked with James Delaney, she imagines. They cover her in a white coating before placing her in the tub, and he can't recognize her. His green eyes wander over her. Putul's hands slide up her stomach in hard, desperate gropes. Under her lover's scrutiny she is small. She pulls her hand away as she remembers that she cannot give in to lust; she must prepare for preservation. Her eyes dampen. Even as her body tremors, the shadow on the wall stays still, too large to mirror subtleties.

Dadi lies at the bottom of a pool of water, preserved. Putul wonders whether life passes above her body so that it remains unobserved and half buried in sea-bottom mud, with orange, red, purple flecks of fish darting over her without pause. She goes to the bathroom, and, without turning on the light, fills the bathtub with water. She stirs the water with her hands, creating small splashes. Her feet resemble narrow rocks in the bottom of the tub. She is far from beautiful this way, Putul realizes. She cannot prevent her corpse from misrepresenting her, for there will be a moment where anger contorts her, sadness crumples her, her depression eclipses all. The skin on the bottom of her hands is shriveled and pruned, her body a listless brown. She thinks of Dadi's bloated body and desperately wants to fish it out of the water. She senses, somehow, that it has gone unnoticed by those swimming by.

The car is parked; that is done. Rumu treats the date like a checklist. With brisk footsteps, she silences her nervousness. At her university office this morning, she filled out the information for the Indian dating service as if it were a doctor's form. Occupation: English professor. Age: (here, she hesitated) early thirties. Ambiguity couldn't be pinned as dishonesty. When she arrived at marital status, she began answering "divorced" but typed in "single" instead. She'd been trained by her mother to deny her deliberate separation from Sunil, to tell others that he'd died a tragic death.

By the afternoon, Rumu had received a response. Single Indian male, 6'1", athletic, 180 pounds, 39, never married, lives at home. The fact that he lived with his parents captured her attention. The picture was conveniently blurry and presented a man wearing a Giants' baseball jersey and holding a football over his head. She wondered if he knew he was mixing sports and whether he'd been instructed by family or friends to wear as many team logos as possible to make his American athleticism known. By five thirty, they'd set up the date. Coffee. Starbucks. Eight fifteen. The fifteen was her addition. Somehow it made the date seem less rigid, less real.

She spots him immediately. The height he gave is about correct, minus three inches or so. If athletic, he's only so in spirit. He'd been sporting the oversized jersey in the picture for a reason; his belly swells under his shirt, too solid to be called mere pudge.

He wears a button-down shirt and wrinkled blue jeans, which are too short around the ankles and look hastily borrowed. When she sits down across from him, she senses by the slight raising of his eyebrows that he's impressed. Her light skin and hazel eyes are rare and coveted in India.

"My name is Udayan," he says. "But please call me Peter. Or Pete, for short."

"I'm Rumu."

The next twenty minutes consist of his self-justifying monologue. *It might seem strange that I live at home, but I'm actually very close to my parents; I may look large, but it's hard muscle; I've had many options to marry, believe me, but I am very picky.*

He speaks in a thick Bengali accent. He keeps his hands close to his face and sits with his legs pressed together too tightly as if trying to fight off the need to expel gas. Rumu studies him, desperate to find something familiar.

"And what caste are you from?" he asks.

"Pardon me?"

"What is your family's caste?"

Her stomach tightens under her costume. When she married, she'd been considered lucky to have been chosen by a Brahmin, a member of the highest caste. There had been another boy she'd known in college who was thinner, softer in tone, kinder. In her family, he didn't have a chance against Sunil's credentials.

They had fought often during the marriage. The reality of living with a woman appalled Sunil; once, he found a bloody tampon floating in the toilet and called her filthy.

"Well, you're a dirty bastard," she retorted, and he threw a dinner plate just above her head. Rumu stared mutely at the pile of glass as if the white splinters on the floor were her teeth, knocked out one by one. Sex with Sunil was like their fights—quick, with staccato movements, and stifling. Rumu called her mother once to complain, and she said, "It is hard, Rumu. But it could be worse. Some husbands burn their wives when they fight. Please try to work it out."

"Why would my caste matter? Especially here?" Rumu asks, her voice cold.

"I can't date a woman of a lower caste."

"What kind of car do you have? I don't date men with cheap cars," she says.

"My car isn't cheap," he says, pinching his chin with his thumb and forefinger. "What do cars have to do with your caste, anyway? This is a bit impertinent of you, don't you think?"

The one time Rumu visited Sunil's parents' house in Calcutta, she'd forgotten that a world existed outside of it. It was so far removed from the bustle of the streets beneath that it virtually eradicated their existence. She'd envied him. In her parents' house, the outside world had been ever present—the marshy land surrounding it, the mosquitoes sneaking in through open windows on particularly hot days. From her view on Sunil's balcony, the water was shallow, the world below distant and innocuous.

Peter clears his throat. "We'll discuss this later. Would you like to meet my parents?" he asks. "I only live a few minutes away."

Rumu agrees without considering this fully. Since the divorce, she's been quick, too quick, to ignore her own instincts.

As they walk toward her car, he rambles. "We should proceed as quickly as possible. Perhaps we can have dinner next week, and I can meet your parents," he says. "There's no need for delay. We're both adults."

"Proceed with what?" Rumu asks.

"The wedding," he answers. Rumu barely suppresses her laughter. "My mother has been impatient for a daughter-in-law. I'm apparently not enough for her," he says, his lips swelling into a childish pout. "She wants a girl to discuss makeup with, I suppose."

His cell phone rings, and he snaps it open. She sits in her car and waits as he leans against his car, cell phone in hand. The image of her mother's body floating in water alongside other corpses flashes through her mind, and she shakes her head to obliterate the thought. For a moment, she contemplates driving away, but then Peter places his phone in his pocket, indicating that the conversation has ended, and she follows him home, the scarf tight around her neck.

Putul rises from the tub and puts on a robe. She dials James Delaney's number with trembling fingers. A woman with a manicured voice picks up the phone, and Putul asks for James. When he answers the phone, Putul desperately searches for a way to express her willingness to sacrifice herself for him. *If I die tonight, it will be because I wanted to save you.* But the words seem flimsy and melodramatic in the safety of their suburban world. She hangs up the phone and stares at it for a long moment. On a pad of notebook paper, she writes in large letters: "For James. And Dadi, so she doesn't have to be alone" and leaves the pad next to the bathroom sink. Putul fetches a knife from the kitchen. She soaks again in the hot bath.

With quick, swift motions, she runs the blade over the surface of her thigh. The slit leaks blood but stops bleeding seconds later. Putul towels herself off and walks out of the bathroom. She catches a glimpse of herself in the mirror. She holds a knife too large for the tiny wound she created. There are not enough opportunities in the world for martyrdom, she thinks. The few positions available for those seeking the perfect death are filled almost immediately.

Her bathing suit, a pink bikini covered with green palm trees, hangs from the shower curtain rod. When she puts it on, her breasts bulge out of the thin bikini top. James Delaney's eyes occasionally rest on them when he passes her in the hall at school with a contemptuous sneer. She puts on her flip-flops, wraps herself in her towel, and walks down the two flights of stairs to the outdoor pool. She needs to be within view of another human being. The pool is lit up, the water a light, inconspicuous green. A man with a hairy chest floats on his back, eyes closed. His chest hairs lightly paddle against the current of the pool. Putul spreads herself out on a lawn chair. Her body is exposed, prepared for the impending abduction, ready for heroic surrender when he violates her. She wants, more than anything, to be touched.

But he doesn't once glance her way and keeps floating, his hands occasionally tapping the water in semiconscious awareness of his surroundings. The night is cold, and her half-exposed breasts are no longer smooth and sensual but dimpled, with goose bumps roughening the terrain of her skin. The man keeps floating, unaware of the June bugs propelling their way toward him. Putul dips her feet in the water, waiting for him to drift in her direction. She sits tall, her stomach sucked in and breasts angled toward the sky. She is certain that, at the very least, he will graze against her foot. Then, she imagines, he will ask her: *What are you doing out here so late? My grandmother died,* she'll say. He'll get out of the pool and wrap his arms around her, feeling the fullness of her body. Then he'll take her to his apartment so he can touch her anytime he wants, while photographs of her face with "Missing" underneath them are plastered on every kiosk in town. Her eyes will haunt the dreams of anyone who passes by the signs.

But when his head collides with her feet, the man wrestles with the water and stands upright. "Sorry," he says, looking at her with surprise. "I had no idea anyone else was here." He swims to the other end, his legs short and froglike. Putul prays for the man to return and brush against her with contempt or desire, any emotion driving him to touch her.

She itches with the desire to fetch Dadi's corpse from underneath the water in India and bring it here. Then, after they all die, they will be together, in their own Pompeii, despite their imperfections and impurities. Dadi and her mother will clasp Putul's preserved hands with their own, smiling. Here, they will finally be recovered; they will not be peripheral but large and looming and inescapable.

Putul can see each individual hair plastered to the man's torso, but she hasn't seen Dadi's body since her death. She wonders whether Dadi was wearing her gold bangles on her wrist when she died, whether her eyes had been open or closed, whether her hair had been knotted back into a bun or loose—thick and gray around her shoulders.

Peter lets himself into his house, and Rumu follows, stepping into a marble foyer with mirrored walls. The decorations stare at her. A wall hanging of an Indian dancer wearing a sari and beaded anklet. A large framed picture of a young woman standing by a man with a smile stretching to his cheeks. The walls in Rumu's house are bare, her mantel lined with only pragmatic items: matches, candles, a vase.

A woman emerges from the kitchen, clothed in a light blue salwar khamese. She is small, but her features have a wise severity to them. Her eyes are weary but kind. She places her hands on Rumu's shoulders. "Peter told me he was meeting you," she says. "You're beautiful. Just lovely. It's such a surprise you aren't married. My name is Deepa."

Peter's father follows her. He is short and portly, with bushy eyebrows raised too far above his eyes so he looks perpetually surprised. "My goodness, hello," he says. "Come into the kitchen. We're having samosas and tea."

At the table, Deepa and her husband sit close together and he places his rough, wrinkled hand over hers. Rumu's own mother and father never touched one another in front of her, and although her mother spoke of him with the highest regard, she never used his name. "He is the most intelligent man you'll ever meet," she'd say. Rumu's recollection of her father is a shadowy sketch of an artist, a humanitarian, a genius.

"Peter said you're an English professor?" Deepa says.

"Yes," she says. "I've been teaching for two years now."

"How fascinating. I am just now working on a Ph.D. in English. I'm focusing on postcolonialism. Naipaul, particularly. Such a condescending bastard, but a genius."

Deepa's husband smiles. The comment surprises Rumu. Her family regards a Ph.D. as a kamikaze mission.

"We moved with Peter when he came here to study engineering," Deepa continues, her eyes scanning and absorbing Rumu's face without embarrassment. "Our other children had already moved out, so we decided to come help him settle."

In her family, it would have been entirely inappropriate for Rumu to come unaccompanied by a husband. She imagines arriving with her mother, waking each morning to her warm face and powdery scent. She would have watched her mother live rather than visiting Calcutta and finding her feebler each time. The steam rises from her cup of tea, stinging her eyes. Rumu pushes it away.

"And your parents, my dear?" Deepa says. "Are they here or back in India?"

"They're both dead," Rumu says. "My mother died very recently."

It's the first time she's said it out loud, she realizes, as Peter places a clumsy hand on her shoulder. Her eyes swell. She expected to feel a jolt when her mother died. She expected the end of her mother's life to send some surge of sorrow her way that would survive the ocean between them. It hadn't. The distance, the surrealistic quality of her death, made it impossible to weep.

"I am very sorry," his mother says, setting down her cup. "How terrible."

"Yes, yes, terrible, absolutely terrible," her husband repeats in such a way that Rumu senses he often echoes his wife's sentiments. "Just terrible."

"I can see the strain in your eyes. It's so hard without family," his mother says.

"So difficult to not have family," her husband adds.

Rumu rises with a flurry of excuses: she has to work early; her stomach is weak; she forgot to take her medication. It is an ideal moment to leave; death makes exits understandable, even desirable. She tries to preserve the brightness on her face as she stands in the entrance, hand on the doorknob. As she starts to say good-bye, she notices another picture in the entrance. In it, Deepa, with a rotund stomach, is likely near the end of her pregnancy and stares straight into the camera. In Rumu's house in Calcutta, a similar picture of her mother rested on the mantel—a solemn photograph of a young woman, barely seventeen, with both hands over her belly as though covering a wound. Sunil had taken a similar photograph of her in her last trimester of pregnancy. Her hands were tight around her belly, as though trying to control the life growing within it. There was no joy in her pregnancy, only a dread of introducing a child to a country entirely unknown to her.

But in this photograph Deepa beams with ecstasy despite the weight of the load she carries. Joy was a possibility Rumu had never realistically considered. Resignation had been passed from mother to daughter like an old family heirloom.

"Rumu, you are a beautiful girl, a *shundor* girl," Deepa says, and, with a swift, single step, wraps her arms around Rumu in a fierce hug before she has the chance to shrink away. "Such a good girl," she says. "I read people well. You are so innocent, so pure." Rumu's face crumples along with her body as Deepa presses her body against hers as though Rumu is a dead battery she can charge with her warmth. Peter stands close behind, making plans out loud for their future. Rumu is much taller than Deepa, but her head rests on her shoulder. The tiny woman's body alone holds her upright.

Deepa's house is full and alive. When Rumu returned to Calcutta last year to visit her mother, the house had already half emptied; their relatives had either died or moved away. More than anything, Rumu wants Putul to have a whole family in India. But that possibility, like the house in Calcutta destroyed by the flooding, has been lost.

When Rumu enters the kitchen of her own house, Putul is sitting at the kitchen table clothed only in a towel and her bikini, her body limp. Rumu sits across from her.

"What happened with your friend?" Putul asks.

"He was okay, nothing special," Rumu says. "But his mother was nice. Dadi would have liked her. I wish she lived here, so she could meet her."

Putul moves to sit closer to her mother. "At least Dadi's holy now," Putul says, "now that she's preserved in the water."

"She's not pure," Rumu says, her voice quiet. "No one can be, completely."

Putul leans against her mother with such force that Rumu nearly falls out of her chair. Putul needs to carve the world into one in which she will never be lost or forgotten.

"I wish her body was here," Putul says, "so we could all be together."

"We will visit India soon," Rumu says, before she remembers that her mother was their last relative remaining in India. They would have no place to stay in Calcutta.

"We might not see her again," Rumu says, after a pause. "But this is our house now, and, somehow, we have to find a way to make it alive."

They remain seated at the table, both of their legs dangling so they look like children forced to sit in chairs too high above the floor, struggling to find their way down.

DAN POPE

Wesleyan Writers Conference

Karaoke Night

The night after my father and I came to blows in the kitchen of our house, he showed up at the bowling alley with a woman named Connie DeLucco. He'd been seeing this woman for over a year but I'd never laid eyes on her until that moment. I knew her name because I'd heard my mother say it countless times over the course of the preceding year in various states of anger and distress, the last time being before a judge of the family court.

From my position at the front counter, I watched my father and the woman move down the aisle—past the trophy cases, the lockers, the pro shop—and go into the lounge. It was Karaoke Night, our busiest of the week. Every lane was filled. All night long I'd been listening to people singing Jimmy Buffett songs. People loved singing Jimmy Buffett on Karaoke Night. It'd be another two, three hours before things quieted down.

I took off my smock and stuffed it under the counter. "I'll be back in ten minutes," I told the owner, Jerry Z. He was spraying a pair of size tens with a can of disinfectant. As I brushed past him, he glanced at his watch—which was what he always did when I went on break.

"Check the parking lot," he said. "Make sure everything's okay."

"Later," I said.

"I don't pay you enough? I ask too much?"

"After I get a drink."

"Drink smink," said Jerry Z. "Thirty-five years and no trouble. Now this."

He was talking about the vandalism. Flat tires, broken headlights, that kind of thing. Jerry Z's Econoline van—fifteen years old, covered in rust, with an engine that gurgled like a speedboat—had its passenger-side window smashed. But he was too cheap to hire a security guard or install outdoor spotlights. Instead he had me go outside every half hour or so to take a look around. Usually I didn't mind. It was a chance to get some fresh air, away from the crash and clatter of balls and pins, and away from the cigarette smoke. Everybody smoked at Jerry Z's Bowl and Dine. You practically had to squint to see the other side of the room.

I went into the lounge. The room was crowded and noisy and lit by tiki lamps, which glowed red onto everyone's faces. I nodded to Vincent the bartender, who flashed me a peace sign. I was nineteen and too young to drink, but Vincent did not abide by the laws of the State of Connecticut, especially not those relating to alcohol or narcotics. He poured a draft beer and placed it in front of me. "Look at that idiot," he said.

A businessman was on stage, belting out "Margaritaville." Under the spotlight his face was flushed and shiny, and there was a big stain on the front of his white shirt. He moved back and forth on the karaoke platform like a cha-cha dancer, directing his vocals toward the tables up front, and the men and women sitting at those tables cheered wildly. Maybe he was their boss. We got a lot of office workers on Karaoke Night. The regulars—punks, junkies, sweetheart couples, VFW members; we got all kinds—sat in the back and smoked and watched the office workers make fools of themselves.

My father was in one of the rear booths. He and the woman—Connie DeLucco—were sitting side by side, holding hands above the table. I took my beer and approached their booth, thinking: People who are middle-aged shouldn't caress each other's hands in public. They should get all that lovey-dovey stuff out of their systems when they're younger and better-looking.

"I didn't know you liked karaoke," I said, sliding into the vinyl seat opposite them.

"Is that what they call it?" said my father. He glanced at the stage and back at me. "I thought it was some sort of amateur hour."

"Maybe you should show them how it's done," I said. "Get up there and sing one."

My father had a strong but off-key voice. He knew most Frank Sinatra songs by heart. We used to sing them around the piano when I was a kid. He said, "I don't feel much like singing."

"Why not?" I said. "You two look pretty cheerful to me, holding hands. Maybe you could sing a duet."

"Don't be smart," said my father. "I didn't come down here to argue with you."

"Did you come to show off your girlfriend in her tight little skirt? Is that why you came down here, Dad?"

His arms tensed, and he raised a finger at me, but Connie DeLucco took his hand and brought it to the table and covered it with her hands. "Don't, Jim," she said.

He exhaled and eased back in his seat. He took his arm off the table and put it around Connie DeLucco. "That's a nice shiner you got," he told me.

I said, "You got a sharp elbow."

"I didn't hit you with my elbow."

"You sure did," I said.

"Well I didn't mean to."

"The hell you didn't."

I slid out of the booth and turned away but the woman reached out and touched my wrist. "Don't go," she said.

"I don't know you, lady," I said, and pulled my hand away.

I'd moved back home six months earlier, after dropping out of college. This was in 1984, in New Britain, Connecticut, home of Pulaski Tools, where my father had made hammers and screwdrivers for thirty years. We lived down the street from the factory in a big, old Victorian that used to be a rooming house. After my mother left he'd allowed the place to get run-down. The paint was chipped and peeling, the floorboards creaked, and the wind whistled through the cracks in the windows and rooftops.

My bedroom was on the third floor and my father's was on the second. He didn't sleep much. Late at night I could hear him below me, coughing, clearing his throat, or getting up to go to the bathroom or down to the den for a whiskey. He didn't bother to hide the bottle after the divorce, just left it on the table in the kitchen or den.

My father wasn't a bad cook. He made steak and potatoes every night. We'd sit across from each other at the kitchen table, chewing and cutting. Eating steak and potatoes put my father in a good mood. He'd say: "How's that steak? Rare enough for you?" Or: "That's a two-inch tenderloin. Cost you fifteen bucks for a cut like that in a restaurant, if you can find it." Or: "Potatoes the way you like 'em?" I'd grunt and keep my head down, shoveling the food into my mouth. Or if I felt like pissing him off I'd say something like: "Yeah, Dad. Just great. A fucking great steak and potato meal." Then I'd put my plate in the sink, grab my jacket, and go out for the night.

I'd moved back home because it was summertime and I liked living rent-free, hanging around with my old friends. I spent the afternoons at Pulaski Park, playing basketball and getting stoned, and nights drinking beer at a college bar near where we lived. I thought: Time is short. Life is precious. Etc. There was no time to waste studying ancient civilizations. I drank until last call, when all the pretty coeds made their blue-jeaned way back to their dorm rooms, calling good night to each other in their singsong sexy coed voices, and I stumbled home alone in the wind to my father's house and passed into beery oblivion on the same saggy bed I'd slept on when I was a kid.

His girlfriend didn't come to our house, but I knew a lot about her from listening to my mother. I knew that she was forty-five years old, that she worked as a bookkeeper for Pulaski Tools, and that she had two teenage boys from a prior marriage. (My mother called her a *divorcée*, among other names I'd been surprised to hear her utter.) Every other weekend—the days her boys stayed with their father—my father went over to Connie DeLucco's condominium and spent the night. He'd return from these visits a bit sheepish and talkative, like a kid who's done something wrong and wants to take your mind off it.

My father believed in the benefits of higher education. He had put fifty dollars in a special bank account for my brother and me every week for eighteen years. He hadn't missed a week, not even when the toolmakers union went on strike for six months back in 1975. He had made sacrifices to give us the chances he didn't have, or so he told me, over and over. So when September came and I told him I wasn't going back to college, that my mind was made up and there was nothing he could do about it, he stopped making me steak and potato dinners and started calling me a lazy freeloading dropout son of a bitch, and I started calling him Jimbo. I'd say, "Pass the salt, Jimbo," and he'd say: "When I was your age I was carrying a hod twelve hours a day. You think that was easy? You think that was some kind of free ride? Well it wasn't." I'd say, "Grab me a beer out of the fridge when you get a chance, Jimbo," and he'd say: "Get a goddamn job, why don't you? I'm sick to death of you hanging around the house like some kind of cripple. That what you want to do with your life? Watch TV?" I'd say anything, and he'd tell me to get a job.

This went on for a month. Then he barged into my bedroom early one morning and turned on the overhead fluorescent light. As a result of my bad habits, mornings were not something to look forward to. I was not accustomed to overhead fluorescent lighting at 7:00 A.M. My nervous system did not know how to react. I squinted at the light, not feeling very well, and said something along the lines of, "Turn off that fucking light."

My father said, "Get out of bed. I don't care if you just sit at the kitchen table and read the newspaper. I won't have any lazy freeloading dropout son of a bitch sleeping till noon in my house. From now on I want you out of bed every morning at 7:00 A.M., checking the want ads. That's the new rule around here, and if you don't like it, tough."

He repeated this performance every day for a week. I took the job at the bowling alley to get him off my back.

When I returned from the lounge, Jerry Z looked up from the eleven o'clock news and glanced at his watch. He kept the TV on at all times, an ancient black-and-white that got a scrambled picture no matter how you adjusted the antenna. He played the audio at very high volume, his good ear cocked toward the screen, but after a while you didn't notice the racket, just like you didn't hear the pins smashing and the office workers singing Jimmy Buffett songs.

He said, "You check the parking lot?"

I shook my head.

"You go fifteen minutes and don't check the parking lot? I got thieves in the parking lot and you don't look? I pay you for this? For nothing?"

"Don't break my balls, Jerry."

"This is not breaking balls, my young friend. If I wanted to break balls you would feel it."

Jerry Z was old and covered with liver spots and he had a large cylindrical wart on the back of his right hand that boys liked to make fun of when they paid for their strings. He spoke with a heavy Polish accent and worked twelve hours a day, more on weekends. Whenever people came to the counter to pay, Jerry Z took his pencil from behind his ear and examined their score sheets, checking off the number of strings they'd rolled. He suspected everyone—boys especially—of trying to get away with rolling more strings than they had marked on their sheets. He kept an eye on all twenty-five lanes, like a sea captain scanning the horizon, and he also watched me and Vincent the bartender and all the other minimum-wagers to make sure we didn't slip into the men's room or out the back door to get high, which we did as often as possible.

I said, "You want a hamburg?"

He said, "Why are you still here?"

"Does that mean you want me to check the parking lot?"

"How many times do I have to say it? Didn't I ask ten times already? I give you five minutes. You're not back in five minutes you might as well go home."

I went outside. November, the night air smelled like fallen leaves, cold and damp. I breathed deep, clearing my lungs.

Silas Deane Highway used to be the main drag, back in the late forties when Jerry Z opened the alley. They built all the buildings on the strip back then—hamburger shacks, diners, one-story motels shaped like the letter L or U. A hotel called the Grantmoor—it had heart-shaped water beds in every room, hourly rates—did good business, but most places were either boarded up or on their last legs. After midnight the gearheads took over the strip, drag racing back and forth. You could hear the howls of the engines—GTOs, Trans Ams, Le Manses—coming from miles away.

Jerry Z's Bowl and Dine was open twenty-four hours, Sundays and holidays included. Jerry Z hadn't closed the doors in thirty-five years—not once, not when JFK got shot, not during the ice storm of '73 or the blizzard of '79, not even when his own wife, Irmine, dropped dead one morning of an aneurysm. "I stayed open then," Jerry Z liked to say, "and I'll stay open until I'm dead, too." Whenever anyone called about our hours of business, Jerry Z always said the same thing: "We never close."

You'd be surprised how many people go bowling in the middle of the night. Like the Grantmoor, Jerry Z's always got a good crowd. People would come to roll a couple of strings, get a beer, play pinball machines in the arcade, or just sit on one of the benches behind the lanes and smoke. The drunks showed up around 3:00 A.M., after the bars closed, and they stayed until dawn, when the third-shift factory workers replaced them, squeezing in a shot and a string before going home to their wives.

On Karaoke Night, the parking lot was full. Jerry Z's Econoline van was parked behind the Dumpster. He thought the van would be safe there, that the vandals wouldn't see it. I walked the length of the parking lot, listening to the cars wailing in the distance. The Dumpster smelled like rotten fish. I stopped and listened for a moment. Then I slipped into the darkness behind the Dumpster and took my

Swiss Army knife out of my pocket. I opened the blade and pushed it into Jerry Z's left front tire above the hubcap, and when I took it out the tire made a hissing sound. I went around to the passenger side and got that tire, too.

I didn't know then that that night would be my last working at the alley. The next day was my day off. I would spend it at the shore with Vincent the bartender trying to find a friend of his who had some Colombian for sale, but we'd get lost and finally have to hitchhike home because Vincent's car got towed from the private road where he'd left it, and the day after that I would stay home sleeping because I was very tired from not sleeping the night before, and the day after that I would spend getting my things together and packing my car and saying good-bye to a few friends, and the day after that I would come into the bowling alley at noon and ask Jerry Z for the paycheck he owed me from the prior week because I was leaving town and wouldn't be working for him anymore and he would throw up his hands and say, "You expect severance pay? Fat chance. This is very simple, my young friend. This is the situation. You quit on me, I owe you nothing. Zero. Zilch. Understand? Nothing. Zero. Zilch."

But I didn't know I was quitting when I popped Jerry Z's tires. I waited until the air stopped hissing and the front of the van rested forward on the pavement. Then I put away my Swiss Army knife and went back inside.

Jerry Z glanced up from the TV set. He said, "You see anybody out there? Anybody suspicious? Anybody looking for trouble?"

I said, "Nope."

My father was a drinking man. Whiskey was his favorite. He'd started drinking in the army—the day he landed at Salerno, to steady his nerves—and hadn't stopped since. He drank every day, but you'd never know it from his behavior. When he and my mother used to argue about the money he spent on booze, he would say, "You've never seen me drunk. Not once in your life. Never."

And that was true. All the time I was growing up, he never slurred his words, never stumbled or fell, never lost his temper, never missed a day of work, never did any of the things drunks are supposed to do. Each evening after dinner he used to sit in the den, watching TV and sipping straight whiskey (no water, no ice). When he finished the glass, he would pour himself another and watch more TV, or help my brother and me with our homework (he was good at math), or sing songs around the piano with my mother while my brother turned the pages of the sheet music and I kept the beat with a pair of maracas we brought back from Miami Beach when I was twelve, or do any of the things we used to do, and all the time he had that glass in his hand, setting it down or raising it to his lips.

I'd never seen him stumble into the house after work, like he did the night we came to blows. I had the day off from the bowling alley, and I'd been looking forward to one of his steak and potato dinners. We'd been getting along better since I'd taken the job. He still wanted me to go back to college and he lectured me on that topic often, but he respected the fact that I was working six days a week. Every morning before he went to the factory he packed my lunch, for me to take to the bowling alley and eat on my break—steak sandwiches with mayonnaise on white bread. And whenever I brought home a bag of groceries from the Dairy Mart, he made a big deal out of it; he'd remove the food from the shopping bag—the carton of milk or eggs or packet of meat—and admire each item as if they were treasures from Arabia. When I showed him my first paycheck, he pursed his lips and nodded, and said: "Two hundred bucks before taxes. Not bad. More than I was making at your age. You'll need that money when you go back to college."

But he was late that night, and I didn't wait for him. I sat at the table, eating the last few bites of a TV dinner. Then he came through the door and staggered to the kitchen table. I thought he was ill, that he'd come down with the flu or something, and I asked him if he was feeling okay.

He steadied himself against the table. "Goddamn right I'm okay," he said. "Never felt better in my life."

His face was red and he was sweating, even though it was a cold November night.

"You're drunk," I told him.

"Like hell I am," he said.

"You can't even stand without holding on to the table."

"Who do you think you are, calling me drunk? Where do you get off talking to me like that?"

I'd meant it as a joke. Being drunk was pretty much normal behavior for me. My father often kidded me about it, asking how my head felt on the morning afterward. *Nothing worse than a beer jag*, he liked to say.

I pushed my TV dinner away from me. "Admit it, Dad. You're drunk off your ass."

"You've never seen me drunk in your life. Not once. Never."

"Look at you. You can't even stand up straight. You can't walk across the room."

"You don't know what you're talking about."

"You can't hold your whiskey anymore."

"The hell I can't."

He moved with exaggerated dignity to the refrigerator and grabbed on to the handle and steadied himself. Then he opened the door and looked inside. "Where's my steak? You eat it all?"

"It's right in front of you."

"You ate it, didn't you? Ate your father's dinner."

"Maybe you're seeing two of them. That makes it harder."

"Don't get smart with me."

He reached into the fridge and knocked over a half gallon of milk, which fell to the floor and started pouring out the top. "For Chrissake," he said. "Who left that open?"

I rose from the table, bent, and picked up the carton of milk, and as I straightened up my father turned and hit me above my right eye with his elbow. The blow rang in my head like a knock on a door, that same wooden sound. I stumbled backward and nearly slipped on the wet floor.

"What the hell?" said my father. "What are you trying to prove?"

I rubbed my head, feeling the pain radiate outward. I found myself holding the carton of milk, and I placed it on the kitchen table. He looked at me with a bewildered expression. He said, "What are you getting under me like that for?"

"What the fuck are you talking about? You practically knocked my eye out, you old drunk."

"You can't talk to me like that. I'm your father."

I said, "You're an old drunk, nothing more."

"You watch yourself. I can still give you a strapping."

He closed the refrigerator door and began fiddling with his belt buckle. My father was thick in the chest and arms. He'd been an all-state football player in high school, the commander of a company of combat engineers that fought in Italy. People who knew him from the old days used to stop him in the street to shake his hand. Seeing him stumble-drunk made me angry.

"Go ahead," I told him. "Try it."

He took off his belt and whipped, but I caught the leather and pulled it toward me and my father came lunging along with it. He lost his footing on the wet floor and fell against me, and we went down. He landed on top of me. I struggled to push him off, and he tried to pin me like a wrestler, the smell of whiskey on his breath, in my face, a smell that reminded me of childhood. I hadn't hugged him for years, for as long as I could remember; we weren't a family that showed affection. I clutched him to my chest, my drunk father, and rolled. In a moment I was on top of him. I grabbed his shoulders and pushed him back against the linoleum. I felt the strength drain out of him, and I pushed him down again, harder, so that the back of his head snapped back and struck the floor.

"Don't fuck with me," I said.

He looked up at me with red-rimmed eyes, then turned his head so that the side of his face was resting in the milk that had spilled onto the floor.

I got up and took my coat off the back of the chair and went out.

Karaoke was still going strong when I came back to the lounge after puncturing Jerry Z's tires. Someone was singing an off-key version of Billy Joel's "Piano Man." I took up a barstool, and Vincent the bartender slid a draft beer in front of me.

He said, "Look at that piece of ass."

"Where?"

He nodded toward one of the tables of office workers. None of them looked pretty to me, but Vincent was not picky when it concerned women. He had a habit of making his fingers into the general shape of a triangle and flicking his tongue into the opening. He liked to say, "They all look the same when you get down to it, kid." In addition to bartender, Vincent was the hamburger chef. Hamburger was the only item offered on the Tiki Lounge menu. When a woman Vincent considered attractive ordered a hamburger, he would go into the minikitchen, place a patty onto the grill, unzip, and piss on the meat while it sizzled and fried. *The special sauce,* he called it. He also regularly pissed on burgers that Jerry Z ordered, and I can't say I objected to this practice because Jerry Z was a stingy old Pollack who docked you if you were ten minutes late and never gave you a day off when you asked for one.

"You got any blues?" I said.

"Sure I got blues. I got the keys to the cabinet, kid."

Vincent's eyes were bulging and alert. He had been a soldier in Vietnam. You could tell by the way he looked at you and everyone else in the world that something inside his brain was no longer functioning properly. Some nights he would drive to the shore and stare at the ocean for hours, seeing shapes in the black waves that no one else saw. Maybe it was all the speed he was doing. Speed, hash, pot, acid: He had whatever you wanted in the trunk of his '75 Impala. At the time, I thought him an admirable person. A few years later—a friend sent me the newspaper clipping—the police would find him in a ditch, beaten to death with a crowbar.

I took a sip of beer. The beer was cold and tasted very good because my throat was dry from breathing cigarette smoke. I looked into the mirror behind the bar and watched my father. He and Connie DeLucco were sitting in the rear booth, their bodies turned toward each other. She seemed to be telling him something, and he nodded slightly while she spoke. I knew they were talking about me, trying to devise words or kindnesses, and I knew that even though I would probably feel sorry about it later nothing they said or did could touch the person I had become.

Vincent tapped me on the shoulder. He said, "Here."

He placed a small blue pill in my palm, and I swallowed it.

Later that night he and I would drive south toward the shore in his '75 Impala. We would pass every car we came up behind but no matter how fast Vincent drove it was not fast enough. We drove with unbearable slowness at a hundred miles an hour. I didn't want to blink. So much happened during that instant of darkness. Vincent drove with the tape deck blasting, drumming his hands against the steering wheel. When we got to the shore he drove up and down different beach roads that all looked the same, trying to find the house of the guy who had the Colombian. Finally we parked, got out of the car, jumped over a fence, and went down an embankment, reaching the beach. We walked along the shore in darkness, passing unlit and shuttered cottages, our sneakers sinking into the sand. We climbed rock walls and ducked under piers, and after a while the cottages began to thin. We came to a highway overpass, with cars and trucks going by above, headlights flashing onto the black ocean for an instant. Later, when the sun came up, we found ourselves on a raised walkway above tall sea grass in a swampy inlet. The edge of the swamp was bordered on all sides by tall pines, off in the distance. A man drifted slowly past us in a skiff, holding a fishing net. He turned toward us, then turned away. The sun was very red against the water. I held my arms around me in the cold light, and Vincent said, "Where's the ocean? Where's the fucking ocean?"

But that happened later. When my father got up from the booth and walked toward the men's room, I took two whiskeys, went over, and placed the glasses on the table in front of Connie DeLucco.

She said, "Your father's not drinking tonight."

"What about you?"

"Yes, I believe I will. Thank you. I don't usually but tonight's a special occasion."

"What's so special about it?"

"Meeting you."

My mother had called Connie DeLucco "cheap" because she was the sort of woman men might notice, with her tight skirts, her long dark hair. But up close you saw the web of lines around her eyes, the smile wrinkles, the streaks of gray in her hair. Her face was drawn and thin, her jaw sharp.

I slid into the booth across from her. "They almost got divorced once before," I told her. "Before you, I mean. Six or seven years ago."

"I didn't know that," she said.

"My brother and I wanted an inground swimming pool for our backyard. My father liked the idea, said it would save him the trouble of mowing the grass. He was always buying us stuff we wanted."

"Your father's a generous man," she said.

I said, "They were always fighting about money, but that time it was worse. That time she went to a lawyer and filed some papers against him."

"She was looking out for you kids."

"We didn't see it that way. We wanted that pool."

She reached across the table and brought her hand near my black eye but didn't touch me. "Your father didn't mean to hurt you," she said.

The speed started hitting my bloodstream around then. It came on like a jolt, like waking up in the morning, that suddenly.

I said, "They always had their problems. You just came along, that's all."

She lowered her hand, and I sat back against the booth. I turned toward the men's room, but my father was nowhere in sight. The office worker finished the Billy Joel song and everyone clapped, and three secretaries got onto the stage and broke into Barry Manilow.

She said, "Your father would never tell you this but I'm going to. He wanted to sell that house six months ago. Did you know that?"

I said, "That's bullshit."

"The only reason he didn't was because of you coming back."

"He told you that to keep you off his back. You probably been nagging him to move in with you."

She said, "You think he likes living in that big house all alone? He's not getting any younger you know."

"He's not alone."

"Of course he is."

I said, "Look, you've got your own family, your own kids. You've got nothing to do with us."

She took a sip of whiskey. "I don't blame you for hating me."

"My mother hates you. I couldn't care less about you."

She smiled, but her eyes welled up with tears. She said, "You know why you came back to town, don't you?"

"Why don't you tell me?"

"To punish your father, that's why. To punish him and me for breaking up your family."

"I just told you, I couldn't care less about you."

She said, "Do you like working in a bowling alley?"

"Sure. It's great."

"Is it? Your father says you were doing terrific at college. He says you got straight As your first semester. He says you're twice as smart as he ever was."

I took the whiskey glass and drank it down, and the whiskey burned in my throat. A moment later I felt my father's hands on my shoulders. I didn't turn around. He patted me on the back and said, "I didn't mean to hit you."

"Forget about it," I told him.

He went around to the other side of the booth and sat down, and as he did I got up. "I got to get back to work," I said.

He winked at Connie DeLucco. "He's making two hundred a week before taxes. Twice what I was making at his age. You should see the groceries he brings home." He turned to me. "You coming home tonight?"

"Tomorrow. I got some things to do tonight."

"All right. We'll have steaks. I got a couple of nice London broils. Two inches thick."

I said, "Good-bye, Dad."

He nodded and I began walking away and even though I didn't turn back and wouldn't have been able to hear him over the music anyway, I knew that he would watch me leave the room and then he would turn to Connie DeLucco and say, "He'll need that money when he goes back to college." And I realized then (or it might have been later when the speed speeded up the workings of my brain and I saw every particle of light like fishing twine hanging from the sky) that he was sixty years old and the only thing I could do for him was leave; and leaving took me away, farther away than I could have imagined that night.

I went out the back door to get some fresh air. It was past midnight. The trees behind the bowling alley were bare and dark. I leaned against the wall, listening to the distant rumble of cars on the strip and watching the branches tremble soundlessly in the wind. Within a week I would be gone. I would gather my things and pack my car one morning while my father was at work, and I would watch the town where I grew up—our house, the park, the factory where my father worked for thirty years—recede in the rearview mirror. Turning onto the interstate, I would picture him coming home that evening, finding the note I left for him on the kitchen table, how he would get out his reading glasses and sit down at the table and read the few words I'd written, how he would purse his lips and nod, like he always did when he knew something was true.

T. GERONIMO JOHNSON

Stanford University

WINTER NEVER QUITS

He has picked a support group that meets far from campus. The fluorescent lights in the room flicker and skip like an old movie. It smells of ammonia and disinfectant, medicinal. The room is square, tiled in black-and-white vinyl, and painted flat white. The walls are bare except for large, white circular posters. Heavy black lines hang across each circle, at a forty-five-degree angle, like bandoliers. In the center of each circle is a silhouette. He recognizes syringes, pipes, and pills. There are also cocktails: a highball, a martini, and a shot. NA shares the space with AA.

The meeting is forty-five minutes long. He is preoccupied with his dissertation. For thirty-five minutes he stares blankly out of the window. His gaze shifts back and forth from the icicles along the top of the window, hanging like daggers, to the coffee shop across the street, Kat's Coffee House. The coffee at NA is watered down. It is Doug's first day, and he refuses to drink it.

Everyone sounds so sad to be clean; he wishes they would start using again.

The meetings are dominated by Stan—a man of indeterminate age; a man with leather skin, mummified by years of religious drug use; a man who likes to talk, a lot, about getting high.

"Most don't last three days. The first day is always the easiest. The first day after a good binge is always the easiest day to quit because the body is still saturated with the bullshit. The first day is easiest for most people who haven't hit rock bottom . . .

"Cocaine is like the bitch who shows out on you, won't be true, but that you can't leave 'cause you *luv* her. Coke is the motherfucker that beats you the night before your new job starts, but you can't leave 'cause you *luv* him. Because it is so good, and ain't nothing better 'an when the white angel fucks you."

Doug idly wonders what rock bottom is. Death, maybe? He goes to the bathroom. He stares at his reflection, his face centered in the mirror. He realizes that he is the only black guy at NA that night. He hums an old poem, "Black like pig's feet, black like greens, black like chitterlings, black like thieves, black like watermelon and dope fiends."

He can hear Stan through the thin walls, "The second and third day are pretty easy, too. After a big binge the body is still shaking off the last of the sickness, still exorcising the devil."

He started using cocaine the last year of his master's program, while writing a paper on the nature of evil in society. He felt that he was "living his writing." He wonders if in five more years he will think of this as the end of an old era, the beginning of a new era, or just a vague point in the middle.

As Doug returns to the meeting room, Stan is momentarily drowned out by an airplane. Doug feels a twinge of gravity and instinctively turns his face toward the bare ceiling. He has a momentary desire to get high, a desire that fades with the noise of the passing jet. He scratches his nose, then jerks his hand away, fearful of triggering a nosebleed.

The nosebleeds were good for meeting women. In school they wanted to mother him, and in a nightclub, the right nightclub, they wanted to share, and were willing to share in return. But he was no Richard Pryor, and coke didn't help his sex life, it only left him feeling impotent. Sex was drab, but scholastics were dynamite. The first paper he wrote on the C garnered him his first A, and every paper without it, a C.

When he got out of the hospital, he knew he had to quit. No more titty-cake, white horse, white pony, white ride, fairy dust, angel powder, Colombian snow, South American sugar, granulated love, powdered angel, white angel, Satan's dried semen, Mexican stucco, blow. The emergency room nurse glared when she read his chart: high blood pressure, low blood sugar, calluses on the nose, deviated septum, etc. She knew. She spoke with the southside accent found in the southside of any town. The southside accent he had worked so hard to discard, but now heard rising in his voice, in response to hers. He felt disembodied, like he was his own ventriloquist, and dummy.

"What is it, cocaine, crystal meth, amyl nitrate, poppers, speed?" she asked.

He weakly admitted that any of the above would be nice right then. She did not laugh but said, "Losing black men every day, and all they can do is try to be comedians. Boy, I've been in the emergency ward for twelve years. I've seen it all and here you come in, should be healthy as a horse, barely twenty-eight years old, a mild heart attack and more tics than a dead deer."

A deal was cut. He would go to Narcotics Anonymous and bring her the chips, or she would report him to the authorities or the counseling center, who would likely report him to the authorities. He did not believe she could enforce the mandate, but her laugh lines and tear trails, and something in the timbre of her voice, spoke to him. She reminded him of his grandmother. It had been years since he had seen his own family. He filled his summers with conferences and his winters with travel. Ostensibly, Dexter State University kept him busy, but the truth was that going home depressed him. His grandmother once told him that the devil didn't chase after the smart ones. She also told him never to look a gift horse in the mouth. So, no more coke.

When the meeting ends, he races across the street, braving the sharp New England wind and the traffic—cars fly through this neighborhood—to get some real coffee.

The first night he walks into Kat's Coffee House his teeth are chattering—he is cold not from the winter wind or constricted blood vessels, but from the empty chill of an *anonymous* support group, cold from being caught in the void between who he is, and who he doesn't want to be, the vacuum between the mask and the veil.

The coffeehouse is brightly lit, and empty. A cowbell jingles when the door opens. A long mahogany counter faces the large windows that overlook the street. Between the counter and the door, next to the windows, are a few small tables. Between the windows, there are mirrors. The floor is painted concrete, and the ceiling is covered with Cuban tiles—mauve and blue on the floor, and silver and yellow and white on the ceiling. A walkway to the left leads around the counter to the back of the shop, where there is abstract art hanging on the unfinished brick walls, and more mirrors, in which he can see that the counter is actually a peninsula and behind the counter there are several more tables and a few Eames chairs. The stool cushions at the counter are upholstered in a faux cow print.

A woman in her midtwenties sits on a stool behind the counter. She takes one look at him and says, "Café au lait." He agrees, though that isn't what he wants. There is a bulletin board next to the register. On the counter there is small chalkboard with one word illegibly scrawled on it. A card taped to the chalkboard reads: KAT'S JEOPARDY—ASK THE RIGHT QUESTION, WIN A FREE ESPRESSO. Doug considers pointing out that the handwriting is almost unreadable, but doesn't want to offend the clerk.

He watches her make the coffee, his new drug of choice. There is a high-pitched whir as she grinds the beans. She tamps the grounds with a metal cylinder, taps the handled filter, careful not to spill even one grain. The cylinder looks like a weight on a triple beam scale. Her hands move with the expertise of a master chef. The precision reminds him of experienced dope dealers as they cut and measure and cut and measure and cut in and measure, hands steady the entire time, even though they are surrounded by a hazy cloud of fairy dust.

She gives him the drink, her hand gently grazing his. Her fingers are hot from handling the coffee. He is shocked by the touch of human warmth. She smiles a smile that he convinces himself is only for him. The cowbell rings and a blast of cold shoots in, followed by an old black man wearing torn and dirty army fatigues. Layers of clothes peek out from his cuffs and sleeves: a green shirt, a black sweater, and red sweatpants. Below the checkered bath towel he wears as a scarf, a cross shows against his neck. Grimy fingers shaking, the old man counts change and mumbles hello. The woman behind the counter cheerfully returns his greeting, and smiles. Doug averts his eyes, and retreats to the rear of the shop. He is surprised to find that Kat's is P-shaped, longer in the back than the front. He finds a barber's chair that he didn't see in the mirror. Sitting in the barber's chair, he is out of the clerk's direct line of sight, but in the mirrors he can watch her work. She gives the homeless man a cup of coffee, but does not accept his change.

He studies her. She has strawberry red hair, with dark roots showing, a small loop in her left eyebrow. She is pale, but not deathly. He remembers that it is winter. She is what he would call healthy. She is not fat, but not so thin as he. She does not appear to be addicted to speed.

He reads the fashion magazines scattered around. He runs his fingers across the pages, and puts them to his nose. He cannot smell anymore, but he remembers the odor of cheap ink mixed with cologne, the scent of desire. He compares himself to the models in the magazines: It's like staring into the back of a two-way mirror as he imagines their features in place of his own. He comes across an advertisement featuring Tyrese. Tyrese is strong, famous, rich, razor-sharp-cheekboned, desired, dark, tattooed, and black. He wonders if Tyrese smokes dope. The bell rings, and another customer enters, bringing a gust of cold air and a few faint wisps of snow. He watches the clerk behind the bar make coffee and decides he will keep coming to NA.

The second night at NA he sits up front, closer to the windows, between the syringe and the shot glass, and watches her the entire evening. He cannot make out her face clearly, but he knows she is not smiling as brightly for other customers as she does for him. Stan's voice relaxes him.

"Anyone who tells you to stay off drugs because they are *bad* for you is full of shit. Only someone who's done it can really know the tragedy. Otherwise, it is like someone telling you to stay away from Vegas because they have seen *Casino,* or stay out of Jersey because they saw *GoodFellas.*

"Anyone who has done drugs knows the truth. Fuck sliced bread, the space shuttle, and penicillin. Fuck microwave popcorn. Narcotics are man's greatest inventions and getting fucked-up is a pleasure so friggin' exquisite anyone would play Faust to this Mephistopheles. Getting blown is the greatest thing there is even when the trip is the worst. Every high is a new trip. So what if you need more and more? Is it any different with cigarettes, sex, coffee, love? Fuck—freedom is a habit. You would kill for it, we do it all the time."

Stan drones on, relentless, indefatigable. Douglas watches the cars zip by like they are on the open road. New anticarjacking legislation gives drivers the right to run red lights in *questionable* neighborhoods. This neighborhood is no longer questionable, but people still run red lights. In this neighborhood, Crystal City—where he scored his first eight-ball, where twelve months ago people were scared to drive after dark, unless it was for a drive-through—there is little foot traffic.

The old buildings have been renovated, redeveloped, recovered. NA meets in the old Velocity Transmission factory, second floor, across the street from, and overlooking, Kat's. Abandoned warehouses and factories have been turned into lofts, salons, and bars, replacing the tenements, beauty parlors, and bars that were there before. The new shops have newer neon signs. They open later and close earlier. They have higher prices. Kat's Coffee House sits in an old mattress factory. The streets have been renamed. This one, formerly Flood Street, is now First Avenue. The gentrification is unfinished, though, and between Crystal City and downtown is another questionable neighborhood—Pine City. Pine City is not fully redeveloped, not fully recovered. Pine City is a stretch of brick and asphalt as mottled as Beirut, a stretch of road that the mayor often refers to as "third world."

An old elm sits in the median, having survived the paving and repaving, the turning of sod, and the cutting of new curbs. Looking as if it has been struck by lightning, it is ashen, thin, skeletal—even for a tree in December. One limb hangs loose. Firewood. He prays for snow. It is the only eyesore on the street, and the broken limb partially blocks his otherwise unobstructed view of Kat's.

He leaves the meeting early, as Stan is saying, "Never quit in winter." That second night she asks him his name, and he lies as he always has lied when asked his name while making a purchase on Flood Street, in Crystal City. He says Peter. Peter sounds to him like a nice, innocent, trustworthy name. She says her name is Trixie, as in Tricia, as in Pat, as in Patricia. She asks him if he wants the same thing and he shrugs.

"Or do you want something different? Be adventurous, hmm?"

He opts for different. She makes him a white mocha. There is no one else in the shop and he searches for something to say as he scans the business cards, movie reviews, and ads on the bulletin board next to the cash register. He wants to let her know that she will not see him on the nightly news. He is not the average black guy. He has been to college. He has been to Greece. He wants to say something intelligent, to let her know that he is smart but down to earth, street-smart but not hardened, friendly but not a pushover or desperate. He wants to tell her that he reads Latin and speaks German, and once, jokingly, used Aristotle's *Poetics* to analyze a gangster rap song, and the paper, written while he was on C, garnered an A, and was published, and won him his current scholarship, and, to this day, stands as one of the finest examples of his academic writing, according to his adviser.

He wants to tell her that he is a fraud.

He wishes he had a tattoo to complement her piercing. They could talk about an alternative band. He struggles to think of one, remembering only Nirvana, but he thinks they might have died in a plane crash. He doesn't want to look stupid. He does not hear her question and so she repeats it.

"Live around here?"

"No, you?"

"I wish. This area is too expensive for me. I remember when it was nothing but drug dealers and gangbangers." She doesn't blush.

"Yeah." Then correcting himself, he says, "Really?"

He scans the bulletin board again—win free passes to a sneak preview of the movie *Dog House*. She hands him his coffee, and he reads the inscription on the cup: THE KAT'S MEOW OF COFFEE.

"Are you Kat?"

"No, I like horses, I guess zebras are my favorite though. I love it when their stripes are symmetric."

"I meant, are you Kat?"

"I wish. I'm Trixie. Thought I told you."

"You wish a lot."

"Who doesn't?"

On the small chalkboard someone has drawn a postage stamp; inside the stamp is written the word *Charade*.

"Cary Grant and Audrey Hepburn directed by Stanley Donen. What's the best Hitchcock film that Hitchcock never made?" he says.

"What?"

He repeats himself.

"Oh, not bad."

"Until about five years ago I was a movie buff," he says.

"I love the old black-and-white movies. What about you?"

"I like *Scarface*."

Another customer enters. Doug retreats to a seat in the back. He is enthused for reasons he doesn't understand. He loves *Scarface:* He can lip-synch every line. Cocaine didn't kill Tony Montana, competition did, capitalism did. At least that's what he liked to think when he was younger, staying up past his bedtime, watching his favorite movie late into the night.

That night he falls asleep reading his dissertation. He dreams of piles of paper filled with an indiscernible black script, the letters jumbled like alphabet soup, shapes shifting like a lava lamp—forming the hieroglyphics of disease.

The third day he is due back at the hospital. He has his chips to show the nurse. He has to cancel his afternoon classes and his meeting with his adviser. He is noticeably nervous. His adviser jokes about predefense jitters. He reminds Doug of an upcoming conference; his adviser has the sullen look of a parent warning a child not to have sex on prom night, and knowing that it will probably happen anyway.

That night, the third, he is anxious to get to, and through, the meeting. He tries to ignore Stan.

"The fourth day is the hardest. It's on the fourth day that you miss it. Just like on the fourth day after your woman leaves, 'cause you know you fucked up everything in your life, the fourth day after your woman leaves, your balls start to ache and you go trawling for a whore. Just like the fourth day after freakin' the whore with your limp dick, it starts to itch. Just like the fourth day after your dick starts to itch, you notice a foul discharge, a burning sensation when you piss—that's the twelve days of Christmas for the speed freak."

Stan pauses and then speaks again. "I love that shit."

Christ, what will he say next, *just like on the fourth day Christ rose again*. Is that even correct?

Doug is bold that night. A storm is headed to town, preceded by light flurries. A biting wind drives clouds so low they seem to roll along the street like tanks. When the occasional flake sticks to the glass, he laughs. He has taken a seat inside the front window of Kat's. He wanted to be able to watch her directly, and he does. He catches their reflection in the mirror behind the counter—a new old movie, of a sort. His nose itches and he wants to lick her back—in the dip where spine meets ass. He wonders if she gives head.

He has brought his dissertation so he can review it. His defense is in one week. He is attempting to reconcile Booker T. Washington and W. E. B. DuBois, both of whom, of late, he finds inaccessible and disturbing. He is shamed by Washington with his proletarian pie-in-the-sky dreams and voluntary servitude. He is troubled by DuBois's elitism: Let the top 10 percent get what they can, then they'll come back to help the rest. Educate 10 percent and turn control over to them, they'll uplift the race. He looks around the new Crystal City. Kat's coffee was in the building that once held Buddy's Pool Hall and the Kit-Kat Lounge. The entire neighborhood is now predominantly white. But before, like every other black area, they probably sent their 10 percent off to Howard, Morehouse, Morgan State, and Tuskegee—but the 10 percent never come back to the Crystal Cities. They set up Randian enclaves in small pockets around the city, exclusive black meccas that one day would be "gentrified" and "rediscovered," too. In sobriety, his dis-ease grows daily. He is resentful of this artificial bifurcation, this cloven path he must negotiate—one or the other, either/or—a life predetermined on some level by the structure into which he was cast. The wind blows under the door, stirring his cuffs, icing his shins like Popsicles.

At the hospital that afternoon he had to wear one of those paper-thin flowered gowns. His ass hung out. He was ashamed, reminded of the bar Bricks and young boys. Boys who swore they were going to be ballers, rappers, players. The bar Bricks, where those same young boys would sell themselves for a line or two. The johns, after loading the kids up with drinks, would lead them to the bathroom, where they would rub a tickle of coke on their puckered asses—just enough to numb them against the reversal of fortune. When the men were spent, they would often charge off without paying, leaving the boys dazed and drunk and cursing for payment. But not so drunk that they couldn't shoot straight. Not high enough to be beyond the pale of shame. Not so dazed that they didn't know they were being cheated when told they already had their bumps, and if they wanted more—lick their underwear. Doug self-consciously fingered his thin gown. The hospital was cold, as hospitals are, but he was sweating. He wondered what Trixie would say—maybe, "hot chocolate."

The fourth day is the devil himself—Stan was right. Doug struggles through class, unable to pay attention or follow any conversation more than a foot away from him. He has to read lips. Comprehension comes slowly, like sound underwater.

He once prided himself on being amphibious. "Socially ambidextrous," he liked to say. He could skate the halls of the university and strut down the avenue with the same ease and comfort. But today, neither feels like home.

At the lunch conference, he is distracted by the sugar and salt on his table. He salivates so profusely he must swallow constantly, which is painful because his throat is sore. Between the presentation on Rhetoric in Af-Am Lit and the reading from the latest enfant terrible of the underclass, his nose starts to bleed.

That evening he decides to skip NA, and work on his dissertation instead. He goes to the library. He chooses the top floor, the fourth, and sits in a cubicle by the window overlooking the dark quad. The text that he has committed the last five years of his life to conceiving, shaping, nurturing; the text his professor had once described as "quite fetching"—which is a compliment coming from a man who thinks that Marxism is sexy and objectivism is a homely ideology made all the more pathetic in its attempts to masquerade under the mascara of second-rate fiction—makes no sense to him now. It reads like a menu in Chinese.

He can only chuckle. He is amused by the challenge of voting in the nineteenth century, the furor over the taking of Hong Kong, and the hazards of ordering food in foreign languages. He is amused, and forlorn. Unforgiving in a sudden assessment of himself as a vile man, a traitor to his race, a man now amused by the very injustices and social ironies he once found heartbreaking. He has lost twenty pounds in the last six months. Outside, flurries. He decides to go to Kat's. He wants to tell her that he is an impostor.

There are spaces out front, but he parks on a side street. There is a string of Christmas lights around the base of the old elm. Kat's is empty when he walks in. The tables are neatly arranged, but the chairs are scattered. When the bell tipped by the opening door falls silent, the background music becomes audible. Trixie comes out from the kitchen. She is wearing the smile that he knows is just for him.

"Early," she says.

"Yeah."

"Hot chocolate?"

He nods. He does not watch her make the drink, instead listening to the sound of blood pounding in his skull and the rush of fever in his chest. Across the street the NA meeting is starting. He turns away so that no one will recognize him, not that anyone ever speaks to him in the meetings. In the mirror, he watches the latecomers race from their cars into the building.

"Quiet tonight," says Trixie.

He wonders why they never speak to him. He wonders what makes him different, besides the obvious.

"I guess so," says Trixie.

He catches up with Trixie and apologizes. "Sorry, the snow has me in a daze is all."

"This is weather for Saint Bernards and brandy."

He nods, confused, as she hands him the hot chocolate.

"Saint Bernards, the dogs, Swiss Alps..."

He catches on. "Yeah, brandy would be cool."

She reaches under the counter, produces a bottle of brandy, and raises her eyebrows.

He pops the top off his cup.

Trixie carefully transfers his hot chocolate into an oversized yellow mug and tops it off with a heavy slug of brandy. She places the mug on the counter next to the register. "Sit up here a minute."

He does. The brandy hits his stomach and he feels a forgotten weight in his loins. She makes herself a drink of half espresso and half brandy.

"What are you studying?" she asks.

"Huh?"

"You're a DSU student, right?"

"How did you know?" He pulls at his left earlobe.

"You had on a DSU sweater and I saw you reading something the other day, last night I think."

"Oh yeah, my dissertation." The last two words he mumbles.

"Can't talk about the writing, right? I've heard that before."

"No, it's not like that. I mean I'm just not sure what it means anymore. It was supposed to be about integration, but I can't keep my ideas together."

The brandy has warmed him. He leans heavily on the counter, upsetting a small pitcher of cream.

"Drunk already?"

"No, not drunk yet, I'm only clumsy when I'm sober."

He tries to explain his dissertation, but it wrestles him like a map that refuses to be unfolded. He brings the ragged explanation to a halt, cutting the mounting tension by saying, finally, "You had to be there."

Trixie laughs.

Encouraged, he follows with, "And, unfortunately, I wasn't."

The brandy has loosened his fingers. He shows her how to make a cat's cradle, and she shows him how to fold back his eyelids. He looks at her intently; she has a faint mole over her left eye and a scar on her chin. Her left earlobe is slightly longer than her right. He sees these things but does not notice them. He does not see the strawberry red hair, the piercing, the way their hands form zebra stripes as he shows her the cat's cradle again, this time with a ribbon from her hair. He sees instead that she is funny and articulate, and in the way she prepares his next drink he divines a certain kindness and he is certain that that smile she smiles is only for him. They talk about nothing until it is time to close, then again about other nothings, until the brandy is gone. "Look," she says, pointing outside.

He turns to see that the snow has picked up. The sidewalk is thinly coated. He wants to make snow angels. The upper branches of the tree are covered in snow, including the sick limb, which now looks like a hand gloved in pearl. Someone, he can't remember who, once told him, *Never quit in winter.*

"The tree looks better now. Uniform," says Trixie.

"Someone turned the floodlights toward it."

"My boss, to warm it."

"Oh."

"He's from California."

She plays '70s soul—Marvin Gaye, the Temptations, Gladys Knight, Earth Wind & Fire. They are drunk on brandy, intoxicated by the freedom of being comfortably unknown to each other. They dance, not touching.

"I better get out of here and let you close," Doug says during a pause between songs.

She insists that he stay while she counts the money. "It's not a problem. It's a questionable neighborhood," she adds. He waits patiently, musing over this fate. Amazed at what he has spent on coffee this week, amazed that he wasn't amazed by what he spent on coke for the last five years. The scholarship covered tuition, and the student loans and grants covered *living expenses.* When she finishes counting the money, he waits for her to lock up and walks her to her car, which is parked out front. She gets into her car and rolls down the window. Emboldened by the brandy, the dancing, the snow, Marvin Gaye, he asks her if she would like to see a movie. "You know, like rent an old Hitchcock film."

She purses her lips and plays with her turn signal. The yellow light flashes against the faded brick wall, ticking off the seconds. He mumbles a hurried apology and steps back from the car. She laughs. "I'd love to, but not tonight. I have a day job, too. Can we make a date for Friday?"

He nods, pleased and terrified at the same time. Time. Friday gives him time to prepare, time to worry, time to relapse, and time to forget. Time to fuck up. Time.

"Bye, Peter, see you Friday."

Doug waves.

He takes the long way home, driving through Pine City to get downtown, where he can pick up the highway. He sees faces he recognizes and that recognize him in return. He drives through and scores, stopping at one corner to pay and the next to pick up.

At home, he sits on the sofa, shuffling the white Baggie from hand to hand. He lays out one thin line on the coffee table, next to his dissertation. He knows that he will not show up on Friday. He knows that he will not return to Kat's because he doesn't trust himself, and so, can't trust Trixie, and he would always wonder whether she liked him because he was black or in spite of it—and both burn like dry ice. He drops his dissertation in the middle of the floor and kicks it as hard as he can. The papers scatter, some settling on the floor by the window. The blinds are open. Outside a blizzard rages; fat snowflakes stick to the glass momentarily, then are blown away, but leave faint white lines. In the dim incandescence of the sodium streetlights, the snow glows fluorescent—burning hot white against the night sky, his dissertation in negative relief. He snorts his line. A smile burns across his face as he begins collecting his pages, mentally making notes for his defense.

CONTRIBUTORS

ANNE DE MARCKEN is a writer, filmmaker, and interactive code artist. Her work is in print, online, and in theaters internationally. Cofounder of Wovie, Inc. (www.wovie.com), De Marcken oversees production design, art direction, animation, and content development for the boundary-pushing digital media arts studio. She is currently working on a collection of short stories entitled *After Life,* is producing the feature film *In the Way of Intimacy,* and is in demand as a speaker on the interplay of writing and digital arts. She received her undergraduate degree in experimental media from the Evergreen State College, and an MFA in Creative Writing from Vermont College.

RYAN EFFGEN has lived and worked in New Orleans, Alaska, Portland, and Washington, D.C., but he considers Chicago his home. He received a BA in English from the University of Iowa in 1997. While completing his MFA, he was awarded George Mason University's Narrative Completion Fellowship and was editor of *Phoebe: A Journal of Literature and Art.* His story in this collection was awarded third prize in *Zoetrope: All-Story's* short fiction contest. He has published both fiction and poetry and is currently at work on a novel.

CAIMEEN GARRETT recently earned her Ph.D. from Florida State University, where she received the Dean's Prize in Creative Writing and a Kingsbury Fellowship. She also holds an MFA from Syracuse University. This is her second story to appear in Best New American Voices. She is completing a collection of stories inspired by the Lindbergh kidnapping.

KEVIN A. GONZÁLEZ was born in San Juan, Puerto Rico, in 1981. He holds degrees from Carnegie Mellon University and the University of Wisconsin-Madison, where he was a Martha Meier Renk Poetry Fellow. His poems have appeared in *Poetry, McSweeney's, Callaloo, The Progressive,* and *North American Review,* as well as in the anthology *Best New Poets 2005* (Meridian). His stories have appeared in *Playboy* (as the 2005 Playboy College Fiction Contest winner), *Crab Orchard Review* (as the 2005

Charles Johnson Fiction Contest winner), *Indiana Review,* and *Virginia Quarterly Review.* Currently, he is a graduate fellow at the Iowa Writers' Workshop, where he is working on a novel.

T. GERONIMO JOHNSON was a University Graduate Scholar in Fiction at Arizona State University, where he was also an editor for *Hayden's Ferry Review.* He is currently a Wallace Stegner Fellow at Stanford. His fiction has appeared in the anthology *Hoot and Holler of the Owls* and the *Los Angeles Review.* He is at work on a novel in stories.

YIYUN LI grew up in Beijing and came to the United States in 1996. She has an MFA from the Iowa Writers' Workshop and an MFA in creative nonfiction writing from the University of Iowa. Her stories and essays have been published in *The New Yorker, Paris Review, Zoetrope: All-Story, Ploughshares,* and elsewhere. Her book, *A Thousand Years of Good Prayers,* won the Frank O'Connor International Short Story Award. She lives in Oakland, California, with her husband and their two sons, and teaches in the MFA program at Mills College.

ROBERT LIDDELL completed his MFA in Creative Writing at the University of Houston in 2005. He continues to live in Houston, where he plays, most days, an unwatchable brand of tennis. He also teaches English at the University of Houston and is currently at work on a collection of stories and a novel.

ELLEN LITMAN grew up in Moscow, Russia, where she lived until 1992. She holds an MFA in Creative Writing from Syracuse University, and she was a James C. McCreight Fiction Fellow at the University of Wisconsin Institute for Creative Writing. Her stories have appeared or are forthcoming in *Ontario Review, Tin House, Best of Tin House, Gulf Coast, TriQuarterly,* and *Another Chicago Magazine.* She recently finished a collection of short stories and is at work on her first novel.

ALICE J. MARSHALL holds an MFA in Creative Writing from the University of Washington. She was a recipient of the Blessing Scholarship. She is a writer-in-residence through Seattle Arts and Lectures' Writers in the Schools program. She is currently at work on a short-story collection.

KEYA MITRA graduated with an MFA in fiction from the University of Houston's Creative Writing Program, where she is currently pursuing a Ph.D. in fiction and literature. Her fiction has been published in the *Ontario Review* and *Orchid.* She received an honorable mention in the *Atlantic Monthly's* 2004–2005 student fiction competition, and she was awarded a work-study scholarship in fiction to the 2005 Bread Loaf Writers' Conference. She won the 2004–2005 Barthelme Fellowship in honor of Donald Barthelme and was the alternate winner for the Michener Fellowship. She has also received a C. Glenn Cambor Fellowship in Writing. Mitra works as a fiction editor for *Gulf Coast: A Journal of Literature and Fine Arts.*

VIET THANH NGUYEN is an associate professor at the University of Southern California, where he teaches literature, ethnic studies, and American studies. A former fellow at the Fine Arts Work Center in Provincetown, Massachusetts, he is the author of *Race and Resistance: Literature and Politics in Asian America*. His short fiction, in addition to being published in *Manoa* and *Orchid: A Literary Review*, has been adapted for the stage by the John Sims Center for the Arts in San Francisco.

LYDIA PEELLE was born in Boston in 1978. Her fiction has appeared in *Epoch* and *Pindeldyboz*, as well as *The O. Henry Prize Stories 2006*. She is at work on a novel.

DAN POPE is a recent graduate of the Iowa Writers' Workshop, where he was awarded the Glenn Schaeffer Award from the International Institute of Modern Letters. He has published short stories in *McSweeney's, Post Road, Crazyhorse, Shenandoah,* and other journals. His first novel, *In the Cherry Tree*, was published by Picador in 2004.

FATIMA RASHID received her MA in Creative Writing from the University of Central Florida. Her work has appeared in *The Paterson Review* and *The Cypress Dome* and is due to appear in an upcoming issue of *The Florida Review*. Rashid has recently completed a collection of short fiction. She is currently working on a novel tentatively entitled *The Bargain* and on a collection of creative nonfiction, snapshots of the author's latest visit to Karachi.

M. O. WALSH was born and raised in Baton Rouge, Louisiana. His work has appeared in *Epoch, Greensboro Review, Phoebe, Pindeldyboz,* and *New Orleans Review,* among others. It has also been anthologized in *French Quarter Fiction* and *Stories from the Blue Moon Cafe IV* and nominated for a Pushcart Prize. He is currently finishing his MFA at the University of Mississippi where he has completed a book-length collection of linked stories and is currently at work on a novel. He and his wife, Sarah, live in Oxford, Mississippi, and are both very happy to be alive.

PARTICIPANTS

The Advanced Fiction Workshop with
Carol Edgarian & Tom Jenks
P.O. Box 29272
San Francisco, CA 94129-9991
415/346-4477

American University
MFA Program in Creative Writing
Department of Literature
Washington, DC 20016-8047
202/885-2973

Antioch Writers' Workshop
P.O. Box 494
Yellow Springs, OH 45387
937/475-7357

Arizona State University
College of Liberal Arts and Sciences
Department of Literature—Creative
Writing Program
Tempe, AZ 85287
480/965-3528

The Asian American Writers Workshop
16 West 32nd Street
Suite 10A
New York, NY 10001
212/494-0061

The Banff Centre for the Arts
Writing Studio
Box 1020, Station 34
107 Tunnel Mountain Drive
Banff, AB TIL 1H5
403/762-6269

Binghamton University
Creative Writing Program
Department of English, General
Literature, and Rhetoric
P.O. Box 6000
Binghamton, NY 13902-6000
607/777-2713

Boise State University
MFA Program in Writing
1910 University Drive
Boise, ID 83725
208/426-1002

Boston University
Creative Writing Program
236 Bay State Road
Boston, MA 02215
617/353-2510

Bowling Green State University
Department of English
Creative Writing Program
Bowling Green, OH 43403-0215
419/372-8370

The Bread Loaf Writers' Conference
Middlebury College—P&W
Middlebury, VT 05753
802/443-5286

Brown University
Box 1852
Creative Writing
Providence, RI 02912
401/863-3260

California College of the Arts
1111 8th Street
San Francisco, CA 94107
415/703-9500

California State University, Fresno
Department of English
5245 North Backer Avenue
M/S 98
Fresno, CA 93740-8001
559/278-2553

California State University, Northridge
Department of English
18111 Nordhoff Street
Northridge, CA 91330-8248
818/677-3431

Colorado State University
MFA Creative Writing Program
English Department, 359 Eddy Hall
Fort Collins, CO 80523-1773
970/491-6428

Columbia College
Department of Fiction Writing
600 South Michigan Avenue
Chicago, IL 60605-1997
312/344-7611

Columbia University
Division of Writing, School of the Arts
2960 Broadway, 415 Dodge
New York, NY 10027
212/854-4391

Cornell University
English Department
Ithaca, NY 14853
607/255-6800

Eastern Washington University
Creative Writing Program
705 W. First Avenue MS#1
Spokane, WA 99201-3900
509/623-4221

Emerson College
Writing, Literature and Publishing
120 Boylston Street
Boston, MA 02116
617/824-8750

Fine Arts Work Center in
Provincetown
24 Pearl Street
Provincetown, MA 02657
508/487-8678

Florida International University
Department of English
Biscayne Bay Campus
3000 NE 151st Street
Miami, FL 33181
305/919-5857

Florida State University
Creative Writing Program
Department of English
Tallahassee, FL 32306-1580
850/644-4230

George Mason University
Creative Writing Program
MS 3E4—English Department
Fairfax, VA 22030
703/993-1185

Georgia State University
Department of English
University Plaza
Atlanta, GA 30303-3083
404/651-2900

Grub Street
160 Boylston Street
Boston, MA 02116
617/695-0075

Hollins University
Department of English
P.O. Box 9677
Roanoke, VA 24020
540/362-6317

Hunter College
MFA Program in Writing
Department of English
695 Park Avenue
New York, NY 10021
212/772-5164

Indiana University
Department of English
Ballantine Hall 442
1020 East Kirkwood Avenue
Bloomington, IN 47405-6601
812/855-8224

The Indiana University Writers'
Conference
Ballantine Hall 464
1020 East Kirkwood Avenue
Bloomington, IN 47405-7103
812/855-1877

Johns Hopkins University
The Writing Seminars
3400 North Charles Street
Baltimore, MD 21218
410/516-7563

The Loft Literary Center
Mentor Series Program
Open Book, Suite 200
1011 Washington Avenue South
Minneapolis, MN 55415
612/215-2575

Louisiana State University
MFA Program
Department of English
Allen Hall
Baton Rouge, LA 70803-5001
225/578-2236

McNeese State University
Department of Languages
P.O. Box 92655
Lake Charles, LA 70609-2655
337/475-5326

Miami University
Creative Writing Program
Oxford, OH 45056
513/529-5221

Mills College
Creative Writing Program
Mills Hall 311
5000 MacArthur Boulevard
Oakland, CA 94613
510/430-3309

Minnesota State University, Mankato
English Department
230 Armstrong Hall
Mankato, MN 56001
507/389-2117

Mississippi State University
Department of English
Drawer E
Mississippi State, MS 39762
662/325-3644

Naropa University
Program in Writing and Poetics
2130 Arapahoe Avenue
Boulder, CO 80302
303/546-3540

New Mexico State University
Department of English
Box 30001—Department 3E
Las Cruces, NM 88003-8001
505/646-3931

The New York State Summer Writers
Institute
Skidmore College
815 North Broadway
Saratoga Springs, NY 12866-1632
518/584-5000

New York University
Graduate Program in Creative Writing
19 University Place, Room 219
New York, NY 10003
212/998-8816

Northwestern University
Master of Arts in Creative Writing
405 Church Street
Evanston, IL 60208-4220
847/491-5612

Ohio State University
English Department
421 Denney Hall
164 West 17th Avenue
Columbus, OH 43210-1370
614/292-6065

Oklahoma State University
Creative Writing Program
English Department—205 Morrill Hall
Stillwater, OK 74078
405/744-9474

PEN Prison Writing Committee
PEN American Center
568 Broadway
Suite 401
New York, NY 10012
212/334-1660

Pennsylvania State University
Department of English
112 Burrowes Building
University Park, PA 16802-6200
814/863-3069

Purdue University
Department of English
Heavilon Hall
West Lafayette, IN 47907-2038
765/494-3740

Rivier College
Department of English
South Main Street
Nashua, NH 03060-5086
603/888-1311

Roosevelt University, Chicago Campus
School of Liberal Arts
430 South Michigan Avenue
Chicago, IL 60605-1394
312/341-3710

Saint Mary's College of California
MFA Program in Creative Writing
P.O. Box 4686
Moraga, CA 94575-4686
925/631-4762

San Francisco State University
Creative Writing Department, College
of Humanities
1600 Holloway Avenue
San Francisco, CA 94132-4162
415/338-1891

Sarah Lawrence College
Graduate Writing Program
1 Mead Way
Slonim House
Bronxville, NY 10708-5999
914/395-2371

The School of the Art Institute of
Chicago
MFA in Writing Program
37 S. Wabash Avenue
Chicago, IL 60603
312/899-5100

Sewanee Writers' Conference
310 St. Luke's Hall
735 University Avenue
Sewanee, TN 37383-1000
931/598-1141

Sonoma State University
Department of English
1801 East Cotati Avenue
Rohnert Park, CA 94928-3609
707/664-2140

Stanford University
Creative Writing Program
Department of English
Stanford, CA 94305-2087
650/725-1208

Syracuse University
Program in Creative Writing
401 Hall of Languages
Syracuse, NY 13244-1170
315/443-2173

Taos Summer Writers' Conference
Department of English
MSC03 2170
University of New Mexico
Albuquerque, NM 87131-0001
505/277-5572

Temple University
Creative Writing Program
Anderson Hall, 10th Floor
Philadelphia, PA 19122
215/204-1796

Texas State University
MFA Program in Creative Writing
Department of English
601 University Drive
San Marcos, TX 78666-4616
512/245-7681

Texas Tech University
Creative Writing Program
Department of English
Box 43091
Lubbock, TX 79409
806/742-2501

University of Alabama
Program in Creative Writing
Department of English
103 Morgan Hall
P.O. Box 870244
Tuscaloosa, AL 35487-0244
205/348-5065

University of Alaska, Anchorage
Department of Creative Writing &
Liberal Arts
3211 Providence Drive
Anchorage, AK 99508-8348
907/786-4330

University of Alaska, Fairbanks
Program in Creative Writing
English Department
P.O. Box 755720
Fairbanks, AK 99775-5720
907/474-7193

University of Arizona
Creative Writing Program
Department of English
Modern Languages Building #67
Tucson, AZ 85721-0067
520/621-7397

University of Arkansas
Program in Creative Writing
Department of English
333 Kimpel Hall
Fayetteville, AR 72701
479/575-4301

University of British Columbia
Creative Writing Program
Buchanan E462—1866 Main Mall
Vancouver, BC V6T 1Z1
604/822-0699

University of California, Davis
Graduate Creative Writing Program
Department of English
One Shields Avenue
Davis, CA 95616
530/752-1658

University of Central Florida
MFA/CRW
P.O. Box 161346
Orlando, FL 32816-1346
407/823-2212

University of Central Oklahoma
Department of Creative Studies
College of Liberal Arts
Edmond, OK 73034-0184
405/974-2000

University of Cincinnati
Creative Writing Program
Department of English & Comparative
Literature
ML 69
Cincinnati, OH 45221-0069
513/556-5924

University of Colorado at Boulder
Creative Writing Program
Department of English
Campus Box 226
Boulder, CO 80309-0226
303/492-7381

University of Denver
Creative Writing Program
Department of English
2140 S. Race Street
Denver, CO 80210
303/871-2266

University of Florida
MFA Program
Department of English
P.O. Box 117310
Gainesville, FL 32611-7310
352/392-6650

University of Houston
Creative Writing Program
Department of English
Houston, TX 77204-3015
713/743-3015

University of Idaho
Creative Writing Program
Department of English
P.O. Box 441102
Moscow, ID 83844-1102
208/885-6156

University of Illinois at Chicago
Program for Writers
Department of English MC/162
601 South Morgan Street
Chicago, IL 60607-7120
312/413-2229

University of Iowa
Program in Creative Writing
102 Dey House
507 N. Clinton Street
Iowa City, IA 52242
319/335-0416

University of Maryland
Creative Writing Program
Department of English
3119F Susquehanna Hall
College Park, MD 20742
301/405-3820

University of Memphis
MFA Creative Writing Program
Department of English
467 Patterson Hall
Memphis, TN 38152-3510
901/678-2651

University of Miami
Creative Writing Program
Department of English
P.O. Box 248145
Coral Gables, FL 33124-4632
305/284-2183

University of Michigan
MFA Program in Creative Writing
Department of English
3187 Angell Hall
Ann Arbor, MI 48109-1003
734/936-2274

University of Mississippi
MFA Program in Creative Writing
English Department
Bondurant Hall C128
Oxford, MS 38677-1848
662/915-7439

University of Missouri-Columbia
Creative Writing Program
Department of English
107 Tate Hall
Columbia, MO 65211-1500
573/884-7773

University of Missouri-St. Louis
MFA in Creative Writing Program
Department of English
One University Boulevard
St. Louis, MO 63121
314/516-6845

University of Montana
Creative Writing Program
Department of English
Missoula, MT 59812-1013
406/243-5231

University of Nebraska, Lincoln
Creative Writing Program
Department of English
202 Andrews Hall
Lincoln, NE 68588-0333
402/472-3191

University of Nevada, Las Vegas
MFA in Creative Writing
Department of English
4505 Maryland Parkway
Las Vegas, NV 89154-5011
702/895-3533

University of New Brunswick
Department of English
Box 4400
Fredericton, NB E3B 5A3
506/453-4676

University of New Hampshire
Creative Writing Program
Department of English
Hamilton Smith Hall
95 Main Street
Durham, NH 03824-3574
603/862-1313

University of New Orleans
Creative Writing Workshop
College of Liberal Arts
Lakefront
New Orleans, LA 70148
504/280-7454

University of North Carolina at
Greensboro
MFA Writing Program
Department of English
P.O. Box 26170
Greensboro, NC 27402-6170
336/334-5459

University of North Carolina at
Wilmington
MFA in Writing Program
Department of Creative Writing
601 S. College Road
Wilmington, NC 28403
910/962-7063

University of North Dakota
Creative Writing Program
English Department
P.O. Box 7209
Grand Forks, ND 58202
701/777-3321

University of North Texas
Creative Writing Division
Department of English
P.O. Box 311307
Denton, TX 76203-1307
940/565-2050

University of Notre Dame
Creative Writing Program
356 O'Shaughnessy Hall
Notre Dame, IN 46556-5639
574/631-7526

University of Oregon
Program in Creative Writing
P.O. Box 5243
Eugene, OR 97403-5243
541/346-0509

University of San Francisco
MFA in Writing Program
Program Office, Lone Mountain 340
2130 Fulton Street
San Francisco, CA 94117-1080
415/422-2382

University of South Carolina
MFA Program in Creative Writing
Department of English
Columbia, SC 29208
803/777-7000

University of Tennessee
Creative Writing Program
Department of English
301 McClung Tower
Knoxville, TN 37996
865/974-5401

University of Texas at Austin
Creative Writing Program in English
Calhoun Hall 210
Austin, TX 78712-1164
512/475-6356

University of Virginia
Creative Writing Program
219 Bryan Hall
P.O. Box 400121
Charlottesville, VA 22904-4121
434/924-6675

University of Washington
Creative Writing Program
Box 354330
Seattle, WA 98195-4330
206/543-9865

University of Wisconsin-Madison
Program in Creative Writing
English Department
Helen C. White Hall
600 N. Park Street
Madison, WI 53706
608/263-3800

University of Wisconsin-Milwaukee
Creative Writing Program
Department of English
Box 413
Milwaukee, WI 53201
414/229-6991

Vermont College of Union Institute &
University
MFA in Writing
36 College Street
Montpelier, VT 05602
800/336-6794

Virginia Commonwealth University
MFA in Creative Writing Program
Department of English
P.O. Box 842005
Richmond, VA 23284-2005
804/828-1329

Washington University
The Writing Program
Campus Box 1122
One Brookings Drive
St. Louis, MO 63130-4899
314/935-5190

The Wesleyan Writers Conference
Wesleyan University
294 High Street
Middletown, CT 06459
860/685-3604

West Virginia University
Creative Writing Program
Department of English
P.O. Box 6269
Morgantown, WV 26506-6269
304/293-3107

Western Illinois University
Department of English and Journalism
1 University Circle
Macomb, IL 61455-1390
309/298-1103

Western Michigan University
Graduate Program in Creative Writing
Department of English
Kalamazoo, MI 49008-5092
269/387-2572

The Julia and David White Artists'
Colony
Interlink 232
P.O. Box 526770
Miami, FL 33152
www.forjuliaanddavid.org

Wisconsin Institute for Creative
Writing
University of Wisconsin-Madison
Department of English
Helen C. White Hall
600 N. Park Street
Madison, WI 53706
608/263-3374